Counterpoint

Other novels of suspense by Isabelle Holland

Counterpoint

Isabelle Holland

RAWSON, WADE PUBLISHERS, INC.
NEW YORK

Library of Congress Cataloging in Publication Data

Holland, Isabelle.
Counterpoint.
I. Title.
PZ4.H735Co   1980   [PS3558.03485]   813'.54   79–91330
ISBN 0–89256–121–1

Published simultaneously in Canada by
McClelland and Stewart, Ltd.
Composition by American–Stratford
Graphic Services, Inc., Brattleboro, Vermont
Printed and bound by Fairfield Graphics,
Fairfield, Pennsylvania
Designed by Gene Siegel

First Edition

Counterpoint

Chapter 1

The night before it all started Kate had a dream that disturbed and frightened her. She dreamed she was lying on a litter, being carried to a small, sealed room by two men. Every time she tried to get up, one of the men pushed her back. Since it was dark she couldn't see their faces, but she was quite sure she knew them and she was also sure they were going to leave her in the room to die. Then they did leave her, and, in her dream, her fear became so overwhelming she knew that she would die from it. Then, as she started to die, she saw that there was a crack in the wall and light was streaming in. She got off the litter, stumbled over to the crack and was trying to pull it apart when she woke up.

Wow! she thought, sitting up. Her next thought was, what did I eat for dinner? She had been to dinner and the theatre with friends and had had—what? Something au gratin. Oysters? Either they or the cheese might have done it.

It was much later that Kate made any connection between this dream and one of Jed's characteristically nutty statements. "Time isn't the way we think of it—a tape or ribbon unfolding from some celestial spool. It circles back. Past and present

3

turn out to be—in some kind of baffling way—one. You think you've left the past for good. And then you discover it's been there all the time. Waiting."

When she thought back she couldn't be sure if she had read it in one of his compulsively successful books, or if he had said it during those turbulent days at the Lamont house. Either way, it went along with the rest of his outlandish metaphysical theories that had sent the sales of his four books up into the ninety thousands, but which nobody at the publishing house that put them out, including Kate, his editor, took seriously.

To Graham Maitland, who had recently bought the publishing house and installed himself as publisher, the content of the books was irrelevant. What mattered were the sales, and the advance sales of Jed Kramer's most recent book—which Kate had not yet finished editing—were already soaring.

"Gratifying," Graham said at a recent sales meeting, looking at the early reports, "most gratifying."

"All Graham cares about is money," Joel Green complained later. He had wandered into Kate's office to borrow the newspaper she always brought in and was leaning against the window sill reading it.

"It pays our salaries, Joel dear," Kate said. She stared at one of Jed Kramer's more intractably obscure sentences. "You know, one piece of overwhelming evidence that our Mr. Kramer has had all the scientific training he claims to have had is his total inability to write understandable, straightforward, standard English."

"I'm glad he's your author, even with all his lousy sales," Joel said, folding back a page.

Her phone rang. Almost immediately her buzzer sounded sharply, making her jump. She picked up the receiver. "Yes? Oh, hi, Dick. Yes, the Kramer manuscript will be ready in time. I've told you before, oh ye of little faith. I promise, I promise, I promise, and I'll charge all the medical costs for my nervous breakdown to the production department." The

4

receiver squawked back. She laughed and hung up. "If you want the paper, Joel, take it to your office. As you just heard, Dick is riding me about the Kramer book. The production department is screaming."

"Under no circumstances would I impede the progress of yet another of those brainless best sellers."

"Jealousy, jealousy!" Kate's head was already bent again over the manuscript.

"He's an idiot," Joel stared gloomily out the window to the street, twenty-nine floors below. He was a tall young man with a brown afro, glasses, and light gray eyes above high cheekbones.

"No. He's not an idiot. Have you ever read any of his books?"

"Of course not."

"Then don't judge. He documents what he says."

Joel turned. "I take it you're a believer."

"As a matter of fact, I'm not. But he's a solid, reliable workman, and I like solid reliable workmen."

"I wish you liked me."

Kate looked at him and her heart melted a little, "I do."

He took a breath. "All right then. Since I have your sealed statement to that effect—I have reservations at that place up in Vermont. There's still some snow there. For two years you've been saying you'd let me teach you to ski. Now's the time."

"Joel, you know I can't. Much as you may hate Kramer, a printer's schedule is a printer's schedule. If I don't have this last part in by the end of the month, the book will miss pub date and the book stores will be furious."

There was a short silence. Then Joel said, "You just refused for the same reason you've refused all my other invitations for an out-of-town weekend or week or even a night. I'm fine to go to concerts and dinner and book affairs with, but nothing further."

"It's just that—"

"No." Joel came over and stood in front of her chair. "Don't give me that. At least be honest. It's 1980, *after* women's liberation, *after* the sexual revolution. Society no longer insists that you go to your marriage bed a virgin."

"Society hasn't insisted on that for some time. And besides," Kate said, "I'm not. A virgin, that is."

"If, at thirty-nine—"

"Thirty-eight," Kate amended. "Don't make it worse than it is. Not that I mind my age. I have great hopes for my forties."

"I know you're not a virgin," Joel went on with the patient persistence of someone following a line of logic, "because of your relationship with our distinguished publisher."

Kate looked up and leaned back in her chair. "You're beginning to sound like a doctor explaining how I managed to catch the measles. What your generation calls a 'relationship'—a disgusting term if I ever heard one, only one degree less revolting than a 'meaningful relationship'—my generation called an affair. My affair with Graham ended years ago, before I came to this house, and even longer than that before he bought it. The fact that we are now back together in the same publishing house is not my doing."

"But since he is now separated from the wife he had then, perhaps you'd be vulnerable to persuasion?"

"Are you playing John Alden to his Miles Standish?"

"No I am not. I'm trying to act in my own interests. And to find an acceptable reason—given today's ambience—why we shouldn't have what *your* generation prefers to call an affair."

"Give me my cane, bring me my walker. Old as I am, I can't understand why you're putting on this act of frothing with frustration. This place is thick with attractive young women, several of whom would be happy to receive your attention."

"It is not an act, and well you know it, and cut out that garbage about your age. You're an extremely attractive woman —although you seem to have a hard time believing that. And you're exactly nine years older than I am. Anyway, you brought up the whole generation thing."

"But those nine years go the wrong way."

"That's mediaeval thinking. Haven't you read . . . ?"

"Yes I have," Kate said, rudely interrupting. "And it gave me a severe case of regression—I giggled all the way through."

Joel turned his back abruptly and stared out the window again at the Hudson River and the New Jersey shore.

"Joel dear—speaking of attractiveness, look who's talking! You're a very attractive man."

"Not to you, evidently."

"That's not true. It's just that . . ." How could she explain the strange hesitation that seemed to afflict her whenever there was a question of commitment? She liked Joel. Contrary to what he believed, she was not bound hand and foot by a puritan ethic of the past. And yet . . ."

"It's Graham," he burst out bitterly. "He hurt you so badly you'll never trust anyone again. I know."

"This is a highly romanticized way of putting it. Graham and I had a long affair. It had the anatomy of most such affairs, starting in passion and ending, finally, in tedium and frustration. It should have finished two years earlier than it did."

And yet, Kate thought, there was a period, towards the beginning and—despite what she said—towards the end when it was agony. Joel might not be all wrong in his diagnosis.

"Did you really think that bastard would divorce his wife and marry you?" Joel said savagely, his back still to the room.

A spurt of anger went through Kate. His shaft went close to the bone.

"I don't think that's any of your business, Joel."

He sighed and turned around again. "My apologies. If it will make it up to you I'll go out and kill myself. I might do that anyway."

"No don't. Your authors would miss you."

"You're right about that," Joel said sardonically. "Without me they wouldn't be published. They don't make enough money."

"Ah, but they bring kudos and prestige, not to mention columns of reviews in distinguished quarterlies by equally distinguished members of the literary establishment."

He walked around her office. "So you won't go with me to Vermont."

"No, I won't. And little though you may believe it, it is because I have to finish editing this book."

"I don't believe you. I mean I don't believe that's the real reason. However . . ." Joel came and stared gloomily over her shoulder. "What's this one about? Ghosts? Seances?"

"No. It's about time, and the past and the present and clairvoyance and precognition and reincarnation. A sort of anthology of philosophy, anecdotes, statements and events."

"Complete rubbish!"

"It's not all rubbish. At least a lot of highly respected people don't think it is. And in his field Kramer is considered the best. His prose may be unspeakable, but his documentation and arrangement are admirable."

"Ummm. What's its title again—just so I can catch it easily and suffer more when I'm looking over the sales reports."

"You're masochistic."

"Not to say rejectable."

"Come on, now. It's called *The Wheel*."

Joel stood there testing the sound in his mouth. "It's a good title," he said pessimistically. "I hope it lays an egg."

"Joel! That's not kind."

"Those cast into outer darkness are seldom kind. What's he like, this nut, I mean?"

"I haven't the faintest idea. I inherited him, as you know, from his editor, who left. I have never met him nor talked to him on the phone. We've only corresponded."

"He probably writes with his fingernail."

"No, with what is almost certainly a manual portable manufactured in 1902 and not touched since."

"You'll be sorry when they fish my body from the Hudson."

8

"I won't have time unless you postpone your suicide until week after next."

Joel slammed the door as he left. Kate grinned and went back to her manuscript. It was then the telephone rang again. She frowned at the interruption, but assumed that Judy Roth, her secretary, would handle it, as she had others that morning.

Kate was therefore a little surprised when Judy appeared in the doorway. "Kate, this is the fourth time that man's called. He says it's urgent. Something about your family."

"My family?" Kate turned and looked at her secretary. "I don't have any—or practically don't."

"Well, he thinks you do."

"Who's he?"

"Dr. Something or other. He's calling from some place in Westchester."

Kate frowned and picked up the receiver. "This is Kate Malory."

"My name is Dr. McGrath. I'm calling from White Falls Clinic in Westchester. A patient, Deborah Lamont, a Mrs. Paul Lamont, who, I'm told, is your sister, has been in treatment here for the past six weeks. A crisis has come up at her home. Her husband, who is in Tokyo and unable to leave immediately, suggested we get in touch with you. You are, I take it, related to her?"

"What's the matter with her?" Kate asked, ignoring his question.

There was a pause. Then, "Six weeks ago Mrs. Lamont attempted suicide and has been hospitalized ever since. A housekeeper has been in charge of the house and the two children. But she left yesterday—more or less abruptly. That was when I got in touch with Mr. Lamont. He said there'd been an estrangement between you and his wife, but you were the only person he could call on."

"Is she going to be all right?"

"Physically, yes." The qualification made the omission seem

all the more obvious. The doctor had a pleasant, rather dry voice, contradicting the urgency her secretary had reported.

Kate took a breath and for a moment felt as though she were pushing a wall of air—or perhaps memory—away from her. Turning, the phone still at her ear, she caught a glimpse of her face in the mirror across her office. If I were a horse, she thought, I'd be showing the whites of my eyes. Her hazel eyes, more green than brown, had a wide, startled look. "Not a pretty face," her father had once said, rather typically. "But a nice one," her mother had countered, also typically.

Kate dragged her mind back to the doctor on the phone. She wondered how long the silence had gone on. "I take it from what you don't say that she—Mrs. Lamont—while physically recovered, is not mentally all right."

"You haven't answered my question," the doctor said brusquely. "Are you related to Mrs. Lamont? Do I have the right Kate Malory?"

He had given her the out she was looking for. All she had to say was, I'm afraid not. You have the wrong Kate Malory. She opened her mouth to speak the words. And then the flash came. It had happened to her fewer than half a dozen times in her life. But it was happening now. She saw two roads forking. At the fork stood a figure, which she recognized as herself. It was a frightening and unpleasant sensation, as though she were viewing it all from a great height, aware, as the figure at the fork was not aware, of how much one of the roads could change her life forever. Panic seized her.

"Hello?" The doctor's pleasant voice sharpened. "Are you there? Have we been cut off?"

You have the wrong Kate Malory. She took another clutch at the words. At that point her intercom buzzed and a third voice—Max Vincenti, assistant managing editor—broke in. "Kate are you counting on Judy to retype the Kramer manuscript? Because another typing job came in for her today."

"I'll be with you in a minute, Vince. Right now I'm on an outside call," she said. Then buzzed her secretary. "Judy, I seem to be talking to two people, one inside the house and one out. Try and keep the lines separate, will you? Sorry," she said automatically to the doctor.

"Paul Lamont mentioned that you were in publishing," the doctor said.

Kate let out her breath. The choice had been made for her. "Yes. I'm sorry. My mind was . . . was somewhere else. I'm Deborah's stepsister." She fought off the beginning of a feeling she was familiar with, entrapment.

"Can you come out here? The neighbor, a Mrs. Fitch, who called and told me the housekeeper had gone, says the place is a mess, and someone has to go and take charge—at least for the time being."

"Dr.—what did you say your name was?"

"McGrath."

"Well, Dr. McGrath, I have a job I can't just say to my boss, to my staff, to my authors, 'Bye now. I'm a woman, so I have to drop everything and rally round the family flag.' Suppose I were a stepbrother? Would you demand my immediate assistance in quite the same way?"

There was a pause. Kate heard him breathe twice. Then he said, "My apologies. I'll concede that I would probably have phrased it differently. I'd probably have asked you if you could come out this evening and make some arrangements for another housekeeper or companion or den mother or whatever until Mr. Lamont comes back. So I'll say that to you, now."

Kate stared at her desk calendar, open in front of her. Next to the hour six, she had scrawled, "Dinner—concert, Joel." It was an all Mozart concert, and she had been looking forward to it. The trap closed a little tighter. "Can it wait until tomorrow evening?"

"It probably could, but I don't think it should. The older child in the house is only fifteen—and not a very stable girl at that. According to the neighbor, she arrived home last night, or rather this morning, around four."

*And what business of that is mine? When did Deb—or Paul—
ever help me?*

"All right," Kate said. "I'll be there. What's the address?"

"You don't know it?"

"No. I don't. As Paul told you, we've not been in touch."

"Forty-nine Wood Lane, Meadowbrook. Are you going to
drive?"

"No, Dr. McGrath. I'm one of the few people left in the
western world who does not drive. I'll come on the train and
get a taxi."

"Then I won't bother with directions."

"No, don't.

She took down the address as he dictated. Then she said, "It
was Paul who told you to call me, I gather. Not Deborah
herself."

"Your sister, I'm afraid, is not in much shape to tell me or
anybody anything. Immediately after she was brought around
in the hospital, she tried to jump out the hospital window and
when she was prevented from doing that, she went into a
depression. She does not respond, or even indicate that she's
heard anything anyone has said."

"Isn't there some way you can bring her out of that?"

"Yes, Miss Malory, there is. And if all else fails, we'll do
whatever is necessary. At the moment we're trying more conventional means."

"When does Paul—Paul Lamont—get home?"

"I'm to call him tonight to tell him if I was able to locate
you. He'll make his plans accordingly."

"Look Dr. McGrath, as I told you, I have a job. It's as much
my life as those children are my sister's or my brother-in-law's.
I've known Paul for a long time, even though I haven't seen
him. If he thinks he can leave the responsibility in my hands
and forget about it, he will. When you call Paul, tell him
I'll try and provide some kind of stopgap for a few nights
only. Then I'm coming back to New York. For anything after

12

that, I'm afraid he'll have to come home and do it himself, or at least make the arrangements."

"I'll suggest that he call you, Miss Malory. You can then tell him yourself." And the doctor hung up.

At 3:30 that afternoon, Kate gathered up the scattered pieces of the bulky manuscript, shoved them into her tote bag, put on her coat and headed towards the outer hall. Passing Judy's desk she stopped.

"I won't be in tomorrow. Apparently my stepsister is in the hospital and I have to go and baby-sit—or child sit—this weekend at her house because her husband is in Tokyo."

"Didn't know you had a sister," Judy said.

"Stepsister," Kate corrected. "An adoptive stepsister whom I haven't spoken to in more than sixteen years and a brother-in-law ditto. Now she's in a mental institution and he's in Tokyo. A meddling neighbor says the house is going to pot—maybe literally for all I know—and the fifteen-year-old daughter comes home at four in the morning. All of this so I will get on my horse and ride off to the suburbs in rescue."

"Lotsa luck," Judy said sympathetically. "You going to take *Wheel* with you?"

I am. I should have gotten the phone number of the house from the doctor. But you should be able to get it from information if you have to. It's Meadowbrook. Paul Lamont. Wood Lane. If I find their number is unlisted or anything stupid like that, I'll call you from the house tomorrow and give it to you. In the meantime cope with what you can cope with. I'll handle the rest Monday."

She walked quickly down a long hall and was about to go out the main door of the publishing house when, her hand on the handle, she changed her mind and went to her left instead towards a large corner office. "Is he in, Cindy?" She asked the woman sitting in the alcove outside. "And not on the phone or in conference."

Cindy, a maternal looking older woman said, "I'm sure he'd be free for you, Kate."

Kate made a face in self deprecation. Then she went to the half open door and lightly tapped with her knuckles on one of the panels. When the good-looking fair haired man glanced up from the papers on his desk, Kate said, "Are you free and available for a minute?"

"For you, always," Graham Maitland said, rising.

As inevitably happened, Kate felt her heart give an extra beat, then seem to stop. This customary reaction was one of the things that made her guarded around her employer. She had left the original publishing house where they had both worked during the years of their affair simply to get away from him and from all the humiliation their relationship had finally, for her, become. Then, a year previously, Graham, a rich man by both inheritance and marriage, had bought Sutcliffe and Wells, the house that Kate had gone to and in which she had risen to the position of senior editor. So now he was her employer, with this difference: he and his wife were legally separated and awaiting a divorce. It was a difference that, if anything, stiffened her reflex action of reserve. For her professional comfort, she had to maintain good relations with him; for her personal ease of mind, she maintained them at as great a distance—both psychological and physical—as possible. The one thing she knew she did not know was how she felt about him.

She stayed near the door and said, "I just came to tell you that I won't be in tomorrow. I have to go up to Westchester to do something about my sister's household. She's in the hospital."

"Sorry to hear it," Graham said with his automatic good manners. He walked around to the front of his desk. "I'd forgotten you had a sister."

"We haven't talked for years. She and Paul, her husband, were traveling for a long time for some big conglomerate, so avoiding one another hasn't been any hassle. I didn't even know they'd come to live in Westchester. But I got a call from a Dr. McGrath this morning who said Deborah was in the

14

hospital with a depression following an attempted suicide, and Paul, who is in Tokyo, had resurrected my name to go and make some other arrangements for a new housekeeper or something. The two children are too young to be left alone."

"Too bad," Graham said. "Do you think that amidst all the *Sturm und Drang* you'll be able to work on *Wheel?*"

"I'm taking the manuscript up there. There's bound to be some time—even if it's the middle of the night."

"Don't kill yourself, but it would help if you could make the production deadline. It would save the house a lot of money. If it misses, we'll have to go on overtime with the printer to get it done, and that costs."

"Aye, aye, sir. I'll do my best."

"Listen, Kate." Graham came up to her and put his hands on her shoulders. "You're the most stable member of the staff. You know it and I know it. And don't think it's not appreciated."

Kate felt the familiar sensation, a sting behind the eyes, a jump in her middle. It happened whenever Graham touched her. She knew she was getting the Distant Early Warning Signal of an old yearning. She should have reflected, she thought now, trying—and failing—to will herself to step back, just how destructive that emotion could be in her life. "Thanks, Graham, those are sweet words to hear."

"As you well know, I mean them." His blue green eyes had lost their usual expression of amused distance. She had a sudden memory of those eyes—not at all distant—bending over her one early morning. The Bahamian sun was pouring through the window, adding a gold wash to the tanned body above her. Her hands were against his chest, feeling the muscles and the hair and the warm dry skin.

"You're very important to me," Graham said now and, ignoring the open door, kissed her.

Her heart scudding and beating, she stepped back. "Don't worry about *Wheel*, Graham. It'll get done."

Leaving him standing there, she left the room—almost fled

from it and went out to the elevator. The louse, she thought. He did that deliberately.

Kate sat in a nonsmoking car of the train and stared out at the 125th Street station. The train had been there already for twenty minutes. The mist and droplets on the dirty windows bespoke weather that was muggy and damp, and the inside of the car had a metallic or chemical smell, she couldn't decide which. A mumbled statement over the train's public-address system indicated that another train had been derailed somewhere and everything had stopped for a while. According to her many friends who had spent their early years of parenthood in the suburbs, the trains between Grand Central and Westchester, Rockland and Putnam Counties and Connecticut spent most of their time waiting for some other train somewhere else to be put back together again.

One former suburban friend (now back in the city) commented that when he was a boy in Montana, he used to go down to the railroad station to watch the Great Northern Express thunder through eight-foot drifts of snow, punctual to the minute. A light dew, he finished acidly, was enough to stop all rail action between New York City and its various suburbs. Kate grinned as she remembered the remark.

Leaning forward, she peered through the murky windows. Outside stretched the gray, dirty, gloomy platform. Beyond the platforms, Kate knew, were steps leading down to the street. Having started underground at Grand Central, and run underground for some fifty blocks beneath the splendor and wealth of Park Avenue, the train emerged at about Ninety-eighth Street and from there ran on overhead tracks till it crossed the Harlem River and the Bronx and headed into Westchester County. At one time New York residents living in the east eighties and nineties, when returning from the suburbs, would get off at 125th Street and take a taxi home, rather than going all the way down to Grand Central and taking a taxi up from there—if they could get one. No longer. Above

16

Ninety-sixth Street had become, with poverty and changing time, a high crime area.

Why was she thinking all that? Because, she thought wearily, she didn't want to think about what might be facing her. Easier to think about the changes New York had gone through since she had come to the city in the early 1960s when she was twenty-two. Afterwards, she was to realize that though New York was not by then the place it was reported to have been immediately following World War II, she had had a year or two of the old style in almost everything—dress, politics and language, commonly held assumptions about the state and society—before the massive explosion of the late sixties changed forever almost everything. Sitting there motionless and sticky with the grime and heat of the car, she felt a beat of nostalgia for the city she had come to and the girl she had been: young, eager and gauche, determined not so much to make a fortune as to make a name for herself.

And what happened? she thought.

Life happened, and she remembered something that someone else had said, life was what happened when you made other plans. . . . Still, senior editor at a top publishing house was not bad. She loved her job, liked her authors—most of them, ego and all—she was proud of the books she had been instrumental in bringing to existence (again, most of them) and—Graham? She pulled her mind away. No use thinking about Graham, not any more. If she was going to sit here and brood, trapped at the 125th Street station, then it would be better to go back to the beginning—back to the reason for coming to New York.

The Garden District of New Orleans was a strange place to go through a youthful dark night of the soul, but it was in the old graceful house on Prytania Street that she had swallowed her first bitter draft of humiliation. Her adoptive father, Keith Malory, a pleasantly unsuccessful broker was neither an aristocrat nor a New Orleanean. He came from a Methodist home in

17

a small town somewhere in the mid-South. Bright, good-looking, lazy and full of charm—and also, of an odd, questing intelligence—he had married the perfect woman for him. She came from the same town and had attended the same Methodist Sunday school. There the similarities ended. Beth Malory was plain, hardworking and rigidly disciplined. She conducted her life and the lives of any who ventured into her sphere of influence with unyielding efficiency. She had also inherited a little money from her mother, who could boast in her bloodline a thin stream of Virginia aristocracy. The rest of her and all of her husband's backgrounds came from the mainstream of Scotch-Irish frontiersmen who felled the forests, tilled their farms, kept their shops and set up an orderly, if segregated, society.

The only thing atypical about Keith and Beth Malory was their apparent inability, as the years passed, to produce a child. Beth went to church and prayed. Keith, when he could get away, went downtown to a crony's house and played poker. Not having a child caused him no distress. What attention he had away from poker was dedicated to his intellectual interests and to a scheme to persuade his wife to hand over her money, which was, in his view, sitting in the bank doing nothing. Once his, he reasoned, he could invest it, make more money, and move to some larger place where his talents could have greater scope. It was a simple, straightforward plan, and since he had no desire to spend his profits on riotous living, but fully intended that Beth should share in his inevitable wealth, he could not understand her recalcitrance.

But Beth had an attitude towards her principal that was worthy of a New Englander.

"We'll always have it, Keith darlin'—a little nest egg we can count on."

And there matters stayed until the specialist in Memphis to whom she had gone informed Beth that it was she who could not have a child, not Keith. That anything as mundane and pedestrian as the ability to conceive should have eluded her

18

filled Beth first with disbelief, then rage. Very well, she announced out of the blue, a week later at dinner, "We'll adopt. That's the thing to do. I'll go down to the Methodist Home tomorrow."

"Come along, honey, we don't need a child. Children can tie you down." In his mind he had already (somehow) acquired enough money to invest and make a killing and was attached to one of the great brokerage houses in a major city —Memphis, perhaps, or New Orleans, or Houston. A child would be expensive and would, he was shrewdly sure, tie him and his wife to this boring small town, which he was determined to leave.

"Yes, we do. And I'm going to have one."

But Beth, who had never encountered serious opposition in her life, met it then. She discovered there was no way she could legally adopt a child without her husband's cooperation—at least not in that section of the country. And the scandal it would cause if she tried to bring one home over his loudly stated objections made even her intrepid soul shrink. She tried all sorts of other devices. She arranged to have the pastor call on her husband to talk to him about Christian duty and homeless orphans. Keith, deadpan, talked back about resignation to the Will of God. She borrowed the babies of her various friends and had them dotted around the house over the weekend. Keith just fled to his poker game. She refused to sleep with him and moved into another bedroom. Keith started taking business trips. She went into a depression and refused to eat. Keith, who had never been overly interested in food, didn't notice. Then she made a serious mistake. She visited the president of the bank that held her money and suggested that he, a deacon of the church, might call on Keith one afternoon at his insurance office. The deacon did. Keith did not come home. He went, instead, to New Orleans. From the moment he got out of the train at Union Station off Rampart Street, and inhaled what he always afterwards called the typical New Orleans smell—composed of swamp, sweet flowering olive, roasting coffee, garlic, people and bayous—he knew he had found his natural habitat. He never left.

Eventually Beth joined him in his pokey little apartment off the Esplanade, where cockroaches the size of mice scurried in and out of the woodwork, where jars containing sweets such as honey and jam had to be kept in bowls of water so that a twisting black rope of ants would not be found leading to and from the cupboard, and where, in her view, the population, high and low, led lax, Catholic and immoral lives.

Eventually they reached a compromise. Keith would be allowed to invest three-quarters of her principal, and Beth would adopt a baby. Before she succeeded she had a bad scare. Between trying to give Mother Nature a chance and their extended arguments they had waited almost too long. Keith was forty-four and Beth was forty-one. But they finally got the infant, a girl, and named her Kate.

By the time Kate was eight they were living in another pokey little apartment on Harmony Street on the edges of the Garden District. The money Keith had made he had mostly lost. His dream of poker-filled days and opulent formal dinners at night and dancing at the great Carnival balls gave way to reality and he took a minor job with a brokerage firm. They were able—just barely—to send Kate to one of the lesser and extremely strict Protestant private schools where Kate made straight A's. She also attended a Methodist Sunday school where, at the age of twelve, she met and fell passionately in love with the son of the pastor, Paul Lamont. When her mother, coming across Kate's secret diary, discovered her violent crush, she decided the time had come to talk to Kate about sex, especially in view of the fact that Kate, an adopted baby, had been illegitimate. Blood, she was afraid, might tell.

Kate listened politely. Despite the fact that every book, magazine and newspaper that entered either her home or her school was vigorously scrutinized and her moviegoing censored, she had managed to pick up a fair amount of informa-

20

tion. None of it quite jived with what her mother was telling her. Finally, she blurted out, "But can you have a baby by kissing a boy?"

Her mother hesitated. If Kate, who had developed far earlier than she herself had and was already bursting out of her first bra, could be prevented from dangerous and indiscriminate kissing by this piece of misinformation, than perhaps Beth's maternal duty lay in allowing it to remain—for the time being.

"It leads to having a baby," she said, comforting her conscience with the undeniable fact that kissing led to other things, which led to a baby.

There were two subjects Kate thought about a lot. One was God and the other was sex. When the time came for her to be received into the Methodist Church, the pastor, mildly puzzled by the self-contained child, asked her if she was interested in religion.

"I'm interested in religions," Kate said, buzzing the plural s.

The pastor thought this was hilarious and told Beth. She did not think it was hilarious and told Keith.

"It's your fault," she said. "You're always talking to her about heathen ideas. Metempsychosis indeed!"

"Aren't you interested in God—whoever He is?" Keith asked lazily.

"I'm interested in church."

"That's not the same thing." Keith loathed church.

"So I have been trying to point out. You're having a bad influence on Kate."

"Oh I don't think so," Keith said. "Why should she care what I think?"

But she did. Kate could never remember when she had not felt different from other people. Most of the time she put it down to being adopted. Sometimes even that didn't seem enough of a reason. She adored Keith but knew that though he would occasionally talk to her about things that interested him, as though she were an equal, she wasn't important to him. She loved Beth, to whom she was important. But she loved her as someone in a fortress would love someone outside besieging it. Beth—metaphorically speaking—supplied her with food and water and affection. But, Kate thought, she lurked outside, waiting to swallow Kate's soul in return.

Years later she realized that when she thought about her mother, she thought about sex, because that became, increasingly, what they talked about. Her mother worried about Kate and sex a lot.

When she thought about her father she thought about God, because that was what she and Keith talked about. Or at least he talked to her sporadically. He had the habit of making a statement that was the end result of some long, involved, inner cogitation, but that fell out of the blue and out of context, such as (on one occasion), "Of course the concept of immortality is fundamentally Platonic, not Biblical."

"How do you know?" Kate asked.

Keith looked annoyed and started to tell her some long rigamarole she didn't understand. But it didn't matter. He was talking to her, or at her, which didn't happen that often.

"Do you like God?" Kate asked, when he stopped talking.

Then he smiled, really looking at her. "Yes, I must, I guess. I keep looking for Him."

"Mom says a poker table is a funny place to find Him."

"No funnier than church."

Kate never discussed sex with any of her friends at school. None of them seemed to have her fascinated curiosity, a fact that she attributed to their not being adopted. Real children—as opposed to adopted children—simply weren't that curious. For one thing, it was lower-class, and her personal state of lower-classness was evidenced not only by her dirty mind—which none of the other children seemed to have—but also by the fact that she got her period when she was barely eleven.

"I suppose it's the hot climate," her mother said. "Back

home our people never started that early. I guess it's because we all came from the British Isles. Of course you're adopted . . ." She stopped there because she truly loved Kate and never wished her to feel anything but totally wanted. In fact, she made the blunder because she would forget for long periods of time that Kate hadn't sprung from the ethnically reliable loins of herself and Keith Malory.

"Who get their periods early—what kind of people?" Kate asked. She was both ashamed of and intensely interested in her own heritage.

"Oh—you know, Italians. People like that."

Kate spent the next year wondering if she was Italian, staring at herself in the mirror over her bureau, poring over any books she could get showing photographs of Italians. But there was nothing about her face or person that could give her a definite answer. It was true both parents had blue eyes, and hers were hazel. Both her parents had shortish noses, and hers, though straight, was disproportionately long. They were thin. She was—not thin. She sighed and looked down beneath her already ample breasts to the ample folds of flesh beneath. She had been a stocky child and had become a fat teen-ager.

Once, at Sunday school, she had clasped Paul's hand in a ring-around-the-rosy game and given it a squeeze before she let it go.

"I like you," she said.

He didn't say anything.

"Do you like me?"

"Not much."

Pain went through her like a lightning bolt. "Why?"

"Because you're too fat."

She went on a diet, trying to keep it secret. Somehow she knew that her mother would oppose any effort of hers to lose weight.

"I'm not having you go on any of those silly diets, Kate. Do you understand? When you're grown up it'll be quite time enough to worry about something like that."

"But boys won't like me," Kate wailed, forgetting her caution.

"So that's what it is! I'm warning you, I won't permit it!"

"Let her lose weight," her father said. "She's right about no boy liking her the way she is. She'll always be bright, but she's never going to be pretty. The least she can do is cultivate a good figure. No man will ever look at her like that." And he went back to his book.

The bolt of pain shot through Kate again. She closed her eyes and wrapped her arms around her body as though it were something obscene.

"Listen to me, Kate," her mother said. "No one will ever love you the way I do. You're my little girl. I *like* fat little girls."

Keith looked up from his book again. "That's a hell of a thing to say to the child, Beth. Come on, now. You're gonna mess up her life."

"Do *you* care?"

Kate remembered that moment; it was like one of those scenes frozen in a paperweight.

Keith shrugged. "No, not that much. It was you adopted her." And he got up and walked into the next room where he could read in peace.

It was the first moment Kate remembered feeling that she wanted to die. It didn't last long, but she never forgot it.

Beth, who hated New Orleans and everything it represented, could not see beyond defying both her husband (who took her there) and sex (which, she was sure, abounded there, especially in the French section) with the same weapon.

"Pay no attention, darlin'. Have a praline. I went especially down to that trashy French Quarter just to get them for you."

But at fifteen Kate was at long last able to go on her diet unimpeded. Beth developed a tumor in her brain that proved malignant and killed her in a very short time.

A year after her mother's death, Keith Malory married Diane Légère and moved with Kate into the great Légère

24

home on Prytania Street.

"And this is my daughter, Deborah," Diane said when Kate came on her first formal visit. "I know you and she will be such friends!"

"Hello," Kate said to the tall child a few years younger than herself.

"Hi." Deborah held out her hand, the palm facing slightly down. A little surprised, because she wasn't much for shaking hands, Kate put hers in Deborah's and gave a shriek. A black spider scudded over her palm onto the back of her hand.

Kate gave another shriek and shook her hand frantically. "Daddy!" she screamed. Deborah was doubled up with laughter.

"Debbie darlin', that's not funny," her mother said, and giggled.

One day, when Paul came by to pick Kate up for Sunday school, he saw Debbie in the living room. He and Kate were only sixteen at the time, and Debbie was only fourteen. But after that everything changed.

The train gave a lurch. A smell of oil and grit filled the car. Then there was another lurch and the train pulled forward, leaving the platform and 125th Street behind.

Kate watched the top floors of the tenements slide past. How many children did Debbie have? The doctor mentioned two. Did that include the fifteen-year-old girl who came in at four in the morning?

Kate didn't know. Not keeping up—or in touch—with Debbie and Paul had been, for a while, the single most important act, or omission, in her life. When that period passed, so did the determination to stay remote from them because by that time she no longer had any interest in them. Her mother, of course, was dead. So were Keith and Diane. Thus, failing desire, there was nothing to tie them.

"Nothing whatsoever," she said aloud.

There was a rustling of newspapers around her. The commuting crowd was thick but, as always when she had taken a commuting train anywhere, self-absorbed.

"The hell with it," she muttered to herself and hauled her copy of *Wheel* out of her tote bag. If anything could prove a talisman against the tentacles of the past, it would be the demands of the present. Extracting a blue pencil from her handbag, she forced her attention to the beginning of the last major segment. After a few seconds, her pencil descended. What a klutz, she thought to herself, marking up a rambling, repetitive and clumsy sentence. But 90,000 people out there, with 90,000 times $10.95 in their hot little hands were waiting to gobble up the expert's latest word. Which made Kate think of Joel. She sighed and her attention strayed. She was telling part of the truth when she said she wouldn't go to bed with him because he was almost a decade younger. The rest of the truth was that she didn't want to. The price, within herself, would be out of proportion to whatever the rewards might be. With Graham, no price had been too high, but then Graham was married. . . .

"It's interesting," a therapist had once said during her brief fling with wisdom according to Freud, "how you always pick unavailable men. . . ."

She had discovered that about herself long before the therapist. Except, of course, for Paul . . .

Back to *Wheel*. This time habit asserted itself. She got caught up in trying to make Mr. Kramer's interesting but miserably written book acceptable. When the trainman bawled out the name of her station, she barely had time to thrust the manuscript into her bag, pick up her overnight suitcase and get off the train.

The house was one of several on a winding street, each house within its generous lot. It was, Kate decided, curiously like the Légère house on Prytania Street, reduced in size. There was the same white frame, the same porch bulging out

26

to the side, the same double garage, the same little columns on either side of the front door. There the resemblance stopped. The huge live oaks of the New Orleans house, some of their branches bending almost to the ground, were represented here by a few Japanese shrubs and what looked, in the semi-dark, like an elm. Another difference leapt to the eye. This lawn was a mess of litter of one kind or another: an overturned bicycle, a wagon minus a wheel, paper bags, a jump rope and dog turds.

Kate walked up to the front door and rang the bell.

From inside there came the sound of disco music, a voice—it sounded like a boy's—yelling above the noise and the phone ringing.

"Turn that thing down," the boy's voice yelled.

"Why should I?" yelled another voice, probably female, Kate thought. "Do it yourself."

There was the sound of steps, then a crash, as though something had fallen, and a yelp.

The boy's voice rose in a wail. "You kicked my dog, you bully!"

The music suddenly stopped and the phone stopped ringing. "Hello," the girl's voice said. In the deafening silence Kate rang the bell again. Then putting down her suitcase she rapped on the door.

"Who is it?" yelled the boy.

"Kate Malory."

There were more steps. The door swung open. Paul Lamont, reincarnated at age about twelve, square of face with short, wheat colored hair, was standing in front of her. Kate felt a curious sense of déjà vu, of time circling back. Could the appalling Kramer be right in his idiocies?

"I'm your Aunt Kate—sort of."

"Oh." Fear showed momentarily in his eyes. Then withdrawal seemed to close off his face. "The doctor said you were coming. We're okay," he burst out. "You didn't have to come."

"I couldn't be happier to hear it. But before I take the next train back, do you mind if I come in long enough to phone for a taxi?"

There was a short pause. Then the boy stepped back. "You won't go round making waves?"

"I'll try not to," Kate said. She stepped through the front door straight into a huge living room. As her toe came down, something soft and liquid gave way under it.

"That's Bones's accident," the boy said. "He's not exactly housebroken."

Chapter 2

Kate stood, one-legged. "How about bringing me a paper towel, damp? Before I step on the carpet."

"There aren't any. We ran out. Anyway, the carpet's pretty grungy, what with Bones not being housebroken."

"Do you have some tissue?" Kate was hanging onto her temper and her balance. Neither was easy.

The boy shrugged. "I don't. Maybe Marie does. Marie!" he yelled suddenly, "Do you have any tissues? Aunt Kate's stepped in Bones's do."

If Marie was the girl on the telephone, her voice went on without interruption.

"I'll get some newspaper," the boy said, and disappeared. In a few seconds he was back holding some newspaper.

"Thanks," Kate said, and dealt with the sole of her foot. "Maybe you'd better bring yet another wet sheet so we can get it off the floor."

"Okay."

She gave him the used paper and put her foot down cautiously, having carefully checked the rest of the parquet around her. Then she looked up. A slender girl of indeterminate age in jeans and a T-shirt was lounging against the far wall, talking on the telephone, her back to Kate, her face turned towards the small passage leading from the living room.

Kate walked into the room, stepping around a T-shirt, a hair dryer, books, a jumble of magazines and some needlepoint. Idly, she picked up the needlepoint. The front didn't look too bad. She turned it over. The back resembled nothing so much as crisscrossed highways. Kate dropped it on top of some accumulated litter on a table by the wall. Behind the table was a mirror. Kate stared at her image and poked her dark, curly hair into place. It had never been hair that responded well to instruction. During much of the sixties she had had it straightened. After the last straightening had grown out, she'd had it set in rollers. It was, curiously, Joel who had changed that. They'd gone swimming and he had ruffled through her springy, drying curls. "Why don't you leave it that way?"

"I suppose you think I should have an afro?"

He'd grinned and reached for his glasses. "Mine's big enough for two."

And what would Joel say about this household? He'd probably be able to cope with it better than she could. And certainly better than Graham. But how could the exquisite Deborah Légère Lamont ever bring up progeny that would produce this chaos? Or Paul? Kate heard the sound of scraping and turned. The twelve-year-old boy was back and attacking the remainder of the smear on the floor.

"Where's Bones?" she asked.

"Out in the kitchen."

"What's your name?"

He stood up. "Ranger."

Ranger? Of course. Ranger Légère was Deborah's father, Ranger being his mother's maiden name.

Ranger stood up and stared at his handiwork.

"You missed some," Kate said. "There." She pointed.

He squatted again, rubbed, and then went back down the passage to what Kate supposed was the kitchen. She waited to see if he would return, but he didn't. That left the girl on the phone, still murmuring into the receiver. That Kate was not particularly welcome was obvious. Good, she thought. The sooner I can go back . . .

She slipped off her tweed jacket, revealing a dark green shirt and tan skirt underneath. It was not only warm in the living room, it smelled. Windows stretched on either side of the front door, all closed. There were more on the other side. Trying one after the other, Kate managed to get three open. The rest were stuck. Furthermore, a dark smear covered one of the once white windowsills. I wonder what that is, Kate thought, fearing the worst. Whatever it was had dried hard.

Putting her jacket over a chair back where it had the greatest chance of safety, Kate then put her overnight bag and tote bag on the sofa beside it. Her eyes strayed towards the smear on the window sill. Would her accoutrements be Bones-proof? On the other hand, would anywhere else be safer? Well, at least Bones was in the kitchen. Ranger had not come back. Kate had an impulse to take the receiver from Marie's hands and place it firmly on the telephone. Fascist, she reproached herself.

She stared at the girl's back. If Ranger looked like the young Paul, there was something about Marie's tall, lissome back and dark blonde curls that spelled her mother. Kate's heart sank and an eerie feeling came over her. Would she have to go through any of those bitter years at the Légère house again—those two years of misery and humiliation, until at eighteen, she finally made her escape?

Of course not, she told herself. Still, it was weird how powerfully that memory came back, triggered by a graceful back.

It was a narrow hall, yet she couldn't help but notice, as she squeezed past the girl on her way to what she supposed was the kitchen, the girl didn't move aside by as much as an inch.

The kitchen turned out to be large, chaotic, messy and pleasant. In one corner, Ranger was squatting, his hand on the neck of a skinny yellow dog. It was easy to see where the dog got his name. Underneath the golden coat, the ribs and vertebrae stood out in ridges.

"You go on the paper, Bones," Ranger said to him. "On the paper."

Bones wagged his tail and jumped up and licked Ranger's face.

"Maybe," Kate said helpfully, "until Bones gets the idea, you could paper the entire floor, and keep Bones in the kitchen until he learns what it's for."

Ranger seemed to explode. "I will not just keep him in the kitchen. He gets lonely. How'd you like to be kept all by yourself. Or maybe you wouldn't care."

"Okay, okay. Sorry! Just a suggestion."

"You're just like everybody else," Ranger muttered. "Don't listen, Bones. Everything's going to be all right."

Kate, who liked animals, walked over to look at Bones. "Hi," she said, when she got within three feet, bending a little and holding out her hand. She was totally unprepared for Bones's reaction. Whimpering frantically, Bones broke loose from Ranger's hand and crept under the table, his tail curved under and beneath his legs.

"Now look what you've done! And he'll probably pee under there or make a mess. That's what happens when he gets scared. Bones, it's all right!" Ranger slid under the table on his knees. But he was right about Bones's reaction. The wretched dog evacuated everything. An unpleasant smell filled the room.

Feeling helpless, Kate stood where she was and said, "Why is it so frightened?"

"Because he got beaten up and pushed into a shed and starved by . . . by people like you who thought he shouldn't be in the house. Come on, Bonesey, it's gonna be okay." The whimpering stopped.

Kate's eye lit on a box of kitchen matches, an ancient remedy for unpleasant odors. Strolling over to the stove slowly so as not to activate any more panic, she struck a match, let it burn almost down to the bottom, blew it out and then struck another. As she watched it burn, she thought about something she had read in a book she had edited: in earlier centuries, before running water and drains, shovels full of smoldering wood and charcoal would be carried through rooms to freshen the stale smells brought on by illnesses such as dysentery. Why do I remember that, she wondered, and not the names of people I've met the week before? She put the spent matches into the sink.

"I'm sorry I frightened him. I'll be more careful in future."

Bones was still under the table. Ranger, with more newspaper, was cleaning up. When he was through he took the balled up paper outside the screen door.

Kate sat down on a chair by the table and stared at Bones, who peered back at her. Taking in the long legs and huge paws and ears, she decided that Bones was probably about four months old and mostly Golden Retriever.

"Where did you get Bones?" she asked Ranger when he came back in.

"At the pound."

"And they told you he'd been beaten?"

"I'm taking him out now for a walk." Ranger took a leash off the back of the door, slid under the table and emerged with Bones, still sitting down and resisting every foot he was dragged. "If you'll just get out of the way," Ranger said, hostility in each syllable, "then Bones will go out the door."

"I'll get out of the way," Kate said amiably, rising from the chair and stepping backwards into the L part of the L-shaped kitchen. "But there's no reason for you—or Bones—to be angry. I went over to pat him. I didn't know about his fears. After all, why should I? Nobody told me. So don't treat me as the enemy. I'm not."

"Okay," Ranger said. "But it'd be better if you just don't

come near him. He doesn't like females—except Marie. And he doesn't like grown-ups." And he and Bones were out the door before Kate could ask anything else.

Why do I feel so guilty? she wondered.

Abruptly turning, she walked back into the major part of the kitchen. Up on a wall a clock gave the time as 3:35. A.M. or P.M.? Kate wondered. She glanced at her watch. It was now five minutes past eight. She had not eaten. She was tired. An overwhelming longing for her own clean, well-ordered apartment on East Eighty-third Street came over her. By this time she would have had a drink, cooked dinner, and would have sat at her own dining table, either watching the news on television, or reading a book. Her windows looked out on that rarity in New York—a garden, with trees just above her window level. On her window sills she had feeders that she left full each morning for birds that congregated there and waited for her. In the course of the evening, she'd probably get two or three phone calls from friends, both female and male. At that, the picture of Joel sprang again into her mind. He had a habit, once or twice a week, of calling around ten, ostensibly about some book, and talking for half an hour.

"I think you look on me as your mother," she'd once said to him.

"No, I don't. And don't say that again. You may not understand your own motive in saying that, but I do. And I don't like it."

"What motive?"

"Think about it," Joel said, and hung up.

He never explained that, and she never asked him. He didn't call back for about three weeks.

And Graham sometimes called. But, by some mutual, unspoken agreement, not often. Kate was grateful that the apartment in which they had conducted their long and ultimately unhappy affair was downtown in the east twenties. One of her final acts when she understood, once and for all, that despite everything he said, Graham would never divorce Danielle and

34

marry her, was to move and to sell most of the furniture she had and buy new. She thought of the new apartment as her celibate self and said that once to Joel.

"Yes," he said. "It looks it."

"I like the way it looks," she had replied, bristling.

"It's okay, but it could change for the better."

When he said that it was the first time she knew positively that this twenty-nine-year-old man wanted to go to bed with her. She turned him down. But it did worlds for her ego, and she had her apartment painted, at vast expense, in newer and brighter colors.

"I take it you're Aunt Kate come to rescue us from our baser selves," a cool voice said behind her.

Kate, snatched back to the dirt, disorder and hostility of the immediate environment, turned. Marie lounged in the door. She really is astonishingly beautiful, Kate thought, and felt the curious mixture of admiration, humility and resentment that great beauty in another woman evoked.

"And I take it you're Marie," she said.

The girl made a mock bow. "You take it right." Her eyes strayed around the chaotic kitchen. "I'm sorry nobody has seemed to welcome you, Aunt Kate," she said, not sounding at all sorry. "But after all, we didn't ask you to come."

"No," Kate said pleasantly, "Dr. McGrath did. But I think you ought to know that this is as much of an imposition on me —as much of an interruption in my life—as it is on you."

"Well then you don't have to stay, do you?"

"Unfortunately—for us both—I do. At least for a day or two, until some arrangement can be made for a companion or housekeeper or somebody. Or until your father gets home. You *are* minor children and you shouldn't be living alone."

"We do okay."

"Not according to either Dr. McGrath or your neighbor."

"Nosey old Fitch-bitch."

"Probably. Still, Mrs. Fitch has a point. Especially if 4:00 A.M. is your favorite time for coming home."

35

"It's none of her business."

"That's debatable. If you were ill and had no one to look after you and she knew it and did nothing about it, she would be severely criticized by just about everybody."

"Didn't you ever come home at four?"

"Yes. But not when I was fifteen."

"What's the difference? Kids of eighteen come home at four all the time. It's so hypocritical to say it's okay at one age but not another. That's like Mom talking about Daddy or me getting drunk or stoned. And all the time she's spaced out on pills. Not that I blame her."

A vision of the exquisite Deborah on the night of her coming out party at the beginning of Carnival sifted across Kate's mind. "Pills? Deborah?"

"Sure. That's why she's locked up."

"I thought—the doctor said something about a depression."

"She's depressed. But she's a pill head, too."

I cannot cope with this and I want to go home, Kate thought. She found she was staring at Marie who was staring back at her. "I'm sorry," Kate said. Questions surged into her mind, but more immediate was the fact that she hadn't had dinner. She said, "I'm starved. Is there anything to eat? Have you had dinner?"

"We don't really have dinner. At least not since Mrs. Brody left. We just eat when we're hungry."

"Well I'm hungry. What would you suggest I eat?"

Marie simply shrugged.

"All right," Kate said dryly. "Never mind. Do you have anything alcoholic around here?"

"We got rid of everything we could find, because of Mom. If she took any liquor on top of her pills, that'd be curtains. Do you have a drinking problem?"

Knowing Marie's insolence was deliberate—a test to see if she, Kate, could be goaded into some overreaction—Kate said calmly, "No, I don't. I enjoy a drink when I get home. Alcoholism is a disease, you know. Or so I have been led to understand." She turned her back and opened the refrigerator. It would have to be a ham and cheese sandwich, she finally decided. Two pieces of bread did not exactly fit into the caloric regimen she tried to hold herself to. But to make an omelette she would have to use the grease encrusted pan she could see on the stove.

Kate put some water in the kettle and set it on the burner. She turned on the jet. Then she started looking in the various cupboards for coffee, determined that she would not, if possible, ask anything more of the sullen, hostile girl still watching her. But at the end of searching through all the wall cupboards, upper and lower, she forced herself to face the fact that there was no coffee. "It's impossible," she said aloud. "There's no coffee. How can I get up in the morning?" She turned towards Marie. "You don't have coffee?"

Hands in pockets, Marie strolled past Kate to the refrigerator in the L. "No, Mrs. Brody drank tea. Daddy's not at home much, and the rest of us drink milk or sodas. I hate coffee. Bad for the tum." And she patted her flat abdomen.

"I don't think I can face life in the morning without coffee. Where is the nearest store or deli or market that would be open at this hour?"

"You are in the suburbs, dear Aunt Kate. Not in the Big Apple, where you can get anything you want somewhere in the city at every hour of the night. We are the pure, pure suburbs. Everything closes down at a decent hour."

"Come off it, Marie." Kate spoke as cheerfully as she could, in view of the fact that she was facing a coffeeless morning.

Ignoring her, Marie turned around and opened the refrigerator. "Sorry, kids, if the cold blast hits you." Taking out a container, she closed the door again, then squatted down.

Irritated but curious, Kate went across the L of the kitchen and peered over Marie's back. In a deep box raised on books was a mother calico cat and six kittens. Still with closed eyes, they looked about a day old and squeaked and groped blindly with tiny paws. A cord led out of the box from something under the layers of newspaper and rags the family was lying on.

"Well, well," Kate said, surprised. Then after a minute, "What's her name?"

"Duchess."

"What's under the paper? I mean, with the electric cord."

"A heating pad. I put it on low at night. Okay, kids. Sleep well." Marie pulled a dirty piece of tarpaulin over the top of the box. Kate could see that because the front of the box was cut lower than the back, there was space between the rim of the front and the cover where air could get in and the mother cat could get out.

"When were they born?" she asked.

"Yesterday." Marie strolled back to the center of the kitchen, picked up a spoon from the drainboard of the sink, and started to walk out.

"Wait a minute," Kate said. "I want to talk to you."

"About what?"

"Don't either you or Ranger realize that if you don't like the idea of having me around, the state can step in and send you both to a juvenile center or foster homes?" Kate didn't know that to be true, but she hauled it out of some crevice of her memory.

Marie started spooning her yogurt. "We'd run away. Anyway, Daddy's getting home some time."

It was like hearing the new echo of an old note. Kate smiled a little. "I ran away," she said. "I was older than you, and it was a different age. But it was still running away."

Marie's blasé manner retreated a little. There was a spark of interest in her face. "Terrific, wasn't it?"

Kate answered slowly. "It had its good points, at least professionally. But twenty years later I still had to cope with the same problem. It didn't really settle anything."

The interested look vanished. "Daddy's getting home sometime, anyway."

"How long has he been away?"

Once again she shrugged. It seemed a characteristic affecta-

38

tion. "A month. But he'll drop in before he goes to see his girl friend. Long enough to hire another sitter." She raised turquoise eyes to Kate. "Unless you're it—our new sitter. But I thought Daddy once said you were some hot shot secretary to a tycoon. Do you sit on his lap?"

For half a minute Kate believed her about the secretary bit. Then she knew she was—again—being baited. Amused, she broke into a grin. "As you well know, I am sure, I am not secretary to a tycoon. I'm senior editor at Sutcliffe and Wells, one of the best publishing houses in the country. What's the matter with you, Marie? Why are you and Ranger so hostile?"

Marie finished the container and threw it towards the overflowing garbage pail. "We just don't want you here. We don't need a keeper."

Kate decided to ignore that. "What time do you and Ranger get up for school?" she asked.

"You'll have to ask Ranger what time he gets up. I don't go to school."

"How come?"

"I was expelled." Marie's triumph in saying that came across to Kate like a wave of warm air. She had obviously wanted to shock and she had succeeded, and she was out of the kitchen before Kate could reply.

Kate finished making her sandwich, poured herself a glass of milk and sat down at the table. It was not until she had done so and taken her first bite that she realized the extent of her fatigue. Depression descended on her. Somewhere she'd read—perhaps in one of Kramer's books—that we thought we made choices but were wrong: our paths were predestined. She had rejected that out of hand, but here she was, back with the Légères and Lamonts and their armory of weapons against her—which hadn't seemed to have changed that much—despite everything she had done to remove herself physically and psychologically from her destructive background. She stared at the second half of her sandwich, her appetite, for the moment, gone. If she stayed here, everything that she had,

39

that she had considered her own, would go: her job, her career, her apartment. She would be back where she was, twenty-two years before, an outsider, an alien, running, running, running, to try and catch something—whatever it was— that for her would always be out of reach.

When she felt a touch on her thigh she nearly jumped off the chair. Looking down she saw the calico cat. The great gold eyes stared up at her. A mournful, muted meow sounded.

Kate had never had a cat, but she thought the message fairly obvious. "Here," she said. She poured some of her milk into the saucer of the coffee cup she had optimistically put out. Then she tore the meat and cheese on her plate into small pieces and put both plates down. The cat sniffed at each, then put her tongue into the milk and started lapping. When she'd polished that off, she ate the ham and cheese, licked her mouth, her whiskers and her paws. Then padded over to her box.

Kate picked the dishes off the floor and took them with her glass to the sink. As she passed the garbage pail its pungent odor registered again on her consciousness. That ought to go outside, she thought. What did people in the suburbs do with their garbage? Ask, she thought. She was about to leave the kitchen and go into the living room when she remembered that Ranger and Bones had been outside for nearly half an hour. Changing direction, she went to the back door and opened it. Light from the door and kitchen windows spilled out on a grayish lawn. There was a belt of trees and something that looked like a kennel. Back of the trees, darkness. There was no sight of boy or dog.

"Ranger!" She called. There was no reply.

"Bones!" Still no reply. She looked at her watch. Twenty to nine. Her own Mother would have had a fit if even at twelve years old she had been out by herself at twenty minutes to nine. Correction, Kate thought wryly. Beth would not have had a fit because Kate would not have been out by herself at that hour. Period. But she had come to realize that Beth, in

40

the 1940s, war or no war, was still, in effect, the Southern Victorian she had been brought up to be.

And what do I do now? Kate asked herself, as she closed the back door. She stared at the latch, then opened the door again and tried the knob from the other side. It turned easily. If she had fur, Kate thought, it would be standing up. No denizen of New York City could view with anything but horror an unlocked door leading into a house. And from what the New York papers reported (with a certain degree of satisfaction) crime in the suburbs was following fast in the footsteps of the metropolitan areas. But if she locked the door, how would Ranger and Bones get in? Well, Kate thought, closing the door, we'll have to have a summit conference on locks. Then she went back through the kitchen into the hall and living room. There was nobody there. Marie was upstairs, from which now echoed a powerful and insistent disco beat.

Kate stood in the living room for a minute, automatically taking in the big, rectangular space, with its well chosen furniture and good colors. Somebody—either Deborah or a decorator—had done a good job. But despite the litter of magazines, old newspapers and books, it had an unfinished look, as though a set of messy transients were in temporary occupation, but the real residents had not as yet moved in.

With an abrupt gesture Kate turned on her heel and went back to the kitchen, which, despite the obvious neglect and clutter, had a pleasanter, more human quality. On the kitchen wall, Kate remembered, was a telephone. And underneath on a shelf some part of her mind had noticed was one of those books for listing numbers frequently in use. On an impulse, Kate looked down the first page. Yes. There they were: Dr. McGrath, followed by two numbers, one marked (o) and the other (h). She dialed (h). The phone rang twice, then was picked up. A man's voice that she instantly recognized said, "Hello."

Kate took a deep breath. "Dr. McGrath, this is Kate Malory, the person you conned into coming out to this home so badly

41

in need of a mother. The present inhabitants, Marie and Ranger, appear about as eager to have me as I was to come. They plainly resent my being here, which I understand—life can't be easy for them at the moment. But I have no more authority to try and make them toe some imaginary line than I would have to make them wear uniforms—even if I wanted to. I will stay tonight and I will talk to them, if I can get them both in one place. But that's about all I can do."

"I'm sorry. I didn't realize it would be that difficult."

"I do seem to remember your mentioning that the house was a mess. But you forgot to add that the two children seem to be in various stages of anger and alienation. It would take a full-time, dedicated therapist to unravel all these hostilities. I learned from Marie, by the way, that Deborah's problem seems to be pills."

"That's true. But she is also depressed. Whether the depression springs entirely from withdrawal from pills or not, I don't know yet."

"But it still requires her hospitalization?"

"Without question. She is also suicidal, as I think I told you."

"Somehow I got the idea that all I had to do was to come out here and supply a warm, adult body on the premises for a few days, at which time another permanent housekeeper would arrive. I didn't know I'd be expected to cope with an anarchic and inimical household. And I can't do it."

"Then what do you suggest?"

"I don't know, Dr. McGrath. That's rather your problem and Paul's, isn't it?"

There was silence. Then the doctor sighed. "All right. Stay tonight and go home tomorrow. I'll make some other arrangement."

Perversely, Kate wasn't much more pleased with this statement than she had been with the previous ones. She was quite sure he was going to hang up. "Wait!" she said.

"All right. What?"

"Where is Paul right now?"

"Somewhere in Tokyo. I have a number here where you can call and leave a message. He'll call back." And Kate heard the sound of opening and closing drawers. She glanced at the clock. A quarter to ten. "Here it is." And he read the number.

"Thank you. I suppose I ought to find out what time it is in Tokyo."

"I have a clock here with international times. Let's see. I think Tokyo is ten hours behind us. I mean earlier."

"That would make it noon there. He'll probably be out to lunch. But I'll try."

"Let me know what he says." And the doctor hung up. There was an odd inflection in his voice.

Kate called the number in Tokyo and prepared herself to wait. She was therefore pleasantly surprised when he answered the phone.

When she heard his voice, she found her heart was hammering. Surely, she thought, after all these years and after all that's happened, it can't be the fossilized remains of that tired old crush. She preferred to think it anxiety.

"Hello, Paul. It's Kate Malory. I'm calling from your house."

"Kate!" he said. "It's wonderful of you to be there! To come to the rescue like that."

"It's not wonderful of me, Paul. Because I haven't done it. I came here at that Dr. McGrath's request with the idea of spending, at the most, the weekend, until he could find somebody permanent. But I didn't quite expect such a generally messed up household—in both the literal and psychological sense. I realize Deborah's been hospitalized for a month. But I take it the housekeeper left only a few days ago. However, I shouldn't hold the mess against her. Your children do not want anyone here, and they're quite open about it. I am calling really to tell you that taking care of this situation requires either you, personally, or a full-time psychologist with a lot of patience and authority. I have a job I have to get back to. And I'm not about to try and persuade your offspring to abate their hostility. By this time—I'm sorry to say—it's entirely mutual."

"Look," Paul said. "I know the kids are . . . they've had a hard time, Kate. Deborah hasn't been well for some time."

"According to Marie her problem is pills."

"That's at least partly true, although I wish Marie didn't feel like advertising it to the world. . . . Well, as you say, it's not your problem. All I can do is thank you for trying."

"When are you planning to come home, Paul? As I said, I feel strongly that the situation needs your personal, paternal touch."

"If you were going to stay, or if Mrs. Brody had stayed, I was going to be here in Japan for three weeks, because there's an exciting possibility that I might be able to visit Peking. A chance like that doesn't come too often. If, though, it really is impossible for you to stay and hold the reins for a bit, then I suppose I could get back in about a week or ten days."

Kate summoned up a picture of Paul as she had last seen him. His nickname at school and college had been the Viking. "All he needs," one admiring girl had said, "is one of those Eric the Red outfits you see in TV commercials, plus spear and leather doublet. He wouldn't even have to wear makeup." It was true. With his gaunt height and fair hair, he looked as though he came straight from a fjord.

". . . So it's really up to you," Paul the Viking was saying over the phone. "I throw myself on your mercy."

Suddenly, as though it were a genie from a bottle, Marie's phrase about her father's having a girl friend erupted in Kate's mind. She opened her mouth, then closed it again. It was none of her business. "By the way, Paul, did you know that Marie has been expelled from whatever school she goes to?"

There was silence. "No," Paul said slowly. "I knew there'd been . . . trouble. Mrs. Brody didn't say anything."

"Did she write to you? Keep you up on what was happening?"

"I called her—often."

They were both silent, as though in respect for what they both knew was either not true, or not entirely true. Then Kate pulled herself together. "Paul these are your *children*. They have an emotionally ill mother who is now in the hospital. You should be here, job or no job."

"If the job goes, Deborah will have to go to a state hospital— and you know what those are supposed to be like, the kids will have to leave their high-priced private schools, and I'll have to find another job."

"That sounds pretty dire. I can't believe that an enlightened corporation today—humane if for no other reason than the rotten publicity that would ensue if they were not humane— would not give you a month's leave of absence to come home and find somebody who can help your family."

"Even if this would be about the fourth leave of absence in a bare two years? My firm is as humane as most. And I am one of the owners. But three contracts were lost because I was there instead of where I should be. It's not that I'm indispensable. I'm not. On the contrary what frightens me is that they'll find me as dispensable as all get out and nudge me out. In which case, bye bye private schools, private sanitariums and standard of living. Do you think that would help?"

"I'm not sure it wouldn't, Paul. At least you'd all be in it together. Right now you want me to do your job for you, and I can't. They're not my children."

Another silence. "All right, Kate. I'll come home. I'll call you tomorrow and tell you when. Just stay until I get there. There's no law that says you can't go into your job during the day. I just want you there at night." He paused. "Where's Marie, now?"

"I don't know. You want me to see if she's upstairs? According to one of your nosey neighbors she came in at four one morning."

"I'm more worried about her than Ranger. She's . . . well,

she's more like her mother. Also, she was supposed to collect the mail for me and hold it. I want to know if the school wrote to me."

"Would she tell you?"

"Yes. She would. You may not like my children, Kate. But they have their virtues, and truthfulness is one. Now please ask her to come to the telephone."

"I'm here, Daddy."

"How long have you been there, Marie?"

"From the beginning. You know how the upstairs extension gives a ping when anybody phones out from downstairs."

"And it didn't occur to you I might be having a private conversation?" Kate said.

"Since it's my father paying for the call from his own house, I don't see why I, his daughter, shouldn't talk to him, too."

"I was going to get you . . ."

"It's okay." Paul's voice broke in abruptly. Then, "Is it true, Marie, that St. Hilary's has kicked you out?"

"Yes. They gave me the final axe about a week ago. There's a letter here from them. You want me to read it to you?"

"Please."

There was the sound of paper being unfolded.

Dear Mr. Lamont, We regret having to take the step of expelling Marie, but feel we have no choice. Her grades are failing, she does not attend school, and when she does attend, she is disruptive and insolent. If this were the first time such a course were under discussion, we might try, as we have before, to avert such a drastic solution. But, as we both know, it is not.

I am truly sorry about this. Marie is bright, talented and has enormous energy which, unfortunately, is mostly directed to activities that are destructive to her and to the other students. As someone once said, energy is neutral, you can use it to build or you can use it to destroy, but you have to use it. I wish with all my heart that Marie would use her boundless resources towards building something satisfying and lasting in her own life. At the moment, she is not doing this, and she is doing her best, while on school premises, to prevent others from doing it. We feel therefore we have no choice: we cannot allow Marie to return to school. Yours truly, Margaret McNair, Headmistress

"That's a pretty good letter, don't you think, Daddy? Mc-Nair can really write."

Against her will—she was furious at herself for not having rung off—Kate said, "Don't you feel any regret, Marie?"

"Why should I? I'm tired of school. You don't suppose that stupid school would have been able to expel me if I hadn't wanted them to?"

"I'm very disappointed in you, Marie," Paul said. And for the first time sounded tired. He doesn't know what to do about this, Kate realized.

"We'll talk about it when you come home," Marie said. "When will you be back?"

"I told your Aunt Kate that I will telephone tomorrow and let her know. And Marie, stay off the phone. First of all, I want to get through. Second, I might like a few private words with Kate."

"About me?"

"And the house, and Ranger."

"I think it would be great if you could fit us in between visits with your girl friend," Marie said. And Kate heard the click as she hung up.

"There are times," Paul said, "when I feel like going straight from here to an ashram in India."

"Why don't you?"

"That was supposed to be a joke. I won't even bother to answer it. I'll talk to you tomorrow. And thanks again."

Kate was standing in front of the phone when the back door burst open. Bones galloped in followed by Ranger.

Kate said, "Ranger, it is not a good idea to leave house doors unlocked. Not even in the suburbs."

"I don't have a key."

"One could be made."

"I'd just lose it. Nobody's gonna steal anything. What's to steal?"

"Well I, for one, am much more comfortable with outside doors locked. Where is the key, by the way?"

"Maybe in one of the drawers there somewhere. Here, Bones! Dinner time."

Kate opened one drawer after another in the cabinet under the sink. She found a box of loose keys in the last drawer. She even found a key marked "back door." Going over to the door she tried it. It did not fit.

"This is marked 'back door.' But it doesn't fit."

"I guess it was to the door in the last house." He looked up. "Look, you can lock it from the inside by pushing that little thing."

"Yes, but—oh never mind. If I get nervous you'll just have to knock. By the way, isn't it a bit late for you to be coming back?"

"I just took a walk for a minute. What's the big deal about that?"

"More like an hour. Ranger, don't be pigheaded. You know it's late. Where were you?"

"Hanging out with some kids from the neighborhood."

They stared at each other. After all, she thought, she was only going to be here a short time. "While I'm here, Ranger, would you try and make it back a little earlier—especially in view of the keyless door?"

"All right," he muttered and bent over his pet who was wolfing down the last of the dog food Ranger had given him.

Going into the living room, Kate picked up her jacket, her tote bag and her overnight suitcase. Then she went upstairs. Be thankful, she told herself, for small mercies. The disco music had stopped. At the head of the steps she paused. Which, if any, room was unoccupied?

Putting down her suitcase on a small sofa in the square

upper hall, she knocked on the nearest door. Marie, in a man's nightshirt, opened the door. She was eating an apple. "Yes?" she said, and spat some seeds into her hand.

Kate hated the somewhat subservient position in which she felt she had somehow placed herself. "Do you know which room I should occupy?"

"Try the one at the end of the annex. That's the one Mrs. Brody had." And she closed the door.

By the time Kate had arrived in the room and shut the door behind her, she found, to her horror, that tears were coursing down her cheeks. They can all go to hell in a handbasket, she thought, groping for the small package of tissues she always kept in her bag. It wasn't there. Somehow, that fact joined the rest of the cosmic plot against her. She sat down on the bed and cried. "I'm leaving tomorrow and they can burn the place down," she said aloud. But even as that thought asserted itself, she had a sudden picture in her mind of the day-old kittens, tiny paws extended, eyes shut in their disproportionately large heads, groping for their mother's nipples. She sighed. "I didn't mean that, God."

Chapter 3

K|ate woke up with a depression, coupled with a queer feeling that she had had an unpleasant and disturbing dream without being able to remember it. Added to that, she sat for a few minutes on the side of the bed and struggled to recall something else that was bothering—or had bothered—her. During a restless night she had half waked once or twice, thinking she had heard a noise. But that could have also been a dream. Sighing, she groped for her slippers.

She had forgotten about the lack of coffee until she actually stood up. Since her usual course was to go immediately to the kitchen and put water on to boil, she was half way to the door of her bedroom before she remembered where she was, and the even more devastating fact that there was no coffee downstairs. For a second she simply stood in the middle of the floor and gave herself up to hating the house, her family, the suburbs, Paul, Deborah and the barbaric attitudes of her niece and nephew. Then, accepting the inevitable, she shuffled off to the nearest bathroom, taking her towel and washrag with her.

Like the rest of the house, it was a mess. Kate closed her eyes to the sodden, bunched up towels on the floor, the rim around the tub, the toothpaste smeared from the squashed tube all over the sink. What made her sit on the side of the tub and take deep breaths was the cigarette stub in the basin. Finally, she removed that, put it down the toilet and flushed it. Then she picked up the used towels and dumped them in a wall hamper. She scraped the toothpaste off the enamel, put the top back on, put various jars, tubes and bottles into the medicine cabinet or on the shelves on the wall, and, when order had been approximately restored, took a shower. It did not help, when the shower was coming down on her, to reach out to the soap dish at hand level and find no soap. Eventually, she got the soap from the hand basin.

By the time she got downstairs, feeling somewhat better, it was forty minutes later. By her watch it was ten minutes past eight. Ranger was sitting at the table eating a bowl of cereal. Bones was sitting at his feet, watching him. When Kate came in and said "Good morning," Bones promptly went under the table. Going to the refrigerator, she opened it and searched for milk and orange juice. Either could be used—however inadequately—as a coffee substitute for the time being. Both containers were empty. Kate turned and looked at the trencherman behind her. Ranger's cereal bowl was filled with milk. In front of him stood an empty glass of what, from the residue at the bottom, appeared to be orange juice.

Well, she thought, no coffee, no milk, no orange juice, and since there was no milk, that would remove cereal also from the list of possibles. Tea?

She found a box of tea bags at the back of one of the shelves, boiled some water, and steeped herself a cup of tea that would have made an Irish grandmother happy. By the time she finished dunking the bag up and down, the center of the liquid in the cup was purple black. She glanced over to the table. Yes, there was sugar. There was no bread in the

51

refrigerator, but there were cookies on the shelf. Not what the diet ordered, she thought grimly, but perhaps sheer rage would burn off a few calories.

Collecting one of the cookie packages, she took her tea and sat down. Before Ranger knew what was happening to his cereal bowl, Kate took it from under his spoon and emptied some of the sweetened milk into her tea.

"Thank you," she said, putting the bowl back under Ranger's nose. Then she helped herself to more sugar.

"That's my milk you've taken," Ranger said. But he sounded a little unsure of himself.

"Since there was no other and you seem to have taken all the milk without regard to what I might want—plus all the orange juice—I felt it quite appropriate to take what I needed from you. Bad manners are inclined to generate bad manners, you know."

"How should I know you wanted milk? You went on and on about coffee."

"How did you know I did? I didn't say anything to you about it."

Ranger put his soup spoon in his mouth and kept his eyes down.

"So you and Marie have been talking. Well, I can hardly blame you for that. Probably under your circumstances I'd do the same."

Some recollection of her uneasy sleep trickled to the surface of her mind. "Do either of you characters sleepwalk?"

Ranger, suddenly still, looked at her. "No, why?" Since he had been sounding hostile all morning, Kate made nothing of the fact that he sounded angry now.

"I'm not sure. I thought I heard someone. But I may have been asleep." She sipped her tea and nibbled her cookie.

With an abrupt gesture Ranger pushed away his cereal bowl, snatched Bones's leash off the back of the door and dragged Bones by his collar out towards the door.

"Where are you going?"

"I'm just taking Bones for a walk before I have to catch the school bus." And he and Bones disappeared out the door. He was, Kate noticed, wearing what was obviously a school uniform: navy blue trousers, white shirt, striped tie and blazer. In a few minutes Ranger and Bones were back. Ranger hung up the leash then knelt down and patted the newspaper spread over the floor. "Okay," he addressed his pet, "Now be good. On the paper, Bones! On the paper." The dog wagged his tail. Ranger got to his feet. Bones jumped up and tried to lick his face. "Stay!" he ordered Bones. "Now stay!" He and Bones looked at each other. Bones put his head on one side as though he were deciphering a code. Then, as though he had suddenly understood, he sat down. "Good dog. *Good dog!*"

Ranger ran to the shelf under the cupboard, got something out of a cardboard box and took it back to Bones. "Good dog!" he said. Bones promptly got up and whirled around him. "No, Bones! Stay! Stay!"

There was the sound of a horn at the bottom of the hill.

"Promise," Ranger said dramatically to Kate, who was leaning against the cupboard unit, watching the show, "Promise you won't go near Bones. He's all right, if you just leave him alone. Like I said, he doesn't like females. Please!"

"I will promise not to hurt or frighten him in any way. Is that okay?"

The horn sounded again. Looking very much like his father in one of Paul's more pigheaded moments, Ranger snatched up an armful of books and went out the front door.

Kate stood in the living room a few moments and considered her options. At the front of her mind was a question: where was Marie? Sleeping, she thought. Should she go up and waken her? What for? her mind answered. So she would have to swallow more obvious hostility? On the other hand, Paul might call at any moment. If he asked what his daughter was doing, how would she feel if she simply said she didn't know. All right. She'd go up and investigate.

But she stood where she was. Her tidy soul longed to clean

and put the place in order. What is it in me? she thought. The Methodist? The Puritan? The orphan who never felt fully good enough? The social inferior with a chip on her shoulder?

Idly she put out her hand to move a small, upholstered chair back from the middle of the carpet. She hadn't noticed the stain on it the night before. It was ugly, obscene really, on an antique chair with a fine needlepoint seat. Bones?

Pushing it aside, she went upstairs and hesitated in the hall. Then she knocked on Marie's door. No answer. She knocked again. Still no answer. Then she put her head in.

If downstairs was chaos, Marie's room specialized in the weird. The walls were painted a dark purple. A huge picture of a monk immolating himself took up one wall. Her bed was a bamboo mat with a blanket tossed to one side. Opposite the burning monk was a watercolor, a delicate pastoral scene, something that would look in keeping with a white or off-white wall in an old-fashioned bedroom. On the purple wall it was so light it looked almost transparent. Bamboo shades hung full length from the window, cutting off almost all light. Even so, it was easy to see that Marie wasn't there.

Kate touched a switch on the wall beside her and then jumped. A glaring strobe lamp started flashing on and off.

"Godalmighty," Kate said to herself, and pushed the switch down. After a minute she went over and rolled up the bamboo blind. Sunlight changed the entire character of the room. What in the dark, or in the dusk, might appear dramatic, now merely looked contrived and tawdry. Kate stood looking, wondering why the room gave her such a feeling of déjà vu. After a few minutes she decided it was the burning monk. Everything he had stood for, all the emotions he was supposed, automatically, to evoke, belonged to the sixties. It was at least thirteen or fourteen years old. Marie was barely born when that conflagrating image helped change a world and nation. Why should she have it there now?

"Isn't he terrific?" Marie said from behind her.

Kate made herself turn around slowly. "Where did you come from?"

"From the bathroom." Marie waved her hand to a door also painted purple that Kate hadn't noticed. At this point Kate took in the fact that Marie was naked. Her slight body, with its pink undertone, with drops from the shower on rounded hip and thigh, was exquisite. Her breasts were small and high, like a child's. Of course, Kate thought. She is a child. She looked up and found Marie's eyes on her, eyes whose expression did not match the innocence and youth of her body. There was no reason on earth, Kate told herself, why she should feel uncomfortable in front of the nude body of a fifteen-year-old girl. Yet she was extremely uncomfortable, as though she had been caught in some lewd act.

Marie walked gracefully over to her dressing table, poked around among the debris of bobby pins, combs, ribbons, makeup, eyebrow brushes and two hair dryers, and found a hair brush. Raising an arm, as though she were a ballet dancer, she started brushing her hair, humming softly in rhythm to the strokes.

"Put something on, Marie," Kate said sharply. And knew instantly that she had made a mistake. Further, that she had been maneuvered into saying exactly what she did.

"Why should I?" Marie said in the same singsong rhythm. "After all, it's my room. I can be naked in my room if I like. If you came in without knocking, dear Aunt Kate, then that's your look out, isn't it?" And she turned gracefully, stuck out her pelvis and posed.

Kate turned and left the room, closing the door behind her. She was, she discovered, very angry, with the worst anger of all—anger at herself.

She was going downstairs when the phone rang. She started to race downstairs, running, she suddenly realized, to get to the receiver first. But somebody must have answered it, because the ringing stopped. Kate stopped at the bottom of the stairs. After all, she thought. It could be for Marie.

Slowing, she turned back upstairs to get her jacket and handbag to go shopping. And if Paul rang while she was out, well, she was the one doing him a favor. He would simply have to call later. But she knew she desperately wanted to hear from him. Hearing from him would release her from having to stay in this terrible house with these aggressive and unpleasant children.

"Aunt Kate."

Kate looked upstairs. Marie, now in a long shirt, was standing at the head of the stairs staring down. "It's Daddy. He wants to talk to you."

"I'll get it in the kitchen," Kate said. "Not that that will stop you listening," she added *sotto voce,* as she pushed through the swing door. "Hello Paul," she said, picking up the receiver.

"Hello Kate. I'm glad you're there. I was afraid, before I placed the call, that you mightn't be there. And I knew that if you weren't I couldn't blame you."

It was embarrassing and inexplicable, this desire to cry that made her throat ache and made her feel like a fool. "No. I'm still here," she managed to get out. And then, "Are you there, Marie?"

"No, I don't think she is," Paul said. "I gave her hell. But you can go and check, if you like."

At that moment the swing door from the dining room was thrust open. "I'm going out," Marie said, not sounding, for once, like her languid self. "So you can have your conversation in peace."

"Just a minute, Paul." Kate said.

Putting down the telephone Kate went into the dining room and to the window and watched Marie in jeans, shirt and clogs go down the short pavement to the sidewalk. As Marie turned to go along the sidewalk, she turned and waved. Kate jumped back. Then again she felt foolish, but watched Marie till she went around a corner three houses away.

Wondering if Paul would still be on the other end of the

telephone in Tokyo, Kate went back to the kitchen and picked up the receiver. "Paul? She's gone. I've just watched her walk down the street." Then, in another voice, "What's the matter with her, Paul?"

"I don't know that anything's the matter with her, Kate, beyond the anger of adolescence." He sounded stiff again. "Why, what seems to you to be the matter?"

Now that he'd asked, Kate knew she couldn't produce an acceptable explanation for her question. "I don't know," she said. "I was in her room this morning. It's—funny. Like something out of the sixties. As though she . . . and . . ." And what, she thought? Came naked into her own room and baited me? Couldn't that be considered normal adolescent defiance?

"Nothing, Paul. I'm afraid you're going to think I've gone bonkers. It just seemed to me . . . as I told you, your children are not in the least overjoyed that I'm here. There's no way on earth I can make them accept me. And there's no way on earth I can make myself stay in a place that will probably drive *me* bonkers before long. When can you arrange to come and take this responsibility yourself?"

There was a silence.

"Paul? Are you there? Did you hear me?"

"I was going to ask you if you could possibly just spend the nights there for the next week or ten days. It might make the difference between whether I'm employed or not."

"Surely your employers . . ."

"It's not my employers, in the sense that you mean, Kate. After all . . ." Almost unconsciously, she noticed that his voice changed subtly. "I'm a considerable stockholder in the business. But we may all go down the tube if I don't stay for a while. There are only about a dozen American competitors cruising around, sniffing out the action, waiting for me to make a false move. And that doesn't even include the English, French and German who are also here."

There was a pause. Then, as Kate seemed gripped by an

odd silence, he took a breath and went on. "I realize I was not . . . I wasn't receptive when you asked what was wrong with Marie. I'm sorry. It's . . . it's a sore point. After all, I can't forget how like her mother she is. . . . But she *is* okay. They may not be acting very well towards you, but please remember, Kate, their mother is in a sanitarium, and they've had to put up with a series of housekeepers, and things are not easy for them either. Before long they'll be in college. That means big fees for the next ten years, to say nothing of keeping Deborah in a decent place where she can get good therapy. So, if I seem to you to be putting business before my family, I'd like you to know why. It's not just greed or irresponsibility. . . ." It sounded, Kate thought, a little like a prepared speech, but she knew that she would do as he asked. She would hate it, but she would do it. Abruptly, almost rudely she interrupted him.

"I'll do as you ask on one condition, Paul. That you give me your word that you'll come here at the end of the week. Is that understood?"

"Of course. Good heavens, Kate. Anyone would think . . . have I ever broken my word to you?"

A silence stretched over the cable miles.

"Technically, no," Kate said.

"We must . . . I didn't mean to bring it up on the international telephone, but we have to talk when I get back at the end of next week."

"All right," Kate said. And hung up.

"Trust me," Paul whispered.

They were parked somewhere along the River Road. Luckily, Paul's car was air-conditioned, so that the closed windows kept out not only the heat and damp, heavy air, but the mosquitoes. The moonlight trickled through the long sweepy veils of Spanish moss that dipped almost to the roadway. A little to the left were houses and a small golf course. But this road was deserted. Both Kate and Paul were seventeen. It was the night after his graduation, and they had come from his class dance at the Roosevelt.

Paul slid his hand up the fitted bodice of her long dress.

"Paul," she said urgently. "Please!"

Obediently he moved his hand to her arm and rubbed the back of his fingers up and down to where the frail strap of fake cornflowers fell off her shoulder. His mouth went back over hers.

She liked kissing. She liked the soft, smooth pressure on her mouth. She didn't like it as well when he opened his lips.

"Umm," she said, and averted her head. "Don't."

He stopped and suddenly sat back, breathing rather rapidly. "I thought you were my girl," he said finally.

"I am."

"Then I don't understand this 'don't' and 'please.'"

She didn't, either. Finally she said, "It's wrong."

"Who says?"

Her mother had said so, not by direct description, but Kate had no trouble identifying what Paul was doing as "taking liberties." The church had said so, too. Paul's church, the Methodist Church, in which Paul's father was pastor. Again, there had been no point by point, item by item, description of what the pastor and the Sunday school teachers called sexual license. But Kate was pretty sure what they meant.

"Your father says so, Paul Lamont. And Mom did, too."

"Aw come on, Kate! For Chrissake, you don't suppose that everybody in that huge church is going around wearing some lily-white pledge? I could tell you they sure as hell aren't. Why, there are at least four of the men . . ." He stopped there.

"What do you mean?"

"Nothing! I mean that everybody isn't such a goody-goody. And that includes some of our sainted Sunday school teachers, too." He started the car and savagely thrust it into gear. Then he stepped on the accelerator, and the car bounded forward.

It was at night and there was no traffic. Even so, he drove at a dangerous pace.

"Paul, please stop! Please slow down! Don't go like that! It's dangerous!"

"Close your eyes if you don't like it," he yelled.

Eventually, because there was nothing else she could do, she did close her eyes and sat, her lids screwed up, her hands clenched in her lap. Only after he had jammed on the brake and she had been thrown forward, bumping her head on the elaborate plastic dashboard, did he slow down.

It was a nasty blow. Kate sat there, fighting a slow nausea that was rising up from her stomach, her mind obsessed with the fear that Paul would now no longer love her. He wouldn't call her. And there was no one else.

"Paul!" she said, pleadingly. The front of her head and her eyes felt funny. But she paid little attention to that. Far greater was her fear that he would take her home and then she would never see him again. Nor could she be certain she'd see him in Sunday school. Paul had stopped going. She knew, because he had told her, that it had caused trouble at his home. "But they can't make me go," he had said to her triumphantly. And they hadn't been able to do so. He hadn't attended for almost a year.

"Paul," she said again.

"What?"

"My head hurts."

"You want me to take you to a hospital?"

"No, of course not. I just want you to be . . . to be nice."

"Why should I be nice to you when you don't even trust me?"

"I *do* trust you, Paul. I'm just scared."

"What are you scared of?"

The easiest fear to identify was the obvious one. "I'm scared of getting pregnant."

"Listen, honey. I promise you, I *promise* you, you won't get pregnant." He slowed the car and turned into a dark street

60

near Audubon Park. "I'm sorry I was mad, Kate. Forgive me?"

This time, when he parted his lips, she didn't pull away. She still didn't like it. She still thought it was wet and messy. But if she didn't let him, then he'd stop calling her, and everything Keith Malory had said about her total rejectability would be proved true. It was unthinkable.

His hand slid up her rib cage. Terror closed in on her. Why wasn't she feeling what girls were supposed to feel when the men they loved made love to them? All she could think about was when he would stop. Maybe, she thought, it was because her head hurt so much and she still felt sick. But she didn't stop Paul when his fingers tickled the bottom of her breast and coyly poked inside her dress. Only the sound of feet on the uneven New Orleans sidewalk suddenly made him straighten and, after the cop seemed inclined to loiter, to drive her home.

"You still like me?" she said pleadingly, as he delivered her to her front door.

"Sure," he said, and left the minute they heard footsteps coming to open the door.

In the remaining two days of the weekend, Kate managed to get the house considerably cleaner, and many of the items lying all over the floor and the furniture put back. No one helped her. But she was prepared for this. By this time she had accepted the fact that if she put the house in better order, it was for herself that she did it. She was, she discovered, literally unable to sit down and read a book—or edit a manuscript—with socks, T-shirts and other assorted litter on the living room carpet, chairs, tables and oven in the case of a pair of Ranger's socks, tucked in above the books in the bookcase.

"Good heavens," she said, fishing them out. She stood, staring at them in her hand.

"At least they were under S for socks," Marie said. She was lying on the sofa perusing the *Village Voice*.

"What do you mean?"

Marie pointed to the books supporting the socks. "Fiction, alphabetically under author."

Kate glanced at the books: Stewart, Sanders, Segal, Sack-ville-West, Saffire, Sayers, Shute, Stendhal, Scott. "Yes indeedy," she said. "That was thoughtful of him. Just where anyone would look—under S."

Marie, her head hidden in the *Voice*, didn't say anything. But there seemed to be a snort of laughter, muffled immediately.

A little cheered by this, Kate said. "There are some questions I'd like to ask, but there's been so much bristling hostility going around I've been scared even to try." She turned and looked at Marie, and found her looking back at her over the top of the tabloid.

"So what do you want to know?" If there'd been a moment of shared amusement it was gone.

"I guess, why are you so defensive? I was asked by your father—through your mother's doctor—to come here. As I said before, if no adult is here, the state can move in and send you both to a juvenile detention place or a foster home. And send *you*, incidentally, to school. In case you didn't know—which I'm sure you do—the school leaving age is sixteen, not fifteen."

"They're not going to do that."

"What makes you so sure?"

"They know Dad'll be home sooner or later."

"And you honestly think that's going to stop them? What if the neighbors complain?"

"That stupid bitch next door complains about everything."

"Okay, so she's a chronic complainer, I still don't see why . . ." Kate stopped. She was getting nowhere. If this were an office problem, she thought, I'd go at it in a more organized fashion. "All right. I understand then that you and Ranger seem to think that you can more or less muddle through by yourselves. I don't think that's true. I think that sooner or later somebody would say something to what are generally

62

called the authorities—somebody at school, one of the neighbors, or maybe everybody all at once if something happens. Suppose the house caught on fire?"

"Why should it?"

"Somebody smokes. I saw a cigarette butt in the bathroom washbowl last night."

Marie shrugged. "Daddy smokes."

"Since he isn't here, I doubt that it was his. And if the house caught fire don't you think your father could be severely critized for not having an adult in charge?"

"He's not exactly your home-loving head of the household, you know."

Kate stared at her.

"I mean," Marie went on. "So he'd get fined for leaving a bunch of kids. He could pay that out of one week's expenses."

"Why are you so angry at him? Because of his so-called girl friend?"

"There's nothing so-called about Angela Griffin. She works in television and has a pad in New York, which Dad spends a lot more time at than he does here. So why should we be in a sweat in case he gets rapped for leaving us alone here?"

"Well, it doesn't take Sigmund Freud to figure out that you can hardly wait for him to get punished. Is this because . . . on behalf of your mother?"

"Mom's been out of it for the past four years. Dad plays around. What's the big deal? This is your ordinary true-blue, red-blooded, one hundred percent American suburban family. Welcome to reality!" And Marie went back to reading the *Voice*.

Kate stood still, her hand still clutching the clothes she'd picked up.

"In that case . . ." she began. She was on the point of announcing her departure for New York when she remembered her promise to stay. By the time she'd remembered it, she also knew that even if she had not given her word, she still would not let Paul down.

"In that case, what?" Marie said.

"Nothing," Kate replied. She went off to the kitchen.

It was during the weekend that there started, somewhere below the surface of her conscious mind, and continued throughout her days there, an eerie feeling of familiarity. After a while it drifted up and became a conscious irritant, and she began to try and trace its origin, if only to allay its annoying presence. Surely, she thought as she vacuumed, dusted, pounded pillows, scrubbed and washed, that despite its outward similarity, there could be nothing in the New York suburban house—or its contents, or its inhabitants—that brought back Prytania Street, or before that, Harmony Street.

Yet curiously, and despite all the shocking dissimilarities, she discovered she was being nagged by a feeling that Marie was running over her old tracks. How on earth, she wondered, startled at this odd occurrence, could the experience of being Beth's daughter be equated in any way with being Deborah's? Unless, of course, the polar opposites met in their very extremes: having, in effect, an absentee mother—absent in mind and attention—could produce the same resentment and rebellion in Marie as the fear of being crushed by a mother who enveloped to the point of swallowing whole had done in Kate. . . . Then Marie's defiance was the reverse side of her own timidity.

And of course . . . of course . . . there were Keith Malory and Paul Lamont, the fathers of herself and Marie. For the first time a similarity between the two men, even to the physical, struck her. They were both tall, well made and fair. They were both ambitious, socially as well as professionally. They were both bountifully endowed with that enigmatic quality, sex appeal. . . . As that aspect of the similarity struck in full force, Kate felt a depression that she had not experienced in a long time. It was to get rid of that, as much as her compulsive cleanliness, that set her to clean yet another carpet, closet, room, floor. *Wheel,* she knew, with increasing guilt, was being

64

neglected. So, after a day of general scrubbing, she sat up at night reworking the last few pages.

The one aspect of her weekend that wasn't entirely negative was her relationship with Bones. She had been careful, at first, to make no overtures to the wretched puppy, since the slightest move in his direction seemed to produce predictable and disastrous results. Her one contribution to the situation was to see that the floor was permanently covered with newspaper.

But after the first day, when she went out to the back garden, Bones's mournful face appeared behind the screen, looking at her from the inside. Saturday afternoon Ranger had gone to the ball park with some friends and had left his pet behind. Bones whimpered and Kate stared back at him. He obviously wanted to go out. But if she opened the door and let him run, he might well dart in front of a car or simply tear out and never come back.

"Sorry, Bones. I'd take you out if you'd let me put a leash on you. But you know how you act when I come near."

Bones whimpered some more. When Kate came back in Bones scuttled back to his corner, but as she stood by the door staring at him, he ventured towards her. The leash was hanging on a hook beside the door. Reaching out, she took it off the hook. "If you want to go for a walk, then you'll have to let me put this on you."

But Bones had other memories, obviously. Putting his tail down between his back legs, he crept under the kitchen table. Terrified that she would precipitate another messy accident, Kate hung up the leash and left the kitchen. The following day when Ranger was going with some friends to a lake to swim, Kate asked, "Why don't you take Bones? He'd love to go out."

"Because somebody would come up to him and he'd run away. He's been lost three times already. All you have to do is leave him alone," Ranger said pointedly.

"Ranger, I knew about dogs before you were born."

"Okay, okay! You don't have to bite my head off."

"If that's the only way to make you be reasonably civil, then I do. I think you owe me an apology."

She didn't really think he would comply. But to her surprise he mumbled, "Sorry," as he went down the back steps.

Later that afternoon Kate decided to brave the worst that Bones could do. "Come on, Bones. Let's go for a walk."

Taking the leash off the hook she squatted, holding it, and waited to see what Bones would do. Plainly he was torn. He whimpered and backed, then poked his head out from under the table, then whimpered some more, and walked to his corner and came back. After about seven minutes, when Kate thought the ligaments of her knees would finally give, he came slowly forward and sniffed her hand. She let him do that for a minute. Then moving as easily as she could, she snapped the leash onto his collar. "Walkie, walkie," she said, feeling stupid.

Once he had recovered from his fright, Bones seemed to get the idea. She took him out into the garden and then onto the street, guiding him towards the gutter when nature or panic called. On the whole it was a successful venture. She and Bones covered a couple of miles, walking as briskly as she could, before she brought him back. No one was at home. No one had seen her leave or return. She decided not to mention her budding relationship with Bones to anyone. It would remain her secret, like a pleasant vice practiced alone.

For Friday's dinner, she made an expandable casserole and put what was left in containers in the freezer. On Friday evening Ranger showed up. On Saturday evening both Ranger and Marie were there. Ranger said, somewhat pugnaciously, "What's for dessert?" There had been only fruit the night before.

"Nothing. I don't eat dessert, and I forgot to ask you. Sorry."

"Better for your teeth, Ranger," Marie said unexpectedly.

"If that's so, how come I saw you eating a double cone with Martha Whatsis on Tuesday?"

"Martha was feeling low and needed cheering up. We all have to make sacrifices," she added piously.

"It's nice to know you can offer such a thoroughly unselfish gesture," Kate said, getting up.

On Sunday evening she had some ice cream which she was going to divide equally between Ranger and Marie. But Marie didn't appear.

"Well, Ranger," Kate said. "Do you think you can manage both portions?"

"Sure," Ranger said.

"Where is Marie?" she asked, as she started to clear the table.

"How should I know?" Ranger snapped the leash onto Bones's collar and opened the back door.

"Just a minute. Turn around, Ranger. Right now!"

Slowly, resistance in every contour of his boy's face, Ranger faced her.

"That's not an answer, and you know it."

Silence. Bones sat down and started to scratch.

"Courtesy—or even lower than that, civility—is what is owed one human being to the humanness of another. It's the basic, irreducible minimum. When you're rude, it doesn't show what you think of me. It shows me what you think of you. I didn't ask you to explain why you didn't know. Just where your sister was. And I'd appreciate an unloaded reply."

"I don't know," yelled Ranger, and slammed out the door.

I feel incompetent and stupid, Kate thought angrily, attacking the casserole dish with a soap pad. Also a prig.

But shortly after midnight, when she heard Marie come in, Kate got out of bed and went into Marie's room, because she realized that what she felt was not so much incompetent as cowardly. And if she gave into it she'd feel worse. The conversation went exactly as Kate had thought it would, as though she had developed clairvoyant qualities.

When Kate knocked on Marie's door there was silence. The moving around Kate had heard stopped. After a short pause, Kate knocked again. This time the door almost flung itself open. Marie, in black jeans, a black T-shirt and four-inch heels stood there. She did not have on much lipstick, but her eyes were heavy with makeup. Above it her fair curls had been gathered in a topknot. A strong smell of cigarette smoke hung about her. All of this served not to make Marie look older, which was obviously its purpose, but about five years younger, despite her height. She looked like a child playing a grownup, which, Kate thought, pushing her way inside, was exactly what she was.

"You have no right to come into my room," Marie said.

"I knocked. Look, Marie, where have you been? It's past midnight. Tomorrow is school. . . ." Kate remembered that Marie had been expelled.

"Not for me."

"You haven't answered my question," Kate said, after a short pause. "Where have you been?"

"I've been with friends."

"Where?"

"At somebody's house."

"Were her—or his—parents there?"

"What does it matter?"

"It matters—I suspect—a lot. What you and your wilder friends might be doing in a house empty of adults is quite different from what you'd be doing if they were there."

"You're just like all adults. You have a dirty mind." And Marie giggled. As she did so, Kate smelled liquor on her breath.

"You've been drinking."

"A little wine. Even Daddy lets me have wine at dinner. What's the big deal about?"

"I should think your mother . . ." Kate said.

"You leave Mom out of this," Marie burst out with unexpected ferocity. "She told us about you. What the goody-goody aunt from New York was *really* like. How you stole . . ." She stopped.

"I stole *what?*" Kate said. Anger came up from the depths

as though from a forgotten volcano. "Stole *what?*" Kate heard herself shout.

"Nothing," Marie muttered. "Do you want to wake the whole house?" From downstairs came the sound of Bones barking. Kate and Marie stood, glaring at each other.

Then Kate took a deep breath. "It's cowardly to make a hit-and-run accusation like that. What did I steal?"

"You *tried* to steal Daddy."

With one part of her mind Kate noted that Marie had been rattled back into behaving like a ten-year-old. "I would have said the shoe was on the other foot," she commented dryly.

"Mom said you'd say something like that."

"Have you been to see her?"

"I'm tired and I'm going to bed."

"Because," Kate went on, "I had the impression from the doctor that she wasn't in any shape to talk to anyone."

"She always talks to me."

"Then I'll try and see her one day this week."

"No!" Marie cried out. "You can't!"

"Why not?"

"Because it would kill her. Haven't you done enough to her already? Get out! Get out!" The high, thin voice rose.

"I'll get out when you ask me to politely and in a normal voice."

The life that had blazed in Marie's face for a minute left. Under the painted eyes the mask was back. "Please go, dear Aunt Kate."

Kate's anger receded before a sense of futility. Even so, she made herself say, "I want you to be in before ten o'clock from now on until your father gets home." She didn't wait for a response, but walked out the door. Just as she left Marie said, "How're you going to make me?"

Which, of course, was the whole point.

"Well," Joel said, coming into her office Monday morning. "How goes the rewrite?"

"It doesn't—for the moment. I was too busy."

Joel draped his lanky body against the doorpost. "The production department will not be happy to hear that. Nor our leader."

"I know. I'm trying to make up for lost time." She tapped the manuscript with her pencil.

"There's a promotion meeting this morning."

"I'm not going. I have to do this."

"Tut tut!"

"Joel, will you get out of here. I'm having a hard enough time trying to concentrate without you distracting me . . ."

"How about dinner?"

"Can't. Have to go back to the suburbs."

"Still playing house mother?"

"Goodbye Joel."

"How did your family turn out? Acceptable?"

Kate sighed. Joel was by no means unsnubbable. If she wanted to she could get rid of him with a couple of sharply honed sentences. But she not only didn't feel like lacerating his feelings, she was finding it hard to concentrate. "I'm having a violent case of the generation gap," she said finally. "I realize I did my growing up in the late forties and fifties. These kids are products of the seventies. I didn't realize they'd be so . . ." Her voice trailed off.

"So what?"

"Hostile. I thought that went out with the sixties. I suppose the truth is, it's not just the difference in era—the generation gap. I'm sure a lot of it has to do with their upbringing."

Joel stuck a cigarette in his mouth and lounged into her office. "What's wrong with their upbringing? What could possibly be wrong in one of our more expensive lily-white suburbs where two car garages and picket fences abound?"

"Come off it, Joel. Money does not automatically mean happiness. You know that."

"Oh. *I* know it. But one of the troubles with our culture . . ."

70

To her own great shock Kate picked up a brass paperweight from her desk and threw it in his general direction. "That kind of garbage is exactly what I don't want to hear. I've come from a weekend of it! Go on, Joel, please leave me alone!"

Joel picked up the paperweight and put it on her desk. "How about lunch?"

"No. I'm going to have a sandwich here."

"You know," he said, mashing out his cigarette in the office's one ashtray, "it's one of nature's greater mysteries that I don't get discouraged."

"I agree. I think you owe it to yourself to pay court to one of the many eager ladies who would be delighted to receive your attentions."

"Maybe I will. See you."

Kate watched his tall figure going down the hall. When he wasn't being deliberately slovenly, he walked with the natural grace of an athlete. Why, she wondered for a minute, did she turn him down so emphatically? He was attractive. He wanted her. They had a pleasant companionship. What was wrong, as far as she was concerned?

It was a problem that had puzzled her for some time, and in some odd way disturbed her. But since that terrible night in Chicago, when she had walked out of Graham Maitland's room, there had been no one who had been able to touch whatever spring opened the lock to her emotion and desire. Other women, Kate knew, took lovers, each time knowing the relationship to be temporary, willing to sacrifice permanence for a brief tenderness. But she couldn't. She had tried, once or twice. And it simply hadn't worked. Not for her . . . not yet.

Kate worked the rest of the day. Kramer's bumpy prose started to smooth out. He believed so much in what he had to say that the clumsy sentences carried an odd conviction. . . . I must be tired to think that, Kate thought, and glanced at her watch, 4:30.

At five minutes to five the door opened and Graham Maitland stuck his head in. "How are you coming along?"

"Fine," Kate said. She added a little desperately, "Don't worry . . . it'll be done in time, I promise, I promise."

"I know. Good heavens, Kate, you're making me feel guilty for even asking."

"Sorry, Graham. I'm feeling defensive."

"What's the matter?" He strolled into the room. If Joel had grace when he walked, Graham had power. As tall as Joel, he was better filled out and looked actually taller than the younger man. Even though his hair was tawny rather than fair, he had the same Baltic blue eyes that Keith Malory had had, and that Paul Lamont had. What is it about men with blue eyes? Kate wondered, as Graham smiled down at her.

"Is it Kramer or your Westchester relations that are getting you down?"

"They somehow make me feel like an idiot."

" 'They' being?"

"Being my niece and nephew. Alienated hardly describes them. They make it plain they don't want me there."

"Then why stay?"

She hesitated. Yes, why? she thought. "I suppose, because they're so young. Because something could happen to them, and most of all, I suppose because I don't want to feel guilty for the rest of my life if something *should* happen."

Graham stared at her a minute. I should say something, she thought. But it was Graham who finally spoke. He got up and held out his hand. "Come along. I have the car and will drive you home."

"I'm not going home. I'm going to Grand Central and thence to Westchester."

"That's where I'm going to drive you. It's on my way," he said as she opened her mouth. "I'm supposed to have dinner in Bedford Hills."

Chapter 4

T hey drove in silence up the drive and onto the parkway. Graham was a skilled driver, soundlessly shifting gears, coaxing the most from his powerful German car, so that he seemed, without particular speed or abrupt stops, to pass most other cars, gliding through knots of traffic as though they had thinned for his benefit.

One of the most satisfying parts of her affair with Graham had been the long, pleasant silences. To be silent with another person, she had previously thought, was to lose one layer of skin. Only with her father—on the rare occasions when they were alone—had there been periods of silence. And during many of those she had had the disturbing suspicion that he did not talk to her, or encourage her to talk to him, because he did not find her interesting. The exceptions to this were her father's periodic rambles into theological speculations, which was undoubtedly the main reason she found them enjoyable. But even then, as she sat entranced, she realized his discourses had more to do with what was on his mind at the moment than with the fact that she was his audience.

But with Graham she knew almost from the beginning that

he simply liked being quiet with her. "It's something I can't really do with anybody else," he'd said to her ten years previously on their first trip together, which made her happy, because "anybody" included his wife. Where did they go that year? Was it to one of the upstate New York lakes? The cape?

It was the cape, she decided now, watching the waning light on the manicured parkway. And it had followed a winter of his spending one or two nights a week in her apartment.

"How do you manage to get away?" she had asked once.

That was the first time she learned that he didn't like being questioned about his relationship with his wife.

"Business," he said briefly, so briefly that she understood she was to drop the subject.

He never volunteered information about his marriage. Finally, when she could stand it no longer, she asked, "Graham, is this just a fling for you? Because if it is, I want to know before I get in any deeper. I'm not very good at flings."

They were in bed, and she had had the forethought to ask him before they made love. He sat there, smoking, not answering. She touched her hand to his thick chest, knowing that if he took long enough to answer, she would lose courage and retract the question. She didn't want to lose him. Above all else, she must not lose him.

But he did answer. "I've known for some time that I was going to have to answer that question, to myself, if not to you. No, it's not just a fling . . . which you must know. Not that there haven't been flings. I'm not kidding anyone. I've always felt monagamy was overvalued . . ." His voice trailed off.

"And how does Danielle feel about it?" It took courage to mention his wife's name, lying beside him in her own bed.

"Danielle is a Catholic," Graham said.

"So am I," Kate said.

"I thought you grew up in one of those strict Southern fundamentalist environments."

"I did. But a few years ago I became a Catholic."

"I see."

74

The statement lay there, unexamined. In a minute or two he put out his cigarette and started to make love to her. How long was it after that when they went to the cape? Six months? She remembered the first time he signed a motel register: Mr. and Mrs. Graham Maitland. Then, in answering some question, the desk clerk addressed her as Mrs. Maitland. More than anything else that bothered her. And it continued to bother her for as long as they went away together. She never got used to it.

"Do you have to sign me in as your wife?" She said once.

"We are a lot closer than my wife and I," Graham said, which was a very Graham-like answer.

"That's beside the point. I feel like a fraud. It literally makes me queasy. Couldn't you just give your name?"

"And maybe have you arrested as a prostitute if the management wanted to get nasty?"

"Would they?"

"I don't know. Do you want to find out?"

She didn't, of course. At the moment of truth, she nearly always retreated.

"You know," Graham said on another occasion when he had registered and she had, once again, protested. "If you were a liberated feminist, I could see your preferring the bold approach—to sign in as yourself and to hell with antiquated and repressive codes of behavior. But given your basic Victorian puritanism, I find your squeamishness strange."

So, for that matter, did she. When she didn't say anything, he came over and sat down beside her on the bed. "The world could have six sexual revolutions and I don't suppose it would affect your . . . your craving for legitimacy. Perhaps that's one of the things I love about you."

"Do you, Graham?" She was overwhelmed by her own ravenous hunger for him to repeat it.

He got up. "You know I do. Let's not . . . you know I do."

Sitting now in the car with him, ten years later, she was gripped by the conviction that if she said to him, suddenly,

75

"Do you still love me?" he would say, in exactly the same tone, "You know I do."

And what would that mean? she thought. Would it mean that during all this time when they had seen each other, if at all, only across a conference room table—what was it now since they had parted, five years?—he had been tortured with unrequited love?

Not hardly, she said to herself. Was he completely cynical? No, not that, either. It was she, finally, who walked out on him in Chicago, where most of the staff had gathered to honor a Chicago author. And five minutes before she slammed the door he had said—and obviously meant—that he loved her.

"You don't know what love is," she had said to him, her voice jagged with despair.

"Perhaps I don't. But at least I don't use it interchangeably with the word 'devour.' "

"I think this is where we turn off for Meadowbrook," Graham said now.

Kate looked at his profile in the twilight. He had grown visibly older in those ten years. A little heavier and a little grayer. But he had not changed in other ways. She looked the same. She was now, at thirty-eight, within two pounds of her weight at twenty-one. Her hair was the same rich brown it had always been. Yet she had changed far more than he.

"Isn't it?"

"Isn't what?"

"Isn't this the right turn for Meadowbrook?"

Why are we in this car driving along as though I hadn't once wanted, with all my soul, to kill him, Kate wondered.

"Yes," she said. "The signpost here says Meadowbrook."

Graham didn't get out of the car when he arrived at the house. He just looked at it and said, "Well, this seems to be it, isn't it?"

"It is. Thanks, Graham, for the ride. It's a big improvement over the railroad." That wasn't entirely true, she thought, as

76

she pushed down the door handle. The railroad was bumpy, smelly and more tiring. But, amidst all the commuters, it gave her a pleasant sense of isolation. In all of New York there was nothing more typical of the city than a crowd of its citizens, locked into a railroad car, bus or subway, each determined to be alone.

Graham was staring out his window. "Somebody seems to be observing you with great interest."

Kate got out and stood up, staring over the car hood towards the house. By now it was almost dark. The light was on in the living room. There was definitely a head staring between parted curtains. From the shape of the hair it obviously belonged to Marie. "That's Marie, my niece," she said.

"See you tomorrow," Graham said, and the car slid almost noiselessly away.

Carrying her tote bag with the ever present Kramer manuscript in it, Kate walked up the driveway. Why am I lugging this here? Kate wondered to herself. It isn't as though there were the least chance I could get any done.

Arriving at the door, Kate rang the bell. Then she waited. After what seemed a reasonable length of time, she rang the bell again. "This is ridiculous!" she muttered. Putting down her tote bag, she backed off the front step far enough to look at the window where she had seen the head. There was no head there now. In fact, the light in the room had been switched off. The front of the house was dark upstairs and down.

For a moment, Kate found herself wishing that Graham had not driven off. Then she went back to the front door and rang the bell. This time it was opened almost immediately by Marie.

"Didn't you hear the bell?" Kate asked belligerently.

"Of course. That's why I answered it." Leaving the door open Marie walked out of the room towards the kitchen.

Kate stepped in, switched on the light and looked around the living room. Her efforts towards cleanliness and order

77

still showed in the washed windowsills and vacuumed floor. But the litter was as abundant and indiscriminate as when she first arrived.

Turning, she went up the stairs and straight back to the room she had occupied the night before. Putting the tote bag down, she removed her jacket, hung it up, glanced into the bathroom and was overwhelmingly relieved to find that it was in the same condition in which she had left it. Then she went downstairs.

Pushing through the swing doors from the passageway, she went into the kitchen. Marie and Ranger were seated at the kitchen table, on which were two packages of french fries, one of them empty, three packages of fried chicken, all of them empty, a package of cole slaw, mostly gone, one rapidly melting container of chocolate ice cream, plus what looked like a small can of chocolate syrup and the empty, cellophane wrapping of a package of chocolate chip cookies.

Nobody said anything. Ranger, who appeared to be finishing a bowl of ice cream, paused, spoon in midair, mouth open. Marie, her feet on another chair, her head back, was smoking.

"Da da dedum." She hummed an approximate version of "Hail to the Chief."

As Kate looked at them, a sense of amusement stole over her, dissipating the irritation that had been growing since she had driven up and seen the face at the window. They were, after all, children, and their determination to show how much they wished her away had a certain childlike exaggeration that was almost appealing. Why have I let them get to me? she wondered. The answer was so obvious that her irritation surfaced again, but this time at herself; she had thought that in some way she could control them. They knew better. Once she acknowledged that, their battle plan would either be neutralized, or they would find other means of attempting to drive her away. For a moment her mind played around with what other means they might employ, and her amusement faded.

Madness lies that way, she thought. Better just play a holding game.

"Good evening," she said. And then, "I'm sorry, Marie, I was so—er—abrasive when you came to the door. I shouldn't have taken out my end-of-the-day humor on you."

Marie had looked up for a moment, surprised, her eyes aquamarine in the fluorescent light of the kitchen. "It's okay," she muttered.

"How is Duchess?" Kate asked.

"Fine."

Going to the refrigerator, Kate took out of the freezer a frozen macaroni and beef concoction that she had stored there, lit the oven and put it in. Then she made herself a salad.

At the end of forty minutes dinner was ready. The kitchen was relatively clean, the empty containers in the garbage and the table cleared. Ranger had taken Bones out. Marie had fed Duchess and helped clear the table. As Kate watched her pile the dishes into the sink she asked, "Why don't you put them straight into the dishwasher?"

"Because it's broken," Marie said languidly.

"Has anybody called for the repair man?"

"Person. Repair person."

"I stand corrected. Repair person."

"No, because we're in school."

"You're not."

"True. But I have other things to do."

"Like what?"

Marie straightened. "Like minding my own business," she said. And she started to walk out of the room.

"Also like washing the dishes you and Ranger used," Kate said. Then, as Marie continued walking, she said, "Please turn around, Marie. I want to talk to you." She was surprised at the sharpness of her own tone. But it stopped Marie, who turned, revealing an angry, sullen face.

"I'll wash my dishes," she said. "But I don't see why I

79

should wash Ranger's. That's a sexist trap. Let him wash his own."

"But it's okay that I wash up for both of you?"

"Well that's what you're here for, isn't it? You're our sitter, our nanny, our keeper. So it's your job."

"You know very well that isn't true. And of course you can get away with it, as long as I'm here because I will not cook or eat in a filthy kitchen with rotted food. Nor can I think it's particularly healthful for the animals that you and Ranger seem to cherish. If you want to live in your private sulks, go ahead. But the rest of the world was not made simply to wait on you. It may be a while before that lesson comes crashing home, but, believe me, Marie, it will. And the later it is, the worse it will hurt. Now you can go." Kate turned her head and started running water over the stacked dishes. Behind her she heard the swish, swish of the swing door.

Angry at herself for being angry, Kate sat down while her dinner was heating and read the afternoon paper she had brought to read on the train. After she finished eating, she washed the dishes, put them away and went to her own room. There was no desk there, so she threw the Kramer manuscript on her bed, climbed on the bed, arranged the pillows behind her back and went to work.

Two days later, while she was having her dinner, Kate heard the front door open and close. She assumed it was Marie, who did not show up for dinner. Then the swing door was pushed open, and Paul Lamont stood in the doorway, "flaming like a god." Her mind produced the remembered line without her being aware of it. The magnificence was still there. She'd always wondered from what Viking ancestor he had inherited his height and big frame and blue and gold coloring. Lamont was certainly a French name, but then the Normans, who had French names, were originally Norsemen.

"Hello Kate," he said. And, suddenly, he looked to her older

80

and tired. There were lines beneath the Baltic blue eyes and beside his prominent nose. And for the first time she noticed he wore a beard—short, squared-off and trimmed, an Elizabethan beard.

He put down his bag. "I can't thank you enough . . ." he started.

But Kate finally came to life and stood up. "You're early," she said, and went towards him. He put his arms around her and kissed her. His beard scratched her face. She kissed his cheek and then felt his mouth slide around to her own. Why not? she thought, astonished at how familiar his lips and face felt against her own. We've been kissing each other for more than twenty years—off and on.

But she pushed away from him, and he released her immediately.

"As I started to say, Kate, I can't thank you enough, I . . ."

"Daddy!"

They both turned. Marie stood in the doorway. She saw us kiss, Kate thought.

"Hello sweetheart." Paul moved towards his daughter, but she stepped aside and went past him.

"Good trip?" she said.

"A long one. Come here, Marie, come give me a kiss."

"Haven't you had yours for the evening?"

Paul walked over and spun her around. "None of that, now. Kate and I have known each other for twenty-five years. What do you expect us to do, shake hands?"

It was like watching a courtship, she thought, as she observed Paul's masterly touch with his daughter. And it *was* masterly for the very reason that it was not contrived, not thought out. It was as much a part of Paul Lamont as his fair hair and height.

"Paul, you're incredible," Kate said, picking up her plate and putting it in the sink.

"How so?" He still had his hands on Marie's shoulders.

"Because you're such a con artist," Marie said, pushing his hands off and moving away. "You're kissing cousins with everybody. Kate, Mom, Angela Griffin, me . . ."

She stood off from him, as though daring him to strike her.

He suddenly started to laugh. Then, before she could get away, he strode over, put his arms around her and gave her a loud smack on her cheek. "I love you," he said. "I'm sorry you have such a rotten life."

Marie burst into tears.

He kept his arms around her. Kate, mesmerized, could see Marie's minimal efforts to free herself. She doesn't want to get loose, Kate thought. She wants to cry on his chest. And then, doesn't everybody?

She walked out and went into the living room where she sat on the sofa and tried to concentrate on the second section of the *New York Times* over a bewildered feeling of blurred time. She felt that in some strange way she and Marie seemed bound together in a fugue-like dance, counterpointing one another. It was disturbing. . . .

Twenty minutes later Marie came through the kitchen door, her face pink and swollen. She didn't glance at Kate but went straight upstairs. In a few seconds Paul came through the door, munching a piece of chicken that had been in the refrigerator.

"Haven't you had anything to eat?" Kate said, delighted she had something practical she could talk about.

"Not really. There was lunch on the plane, followed by what they graciously call a snack, which was two tired pieces of bread on either side of an exhausted piece of luncheon meat. But I got a sandwich at the airport before I went to the hospital."

Kate was aware of a stab of disappointment. "You've already been there?"

"Yes. I wanted to catch McGrath before he packed it in for the evening, and I wanted to see Deborah. I felt I had to have a clear picture of what's going on now and what I can expect."

"What did you find out?"

"That Deborah's not about to be ready to come home and that I'm going to have to do something about getting a sitter in for the time being." He chewed the last of his chicken leg, wrapped it in the paper napkin he had in his hand and sat down. Pulling a cigarette from the pack in his shirt pocket, he lit it, inhaled deeply, then snatched the pack from his pocket and held it out towards Kate. "Sorry!"

She shook her head. "No, thanks. Is it all pills, or does Deborah have an underlying emotional problem?"

He put the cigarettes back in his pocket. "I'm not sure. Neither is McGrath. Of course, one can feed the other."

"When did she start taking the pills?"

"When we were first in Japan. Lots of perks over there, including servants. She didn't have much to do. She was lonely and didn't know many people. I was away a lot. You can fill out the rest."

Kate studied him. He looked tired and he looked his age, which was thirty-eight—the same as hers. Sitting a few feet away from him, she could see that some of the fairness of his hair was gray. Yet he seemed as packed with vitality as he always was. His body was as lean as when she had last seen him, which was at his wedding.

"Do you realize how long it's been since we've seen each other?" Kate asked.

"Yes," he said promptly. "It was my wedding day."

"Speaking of which, you don't seem to be bowed down with grief that your wife is in the hospital, suffering from narcotic addiction and depression, following a suicide attempt."

"I might if this hadn't been the third time it's happened. And if I hadn't been living with her being spaced out for the past several years." He leaned back in his chair and drew on his cigarette. "They say you can get used to anything, and I suppose I am used to it." He glanced at Kate. "I dare say that sounds hard-boiled to you."

"Yes, it does."

"Too bad! For your information, I am very concerned indeed about my children. Which is why I haven't sued for divorce. Until now it always seemed to me that to keep up at least the structure of marriage was the lesser of two evils. Now I think the scales are falling in the opposite direction. I'll take custody of the children and will try and give them a more stable home."

"You mean you'll just divorce Deborah and let her sink or swim."

"Deborah is rich in her own right. You know that."

Kate did. "I always thought that was . . ." She stopped, whether out of tact or cowardice she didn't know.

"That was the reason I married her?"

"Yes."

"No, you didn't. You told yourself that was the reason. But you knew better. I married Deborah because you told me to go to hell. In those days Deb was a dazzler. She was beautiful and glamorous and headed straight for being queen of Carnival. To a kid from the sticks, which was what you and I both were, that was heady stuff. And she made it clear she liked me. Sure I took her out and played around with her—as did a couple of others. You went out with other people, too. But I loved you and wanted to marry you just the way I said. I won't buy that bit that I deserted you for money and family and the house in Prytania Street. That's what you told yourself. But that's not the reason."

"Then what was the reason?"

"I don't know. I'm not sure. I've never been sure. And the few times I've been in New York and tried to reach you, you wouldn't even return my calls. You started acting strange when you were a sophomore in college. It was like another person had taken possession of you—had started to live in your skin. I couldn't get through to you. After the beginning of your junior year you only came home twice: when you came down for the disastrous party when you read me out of your life and on the day Deb and I were married."

Kate was still absorbing this statement when the kitchen door opened.

"Dad!" Ranger came in.

"Hello son!" Paul got to his feet, putting out his cigarette in the ashtray on the table beside him. Then he reached out, tousled Ranger's head, shook his hand and gave him a brief hug, all in one quick movement. "How are you?" he said.

"Okay." Pause. They both seemed to be waiting for something. Then, in a burst, Ranger said, "Bones is almost housebroken."

"Almost isn't enough, Ranger."

"He'll be fine. Honest."

"You know how your mother feels about animals in the house."

"Dad, one reason he's the way he is, scared, is because he had to sleep out there in the back. He's only a puppy."

"He's really going to be okay, Paul," Kate put in. "He's improved a lot even since I've been here."

A look of astonishment passed over Ranger's face. Quickly it turned to gratitude. "You see? Even Aunt Kate says so."

"All right. But keep him in the kitchen. If he messes up—out he goes."

Kate understood then Ranger's anxiety on the point. She glanced at the boy and smiled.

"Don't tell me you're in on this conspiracy," Paul said.

"No conspiracy, Paul. I've been very glad to have Bones here. I never knew Deborah to be so opposed to animals."

"None of us knew Deborah," Paul said. Kate saw Ranger get red.

"Done your homework?" Paul asked his son.

"I'm almost finished."

"I didn't ask if you'd finished. I asked you if you'd done it." Ranger mumbled something.

"Because if you're fooling with that mongrel instead of doing your work, then the dog will have to go. Better get at it."

Kate watched unbelievingly as Ranger escaped up the stairs.

"My God, Paul, you're tough on Ranger. As tough on him as you're easy on Marie. At least he's in school. Marie isn't even that."

Paul's eyes suddenly looked arctic, reminding Kate of times when she'd seen them like that before. "The problem lies in your head, Kate, not in mine. One of the things that drove Deborah round the bend was Ranger bringing home a series of animals, none of whom had any training, all of whom seemed to evacuate over everything in sight. Some of the things those dogs ruined—chairs, small carpets—were family pieces that meant a lot to her. Asking Ranger didn't do any good. I'd come home and find Deborah in tears and—of course —zonked. At least Marie tried to help her mother. The prejudice—if there is any—lies as much in the way you see the children as in my way." He got up suddenly. "I'm going to bed. I've been up for twenty hours, and the night before, I had four hours sleep. I want to talk to you about what to do. But I think we'd better postpone it till I've had some rest. In the meantime, I'd appreciate your staying here."

"If you're here you don't need me," Kate said. "I'll go back to my apartment tomorrow. Anyway, wouldn't the neighbors think it funny?"

"I don't care what the hell the neighbors think. But just for the record, I imagine they'd think it was funny if Deborah's only sister didn't come to help out when she was in the hospital. You always did have a mind surrounded on all sides by middle-class values. Good night."

Kate lay in bed, reliving as much as she could remember of what Paul called "that disastrous party."

Since he had first laid eyes on the fourteen-year-old Deborah, when he and Kate were sixteen, he had obviously (at least it was obvious to Kate) been as bewitched as the goose-boy in a traditional fairy tale when he had first glimpsed the princess. For the two years following, this had been revealed to Kate mostly through watching his face when Deborah came into the room while Paul was there, picking Kate up, or bringing her home . . . and Deborah managed to be hanging around on almost all those occasions, though "hanging" was too gross a description of her gossamer, graceful presence. With rage and a sense of impotence Kate would watch the metamorphosis of Paul's face. His eyes would become fixed, a red would creep up right under his high cheekbones, and what Kate would think of as a "goofy" look—an expression she later defined to herself as moonstruck rapture —would slide over his features, or rather, all other expressions would simply disappear, leaving the bewitched expression that made him appear younger and more vulnerable, and made Kate both want to cry and to kick him.

As a result of her straight A record in her socially tacky but academically stringent school, Kate went off to Barnard. Before she left she exchanged with the reluctant Paul—who was heading for Stanford—assertions of love and fidelity, which, however, allowed for the facts of life including one obvious one—that they'd both be free to go out with others. Kate would have been perfectly willing to go further and renounce all dating. But some small remnant of wisdom made her see that even to suggest such a binding contract would do more harm than good. She hadn't been in Morningside Heights for more than a month when Paul, who at the last moment and with help from his father's considerable local clout, had changed from Stanford to Tulane in New Orleans, started taking out Deborah, a fact that was conveyed to Kate in the letters from various friends.

He took out plenty of other girls also. As a rising athletic star he had his pick of the assembled beauties of Newcomb— the women's college of Tulane. He didn't take Deborah out often. She was, after all, only sixteen, and still at McGehee's— New Orleans' private school for the female Protestant elite. But they saw each other steadily—a fact that was also conveyed to Kate. After many tears and much conflicting advice, Kate decided to ignore the issue. When she went home the

the first Christmas Paul telephoned immediately. They went out. Having had it drummed into her that she should not make an issue of Deborah, she managed not to mention the matter. But the effort killed all spontaneity, and with it the evening. She went back to Barnard and did not return to New Orleans until June, by which time she'd put on twenty pounds.

Keith, who was slowly dying of emphysema and seemed in some world of his own, stared at her out of his ice blue eyes. She felt as though he was looking through her to something beyond.

"That's no way to get him back, Kate," he said when she went up to his room to see him. Neither mentioned Paul's name. But both knew what he meant.

"I can't help it," she said belligerently. "I get the hungries when I study."

"It certainly takes you away from competition—not that you could offer Deborah any. Or anyone else, for that matter," he finished cruelly. His eyes were as detached and impersonal as though he were looking at a plastic clothes model. Then he turned to stare out of the window.

"Look," she said, making a last desperate attempt to bridge some gulf that had always been there. "I'm your daughter."

He did not turn around. "No, you're not. You never have been. You're an unwanted child that Beth adopted." He was not angry. Just indifferent.

Kate went back to New York. She no longer wrote Paul, and he did not write to her. When her father died a few months later, she came down to the funeral. When Paul called her to express his sympathy and invite her out to dinner, she refused. The twenty excess pounds had grown to twenty-five.

If Keith Malory had found in the house on Prytania Street his native milieu with which a right-thinking world should have surrounded him from birth, Kate found herself confronted with a mirror that constantly reflected her ugly-duckling image. Until then, she had been borne up by an unspoken hope that time would turn her into a swan. It was at Prytania

Street that Kate became convinced that she would never become a swan; swanness was born, not made. She also learned that Paul saw the difference immediately.

When she returned to Barnard after her father's death, Kate had relinquished all claim to Paul.

It was two years later that Diane's letter arrived, asking her to come down for Deborah's coming out party—"just for old times' sake," as Diane put it. Kate's first impulse was to refuse. But she changed her mind, mostly, she realized later, because in the intervening months she had changed her own appearance considerably for the better and was not averse to all her old competitors in New Orleans knowing it. She had starved herself and was now slender and had learned how to dress to her own looks in bright colors and simple, rather sophisticated lines.

So, against a nagging voice that told her she was not ready to go down to New Orleans, she wrote to Diane and said, with carefully contrived casualness, that she might be able to fit a visit into her busy schedule. Then she went to Lord & Taylor and blew her savings on a long, flame colored silk crepe that emphasized her fine neck, small waist, and made her eyes look green.

She arrived the same day of the party, a few hours before it was due to begin. And that was her first mistake. Excitement and anxiety had rendered her somewhat underslept and overstrung, although afterwards, in the despair of the aftermath, she decided that that might not have made any difference. In any case, she had steeled herself for her first sight of Paul with recollections and reminders of the various men who had taken her out in New York, some of whom continued to show flattering interest. She did not consider relevant the fact that she found none of them attractive.

In the months during which her own body had grown more comely, she had persuaded herself by some alchemy of hope and optimism that, undoubtedly, Paul had grown less so. That comforting myth was ripped from her the moment he walked in, tall in his tails and white tie, his wheat colored head rising above those of the other men around him. He came almost immediately over to her, kissed her cheek, squeezed her hand and said, "Why Kate, darling, you're beautiful!"

It was devastating. The psychological work of years, the mental pep talks, the ramming home to herself of her central thesis—Paul was an over-muscled lout on the make—all was swept away by the sight of his head bending towards hers, the feel of his lips on her skin, his strong hand holding hers.

"Here's to you, Kate," he said, handing her one of two champagne glasses he had taken from a perambulating waiter. "Here's to your lovely green eyes."

The old pain throbbed. The old love rose up from the ashes, undiminished and undaunted. After the New York voices, Paul's flat, New Orleans vowels were as seductive as love itself. She drank down her champagne. It was the first champagne she had ever tasted, and after her initial impression that it was grossly overpraised, she found she liked it. When Paul took a second glass for them each from another tray, she drank it almost at once. Paul laughed down into her eyes and gave her another one.

"It's a long way for us both from the Methodist Sunday school, isn't it?"

"Here's to distance!" she said gaily, draining her glass.

"That stuff's a mite more potent than it tastes," Paul said.

"I've discovered I have a hard head," Kate said, who had discovered no such thing, largely because she was, by instinct and habit, a modest drinker.

"Good for you! If there's one thing I can't stand it's a female who's had too much."

"Only hicks do that," Kate said.

"You know, it's been too long," Paul's fine blue eyes smiled down into hers.

Her heart was behaving in such an erratic fashion she thought she would choke.

90

And then Deborah came down the stairs, radiant and grace-ful in the classic debutante dress, with its small waist, billow-ing tulle skirts and off-the-shoulder neckline.

"Paul!" she said in her low, pretty voice. And he left Kate immediately.

An hour or so later, when Deborah was dancing with some-one else, Paul cut back in on Kate.

"Now where were we?" he said, slipping his arm around her.

Kate was angry. Over the shoulders of the men who had cut in on her, she had watched Paul either dance with Deborah or hover around waiting to cut back in on her. For the first half hour she told herself that since it was a party for Deborah, it was only right that such an old friend of the family should dance attendance on her. For the second half hour, Kate de-cided he was overdoing the dutiful bit. For the remaining forty minutes she struggled with an old dragon that she thought had been slain for good and all by the years in New York, the lost pounds and the new boyfriends—the forgotten gnawing conviction that she herself was the intruder, the alien fowl in this household of swans, and that Paul, along with all the other men in the room, was dancing with Deborah not only because the party was in her honor, but because, once they had seen the real gem, Deborah, they knew instantly that she, Kate, was a fraud, a piece of paste, a throwaway. Fueled by several more glasses of the unfamiliar ethyl alcohol disguised as a bubbling wine, she felt the beginning wildfire of growing rage.

"I don't know," she said with a forced laugh. "It's been such a long time."

"Yes, I know. I, too, have thought it was long. But this is Deb's party, and I owe the Légères a lot. You understand, don't you? Well, I'm sure you do." He smiled, that appealing crooked smile that had pulled her heart out of her chest across a Sunday school classroom. "After all, that's why you're down here, too."

She wanted so much to believe him. Eagerly she accepted his statement. "That's right," she said, gazing up at his face. "It is Deb's party, we have to remember that."

He put his face next to hers and danced, holding her close.

If he had felt his duty towards Deborah sufficiently executed, if she had not drunk so much champagne, if the music had not stopped a moment later, then there was still time for the evening to veer from the disastrous course that lay ahead. But none of those contingencies occurred.

"Let's collect some champagne and go out into the garden," Paul said, looking around for a waiter as the musicians rested their instruments and wiped their brows.

Warning bells were sounding in Kate's head. But they were distant and muffled. "Yes, let's."

Two glasses of champagne later, they were kissing passionately under the great boughs of the live oak, more or less sheltered by the branches that dipped almost to the ground.

In the midst of this sounded the gong. "Supper, everyone," someone called.

Paul unglued himself. "I'm supposed to take Deb in to supper," he said, and without further ceremony ran towards the house.

Kate walked slowly towards the French windows of the ballroom. For one of the few times in her life the thought of food was not attractive. In fact, it nauseated her. By the time she wandered into the ballroom, the last guests were filing into the dining room beyond where, Kate remembered being told, a buffet supper with more champagne was to be held. The ballroom had an abandoned end-of-party look that Kate had seen after many festivities, but she knew it was only a pause before the musicians, then being fed in another room, and all the guests would be back and the second half of the dance would proceed. Even the waiters had gone, undoubtedly now on duty in the dining room. The long table that served as a bar was deserted, champagne bottles, many of them upside down, shoved into buckets of melted ice. But some bottles were still right way up. Walking slowly over to the table, Kate took a glass at random and picked up one of the bottles. It was almost full and still cold. With no more ado, she poured herself a glass, filling it to the top and watching the white foam flow out and onto the floor. "Lovely," she said half aloud, and drank it off. Then she filled it again.

She could never remember the sequence of events that followed, just separate scenes: there was herself in the downstairs bathroom, staring at her image in the long mirror, and deciding that the flame color was strident, or perhaps kitschy, or both. There was the man with glasses with whom she danced and to whom she confided this great worry and who reassured her so well that she found herself with him back under the live oak, her tormenting self doubts being reassured in the most direct way. There was more champagne . . . Paul cut in again. .

There was a confused jumble of sights and sounds, a high voice going on and on . . . The next memory was unmercifully clear; somebody was helping her upstairs . . . she was in a bedroom . . . and then she was in the bathroom being terribly sick again . . . *again?* . . . She looked down the red dress and saw the smear of vomit.

The next thing she remembered was the following day. She awoke with a burning headache, a retching stomach and a sense of total devastation. One of the maids came in and said Mr. Lamont was on the phone. Kate refused to speak to him. She knew that whatever dreadful thing had happened had involved him, even though it was she (she also somehow knew) who had been humiliated. In fact, whatever it was (she became suddenly convinced) had been caused by him and by his characteristically treacherous behavior; when she had come South she was prepared—in fact eager—to let bygones be bygones. But he had treated her like his long lost love, had led her on to believe she still meant a great deal to him. He had flattered her so that she had lowered her guard . . . and then when the rich, all-conquering, socially prominent Deborah beckoned, he flew to her side. She had been right all along; he was a good looking muscle-bound lout on the make. There were a lot of nicer men in New York . . . men who had no terrible, degrading memory to hold against her. She could not —would not—remember the details. But she knew in the depths of her bones that, because of what happened, everything was beyond repair.

The last time Paul called she sent a message that he was to leave her alone. She had no wish to speak to him. After that she felt a little better, somewhat restored. Neither Diane nor Deborah mentioned what had happened. There was total silence from her old friends who had attended the party.

The day after, she flew back to New York.

Following that debacle, she went through a period, which she preferred now to forget, when, restless, angry and determined to justify herself before some unseen judge, she passed rapidly from job to job, and from man to man. Which was one of the things that made Joel's periodic lectures on the benefits of the sexual revolution so—to her—amusing and ironic. She had had her revolution and come out the other side.

Except for Paul and Deborah's wedding, she never went back to New Orleans.

And now she was lying here in Deborah's house with Deborah off at the nut house and Paul—looking better than he ever had—upstairs. What did he mean by that crack about middle-class values? If anyone's home, location and lifestyle was the epitome of the affluent middle class it was Paul's—up to and including his depressed, pill addicted wife.

Kate slept fitfully and was up before anyone else in the house. Sometime in the course of her sleep she had reached a decision. After a hasty cup of coffee she packed her bag, called a taxi and went to the station. Paul could take care of his own family now that he was back.

Chapter 5

B less me Father, for I have sinned. My last confession was . . ." Kate searched her mind, panicky that she had not thought to figure that out before she arrived at the confessional. "Well," she finally said, "a long time ago. Maybe a year."

"Not at Easter?" the priest asked in a slightly shocked tone. Easter had been about three weeks previous.

"No."

"Go on," the priest said.

Kate peered through the mesh into the dimness. Something about the way the priest spoke—more a rhythm in his speech than an accent—denoted the foreigner. Well, she thought, wasn't that what she expected? She had come to this midtown church during the lunch hour, a church that employed a great number of Filipino, Asiatic and Indonesian priests.

"Go on, please," the priest said again.

But her mind had frozen. She knew she could run through the list of sins of omission—I have not been kind, I have not been unselfish, I have not been pure in thought, I have not been silent when I should have been—plus the sorry, inevitable trespasses of being human—I have been angry, full of pride, unforgiving, happy over someone else's misfortune, I've gossiped in the office, was rude to the cleaning woman, etcetera, etcetera, etcetera—that could be reliably produced in the absolute certainty that they had been committed.

I have lusted—but at that, as though a lid had flown off her mind and memory, Kate knew that was not her problem at all. Not now, anyway. Or at least not in the usual sense. But what about the pounding heart, the uneven breath when either Paul or Graham was in the vicinity? Couldn't that be called desire? At that moment, kneeling uncomfortably in the confessional, Kate understood something about herself. Whatever those physical symptoms indicated, they were not, for her, desire. Whatever else they portended, they were not signs that she had the slightest wish to climb into bed and be made love to by, or to make love to, either Graham or Paul. In that case, desire for what?

"Are you there?" The priest tapped his side of the plastic mesh with one finger.

Kate wondered what his reaction would be if she said, Father, you may not believe this, in fact, I'm sure you won't, but I somehow feel sure that my real transgression is that I haven't truly desired anybody for at least five years.

What would he say to her? She decided not to find out. "I'm sorry, Father, I've changed my mind." And she got up hastily, fumbled with the door and left. There was a line of penitents waiting to go in on both sides of the confessional, so the priest —Kate looked at the sign hung on the door, *Fr. Francis Lo*— so Father Francis Lo should be too occupied to open the door of the confessional and call her back, even if he would. Kate wasn't sure that that would be allowable, although the saintly Curé d'Ars was supposed to have reached out of the confessional and all but dragged those in he thought in need of the sacrament of penance.

Instead, she went and sat in a back pew of the church, well

out of any line of vision he might have. Now what? she thought. And why did she come here in the first place, after more than a year since her last attempt to set matters straight?

She stared at the old-fashioned, overly ornate altar, at the rather hideous painting over it of the Last Supper, and the small, surprisingly beautiful statue of the Virgin to the side. Delicate, the features and hands indicated rather than carved in detail, it was artistically out of place in the picture-postcard decor of the rest of the church. Yet it was here, many years before, that she had crept in, lunch hour after lunch hour, finding among the plastic images and rattling rosaries a peace and sense of otherness that she had never before encountered. Where was that sense now? Vanished, and had been vanished for some time. Was it because of her protracted affair with a married man, doing her best by word and act, in bed and out, to break up his marriage? Yet she had confessed that long since, and, according to church belief, had her sin (and sins) wiped out. But, she remembered her instructions, absolution didn't mean that the temporal punishment was removed. Was this sense of nothing, then, of absolute nothing, and of boredom and frustration on the few occasions when she attended Mass the temporal punishment? That somehow didn't seem kosher . . . Kate grinned at her use of the word in such a context. But then, she thought, she didn't make the rules.

"Where were you when I made the Pleiades?" said God.

"You have a point, Lord. I don't know," Kate answered within herself, and left the church.

When she got back to the office she found her secretary still out to lunch and a message planted in the middle of her desk. "Call Dr. McGrath." Underneath that line was the number.

The desire to have nothing further to do with Deborah and Paul—especially Paul—to say nothing of those debilitating children, whom she thankfully left the previous Thursday, struck

97

Kate so overwhelmingly that it shocked her. Without volition, her hand was already out, crumpling the paper, when the phone rang.

Anything for an escape or reprieve, she thought and picked up the receiver. "Hello."

"Miss Malory?"

Recognizing the voice, she almost slammed the phone down. Instead, she took a breath and said, "Yes? What is it, Dr. McGrath? My brother-in-law is back, you know."

"Yes. I know. He came back sooner than I thought he would."

"Surely that's to his credit. They are, after all, his children."

"Yes." He, too, seemed to pause and take a breath. Then, "I will be in the city later this afternoon, Miss Malory, seeing patients of a colleague who is away. I would like very much to talk to you. Would you be willing to come to his office?" He didn't wait for her assent, but went on, "I'll give you the address," and proceeded to name a Park Avenue number.

I'm not about to go to an office and have him talk to me from behind a desk, Kate thought. "I'd rather not do that, Dr. McGrath. If it is necessary for us to talk, then we can arrange a meeting place, or you can come to my apartment." The moment she said that she regretted it. At a neutral place— such as a hotel lobby or lounge—she would at least be free to get up and leave. But it was too late.

"Certainly," he said. And the dry note was back. "Where do you live?"

She gave him her address in the east eighties.

"What time would be convenient?"

She glanced at her desk and at the barely touched Kramer manuscript. Well, she'd work on it at home after the doctor left. "Six o'clock?"

"I'll be there," he said, and hung up, almost, she thought, as though he were afraid that if she lingered at the other end she'd change her mind. Which I might have done, she thought, putting down the receiver. Probably would have done.

She worked on the manuscript behind a closed door, and with instructions to her secretary to hold all calls, for the rest of the afternoon. Then at ten minutes to five, she gathered up her papers, put the bulky book into her tote bag and left the office.

"Any messages?" she asked Judy as she passed her desk.

"Lots," Judy replied, and held out some message forms clipped together.

Kate looked at them first with distaste and then a tinge of hope. "Any from Dr. McGrath?"

"None. Were you expecting him?"

Kate remembered that Judy had been out when he'd called before. "Wishing is more like it. I'm supposed to meet him later, and I had a faint hope that he might have called to break it."

"Sorry. No luck there."

When Kate got home she watered her plants, checked on the bird feeder outside her window, found it pecked clean and stared down into the gardens below. How wonderful it was to be back! The townhouses opposite were only one floor higher than the apartment she occupied in her own building, so that when she looked out and around the trees, she could see an expanse of sky—another rarity in New York—especially for an apartment on the third floor. Putting the manuscript on her desk, she made her way back to the small kitchen to make herself some tea. She was sipping this and reading the afternoon paper when her buzzer rang from downstairs.

Suppressing an impulse to pretend she wasn't there, Kate got up, went over to the intercom and told her doorman to send Dr. McGrath up. Then she waited, with, she admitted to herself, some curiosity.

He was younger than she had thought. For some reason she had imagined him to be past sixty, why, she couldn't now understand. Facing her in the doorway was a well-dressed man in his late forties. He had straight features and was surprisingly good looking.

"Come in," she said. "I'm having some tea. Would you like some? Or would you prefer a drink?"

"No, thanks. Tea will be fine."

She went to the kitchen and, adding some water to the kettle, put it on the stove. From there she watched him move around the room, examining her books, her pictures and her plants. Then he looked out the window.

"This is a nice apartment," he said, when she brought in a small tray with the teacup, milk and sugar. "You're lucky with that view of the gardens."

"I know. That's why I'm willing to pay more rent than I can afford. Please sit down." As he did so she squelched a desire to say, "You don't look like my idea of a psychiatrist." It might be true, but it would sound jejeune.

"What did you want to see me about, Dr. McGrath?" she asked instead.

For a moment he didn't reply, just sat there, staring down at his half empty cup. Then he put the cup down on a side table and looked up at her.

"I think we've already talked about the fact that your sister is seriously depressed and a drug addict." He paused.

"You call her my sister. You do know, don't you," Kate said, "that she's my stepsister?"

"Which places you at two removes from any responsibility." It was a statement.

"Yes." Kate matched his bluntness. "It does. And that doesn't go into . . ." Suddenly, as though an old movie was superimposed over the present, she saw the sixteen-year-old Deborah swing gracefully into the big, high-ceilinged Légère living room. "Hello Paul," Deborah's ghost said, eyes shining. With an effort Kate banished the shadowy movie. ". . . ancient history," Kate finished dryly. "Anyway, Paul Lamont's now back . . . as I said before."

There was a silence. The doctor's light eyes seemed to probe, almost, Kate thought, as though they were weighing or assessing her. "Could you find it in yourself to help her at all?" he said. "Or is your dislike too total? If she had any close friends I wouldn't be bothering you. But she appears not to."

"Why does she need help? I mean now that her husband is back."

"You don't look unintelligent."

It was a curious statement. By themselves the words were a snub. But the smile that went with them made them into a compliment. She had an odd feeling that she had underestimated this man's intelligence, perhaps because he made her think of an actor—a leading man—taking the part of a psychiatrist.

"I'm not sure what you mean."

"I mean that—as I'm sure you know—a family member isn't always the one who can give the most help."

It was a perfectly good answer and quite true. But Kate thought that if she had responded in a different way he would have had ready a reply different not so much in content as in style.

A smile then touched the corner of his mouth. "In your reflex action to any mention of your sister—sorry, stepsister—you remind me strongly of Azucena, our family cat. She took an instant dislike to a puppy that was brought home. Every time the puppy came within five feet of her, she stopped whatever she was doing and hissed. It was quite automatic and continued, even though, when he braved the magic five-foot circle and came up to her, she started licking him as though he were her kitten."

As a comment it had charm. Deliberately so?

"Well, I'm not about to do the human equivalent as far as Deborah is concerned. Yes, I dislike her. In a general way I'm sorry that she's having trouble. I'm sorry for anyone who's having trouble. But I'm not the person to assist."

"All right." He got up. "I won't bother you further. Thank you for the tea."

Even while he was walking to the door and Kate knew that she would stop him, she acknowledged his move as masterly.

It removed from him the onerous role of solicitor and placed it on her. "Very well," she said, "I'm curious. Come back and tell me why Deborah needs my help. If that was a ploy or a game it worked."

"It's not a ploy. I don't play games. I may take a tack with a patient if I think it's for the patient's good. But I don't manipulate other people."

Oh don't you! she thought, but was willing to give him the benefit of many doubts. "I'm sorry. Since my father married Diane Légère—Deborah's mother—I've always taken it for granted that I existed for them only as some kind of aid for their interests. Which puts my back up."

"So?"

"So, tell me how you think I can help Deborah."

"Curiosity or concern?"

"Does it matter?"

"Of course."

"About ninety-five and a half percent curiosity."

"All right. I'm willing to go with the four and a half percent interest."

Dr. McGrath closed the door and came back in, putting his brief case once more down on the side table. After he sat down, he stared for a moment at his linked hands. "The truth is, Deborah—Mrs. Lamont—is not responding to treatment the way she should. It's true it's only been six weeks and narcotics withdrawal combined with depression can have devastating effects on a patient's vitality—even will to recover. Yet her continued lethargy, alternating with wild, almost manic periods, is puzzling. We've given her every test we can. We watch her carefully. I've had two outside consultants examine her. She should be showing more improvement than she is." He frowned.

"Well, doctor, forgive the bluntness, but if you and two other doctors—and her husband—are stymied, what can I do about it?"

He looked up. "Nothing, of course. I'm sorry if I sounded

as though I were handing you a strictly medical problem. I'm not. But she does have her rational moments—periods when she is neither apathetic to the point, almost, of paralysis, nor manic. And in those moments she frets about her children, especially when she learns—as she did recently—that their most recent housekeeper had left and they were alone. In her own way, and within her terrible limitations, she tries to be a good mother." He hesitated. "I realize the evidence doesn't point in that direction, and I know the children—especially the girl—are completely out of hand. But aside from her fears as to what they might do to themselves, there is also her fear that the state child welfare bureau will come and take them away. Certainly, if the nosey neighbor has anything to do with it—or so Deborah thinks at any rate—they will."

"But Paul's there."

"I know. And I have explained that to her. She's aware, though, that he does still have to travel some." The doctor looked at her and smiled dryly. "Yes, I know, it doesn't make total sense. But then she is in no condition to make total sense, and my first obligation, as her physician, is to do the best I can for her."

"I take it you mean that if I were there, holding the fort, even with Paul in the country, Deborah would be easier in her mind."

"That's exactly what I mean. It's difficult for you, I know. But it might make the difference."

Kate realized that if someone were putting this to her in a letter, she would, by this time, be having the feeling of entrapment that she so hated and would therefore find it possible to refuse. But with the personal and enigmatic physician there, she felt herself acceding to his request. Which is why, she thought dryly, he is here.

She got up. "I feel that I am being overpersuaded against my better judgment. You are a powerful advocate, Dr. McGrath, and I think you must know it."

He had the grace to blush, which did not detract from his

charm. "I'll plead guilty to that. I'm asking a lot of you. You showed yourself unwilling right from the beginning. I'm intruding on your life. Your obligations towards the Lamonts are not . . . are not the same as if you were related by blood. All of these facts, I know. I decided to throw whatever powers of persuasion I have on the other side. I am intensely sorry for Deborah Lamont, and I'd like to give her recovery every chance." His manner—rather than the actual words—carried so much conviction that another suspicion crossed Kate's mind.

"Et tu, Brute?" she said, not expecting him to pick it up.

He frowned. "Meaning?"

"It's a quotation."

"I know perfectly well it's a quotation. I'm not illiterate. I studied something in school besides anatomy and the nervous system of the frog."

"Sorry. No offense."

"None taken. But I still don't know what you mean."

Kate, who had been moving around the room, sat down again. "When I knew Deborah, she was one of the most staggeringly beautiful young women I'd ever known. Men—all ages of men—went over like ninepins. Including Paul. I was wondering if, sick as she is, she still has the old magic."

A curious look passed over his face, but was gone before Kate could identify it.

Then, "I see," he said dryly. "Well—drug addiction and depression are not beauty treatments. From time to time, I've seen glimpses of what she must have been like, once. But she looks now like a tired, middle-aged, overweight woman who's neglected herself for the past ten years. I don't know about your relative ages, but she looks fifteen years older than you."

Kate's first sensation was a fierce thrust of pleasure and vindication, followed by shame at herself. Both feelings were so strong that Kate looked quickly at the doctor, as though he could read her thoughts.

104

Evidently he could. "You have what used to be called a 'speaking countenance,' Miss Malory."

"Meaning I do not have a poker face."

He laughed. "No. I don't think you'd do well in that game." He looked speculatively at her. "Was she that beautiful?"

"Yes. And rich. And wellborn. Everything I wanted to be. She was a swan and I was a crow. And every time I looked at her I felt more of a crow. She was gossamer and I was a lump. She and her mother, Diane, were exactly what my father admired and went after—not me."

There was a silence. "Dear me," Kate murmured, "that sounds remarkably like an acute case of self pity. I apologize."

"No need to apologize, but your roles are now reversed. You would appear to have a great deal—good looks, good job, nice apartment, and Deborah has nothing—not even her sanity."

She still has Paul. The words were in Kate's mind before she could stop them. She glanced at her cup and saw it was empty. "I think I'm going to have a drink. Would you like one?"

"All right. Thanks."

"Scotch?"

"That'd be fine. On the rocks."

Kate mixed the two drinks and brought the glasses in, handing one to the doctor. "I'll take your cup," she said, and put it in the kitchen.

When she was back in her seat she started, "All the same . . ." All the same—what? she wondered. Doubts were littered around in her mind like debris. But she couldn't put them together into a coherent statement. The trouble with me, she thought, is that my reservations have reservations.

"All the same, what?"

"Nothing." She took a breath. "All right. I'll go back there—for a few days, anyway. But I think you ought to know that I didn't just envy Deborah Légère. I hated her."

For a second he looked startled.

"Paul didn't tell you that?"

"No. His great concern was his children."

And yours? Kate thought. What was the doctor's great concern? Why was he here? Deborah—as he kept insisting? Odd, she reflected, she had no trouble at all believing that he wanted her in the Légère house. But his stated concern for Deborah had a curiously unreal quality. Still, he had made a strong case. Paul might be worried for his children. But Kate knew it wouldn't prevent him from being away. And there could be no doubt in anyone's mind that those children should not be alone. However, she felt that there was one more thing she must make clear to Deborah's physician.

"Among the other things that Deborah had that I didn't—although I had him first—was Paul Lamont."

"I see," the doctor said. He took a swallow from his glass then turned it round and round in his hand, "Would that still be a problem?"

"Meaning, am I still in love with him? I don't think so. Technically speaking, I walked out on him. But I did it only when I realized I had lost the contest for good and all. He's still attractive, as I am sure you realize. I'm merely saying this because, since you are Deborah's shrink, you ought to know that. It's an element you can't leave out in your calculations."

"To be blunt—you're saying you might, in the void left by Deborah's state of the past years, take up where you left off."

"No, I don't think I mean that, doctor. And I'm not sure, by the way that there's been a void. I meant just what I said. It was an aspect of the long complicated relationship between the Légères and myself that you should at least be aware existed."

He swallowed the last of his drink and stood up. "Don't go if you feel it to be wrong or unwise."

"Oh I'll go. I've said I would." She stood up. "As I commented before, you are a powerful persuader."

As she opened the door she said, "By the way, what's this establishment of yours called?"

He picked up his brief case. "White Falls Clinic. Named after the estate that used to be there."

"I haven't heard of it—although there's no particular reason why I should. Have you been there long?"

He smiled. "A few years. Although sometimes it feels longer."

"I take it you specialize in drugs?"

She had made the comment idly, thinking of Deborah, so she was disconcerted when he stopped short and said, "What do you mean?" His brows came down, masking his eyes.

"Well . . ." she paused, a little startled. "Deborah's problem. Pills."

"Oh . . . I see. Well, not really. Certainly not exclusively. White Falls is a kind of sanitarium for people who . . . who suffer from stress in one way or another and take the wrong way out. Pills, alcohol, other things. We try to help them get back on the track again."

"Helpful," she said, thinking he sounded a little like a brochure. "There seems to be more and more need for it."

He walked to the elevator and pushed the button, then turned back and smiled at her. His smile, she thought, had all the substance and warmth that his words—or at least some of them—lacked. The elevator came almost immediately. "Good night," he said, and got in.

After he'd left she made herself dinner and watched the news on television while she ate. Then she cleared up the table, got out the Kramer manuscript and forced herself to work for the next three hours. After that she took a hot bath, went to bed and lay awake half the night.

She had expected to be thinking about Paul; one way or another, on one level or another, she had thought about him a large part of her life. What she hadn't expected was to find her mind focused on Dr. McGrath. There were contra-

107

dictions there she found profoundly puzzling. On the two occasions when she'd talked with him on the phone, he'd sounded brisk, competent and somewhat harassed. She had had no trouble in stating her point of view and the limits to which she was willing to go. Tonight . . . she had conceded within a few minutes of his walking into the room. Why? It was not what he said, which was not that different from what he'd said before, and there was a great deal left unsaid as to Deborah's illness, her treatment and her lack of response to that treatment. Further, his statements, in retrospect, had a curiously rehearsed quality. So where did the doctor's power lie?

Ruefully, lying there in the dark, staring up at the ceiling, Kate acknowledged that Dr. McGrath had considerable presence, a power that was almost intimate and went beyond his sophisticated good looks and exquisite tailoring. And no matter what he said that impact did not falter, except, perhaps, at the very end when Kate's idle question as to his specializing in drug abuse treatment seemed to throw him.

I suppose, she reflected, everybody's jumpy about pills these days. . . . Then, how funny to find such a man in the backwoods of Westchester! As she was on the edge of sleep she remembered the look on his face when he spoke of Deborah's appearance. At the time she couldn't define it, but now she recognized it as distaste. Odd, she thought, that such a powerful advocate on Deborah's behalf should feel that way about her.

She called Paul the next morning after she got to the office. "How're things?" she said.

"Lousy, thanks. It would be a big help if you were here. At least I'd know the kids had somebody around."

"You're around, and they like you better than they do me."

"I would like to be able to go to a conference in Chicago. If I can't, I can't. But it doesn't make my work easier. I'm sorry I have the job I do, requiring the traveling I do. But I

108

can't get another one by tomorrow morning. I can stay in New York, but I would not be doing what I am paid to do.

"They—the corporation—let me come home. But I'm still supposed to oversee plans from time to time. If I could get a good housekeeper I would. But no one that we've had before and that I trust can come. End of story."

"All right, Paul. I'll come and stay awhile. Between you and that con artist Dr. McGrath, I've been shamed into it. I'll be there this evening."

There was a short pause. Then, "Well, I'd be a liar if I pretended not to be relieved. There's no way, at the moment, I can repay you. And the house isn't much better than it was before. In fact, it's worse. I have to do something about Marie and I'd like your help." He sounded moved, and despite her strongest resolve, Kate found herself responding to that. "Okay, I'll see you this evening."

After she hung up, Kate found herself thinking about Paul's girl friend. What was the name Marie had said? Angela Griffin. For a moment she toyed with the idea of suggesting to him that he ask his girl friend to lend a hand. The resulting fracas should be interesting, she thought. And then plunged into work.

She worked through the lunch hour, sending out for a sandwich. At three o'clock her phone rang for the umpteenth time. She had told Judy to disturb her only for something cataclysmic, so she was surprised when her buzzer sounded.

"Tell them to call tomorrow," she said. "Whoever it is."

"It's Jed Kramer. And he's outside in the foyer."

"In the foyer? He lives in California with the other kooks."

"Right now he's sitting in the red chair gazing at the jacket of his new book up on the bulletin board. He says he just wants to meet you and say hello."

Kate groaned. "Why today of all days? Why does this happen to me? Why didn't he stay in California?" She thought feelingly of one of her former colleagues working in the publicity department of another publisher. "Fortunately," this publicist had said, "in this house, most of our authors are dead or in England."

"Give me a minute to think," she said now to Judy.

"I don't know what you have to think about," Judy said. "You can't brush one of our best-selling authors under the hall carpet. Suppose he got offended and went off to another publisher? They'd snatch him up in a minute, him and his ninety-thousand copies."

"True. What a company girl you are! Give me a minute then send him in."

Hastily she shook together the scattered sheets of his manuscript. Since she had inherited Kramer from an editor who had left, she had never met the man before and tried to imagine what a devout reincarnationist would look like. All she could visualize were vague, wispy tendrils, mostly taken from arty drawings of seances. Yuch, she thought to herself. Hearing Judy's voice in the hall and footsteps, she shoved the manuscript into her bottom drawer and turned towards the door.

I should stop trying to visualize people was her first thought. She'd been way off with Dr. McGrath and she was way off now. Jed Kramer, so far from being a wisp, was very corporeal; he was a short, square man with a face like a bright monkey and thick, curly brown hair.

"Mr. Kramer?" she said, getting up and trying to keep the surprise out of her voice.

"Yes. That's right. I hope you don't mind my dropping in. I should have called first, but I didn't think I'd be able to get away from the convention. I'm delighted to meet you." He looked at her out of small, cheerful brown eyes.

"Do sit down," Kate said, still coping with her surprise at the way he looked, and wondering how long he would stay.

"I won't stay long, don't worry. I have to be back at the Hilton in an hour."

Kate felt the betraying blush rush into her cheeks. "I wasn't . . ."

110

"Yes you were and I don't blame you. You're probably still trying to rewrite my book. I never could write and the terrible thing was that when I was a boy at school when maybe I could have learned, I was too busy taking extra science courses and practicing my magician's tricks to bother to learn. Besides I have a poor ear. And good language is so much a question of ear, don't you think?" He beamed at her.

"I've never thought about it. But . . . now that I do, I think you're right. You don't mind that your books are rewritten, then?" Kate asked, remembering countless authors who commonly treated their editors to tantrums before submitting to the change of a comma.

"Not a bit. Why should I mind? What I have is the belief and the documentation. You put it in readable form."

Kate could feel the chasm of belief yawning between them and wondered how she could divert the conversation. "I take it you're here for a convention," she said hastily.

"It's all right. I know you think my views and theories are a lot of nonsense. Most people do. They will be in for a surprise! Never mind. Yes, I am here for a convention."

Kate felt the fatal blush start up again.

"And there's no need to feel embarrassed. People progress in their beliefs at their own paces."

Kate suddenly felt as though she were undressed. "Do you always read minds like that?"

"Yes. It's just a knack. I can do it the way a person with perfect pitch can tell you exactly what a note is. Or people with photographic memories can reproduce whole printed pages immediately after reading them."

She smiled. "You must be an uncomfortable person to be around, sometimes."

"That's what my dear wife used to say. But after a while she discovered it wasn't really true. Most of the time people— that is ordinary people of good will—don't want you to know what they're thinking out of kindness and because they're trying to make you think something else." He glanced at

111

Kate's somewhat puzzled look. "Supposing you said, 'how do you like my new red hat?' and I said, 'it's lovely,' but was really thinking you shouldn't wear red, not with that troubled orange aura, and you read what I was thinking. You'd be angry because I was saying one thing and thinking another. But if I said what I was thinking and you knew it was out of admiration and affection, you wouldn't be upset at all."

Kate found herself fascinated. "Suppose you were thinking, she shouldn't wear red because she's mean as a witch. And anyway, what's this about aura?"

"If I thought you were mean as a witch and you could read that, then you'd want to know why and I'd tell you, or you'd read it, and then maybe I'd discover that you only seemed mean because you'd been hurt and didn't understand something that had happened. And everybody has an aura. I'm sorry about whatever's troubling you." He looked unhappy.

"It's all right." Kate felt rather stunned.

Kramer suddenly stood up. "I'll be leaving now. You have a lot on your mind and a lot to do. Try not to worry too much . . ." His face screwed up. "In the end all will be well, as Blessed Mother Julian said."

Kate made a firm grab at something material. "Don't you want to see the changes in *Wheel* I've made before the manuscript goes to the printer, or ask about money or royalties or anything? I can't believe that an author from three thousand miles away would leave without even mentioning the matter!"

"Oh no. I make an adequate living at my profession. All the royalties go to the foundation." Bounding over to her he patted her arm with a stubby hand. "Don't worry. Be brave. Goodbye." Then he disappeared, a little, Kate found herself thinking, like Alice's rabbit down a hole.

In a minute Judy came in. Kate was still sitting there in a state of shock.

"Well?" Judy said. "How was he?"

Kate stared at her. "I can't believe him. He's . . . he's incredible."

Judy grinned. "He told me I had a lovely blue aura."

"He didn't like mine at all. He said it was orange for troubled."

"You don't have to be a psychic to know you're troubled. The receptionist could have told you that."

The two women looked at each other for a minute. Judy Roth was an intelligent young woman in her early twenties, who served as Kate's secretary in her office hours and read unsolicited manuscripts—known as the slush pile—on her own time and for no pay, for which she wrote excellent reports.

"Thanks a lot," Kate said dryly. "Has it been that bad?"

"It hasn't been bad. You've just been walking around looking as though somebody'd bitten you."

"Are you also a psychic?"

Judy grinned. "No but my boyfriend's into that."

"On the whole," Kate said, getting the manuscript out again, "I'm glad that I can't read minds the way Kramer can. I'd probably commit suicide over what people were thinking about me."

"No you wouldn't. Why be so negative?"

"What ever happened to reverence for elders—the quaking knee before the boss?"

Judy grinned. "It went out in the sixties," she said, and left the room.

Kate went back to work. Rather to her surprise, she found she was feeling a lot better.

When Kate rang the doorbell of the Lamont house that evening, Paul answered the door.

"Welcome," he said, holding the door open.

She stepped into an immaculate living room.

"No needlepoint, no T-shirt, no socks? What's come over the place?"

"I have. With my pan, brush, mop and polisher. If you even start to say anything to me about women's lib I'll shove the whole brush down your throat."

113

"I wasn't about to. Are you averse to a compliment? It looks," she sniffed, "and smells wonderful. Lemon furniture polish."

"Thank you. Your words are appreciated. I'm now about to go and have a bubble bath and put my hair up."

Kate burst out laughing and put down her suitcase. "I'll see about dinner. Where are your children?"

"Upstairs, doing their homework. Marie has been re-installed in school. Public school this time."

"Did she go willingly?"

"She did not. But I didn't ask her. I just put her in the car and drove her there and told her she'd stay or—or I'd take methods of reprisal."

There was something in his voice that made Kate glance at him. For a minute she felt sorry for Marie.

"Dinner?" she said.

"I didn't get to that. There's chicken and chopped meat in the refrigerator, plus assorted vegetables. If you hate cooking, I'll take you out. There's no reason why you should cook for a family."

"No. I don't mind. I'll go and get started. You take your bubble bath."

"Actually what I'm going to do is take the car down to the village and have it serviced and the tank filled. I'd rather drive to this convention than fly. Do you mind? If you need a car, there's a hire service in the village or you can call a taxi and charge it to me. Deborah did for the past couple of years."

"It'll have to be a taxi. I don't drive. I once took lessons and even passed the test and got a license, but since I never drove I let it lapse. To know how to drive you have to drive."

"True. Well, if I have a chance, I'll teach you. See you later."

Kate got out the chicken, sauteed it lightly, then put it in a casserole and started chopping up some vegetables to put on top. As her hands worked, leaving her mind free for the first time that day, she pondered the unwelcome but undeniable fact that this evening, as Paul opened the door to her, she felt again the same visceral reaction, the same midriff jolt that she always had whenever she saw him.

Which seemed to prove that she hadn't changed—whatever that meant, she thought, finishing the zucchini and going on to the carrots. But did it mean—God forbid—that she was in love with him? Who knows? She asked in her dialogue with herself. But it was disturbing. Disturbing enough to add a slight chill to the otherwise pleasant atmosphere. She was touched and pleased at Paul's vigorous housecleaning. Yet . . . there was something that was bothering her. She put down the knife. Something was missing. The kitchen was undoubtedly more antiseptic than it had been the previous weekend. The garbage was emptied, the garbage can closed neatly over its fresh plastic bag, the papers thrown away. . . . The papers had been there for Bones. . . . Bones . . . where was Bones?

It was then she became conscious of a noise that had been tapping at her attention for some minutes. Somewhere from outside the house a puppy was crying. Bones, she thought. Going over, she opened the back door. The sound became much clearer. In the back under a tree was what looked like a dog house. Kate went over calling softly, "Bones?"

The noise rose. "All right, all right," she said, reaching him. He seemed distraught and tried to leap up at her as she approached only to be yanked back by the chain. Patting and soothing him, she felt around the collar and found the snap of the chain that held him. She knew beyond question that Ranger would never put his pet out here. She glanced around. It was evident that Bones had reacted to his banishment in his characteristic way. Yet, she remembered, not once in the days when she was making friends with him, had he suffered a mishap. She recalled suddenly Paul's eyes when he had looked at Ranger the night he returned home, and his strictures about Bones and she shivered. It came to her that he was not a patient or tolerant man. But perhaps, she countered to herself, it came from living with Deborah. She hesitated. Should she go upstairs and talk to Ranger before she did anything? Probably.

115

She was turning away when she heard the sound of a car. Pausing, she waited until the car passed the house. It wasn't Paul. But the possibility that he might return at any moment made her come to a decision. Unsnapping the chain, she managed to hang onto Bones's collar as they went back to the house, Bones now beside himself with delight and making holding him extremely difficult. "Quiet, Bones. It's going to be all right!" Evidently her voice had some effect; he trotted the last few feet fairly quietly. Luckily, she had brought her tote bag back to the kitchen with her, and she started to put down the various sheets of the morning and afternoon papers she had brought to read on the train. When the floor was covered, she went to the foot of the back steps and called Ranger.

He didn't answer at first. So she called again. "Ranger, Bones is waiting for you in the kitchen." Then she went back to her vegetables. For a minute there was silence. Bones went to the foot of the steps and pointed his muzzle up, making a whinnying noise. Then he barked.

"Quiet, Bones!" Kate said, "let's not make waves."

All of a sudden there was the sound of rapid steps above, a joyous bark below and paws on the stairs mixed in with the sound of sneakered feet.

"Bones, how did you get in. You've got to get back!" It was an anguished whisper. Then there were more steps and Ranger's head appeared. He was holding Bones by the collar, but when he saw Kate he stopped.

"I suppose you'll tell Dad that Bones got loose!" There was so much anger and misery in Ranger's voice that Kate, startled, looked up. Ranger's face was dry, but it was obvious from his red and puffy eyelids that he had been crying.

"No, I'll tell him that I went out and got him. I heard him crying and brought him in. Why did you say that?"

"Because it was on account of you saying that you wouldn't come here if he was in the house that Dad said he had to be outside and if he made any more messes out there then he'd have to go to the pound tomorrow."

116

"I didn't . . ." Kate started, then she stopped. Ranger's eyes, painfully intense, were on her. He was standing there, his hand on Bones's collar, waiting. How could she tell him his father was a liar? A strange pain filled her. Finally, she said, "Ranger, he must have misunderstood—completely misunderstood—something I may have said in passing, as a joke. I like Bones. I want him here. During the day when I was here before he was fine. Just leave him."

For a minute he stared, plainly unbelieving. "D'you mean it? For real?"

"Yes, for real. Bones stays. Has he had his dinner?"

"I tried to feed him, but he wasn't hungry. Maybe he'll eat now."

"Don't give him the full amount. Just half. He could probably throw up as easily from being happy as being unhappy."

The anxious look came back over Ranger's face. "What if Dad says he can't stay?"

"Don't worry about it. I'll talk to him."

"That's terrific. I mean—well, thanks a lot. I'm sorry I said what I did."

"It was all a mistake. Now, I was thinking. When you've fed Bones, why don't you set the table in the dining room. We didn't use it the whole time I was here. It'll be better all round."

"Okay. I'll just give Bones his dinner." In a moment he put the half-filled dish on the floor. Bones, looking like an agitated shag rug, gathered himself up and loped over to smell the dish. Then he started to wolf it down, looking up and around every few bites to reassure himself about something. Seeing Ranger and Kate standing there, the plumey tail wagged and his nose went down.

"Okay," Ranger said. "I'll set the table now."

Twenty minutes later Kate was taking rolls out of the oven when the kitchen door opened and Paul walked in. "Well, the car's fixed and . . . damn it to hell! Ranger!" He stalked to the foot of the back steps.

"Paul," Kate said. "Please lower your voice. I brought the dog in because I like him and because when I'm with him—and I've been with him for two or three days at a time—he has no accidents at all. It wasn't Ranger's idea, it was mine. So please—lower the decibel level, or you'll bring about exactly what you don't want."

Putting down the salad dressing, Kate went over, reached a hand under the table, where Bones had retreated, and stroked his head, "It's all right Bones, it's all right." She glanced at Paul out of the corner of her eye. "Nasty man will be quiet."

The look, hard as a knife, that had slipped over Paul's face retreated. Slowly he went over to the sink and poured himself some water. "If Ranger wants a dog, I'll get him a decent one from a kennel. One that's been obedience trained. Not that incontinent mix."

"He's perfectly all right when he's not frightened. And he's only a puppy."

"I don't see why . . ."

"No Bones, no me."

It was delicious, Kate decided, having such bargaining power. Waifs of the world unite, she thought. We have nothing to lose but our inferiority complexes.

Paul shrugged. "Okay. If you don't mind cleaning up after him. But I'll be damned if I'm going to eat in a room that smells of diarrhea."

"You don't have to. We're eating in the dining room. Ranger's setting the table now."

"Well, well. What magic did you use to achieve that . . . no," he said, glancing at Bones, still under the table. "You don't have to answer that. By the way, I forgot to ask. Would you like a drink?"

"Not now. I'm hungry."

"Well, I brought home some wine. We can have that."

"That sounds delightful. We . . ."

Ranger came plunging back into the room from the dining room entrance. Seeing his father he skidded to a stop. His face closed up. "Hello, Dad." He turned alarmed eyes towards Kate.

"It's all right, Ranger. I've explained the mistake, and your father is quite willing that Bones can be here. Now just take this salad bowl into the dining room."

"That's a rather loose interpretation of the blackmail you exerted, isn't it?" Paul asked when Ranger had left.

Kate faced him. "Ranger said that you put the reason for Bones's banishment on me—that I had said I wouldn't stay here unless he were outside or sent to the pound." She paused, waiting to see what he would say, but he just went on sipping from his water glass, watching her. "Since I didn't want to call you a liar in front of your son, I decided to say that you had misunderstood something I said and that I would put it right. You heard me doing so."

"How very moral of you. I put it on you, as you state, because I thought that matters between Ranger and me were bad enough without my just telling him to get the hound the hell out of here. I don't like him and I don't want him around. However, you've got me by the short hairs as you very well know. If you can keep the dog on an even keel, then he can stay."

"Life is not exactly easy for Ranger right now, what with his mother in the hospital and you away so much, and one sitter after another coming and going."

"I'm their father, Kate. You don't have to explain it to me. Is dinner ready?"

"Sorry. Yes. Why don't you alert Marie to come down. I doubt if she'd listen to me."

Considering all the circumstances, Kate told herself, dinner passed off reasonably well. Ranger and Marie were both silent, although probably for different reasons. If Ranger looked apprehensive, Marie was sulking. Both looked as though they'd been crying. Kate and Paul kept some kind of conversation going, with Kate leaving occasional gaps in case either of the children wanted to say something. But neither did. Right after they'd finished Paul said, "Okay kids, the cleanup is on you. Your aunt and I are going to sit in the living room."

As they sat drinking the coffee that Kate had bought and prepared, Paul lit a cigarette and said dreamily, "I gave up coffee a year or so ago, but I must say this tastes good."

"Why did you give it up?"

"Because Deborah didn't like it, couldn't fix it, and usually had forgotten it. So, through necessity, I gave it up. She kept tea on hand, so I used that."

"That's very accommodating, for someone who sounds as dictatorial around the house as you do."

"Look, I'm not Attila the Hun. But since no one was setting any limits around here, I've had to do it."

"All right. You don't have to get your dander up. It can't have been easy."

"It hasn't been."

Kate looked at him. "And what about Miss Griffin?"

Paul didn't answer for a minute, drawing once or twice on his cigarette. Then he said, "You haven't seen Deborah, have you?"

"No. But Dr. McGrath did say, when he came to my apartment, that her looks have deteriorated." Again Kate felt the mixture of pleasure and guilt at her own reaction. But this time the guilt predominated simply for having made the statement. "*Schadenfreud,*" she murmured, remembering that the Germans had a name for rejoicing in someone's downfall.

"Ah yes," Paul said. "How are the mighty fallen!" His mouth twisted. "Don't look so shamefaced. We're all guilty of it. If it's any consolation to you, you are about five hundred percent better looking than she is now."

For the first time, pity stirred in Kate. "Poor Deborah. I'm not all that consoled by the thought of what's happened to her."

Paul looked at her. "When was McGrath at your apartment?"

120

"Yesterday evening. He came to lend the power of his presence to persuading me to come back here."

He grinned. "Nice of him. I see he succeeded."

"He's a potent persuader, Paul. And the funny part is, I'm still not sure how he did it. It's not so much what he said—he'd said a lot of it before, anyway—but something about him, personally."

"There *is* something of the swami or guru about him. Still, he seems to get results."

Her own vague discomfort at having yielded too easily to the doctor's persuasions came back to her. Was there some reason, other than Deborah's health and ease of mind, that he had been so insistent on her staying in the Lamont house? Or was it her suspicious imagination? She said now to Paul, "You know, according to him, Deborah isn't responding to treatment the way he thinks she should. She's still vacilating between extreme lethargy, or depression, and manic periods. Apparently she does have rational periods also, when she frets about Marie and Ranger, which was why he was trying to get me to come out again."

"And you feel there's something strange about his concern?"

"I wondered."

Paul stubbed out his cigarette. "Well, give him the benefit of the doubt. Maybe it was conscientiousness. As for Deborah—she's been on drugs a long time. You don't bounce back from that in a hurry."

"What do you know about McGrath?"

"Not a great deal. He has a good reputation locally. As I said, he gets results. And he's been good with Deborah. It's true there are those in this area who, if the need arose, would take their husbands or wives or whoever into the city to one of the big psychiatric institutions, or to the Payne Whitney branch out here in Westchester. . . . But that's probably because McGrath's place is new. You know how people are, particularly in a conservative area like this."

"But . . ." Kate stopped, trying to remember something.

121

Paul looked at her. "But what?"

"He said—or at least implied—it had been here several years."

"You must have misunderstood. It opened up about eleven months ago—something like that." He grinned. "Maybe you were so dazzled by his charm you didn't hear right."

"Maybe." It was true that she didn't remember exactly what McGrath had said.

"There was something else, though. I was asking him about the place—what's it called? High Falls? No—White Falls Clinic—and said something casually about his specializing in drugs. We were walking towards the door at that point, but he stopped cold and snapped out 'what do you mean?' I was taken aback. When I told him I meant Deborah and others like her, he figuratively backed off and after a little speech about helping people get on the right track, left hurriedly."

"What's funny about that? With doctors being hauled into court by every patient who ever abused a legitimate prescription, you can hardly blame him for jumping. It's open season on your friendly neighborhood physician right now. And every time an ex-patient opens his mouth or writes an article, malpractice insurance soars up."

"So you don't have any doubts about him?"

"For heaven's sake, Kate, if I did I wouldn't have permitted Deb to stay there. She made her suicide attempt while I was away, and Marie sent for the police, who took her to White Falls when they learned McGrath was her doctor. But when I got here, if I'd had any major reservations, I'd have taken her out."

Kate absorbed this. She was still not satisfied. But there was truth and common sense in what Paul said, and she decided she was just being overly fussy to worry any further.

After a minute she said, "You didn't answer my question about Miss Griffin."

He lit a second cigarette. "I thought I did—when we were discussing Deb's deterioration. When Deb was depressed, there were days, sometimes weeks, when she never seemed to get out of her nightgown. Not exactly what a man looks forward to coming home to. So—Angela, and before Angela somebody else. Actually, Marie is out of date with her information. Angela and I are pretty much finished."

"So you don't love her."

"What's love?"

"You tell me, Paul."

"Love was what I felt for you. Only you ran away to New York, so I married Deborah. Then Deborah started to fall apart. Neither your life nor mine has worked out too well—at least from the emotional standpoint. Maybe the old idea was right; an arranged, unromantic marriage had the best chance of success. No one expected too much."

They were sitting in armchairs facing the fireplace, which Paul had lit. Suddenly he threw his cigarette in the fire and put his arm out. Without her volition, without even thinking about it, Kate put out hers and clasped his hand.

"So it's still there a little."

Somewhat out of breath and thoroughly confused, Kate detached her hand.

"And you still pull back when anybody gets too close, don't you?"

Kate got up. "Somehow the burden of the breakup of whatever it was we had seems to be my fault; I ran away to New York, I pulled back whenever anybody—meaning you, I guess —got too close. There are more ways than one, dear Paul, in which you haven't changed; you still have the power to muddle something I thought I had straight. And I'll have you know," she finished somewhat belligerently, "I have not *always* pulled away. There are those to whom, or with whom, I have, as you delicately put it, been close. I resent this picture of myself as the frozen maiden that you and Joel seem to draw every chance you get."

"Who's Joel? One of the lucky ones with whom you have— er—not been the frozen maid?"

123

"That's not the point," Kate said, wishing now she hadn't brought up anyone's name. Also, this conversation was bringing back to her mind the curious dialogue with the Deity that she had when she came down the church steps. Strangely, at that moment, she felt suddenly as though something different —different from the desert of the past five years—were going to happen in her life.

Paul stood up. "All right. I won't tease you anymore. Just let me say that I, too, as well as the good doctor, am glad you're here. Not only for the children's sake, or even my own, but Deborah's."

Chapter 6

Kate woke up suddenly. Lying there in the dark, she knew something had wakened her, but she didn't know what. She had been dreaming, and the dream, which she could not remember, must have been frightening. Her heart was hammering and, against all logic, she had an overwhelming sense of being in great danger.

Then, slowly, the dream started to come back; she had dreamed she was lying on something like a stretcher, strapped down, unable to move her legs or arms, and also unable to talk. Something was wrapped around her mouth. Two figures were carrying the stretcher. She was trying desperately to free herself so she could tell them they were making a fearful mistake. But she could not budge her hands to untie the bandage around her mouth. As she struggled the realization came to her that these figures, whoever they were, believed her to be dead and were taking her to be buried. She was overwhelmed with urgency. If she could not get their attention before they took her to the tomb, they would bury her alive. But, in this horribly vivid dream, she continued to be unable to move or to make a sound. Then she saw the door to the tomb. Frantic, she struggled harder, making all the noise that the tight band around her mouth would allow. But she knew that whatever sound came from her throat did not reach the ears of the carriers. Then they were in the tomb, a square, gray room like a vault, empty, except for a coffin on the floor. The two men put her, still tied to the stretcher, into the coffin. As they bent, she tried to see their faces. But a mist covered them from the shoulders up, so she could not recognize them. They started to leave. She thought her chest would break in her effort to scream. Then one of the carriers made a noise, the sound of something scraping nearby. That was when she woke up. Was it the noise that had wakened her?

She sat up in bed and fumbled to find the light on her night table. Finally her finger connected with the switch. The light went on and she stared around the room. It was the last of two rooms in an extension built onto the back of the house and had three exposures. Outside the windows it was black, punctuated by the shape of trees and branches and by the diamond points of stars. Two windows were open, and a fresh breeze blew the curtains. It was a chilly, impersonal room with hard blue walls and plain furniture chosen *en bloc* from a department store show room: bureau, two night tables, a small desk and chair and an armchair in an equally hard, though deeper, blue. There was a print of Notre Dame in Paris on one wall and a tired-looking sampler on the other. What did the sampler say? Appropriately enough, "A stitch in time saves nine." It seemed an odd room for Deborah to have furnished, Kate thought. She had grown up with exquisite furniture, crystal and china, much of it inherited through several generations of Légères. Some of the furniture downstairs had come from the house on Prytania Street. But this room—Kate looked around and found herself thinking that Deborah could have chosen more imaginatively from a thrift shop.

What time was it? Kate glanced at the night table where she had put the electric alarm clock she had brought from her apartment. It was 4:00 A.M., the low point of the twenty-four hours when—a phrase slid through her mind—people died and others were born. Suddenly she shivered and got up to close one of the windows, padding across the room barefoot. But as she raised her arms to pull the window down she paused. What little moon there was was small, dim and high up, yielding meager light. But the stars were bright. Underneath one of the trees was a shadow. It could, Kate told herself, easily be something quite ordinary. Like what? Well, there was the remains of an old swing back there. There was also a post with a basketball basket on top, but that, she thought, was the other side. And the noise was much nearer to her than that.

Returning towards the bed, she turned off the light. Then she crept back to the window. Certainly the shadow was not a post because it moved, sliding rapidly across the small patch of dimly lit lawn. She looked down. Below her window was the roof of the porch that went around one side and the back of the house. Angry at herself for not having noticed that before, Kate shut the window and slid the lock on top across. Then she went to the other windows. No, the porch did not extend beneath them, and the only branches were thin and supple, sturdy enough, perhaps, to support a cat, but nothing heavier. Leaving one window open, Kate put on her robe and made her way to the nearest bathroom. Evidently the children had been put on notice not to use it, because, in contrast to the time she had been here before, it was immaculate. Returning to her bed, Kate took off her robe, got in and lay down. But it was near six before she got to sleep, and when she woke up, it was not to her silvery alarm, but to see Paul bending over her, shaking her shoulder.

"Don't you plan to go to work today?"

"Of course." She sat up. "What time is it?"

"It's eight o'clock."

"Good heavens! What happened to my alarm?" She put her hand out to the clock and discovered she had forgotten to press the lever down. "Damn! I forgot to turn it on." Then she remembered waking up during the night, and the shadow outside that moved. She sat up. "Paul, somebody was outside on the lawn last night. And I have an awful feeling that whoever it was—I know this sounds crazy—but he may have been in my room. A noise quite near woke me. And the porch roof is outside and the window was open."

"What? What are you saying?"

Pulling her robe around her, Kate told him. "Whoever it was made a noise waking me up. Then I saw him out the window."

"Are you missing anything?"

Kate looked around the room. "There's not a lot to miss, because I didn't bring much."

"Well, check your bag and your suitcase. If there's anything missing at all I'll call the police."

"Why don't you call the police anyway? It's not exactly soothing to think that people are getting into the house in the dead of night."

"Because if there's nothing missing, then I'll think twice about calling the cops. It's true there's been prowler around here off and on for the past couple of years. Nobody's ever caught him, and not a lot has been stolen—some pocket money here and there, a little costume jewelry, and a credit card or two."

"And you think that's okay?" Kate stood up and tied her robe around her.

"Of course I don't. But after the first reports, everybody got in on the act. It's the same as when the police circulate or broadcast a description of a wanted criminal or missing person. Thousands of callers suddenly claim to have seen him. After the first report of the prowler, everybody said he had seen him—including Deborah. But he was never found, and quite frankly, Deborah's fantasies were so frequent that I could never be sure whether she was in reality or out."

"Well I don't suffer from that kind of problem, thank you."

"I'm not saying you do. How about checking your bag, your

suitcase and any drawers you may have put your things into."

It didn't take long. Nothing was missing.

"Do you still want me to call the police?"

By this time Kate was beginning to feel foolish. But she disliked backing down completely. "In view of the fact that you're going to be away at this convention, how many other rooms have windows opening onto the porch roof?"

"Only Marie, and she does not share your mania for the night air. But I'll tell her to keep her porch window closed."

"All right. You can leave the local constabulary alone. Now please leave so I can get dressed."

Paul paused with his hand on the door. "If it were an hour later and the children in school, I might turn down that suggestion. Do you have to get to the office right away?"

"Yes," Kate said. She felt rattled. "What's the next train I could possibly catch?"

Paul grinned and then sighed. "*Quel dommage!*" He glanced at his watch. "If you're willing to go minus coffee or breakfast and think you can get ready in ten minutes, then I can run you to the station in time for the eight thirty."

"I'll be ready," Kate said.

The ends of her hair still curling wet from the shower, she was downstairs in nine.

"You'd better put these on," Paul said, handing her a pair of short rubber boots and a fire-engine red slicker. "It's pelting outside. You can stick your shoes in your tote bag. I'll call you next week on Tuesday."

On and off for the rest of the day, when she was not grinding to the end of Kramer's opus, Kate's mind returned to tease at the dream. It was a dream, she kept reminding herself, only a dream. The mind dealt in strange symbols. During the lunch hour she found herself groping through the library in the conference room to see if there were any work—legitimate and scientific, or crackpot and dismissable—on dreams. She found, in various books of psychology, more material than she bargained for. Yet none of it helped because none of it seemed to

129

apply to her or to her dream. Then there was that odd and disturbing shadow outside her window, which may, or may not, have moved. "I saw it move," she muttered to herself more than once.

On one occasion Judy came in. "Did you say something?"

"Not really."

Judy lingered at the door. "You're all right, aren't you?"

At that Kate emerged from her preoccupation. "Yes. Why—do I seem strange?"

"A little spacey."

"What does that mean?"

"Somewhere else." Judy grinned. "Like on another planet."

"Thanks a lot."

For some reason that made her think of Deborah, and when Judy left, she sat back, staring at the finished manuscript and thinking about Dr. McGrath's statement that Deborah was not responding to treatment. On an impulse, she pulled the telephone towards her and dialed the number of the hospital.

"Hello?" he said when she had been put through. "Miss Malory?"

"I called to see if Deborah's any better, if she's responding more to treatment."

"I'm afraid not—at least not yet. But when she's herself, rational, she feels much easier in her mind knowing you are there with the children."

"I take it you told her I was going back."

"Yes, of course. But she also hears this from Marie and Ranger."

"Do they visit her often?"

"One or the other comes almost every day."

"That's nice." She found she was a little surprised, pleasantly so.

"Yes. They're very good with her."

"Then you were right when you said she tried to be a good mother."

"You sound astonished."

130

"I suppose I am, which is obviously unjust. I owe Deborah an apology—and the children."

"Would you like to see Deborah yourself?"

She did want to see Deborah. But she decided, on the spur of the moment, and pushed by motives of which she was not entirely clear, not to announce her intention.

"No, not at the moment."

"As you wish." His voice was chilly, more the way it had been during their conversation when he first called her at the office. Plainly, she reflected, he didn't think her much of a sister. She started to justify herself, then stopped. She owed him no explanation. If anything, she found herself thinking, with the return of her sense of unease concerning him, the shoe was on the other foot.

It was that night, when Paul was away at the convention in Chicago, that the dream, identical in every detail, returned. Only this time she didn't know what wakened her. But once again, all of a sudden, she was awake, sitting up in bed, her heart hammering. Quickly she turned on the light. The window giving out onto the porch roof was closed. The other two windows were open and the room filled with cold air. She glanced at her clock, 3:45. She turned off the light, got out of bed and went to the closed window, looking out onto the tree where she had seen a shadow. It was very much the same kind of night as before: a high, thin moon and bright stars. She could see the same tree as she had looked out on before. But this time there was no extra shadow, no slighter darkness that moved. After a minute or two she went back to bed, started to get in, then, on impulse, decided to check on Marie's whereabouts. Marie had gone up to her room after dinner and had not reappeared. Kate assumed that she had gone to bed. I should have made sure, she thought now. Marie could have slipped out when she, Kate, was in her own bedroom and only now be coming back in. Or could be going out now. It wasn't impossible—just exasperating, she thought. Putting on her robe, she made her way to the main part of the house. By this time she knew which rooms belonged to Paul, Marie and Ranger, but the hall light was not on, and she waited for a few seconds to get accustomed to the gray murk. Finally she thought she could make out the doors. Paul's was open. With no hesitation, she went in, switching on the light. Then she went over and pulled down the shades.

It was a big room, almost dwarfing the wide, massive bed. Everything was in order: the bed made, with a striped beige and gray cover, the bureau with a photograph or two on top, a dressing table, looking curiously bare, a desk with papers under a paperweight, note paper, and envelopes stacked in a rack, a door that probably led to a closet, another door that probably led to a bathroom, dark green walls with anonymous-looking water colors spaced regularly around, and a plain wall to wall beige carpet. Kate thought of Marie's room. It was difficult to believe the two rooms existed within the same household. It was as though the occupants came from different cultures or even different planets.

The master bedroom was an oddly masculine room, Kate decided, standing there, as though Deborah's presence had had no impact on it whatsoever. How could the girl Kate remembered, nothing if not feminine, have lived in this almost male clubroom atmosphere? For the second time Kate felt a stirring of something approaching sympathy for her stepsister and she decided that she would go to see her that day. Was it reluctance that had kept her from going sooner? She had told herself that she didn't want to interfere with whatever treatment Deborah was getting. Nor did she want to upset her by activating old memories. . . . Or was it all rationalization? Was it that, even after all these years, and even though she had been called on to help, she still did not want to see the woman who, she believed, had stolen from her what she most desired? "You're an unforgiving witch, Kate," she admonished herself now, standing in the middle of Deborah's bedroom. She was about to go out when, on impulse, remembering

132

Deborah's long bondage to pills, she decided she should go and look in the bathroom medicine closet . . . to see what, if anything, she had left there, and whether she, Kate, should question Paul as to whether or not they should be there when Deborah came home.

Closing the door behind her, Kate went to the door she thought might be the bathroom and opened it. What faced her was one of the largest walk-in closets she had ever seen.

The huge closet looked like a model of efficient storage.

Clothes bars ran along each side, one side filled with Paul's suits, the other, with Deborah's dresses. Her shoes and his were propped on racks beneath. Above the bars, shelves with built-in drawers rose almost to the ceiling. In the ceiling itself was a rectangular panel, on one end of which was a handle. In the far corner of the closet, built with more shelves and drawers, was a pole with a hook on the end. Without forethought, Kate took the pole, raised it, fitted the hook over the handle and pulled. Down came an aluminum folded stair that unfolded as she took hold of the bottom steps and lowered it to the floor. A black rectangular hole yawned above her. She stared up at the hole and felt chilled air on her face. At that hour it was far from inviting. Until that moment Kate, who had lived in apartments throughout her adult life, did not realize how much she had retained of her childhood dislike of the dark. The dark of an apartment, nestled in a building with other thin walled apartments, where all sounds were immediately audible to neighbors, somehow had a different feel from the dark yawning at her from the unheated attic of a house in a suburb.

Castigating herself for being a pantywaist, Kate gathered up her robe and started to mount the stairs.

She could never afterwards be entirely sure what had stopped her three steps from the top. Because she had come to a stop, unable to go on, when she thought she heard a noise from somewhere downstairs, followed by the unmistakable sound of Bones's whimpering. Turning, she started down the ladder, caught her foot on the corner of her robe and almost fell, knocking her naked foot and cracking her shin. For a minute she sat on the second step, her injured foot caught up in her hand, waiting for the pain to go away. When she rose, she pushed the ladder up and, using the pole, folded the whole contraption back into the ceiling. Then, gimpy with pain, she left the closet, closing it and turning out the light, went over to the door of the room, turned off the lights and went out into the hall. It was only when she reached the hall and had crossed to the top of the stairs that she realized how much better she felt out here, as contrasted to the way she had felt in the bedroom and the bedroom closet. What did I feel there? she wondered. It was hard to define. Depressed? Anxious? She paused at the top of the stairs. Neither of those expressions quite defined it. She shook herself. Facts before fancy—that was one of her mother's numerous sampler-type maxims. The fact was she had heard a noise and was going down now to investigate. There was nothing either ghostly or psychic about that.

But there was nothing unusual downstairs. Turning on all lights, she inspected every corner and cranny and both the front and back doors. There wasn't the slightest evidence to make her think that anyone had been in the house. When she went into the kitchen, Bones, who had left his basket and retreated to his hideout far under the kitchen table, made the whimpering noise that she had heard from above.

"It's all right, Bones," she said. "There's nothing here to frighten you."

She spoke as much to herself as to the dog. Eventually he crawled forward, and Kate squatted down and scratched his head. "There's no reason to be frightened," she repeated, more loudly this time. But it was no use. Despite everything she tried to make herself and Bones believe, she could not overcome the conviction that someone had been here, in the kitchen, within the past hour.

It was not a feeling that made her comfortable. In fact, she felt decidedly uncomfortable. Finally she stood up and stared out the back window. With the light on inside, it was, naturally, as black as tar paper.

"Come on, Bones. I'm taking you upstairs."

Common sense told her it was a rash decision. As a nod to fact over fancy, she scooped up several sections of yesterday's newspaper. Then, with Bones jumping around her, she started to go up the back steps. Bones, still at the bottom, whimpered. His ears, even more of a thermometer than his tail, drooped.

"I told you. Come on!" she whispered.

He could hardly believe it. With one paw on the bottom step, he paused again. She bent over, patted him on the head and said quietly, "There's nothing to make you afraid," and hoped that Bones would not detect her feeling, on some bottom layer, that she was not telling the truth.

When they got to the top of the back steps, Kate hesitated, suddenly smitten with an uncertainty as to whether or not she had turned out the lights in Paul's and Deborah's bedroom. She decided to make sure. With Bones beside her she headed for the center hall, switched on the hall light and went over to Paul's door. She had half opened the door, just enough to see that it was indeed dark inside, when the most desolate whimpering broke from Bones and he seemed to be trying to crawl downstairs.

"Bones!" Kate closed the bedroom door hurriedly and went after the dog, putting her hand on his collar just as he was about to head down the back steps.

"You're coming to my room with me," she said, a little surprised at how firm she felt about it. But she was not going to force him. Loosing his collar, she turned and without entering the center hall went back to the extension and turned down the narrow hall that ran along one side of it. As she was about to enter her bedroom she heard paws on the parquet and saw Bones hurrying along after her. "That's a good

135

boy!" she said, ridiculously relieved that he was there with her. First she put the newspaper sheets down on the carpet, so that the whole area under the bed and most of the rest of the carpet were covered. Then she took off her robe, turned out the light and got into bed, wondering whether Bones would choose the little arm chair or the straight chair on which she had placed the second pillow for his bed. He chose neither. She had no more than pulled the covers up to her chin when there was a huge plop beside her. Bones had chosen his sleeping place.

"Good Bones!" she said, extracting an arm from under the cover and patting him. He licked her face. She got out her other arm again and gave him a hug. His tail thumped wildly against her sore shin. But she bore the pain without a murmur. "Sweet are the uses of adversity," she muttered, wondering where the line came from. And then, "in a pig's eye."

With Bones at her back, Kate lay and watched the dark outside become first charcoal gray, than gray, than pearly gray with pink streaks. She found that with the warm, living presence of Bones, now beginning to snore gently, and with his doggy smell in her nostrils, she could bear to think about the unthinkables: the repetitive dream of being buried alive with all of its suffocating reality and sense of hopeless desolation and the fact that Bones seemed to go into panic in front of the bedroom door. Perhaps he had been mistreated there after suffering one of his mishaps. Without thinking, she patted his silky side. Then before he could wake up, she put her hand back under the covers. Glancing at the clock she saw it was a quarter to five. If she went to sleep right now, she'd have three hours before she had to get up and order a taxi to take her to catch the 8:30 train. Firmly she closed her eyes, her nerves relaxing as the sights, sounds and smell of morning pushed back the fears of the night. Nevertheless, the next to last thing she remembered before she went to sleep was the yawning black rectangle of the attic. The last thing was her realization that she had been on the way to check on Marie's room when she opened the door to the master bedroom. Why was she going there? She fell asleep before she could come up with the answer.

She didn't think about the matter until she was on the train the next morning. From the time her alarm went off and throughout her headlong breakfast rush to catch the train, she hadn't had time to think of anything except getting to the station. Since she didn't stop in the kitchen for as much as a cup of coffee, she had to assume that both Marie and Ranger had got off to school. Marie: she had been on her way to check on Marie's room when she went into Paul's and Deborah's bedroom. But, diverted by the master bedroom and its closet with the trap door, she had forgotten to check on Marie and her whereabouts. Now, again, she wondered. Having overslept herself, she still didn't know for sure whether or not Marie had spent the full night in her own bed (or on her own mat!).

More questions pushed themselves at her. Why did she keep having this strange dream? Why should she have that unsettling but powerful feeling that somebody had been in the kitchen? She didn't know any of the answers. Furthermore, she didn't know why, immediately after the train pulled in, she found herself in a phone booth in Grand Central Terminal looking up the telephone number of the Hilton Hotel.

As she heard the phone ringing at the other end, she realized she had no idea what convention Kramer was attending because he had not told her one word about his professional calling. Was it in his questionnaire? She had checked on that document when she had inherited Kramer from the editor who had left, but could remember nothing that would give her a hint of what he did with his time when he wasn't writing about reincarnation and related subjects.

"Mr. Jed Kramer," she said, when the hotel operator finally answered.

137

"We have no such person registered," the operator said after a moment.

Damn! Kate thought. The convention's over and he's gone home. "I suppose the convention's come to an end?" she said to the operator.

"Which convention? We've had three meetings here in the past two weeks."

"What groups were they?"

"Let's see." The operator was polite and helpful. There was the sound of rustling paper. "Doctors, plumbers and undertakers."

Surely, Kate thought, not an undertaker. She rejected out of hand the idea that Kramer was a doctor and settled, reluctantly, on plumber. "Could you check and see if a Mr. Kramer was registered there as recently as . . ." she hastily figured backwards, "last Tuesday?"

After another moment's silence, during which time Kate was envisioning Kramer in a boiler suit with a plumber's snake in his hand and a monkey wrench in his pocket, the operator said, "We have a Mrs. William Kramer. Would that be the person?"

"No. Thanks."

"And anyway, Kate said to herself as she sped across the immense station towards Fifth Avenue, what would I have said to him if I had got him? She still didn't know why she had called him.

Ten minutes later she was walking past Judy's desk.

"Your leading author called," Judy said. "He's eager for you to return his call."

Kate wheeled. "Kramer?"

"No other. Himself in person."

Kate flew over to her desk and found the message propped against her phone. She recognized the number immediately. It was the one she had called from the station. Beside the hotel number was an extension number, which she gave the operator.

"I want you to know," she said, before he could say any more than "hello," "that I called you from the station and they not only did not have a Jed Kramer listed, they said you had not been listed for the past two weeks."

"That's because Kramer's my pen name," Mr. Kramer said, as cheerful as ever. "Can I come over to see you?"

"All right. But I think I ought to know all your aliases."

"Certainly. I'll be right over."

He was there in a surprisingly short time. "You see," he said, as he walked in, "My name's not Kramer. It's Marker. Kramer is an anagram of Marker. I'm afraid if my patients knew about the kind of books I wrote, they'd all leave. Or at least most of them would."

Kate stared at him. "I had decided you were a plumber. The operator said there were three conventions there—undertakers, doctors and plumbers. I was sure you couldn't be either a doctor or an undertaker."

"Nobody ever thinks I'm a doctor." He seemed totally unfazed by this. "May I sit down."

Kate waved him to a chair. "Sorry. Of course. What kind of a doctor?"

"Family. Used to be called a general practitioner."

Kate looked into his monkeylike face, and, just as she had seen the impatience and intolerance in Paul, she saw now the kindness in his. It lay not only in his brown eyes, but in all of his simian features.

"No, I know I don't look like Dr. Welby."

Once again she felt her cheeks get hot. "I had forgotten that knack of yours. It must help you in your diagnostic work."

"It does—to a point. But no more, really, than any experienced physician. Most people lie when they tell you about themselves—not meaning to, you understand. But because they're afraid it's worse than you are telling them, or they want it to be worse than they think it might be, or because they think I will be angry if it's not terminal, or because they're lonely and want attention."

139

"Who on earth would want something to be worse?"

"People who are both hypochondriacs and timid. They need desperately to be sure that the slightly infected cut on their finger is not going to lead to blood poisoning and death within the next few hours. On the other hand, they have experienced constantly—because of their hypochondria—the impatience and rebuff of doctors who find them time consuming and let them know it."

Kate thought about that. "I suppose so. Why did you call me?"

"Because I had a couple of strong feelings about you. One was that you were trying to get in touch with me. And I knew that you wouldn't be able to because you had no way of knowing my real name. Why were you, by the way?"

Her mind was a blank—a situation not at all characteristic of herself. "I'm not sure. I just got off the train and headed for a phone. It does sound crazy." She paused. "I supposed because weird things seem to be happening. And you seem to know about them." She hesitated again. "You said you had two strong feelings that made you call. What was the other one?"

"The other was . . ." His voice trailed off as he looked at her. "The best way I can put this is that I want you to be careful."

That jarred her. "Why do you say that?" Hearing the sharpness in her tone, she said, "I didn't mean it to sound like that. But it was . . . well, a shock."

He said simply. "I have the feeling that you're entering an area of danger." There was silence for a minute. "Are you?"

"I don't know. I've had—I've twice had—a really horrible dream." She told him about it. And then found herself saying, "Each time I've been wakened by something. The first time, when I looked out the window, I thought I saw someone. And that window looks over the roof of a porch. I'm not at my apartment in the city. I'm staying at my sister- and brother-in-law's in a Westchester suburb. Anyway, the second

140

time also I was awakened abruptly, although I don't know why. I went out to the main front hall to look and then found myself in my brother-in-law's bedroom. . . ." She glanced at Kramer, "He's in Chicago and my sister's in the hospital, which is why I'm there. . . ."

Her voice trailed off for a minute. "I was about to say that I went into what looked like a walk-in closet that opens off my sister- and brother-in-law's bedroom and found there a trapdoor leading to the attic. I pulled it open with a pole. Some aluminum steps came down and I started to go up. . . ." She paused. "It's hard to figure out what happened next—at least not *what* happened but in what order. I know that when I was about three steps from the top of the stepladder I stopped cold. It was as though a wall were in front of me. But I hadn't really had time to absorb that before there was another noise downstairs. I almost fell down the ladder making a loud racket myself, so if there was somebody there, I could have given him all the notice in the world. When I got downstairs I found Bones, Ranger's dog, terrified as usual. So there was nothing strange about that. He's a neurotic half-grown puppy that my nephew, Ranger, has adopted and claims was once abused. Anyway, there was nobody there—then. But I couldn't get rid of the feeling that somebody had been there recently. I took Bones up to bed with me."

She glanced at her author, a bewildered look on her face. "It's incredible for me to be telling you all this when I hardly know you and you can't possibly know all the circumstances and I don't know why I am." She smiled. "And it's hard for me to switch from Kramer, the author of books on reincarnation, dreams, psychics, etc., to Dr. Marker, family physician."

"Why not call me Jed? It would settle the issue. That's not my name either. But it comes from my initials, Jonathan Edwards David." He smiled back at her. "Yes, my parents were deeply religious."

"What do your friends in California call you? Not the reincarnation ones, the other ones."

141

"They all call me Jed, because of the initials. I sometimes wondered if my colleagues in the medical world—knowing my nickname to be Jed—would fall upon the fact that I was Jed Kramer, the writer on reincarnation and related subjects. But I needn't have worried—not that I did, I wasn't and am not ashamed of my beliefs. But I had overestimated doctors' reading habits. It's not their fault. By the time they've taken care of their office patients, visited their other patients in the hospital and kept up with the various journals they have to read, they barely have time to talk to their families."

"You manage. Not only to read—you've obviously read a lot about your subject—but to write books on it."

"True. But I had an overwhelming drive to do so."

"How did you manage? After all, you have patients in your office and in the hospital and journals to read?"

"I set my alarm each morning for one hour earlier than I would normally get up."

"Just that? Four books' worth?"

"It's amazing how much you can get done in an hour. And now I'm a widower I have even more time. It's different with most other doctors."

Kate smiled. "You take a determinedly rosey view of people, don't you?"

"Yes. Though I'm not unrealistic. It makes me happier to take what you call a rosey view, and if happier I do better service for people. Also, most people are inclined to be the way you treat them. Concerning your dream, it means that I was right to tell you to be careful." He paused. "Why are you in your sister- and brother-in-law's house?"

Kate sighed. "I'd better start from the beginning." She did, telling him everything including Dr. McGrath's recent call and visit to her apartment.

"And you never did check on whether your niece was in or out of the house?"

"No. By the time I finally got back upstairs I had forgotten about it and didn't think of it until I was on the train this morning."

"I see. And this psychiatrist seems to think that your sister, Deborah, is not responding to treatment?"

"Yes."

"Have you seen her?"

"No. I'm . . . I'm ashamed to say I haven't. I've always resented her, feeling she got the best of everything, including . . . including the man I wanted. It's funny," Kate went on in a musing voice. "From something that her daughter, Marie, said, and also from something Paul said, they seem to think it's the other way around—that Deborah only got him because I was the one to leave." And how astonishing that I am telling this slightly comic stranger things I've never talked about to anyone else, Kate marveled to herself.

"We sometimes see things as we need to, rather than as they are, or would appear to be. And that applies to other people, too."

"You mean I need to feel jilted?"

He smiled. "Not so much need to. Perhaps it's a deeply ingrained mental habit. You've always seen yourself that way."

Kate made a wry face. "I suppose so."

"Tell me about your parents."

And somewhat to Kate's surprise, she did, remembering things she thought she'd forgotten.

"Umm," Jed said. He had, Kate thought, a quality of totally unsentimental kindness. "Which brings me to the present," she said finally. "In answer to your question of a while ago, I have not seen Deborah for eighteen years. I was halfway planning to go this afternoon."

"You wouldn't have anything of your sister's here, would you? Some article?"

"No—Yes I do." Kate got up, opened a closet door in her office and pulled out the boots and red slicker that Paul had made her wear. "My brother-in-law insisted I wear these the

143

other morning." She handed them to him. "Are you going to go into a trance?"

"Oh no, nothing like that. But sometimes I can get a clearer picture of a person if I can hold something that belongs to him."

Half-amused, half-interested, Kate watched as he turned one of the boots around and around in his square hands. His round eyes seemed to stare out the window. Kate found in herself a queer fondness for him, quite different from anything she'd ever before felt for a man. He might be absurd, but he was trying, in his way, to be helpful, and he was doing it, she noted to herself, with a small stab of gratitude, without subjecting her to some kind of psychological or verbal barrage.

"Your sister is, I think, in danger."

"What do you mean?"

"I'm not sure. But I also think you should see her as soon as you can."

"All right. I said I was planning to go this afternoon. What else does your crystal ball say?" And why, she wondered, am I being so surly all of a sudden? "I'm sorry. I don't know why I said that. I mean it's a difficult and awkward time. But there's still no reason for me to bite people's heads off—particularly when they're as helpful as you."

He rose. "Let me tell you something about prevision, or crystal balls, as you put it. No—I know you didn't mean to offend me, and you didn't. You're going through a lot more now than you realize. But when people tell you something's going to happen, they should be truthful and tell you it's almost impossible to say whether something is going to take place or has already taken place. That's because in that area time as we know it, the chronological unfolding ribbon, doesn't exist. The past and the present are the same. Goodbye now, let me know what happens and how you're getting on. I'll be in the hotel a few more days. Here is my direct number. I wrote it down for you." And having put the paper down on

144

her desk, he was gone. Once more he put her in mind of Alice's white rabbit.

"Did you tell him you'd finished his opus?" Judy said from the door. Kate had given her the last eleven pages with all the corrections to send to the typist.

"No, I forgot."

"You *forgot?*"

"I wish you wouldn't say it in that tone of voice."

"What on earth did you talk about?"

"Precognition."

"I see." There was a funny look on Judy's face when she left.

Kate walked out of the station and got into one of the waiting taxis. "White Falls Clinic," she said.

The hospital turned out to be a new stucco building behind high walls some miles away from the village. It was, as Dr. McGrath had said, not large, but the grounds looked well kept and there were numerous benches and walks that gave it a friendly atmosphere. Kate walked up front steps through a glass door and found herself facing an information and reception desk.

"I'd like to see Mrs. Paul Lamont," she said.

"Do you have an appointment? I mean . . ." the rather severe looking receptionist smiled a little, "is she expecting you?"

"No."

"May I have your name?"

"Kate Malory. I'm her sister."

"I see. Just a minute please. Please take a seat over there and I'll let you know if you can go up."

With a strong feeling that she was being dismissed, Kate sat down on one of the sofas in what was plainly a waiting area. Wanting not to appear anxious, she picked up a magazine.

"You can go up now," the receptionist said, after talking into a telephone. "The elevator is over there. Fifth floor."

145

There was another receptionist on the fifth floor. "Mrs. Lamont is in her room," she said, beaming. "Just down there, the third to the right."

The door was closed when Kate got there. She found herself standing outside, staring at the visiting card stuck in the slot to the side of the door: "Mrs. Paul Lamont," written in the finest italic script. Without even thinking Kate ran her finger over the lettering. As she suspected, it was properly engraved. What else would Deborah's card be? she thought, and knew that she was standing there, postponing the moment when she would put up her hand and knock. For a second she found herself thinking, incongruously, about the black, rectangular hole in the ceiling of Deborah's closet leading to the attic. Then she put up her hand and knocked on the door.

"Come in, Kate."

So they had told Deborah who had come to see her. Which was natural and proper, she pointed out to herself, reaching for the door handle. Unless there was a peephole. With her hand on the knob, Kate looked at the smooth white painted surface of the door. No peephole. Did the patients have closed circuit television or something of that kind? Why should she be beset with these cloak and dagger thoughts, she wondered, pushing the door open? She froze in shock on the threshold.

Only the large blue eyes were the same. The heavy woman sitting in a food-spotted robe in front of her seemed to bear no echo of the Deborah Légère Kate remembered. Hair, showing two inches of gray brown and the rest streaked blond, fell to her collar. But she's younger than I am, Kate found herself thinking indignantly.

"You needn't look like that," Deborah said. "I know I'm not what I used to be. I've been ill." Her voice had a slight drag to it. "Mama was completely gray by the time she was forty," Deborah went on. "Only she kept it frosted so nobody knew. Lulu told me."

And we're back where we started, Kate thought. Two adolescents spitting at each other. "Lulu?" she said. Lulu was Diane's personal maid, a strong, gentle-eyed black woman and the only person in the Légère household that Kate had ever liked or trusted. Funny, she thought, that Deborah should mention her now, and she looked quickly at Deborah, catching an expression she's forgotten, an odd, sly look, a secret satisfaction that she had gotten away with a lie.

"Lulu would never have done that," Kate said now, coming in and closing the door.

"Maybe it was Lianne." Lianne was the French girl that Diane had brought back once from a visit to France to take Lulu's place.

"Yes," Kate said, coming into the room. "That sounds more like it. It's the kind of thing Lianne would have loved to tell you, especially if you bribed her."

Deborah's laugh was the same. Whenever Kate read the cliché phrase, "a musical laugh," she thought of Deborah. Except for Deborah she would have dubbed it a meaningless metaphor. But Deborah's laugh had a natural, melodic quality.

"You still have a laugh like a music box, Deborah."

"It was the only thing you ever liked about me. Why don't you sit down?"

Kate sat in the room's only other chair. It was a pleasant room with pale blue walls, watercolors and blue and yellow print curtains. There was a single bed that looked more like a daybed than the usual hospital variety, book shelves, a bureau and a blue and beige carpet. A half-open door revealed a bathroom. Visible were a washbasin, a medicine cabinet, what looked like the front of a metal clothes hamper fixed into the wall, and on the shelf above that a room spray, talcum and something else that Kate couldn't quite make out.

"Not bad for a looney bin, is it?" Deborah said.

"No, it isn't." She was beginning to see what Judy had meant by the word, "spacey." In one sense Deborah seemed sharp. They were already talking as though there had not been gap of years. There had always been a slight snipe-and-run quality about their conversations, the scatter shot of near siblings, which was somehow worse than true siblings, mutually suspicious, hostile and competitive, brought together by the whim of widowed parents who had decided for their own reasons to merge the households. Yet there was another quality about Deborah that Kate found disturbing. It was as though most of her were in another world. Kate decided to force the conversation back to the here and now. "How are you, Deborah? How do you feel? When do you think you'll be able to go home?"

"Home," Deborah said. Her expression changed. Without quite knowing how she knew, Kate realized that Deborah was, for the moment, in her right mind and rational.

"Marie and Ranger send their love," Kate said, making it up, but feeling that it was appropriate and probably true. "They're fine."

"Kate . . . I really tried to be a good mother. But. . . ." The large blue eyes filled with tears.

"I know," Kate said, filled with a wrenching pity.

"After I was ill . . . that's when I tried. But . . ."

"When were you ill?"

Deborah rubbed her head. "A year . . . two years ago."

And do you mean mentally or physically ill, Kate wanted to ask, but didn't.

Deborah lapsed into silence, shifting heavily in her chair. She seemed restless, Kate thought. Then Deborah got up. "Excuse me," she said, and went into the bathroom, closing the door.

Kate stared around the room. For a room that had been continuously occupied by the same person for nearly two months, Kate thought, it had remained strangely impersonal. There were no pictures, papers, books or magazines.

There was the sound of flushing and then of faucets being turned on and off. Deborah came out of the bathroom. Her mouth and chin were wet, as though she had been drinking water. Kate had a glimpse of the basin and metal clothes hamper before Deborah closed the door.

148

"Umm, thirsty," she said, and wiped her face with her hand. Then she sat down. For a minute they sat in silence. Still relatively numb with shock and pity at what Deborah Légère Lamont had become, Kate wracked her brain for something they could talk about for a few more minutes. Everything seemed unwise—Paul, the true state of the children, the state of the house, even Bones. Furtively Kate glanced at her watch and saw that only about eighteen minutes had passed. Five more, she thought, and I can go. She glanced at Deborah who was staring at the twilit sky outside the windows.

Why is it, Kate thought, that I am becoming more uncomfortable than when I came in? It was almost, she reflected idly, as though something else had entered the room. Then she nearly jumped because she found herself thinking about Jed. For a moment he seemed as clear as Deborah herself. Have I let his crazy theories got to me, she thought? And then, well, I did call him. . . .

Suddenly Deborah spoke. "Did Paul send you to find out about me?"

Kate was startled. "No, of course not. What do you mean, find out about you?"

"He doesn't want me to come home. He wants me to die."

"Deborah, you don't mean that! That's a terrible thing to say."

"You're still in love with him!"

"No. No, I'm not. And anyway, he has some . . . no, I'm not."

"Oh, I know about his girl friend, Angela. That's not serious. He wasn't serious about any of them—except you."

Deep within herself, Kate felt that bittersweet tug. But it was, she knew, more the memory of the hold Paul had once had on her rather than present fact. It was the injured child within her responding. But, she realized with an odd sense of revelation, that child was now grown up, healed. She said a little dryly, "You mean there've been others? Other girl friends besides Angela?"

149

"Of course. Paul hasn't changed. He always liked to have two or three going at once. But the only person he really wanted permanently was you."

This time the words had no effect at all. She simply knew them to be untrue. "Deborah—that's simply not the case."

"Yes it is. You're trying to pretend. I know what's happened. The two of you are in it together. You're going to kill me. Paul will get my money. Then you two will marry. And you'll kill my children so they won't get the money. I know about you. You don't think I do. But I've known for a long time. You and Paul have been very quiet about it. All these girl friends are just cover for you so that when I'm dead nobody will suspect you. But I know . . ."

"Deborah!" What was happening was incredible, impossible to believe. Kate found she was shouting. She struck the arm of her chair. "What's happened? You weren't like this when I came in!"

A look of terror came over Deborah's face. "I think I'm losing my mind," she whispered. "Kate, help me!"

A sense of shock went through Kate. For a moment she felt as though through folds of concealing curtains she had glimpsed a reality, and her flesh moved with horror and pity.

"Deborah . . ." she whispered.

Then Deborah's expression was gone so fast Kate couldn't be sure that she had seen it or what it meant. Deborah's hand went out. She groped under the pillow of her bed near her chair. Belatedly, Kate realized that Deborah had rung a bell pinned to her bed.

When a nurse came in, Deborah cried, "Take this woman away from me. She's threatened me. I'm frightened. I don't ever want to see her again. Take her away . . ." Deborah's voice was slowly rising in a steady crescendo.

"Come along, miss." Kate felt a hand under her elbow. Willy-nilly she rose to her feet, then snatched her arm away. "I don't have to be led out," she said. "I am perfectly capable of leaving under my own steam." She turned towards Deborah. "I just wanted to say . . ."

The noise when it came was frightful. Somewhere between a shout and a howl, it poured from Deborah's throat. Her mouth was open round, like a funnel. The sound was coming out in a steady scream. Kate found herself being marched to the door. The moment she and the nurse were on the other side of the door the noise ceased.

"You should never have upset her, Miss Malory," the nurse said accusingly. "You are her sister so we didn't think she'd be excited like that."

"I didn't say anything to upset her. I . . ."

The noise had started again.

"Come along," the nurse said. Her fingers again gripped Kate's elbow.

"Damn you! Take your hands off me! I'm going!"

Kate felt the nurse watching her as she marched back down the hall and pushed the elevator button. The receptionist behind the desk looked at her with what Kate felt was reproach. She pushed the elevator button again, and then, when there was no sound of one approaching, twice more. Finally it arrived, and the doors opened. Kate got in, more relieved than she would have believed possible.

When the elevator got to the bottom Kate went over to the receptionist behind the main information desk. "Where could I find Dr. McGrath?"

"He might be in his office. On the other hand, he often goes to check on his patients at this house. Do you want me to page him?"

Kate thought for a minute. 'Yes. I'd like to talk to him."

"You can sit over there while I find out where he is," the receptionist said, dialing her desk phone.

"It's all right. I can stand here. I don't mind. I spend an awful lot of the day sitting."

"As you wish," the young woman said, managing to convey extreme displeasure.

Kate stood there, ostensibly turning the pages of the afternoon paper she'd brought from the city. The operator murmured into the receiver. Then she lowered the instrument and said, "Your name, please."

"Kate Malory."

"Would that be Miss, Mrs. or Ms?"

"Mr."

"Miz Malory," the young lady said soothingly into the phone. But her eyes above the receiver were full of reproach. "Dr. McGrath will be here in a minute," she said sadly. "Please sit down in the waiting area."

But at that moment the other elevator opened and Dr. McGrath appeared. "Miss Malory," he said stiffly. "Please come to my office."

The size and grandeur of the office somehow surprised her. One long wall was covered with bookshelves, another with files. She noticed, on the desk, the back of a picture frame and found herself wondering if it held his wife's picture. Did he ever mention a wife? A child? No, only Azucena, the family cat.

"I've just been to see Deborah," Kate said.

"So I gather."

"Since you seem to have heard that I was up there, I would like to tell you that I did nothing, absolutely nothing, to get Deborah upset. She did it to herself." Kate put her hands to her face. "I can't believe what's happened to her. I can't believe what occurred up there just now."

"You don't have to explain it to me. I've seen her do the same."

"What I want to know is, is it for real? She seemed at first abstracted. Then normal—sad, but perfectly rational. Then out of the blue she went crazy. Except for one really horrifying moment when she seemed to see what was happening to her and pleaded for my help, she was completely out of her mind. She took off about Paul and me, saying she thought Paul was trying to kill her so he could marry me. She brushed aside his girl friend—and other assorted girl friends of the past—as of no significance. Then she came back to Paul and me and the fact that I was the only person he ever loved. Doctor, it was weird. Even granted that my own memories are distorted, hers bear no relation to what could be remotely called reality. And yet I had the queerest feeling that underneath all of that insane rambling, she knew exactly what she was doing."

"Yes. Sit down." He went to another chair and sat. Suddenly he looked tired and drained, a lot of the vitality and power she had remembered in him seemed to have vanished. "I've had the same feeling, too." He reached out and picked a pencil off the desk, turning it over and over in his hands. "Beyond a certain point, we can't know what's truth and what's not—whatever truth is. There are times when she seems in a complete fog, times when she seems like a child playing games. There are times she seems rational. I don't know what to think. Once you know what kind of disturbances they have, most people fit into some kind of pattern. That sounds in the worst tradition of bureaucratic thinking. But within certain parameters people—even disturbed people—are predictable. But Deborah isn't. That's why I say she's not responding. That's why I wanted you to see her." He glanced up from the pencil. "Is she very different from what you remember?"

"If I hadn't known it was she, I don't think I would have recognized her. She must be terribly ill."

He sighed and got up. "Yes I'm going home now. Can I give you a lift?"

Kate gave herself a mental shake. The spell from upstairs was hard to break. "Yes, thanks. I had to get a taxi here."

"I'll be with you in a minute."

The doctor walked over to a door behind the desk, opened it, and shut it behind him. Unable to stop herself, Kate got up and went over to the desk and turned the photograph around. It showed an attractive, intelligent looking woman in her thirties with a boy of about twelve, who looked very much like Dr. McGrath. Kate was still holding it, staring at it, when

153

the doctor came out. Feeling as guilty as a child caught stealing a cookie or, worse, a teenager sighing over her latest crush, Kate put the photograph down. "She's attractive," she said, feeling foolish.

"Yes." He didn't look up. "We're divorced. I keep the picture there because of David. It's the best one I have of him. This way." He had taken off his white coat and had on a tweed jacket. Kate walked out of the room ahead of him. As they passed the reception desk he said to the woman there. "I'm going home now and will be there if I'm wanted."

"Yes, Dr. McGrath," the receptionist intoned. Her eyes went to Kate before they returned to her typewriter.

His handsome foreign car was parked to the right of the driveway. Punctiliously, he held open the passenger door and then went over to his side. All this time they hadn't spoken, but when the car nosed back into the main road Kate said, "I don't know why, but I was surprised to hear from both Paul and Deborah that Marie and Ranger visit her often. I think that's nice."

"Yes. Marie sees her every other day, and Ranger about twice a week. How are you getting on in the house?"

"All right. The kids are a degree or so less hostile than they were. I find, to my surprise, that I'm quite fond of them. But I must say, sleeping there leaves a lot to be desired."

"What do you mean?" His voice was suddenly sharp, reminding her of the moment by the front door of her apartment. The car spurted forward.

"Just that I get awakened by noises—wherever did the country and the suburbs get their reputation for the crash of quiet? I can sleep through sirens and the gentle sounds of people haranguing each other in the next apartment, but things that go bump in the night have me sitting upright with my hair also upright with fright."

He laughed. The car slowed. "What has startled you?"

"I don't know. I thought I heard a noise one night and got up. I noticed then that the porch roof is under one of my

154

windows—not the most consoling thought in the world—and also I thought I saw a shadow move outside. But by the time Paul had finished pooh-poohing it, I felt a little foolish. The worst are my dreams—I've had at least one real nightmare."

"Oh? What was it?"

Kate told him.

"Unlike many psychiatrists, I don't attach much importance to dreams. The one you had just seems to me to be expressive of anxiety, probably with specific reference to your being in the Lamont house, where you don't wish to be. Here we are."

Kate looked out. McGrath slid the car along the curb. "I haven't thanked you, by the way, for coming," he said rather formally. "Considering the way you felt about it, your presence is above and beyond the call of kindness. By the way, would you like me to prescribe something to help you sleep?"

"No, thanks. Some form of aspirin is the strongest thing I ever take."

"How wise!"

"It's getting late," Kate said. She still felt somewhat disoriented by the shocks of the past hour. She opened the door. "Good night, and thanks for bringing me." Slamming the door, she walked rapidly towards the house, oddly relieved to have left the doctor in his car.

Chapter 7

When she got back to the kitchen, she found Marie rinsing off the dishes and putting them in the now mended dishwasher. Marie was, Kate noticed, wearing her habitual sulky expression.

"I'm sorry I'm late," Kate said, and then added, "I went to see your mother."

Marie muttered something, put a rinsed dish in the machine and reached for a pan.

"What was that?" Kate asked.

"I said big deal."

"What does that mean?"

"It means thanks a lot for being the gracious lady."

Marie was so obviously expecting a sharp reproof that it was almost funny, or would have been if Kate hadn't been startled by the sense that this scene was an echo or replica of one she had known before. But known where? A second later Kate was again shocked, this time by hearing, in her memory, her own voice saying belligerently to Diane, "I'm tired of playing Toad to your Gracious Lady." And she saw the whole moment as

156

vividly as though she were watching an old movie. It was 1955 and she was seventeen, dressed in sweater, skirt and saddle shoes. In front of her stood Diane Légère, offering . . . offering what? The ironic part was that Kate couldn't now remember. It wasn't important. What lived on was her angry sense of being the object of charity, of Diane's (as Kate saw it) arrogant desire to play the lady bountiful. And how she resented the expensive clothes Diane bought her, the cashmere sweaters . . . all the things that made her feel not loved, but inferior.

Odd, Kate thought. It was truly odd that now that life, in the person of Marie, had come full circle, she herself could see, for the first time, that perhaps Diane really was trying to be helpful, to win the friendship, if not the affection of the difficult, thorny creature who had become her stepdaughter.

"It's funny, Marie," she said. "In a way, and probably not meaning to, you've made me see another side of your grandmother—and of myself. Years ago I said to her more or less exactly what you've just said when she wanted either to give me something or do something for me. I've always thought that that impulse in her sprang from some devastating snobbery. She's long dead, but wherever she is now, I offer my apology."

"I don't know what you're talking about," Marie said, still surly.

"I accused her of playing the lady bountiful, just as you've just accused me of being the gracious lady in visiting your mother." Kate took the pan from Marie and started to dry it with a dish towel. "I really wasn't being the gracious lady. If I haven't visited her before . . . well, it doesn't do me much credit to admit it, but I guess I've always been jealous of her."

Marie, who had looked on the point of taking flight, lifted another dirty pan off the other side of the drainboard and plunged it into the soapy water in the sink.

"I guess you don't put pans in the dishwasher," Kate said.

157

"In the newer ones you can. But this is sort of ancient."
Marie went to work with a soap pad. Then she said, "Because
of Daddy?"

"Yes. Your mother was very beautiful and I felt like . . .
well like Toad by comparison."

Marie glanced at her. *"Wind in the Willows* Toad?"

"More or less. Generally unglamorous. And your mother
would come in and stare up at him with that soft look and
say, Good evening, Mr. Lamont, in a way that would have
seduced Scrooge."

Marie's sulkiness vanished for a moment as she broke into
a giggle.

Kate was just congratulating herself that she and Marie
seemed to have reached some kind of a rapport when the defensive look came down onto the girl's face, like a screen.

Abruptly, Marie took the rubber stopper out of the sink
and rinsed and dried her hands. "Sorry about not waiting to
eat," she muttered.

"It's all right." A little puzzled, Kate tried to see Marie's
face but the girl had her back turned. "Did I say something
wrong?" she asked.

"What's to say?" Marie replied in the same mumble, and
left the kitchen. She was pushing her way through the swing
door when Kate said, "Is Ranger upstairs?"

"Where else?"

"Bones?"

"Upstairs with him." Marie seemed to hesitate. "Thanks anyway, for making Daddy let Ranger keep Bones."

"You're welcome. I like Bones. He's going to be a fine dog.
By the way, I haven't interfered with Duchess and her family.
But I take it she's all right? I've been told not to go snooping
around mother cats with new kittens, or the mother will carry
them all somewhere else. So I didn't go over to investigate
the box beside the other refrigerator."

Marie turned a little then. "As a matter of fact . . ."

"Yes."

"She has carried them somewhere else."

"Oh? Somewhere safe, I hope."

Marie flashed one of her lightning smiles, "I hope you think so when you see it. Bye now." And she was gone.

Feeling she had made a little headway, Kate rummaged in the refrigerator for something to eat. Obviously Paul had become a good housekeeper. Kate found some fresh hamburger and the makings of a salad. Ten minutes later she was sitting down to hamburger, peas and mushrooms and salad, plus coffee. A half hour after that she finished washing the pan she had used, placed her dishes and silver in the dishwasher, and started it off. Then she went up to her room.

On the way she knocked on Ranger's door.

"Who is it?" he yelled.

"Me. Kate Malory."

"Oh." There was the sound of a chair scraping, feet and paws on the wooden floor. Then the door opened a crack. Above was Ranger's face. Below was Bones's muzzle.

"Everything okay?" Kate inquired.

"Sure. Fine. And thanks for helping with Bones. Do you want to come in? I'm holding the door this way so he won't get out."

Actually, what Kate wanted to do, in view of her plans for later in the evening when everyone was in bed, was to take her own hot bath and a nap. But this was the first time that Ranger seemed friendly, so she said, "Thanks. Just for a minute. I'm on my way to have a bath."

If Marie's room was straight out of the sixties, Ranger's was as near to an animal park as photographs and pasted up pages could make it. All four walls were covered with pictures that obviously came from books, newspapers, magazines and calendars, all of animals both domestic and wild. Besides dogs, cats, horses, lions, tigers and elephants, half of one wall was devoted to birds, another half to reptiles, and half of a second wall to insects. After a swift glance, Kate decided that dogs of various colors, sizes and types, including their near relatives, wolves, seemed to predominate with the equine and feline families coming a close second.

"I like your animals," Kate said, somewhat surprised to find how true it was. Odd, she thought, I've never given them that much thought—at least consciously.

"Do you have a dog?" Ranger asked.

"No."

"A cat?"

"No."

"That's funny—if you like animals."

Kate pondered his remark. Beth Malory had not admired nature in any movable form. She felt it was untidy, germ-ridden and unredeemed. Diane Légère would not abide animals in the house. She once said, "I didn't have tapestry covers for my chairs made in France just to have some flea-ridden creature scratch them."

Why did she recall that? It wasn't said to her. Suddenly, in her memory, she saw an uncharacteristically disheveled Deborah holding a filthy ginger kitten, tears streaming down her face. What happened to the kitten? She never saw it again.

"I recall once when your mother wanted to keep a kitten she'd rescued and brought home. But her mother wouldn't let her."

"Well then you'd think she'd understand about Bones and let him and Duchess stay in the house," Ranger exploded.

Kate wandered over and looked at a picture of a lion cub. "An experience like that when you're young can push you in one of two opposite directions. You can rebel. The moment you have a place of your own you acquire a live in zoo. The other way of coping with it is to take on the prejudice and make it your own. Which I guess is what your mother did. She's having a difficult time, Ranger. Try not to be too hard on her."

He exploded again. "You don't know how mean to Bones she was. She . . . she beat him. And not just once."

Bones himself had wandered over and was looking at Kate

with soulful eyes. Then he got up on his hind legs and tried to lick her face. As Kate patted him and tried to avoid the more ardent licks of his tongue, she saw again in her mind the round hole of a mouth with the steady, horrifying stream of noise coming out. It was hard to find something to say in defense of that particular Deborah. But somewhere there was also the Deborah with the kitten, and the Deborah who did not see herself as the all-conquering princess, which role Kate had ascribed to her. "Tell me," she said suddenly, "do you remember any time when your mother was kind and warm and fun?"

Ranger stared at her for a minute. "Yeah," he said finally. "When I was a little kid. She and Marie and me used to go out on picnics sometimes by a lake near here. We'd sit around and play games. Sometimes I could bring another kid along, or Marie did. It was Mom who made me first like animals. It was on a picnic, and a guy I'd brought along and I were teasing a chipmunk we'd caught. Mom made us let it go and then came home and read me a long piece out of a book about chipmunks. Funny. I'd forgotten that."

"Well, that's what I mean. She has that other side. And she just hasn't been herself lately. Lots of times all of us do things that aren't very nice when we're upset or scared."

"What'd Mom be scared about?"

"I don't know. People can be scared about lots of things—adults as much as children. And sometimes the things are out of your own imagination, and sometimes they're real. But you're scared in either case."

Ranger received that in silence. Opening a drawer, he got out a brush. "Here, Bones. Come let me brush you."

Kate, who knew she should leave and let him get on with his homework nevertheless stood there, still leaning against the bureau, watching the boy's hand—at the moment much too large for his size—swing the brush in firm strokes along Bones's tawny coat. And then Ranger took Kate by surprise.

"Do you think somebody's giving something to Mom? I

mean, like a drug, like in the movies, to change her personality?"

It was an idea from nowhere. Yet . . . "What made you say that, Ranger?"

"She's so funny. Every time you see her she's different."

"So that made you think somebody might be giving her something."

He didn't look up. "Well, actually I dreamed it."

"What did you dream?"

He turned Bones around and started on the other side. Obviously the dog found this an ecstatic experience. He was standing, nose up, eyes three-quarters closed. "Well," Ranger said. "I had this spooky dream. I dreamed that I saw Mom in her room sitting beside a table filled with little boxes and bottles—you know the kind the drugstore sends pills in. Anyway, she took a swallow from every bottle and a pill from every container and swallowed them all. Then somebody came into her room and I turned around to see who it was only I couldn't see. Whoever it was was standing inside a big column of smoke. And I was yelling, 'Look out, Mom, he's gonna put you on fire.' Then I turned around and she was dying. I mean she was rolling on the floor saying, 'I didn't know it was poison!' And then this man with the flames and the smoke all around started to walk up, and in my dream I yelled at him 'cause I was standing there somewhere. Only I was really yelling and Marie was shaking me."

"This seems to be a house of strange dreams," Kate said.

"Why? Did you have one, too?"

"Yes. I dreamed I was being buried alive."

"Yuch!"

"Your mother's getting treatment, Ranger. That's not the same as being given something to make her different." Or is it, she wondered? Her discomfort at how little she knew about Deborah's recovery program increased. She was leaning against the bureau, thinking about this, when Ranger asked suddenly,

162

"Are you having a thing with the doctor?"

Kate stiffened, then relaxed, amused. "No. Why?"

" 'Cause I saw you drive up. Then you sat there for a minute and you looked terribly close. The front's right out the window there, and there's a streetlight. I wasn't snooping. If you happen to be looking out the window you couldn't miss it!"

"I wasn't accusing you of snooping. No, I'm not having a thing with the doctor. Would it worry you if I was?"

"That's all Bonesey. I'll brush you tomorrow, if I remember." Ranger pulled the hairs out of the brush and put it in his drawer. "I don't like him."

"Why don't you like him?"

"I dunno. He's funny." Pause. "He came here once when Mom started being sick. Bones didn't like him at all."

"Well Bones didn't like me at all, either. I don't think that's some kind of infallible litmus test."

"What's a litmus test?"

"To tell you the truth, I don't know. It's some kind of a chemical test that tells you something definite one way or another. Anyway, it's become an expression meaning just that —a definitive test."

Ranger's blue-green eyes, so like his father's, were trained on Kate. "Bones was only scared of you because he didn't know you. He didn't *like* Dr. McGrath. There's a difference."

"Maybe the difference is that I had time and was around and could coax him into liking me," Kate said.

"You *do* like the doctor," Ranger said. "I was afraid you would."

Kate found herself annoyed and was having trouble not showing it. Then Bones waved his plumed tail and came over and quite abruptly sat up on his haunches.

"You see," Ranger said proudly. "He only does that when he likes people."

Kate laughed. Then she leaned over and hugged Bones. "His ribs aren't showing nearly as much," she said, straightening.

"No, Bones, you don't have to be hysterical. Anyway, Ranger, you must be doing something right. Good night."

She was about to leave when Ranger said, "You aren't mad, are you?"

She looked over and caught an anxious expression on his face. It came to her that he was a twelve-year-old boy without the consistent, balanced attention of a mother, and that whether he knew it or not he was suffering a great loss.

"No, I'm not mad," she said, and went over to where he sat and hugged him.

To her considerable surprise, she got a hug back and a swift shy kiss on her cheek. "I like you," Ranger said.

"It's entirely mutual! Good night!" And she smiled and left.

She discovered what Marie had been talking about when she started to undress and reached into the closet to hang up her skirt. A faint meow came to her ears. She peered in. At first she was unable to see anything because Deborah had obviously used this closet to store out-of-season clothes, plus blankets and hangings of various kinds. But Kate squatted down and peered under the clothes. There, at the back of the closet, Duchess had placed her family, having first managed to pull down someone's sweater for a nest. Duchess gave another meow. She looked, Kate thought, anxious. "It's okay, Duchess," she whispered, and stood up. Then she pushed the door to within three inches of closing. After some more thought she took a china dish, obviously meant as an ashtray, washed it out, filled it with cold water and placed it just outside the closet door. Then she took her bath, set her alarm for 2:30, and climbed into bed with a bulky manuscript, fully intending to read until the alarm went off.

When the alarm went off, she awoke to discover she'd gone to sleep with the light on and the manuscript on her lap open to page 103. Well, she thought, she'd at least read a hundred pages.

Putting her bare feet on the floor, she slipped on her robe

164

and went out into the hall. By this time she had no trouble finding the master bedroom. Inside, she turned on the light, lowered the blinds and went into the closet. Then she took the pole, hooked the end over the handle of the trap door and pulled. And pulled again. It didn't budge. She stood staring up at it as the obvious dawned; someone had locked it.

"Where's the Kramer book?" Dick asked the following Monday, coming in. "I heard a rumor you'd finished it, but production hasn't seen a page, and time is running low."

"It's with the typist," Kate said. Feet propped on the open lower drawer of her desk, she was busy perusing a lengthy saga of the Napoleonic wars.

"I take it Kramer okayed all the changes and revisions?"

"Didn't even want to see them. Admitted immediately he couldn't write and thanked me—and the house—for doing it for him. Couldn't have been nicer."

"Well that's something. We don't have time for him to have an attack of author's ego. It may be a crummy book . . ."

"It's not a crummy book."

"Not after you've finished with it. I meant before."

"It wasn't a crummy book then. He just isn't a writer. Doesn't pretend to be."

"No matter how nice he is, anyone who believes that nonsense has to be retarded. He probably doesn't. Just knows a good scam when he sees it. As Barnum said . . ."

"That's an outrageous accusation, Dick. He does believe it. And it's not a scam. He told me all the money goes to some foundation. He makes a perfectly good living . . ." At that moment Kate remembered Jed's pseudonym and how much it might affect his medical practice if it were known that he wrote books about his esoteric theories.

"Don't stop. What is his profession—don't tell me. Let me guess. He's an astrologer? A dowser?"

"I'm not going to tell you, Dick. It's confidential."

"Hey—you've changed. Nobody made any more fun of this kook than you did. Judy said he'd been in. What is he? Mr. Sex Appeal?"

Kate suddenly had a mental picture of the tubby doctor. "My lips are sealed. You'll get the manuscript as soon as the typist has finished with it. Now run along. I'm working on another overdue book."

"I'll ask Judy," Dick said. "She won't hold out on me." And he left the room.

An hour later Joel wandered in. He had made himself somewhat scarce since their last meeting, a fact Kate had been only dimly aware of until this moment.

"Hello stranger," she said. "Have you been away? Pursuing authors with contract and pen in hand?" She smiled at him. For some reason he looked different.

"I have and signed up a few you might be interested to know."

"Are they readable by such common clay as myself?"

"If you mean garbage . . ."

"No dear Joel. I just mean readable. You look different. I wonder why?" She put her head on one side.

"I cut my hair. Something told me that the more I looked like a bank executive the better you'd like me."

"You're full of blarney, as usual. Yes, it makes a lot of difference. And if that's what's called the bank executive's cut, then I have been neglecting a whole area of men that I should have known about before."

It was astonishing, how different he looked. The wild fuzz had been tamed or grown out or something. Naturally, his hair was wavy rather than corkscrew curly. Now that it was (relatively) short—above his ears and not too long at the back —Joel looked older, slightly less lean in the face and, curiously, more immature. Perhaps it was the white shirt and striped tie under the tweed jacket, plus the bank haircut. But such conservative garb served to emphasize a curious boyishness that still hung about him. He reminded Kate of all the prep school boys in the sixties who had flocked into the various radical causes. So many donned the uniform of the street—dirty jeans, torn T-shirts, unwashed hair—only to open their mouths and utter the purest vowel sounds of Groton, Exeter, and Andover.

"How about dinner?"

Kate was about to refuse when she paused. Why shouldn't she have dinner with him? It would make a nice change from having to cook for three or a TV plate. "Thanks. Love to."

His face broke into a beam. "We can leave here for a drink around five thirty and go on from there."

"Just as long as you remember I have to catch a train back to exurbia not later than eight."

"What happens then? You turn into a pumpkin or a street rat?"

"I turn into a tired, underslept and therefore probably cranky editor. Commuting is a lot more tiring than all those old magazines used to let on."

"What magazines?"

"The ones that were stuffed with fiction about young marrieds in the suburbs. You wouldn't know. You were just born about that time."

"Then why do you know? I don't buy that you were reading the *Lady's Own Compost Heap* at age eight or ten."

"I was precocious."

"Backward is more like it."

Kate sighed. "Joel—for the sake of our evening, I think it would be better if you left now. The auguries are not falling well."

"That's only because your desire for me threatens to overcome your sense of decorum. What you really want to do is to rush hungrily into my arms. After, of course, closing the door." He smiled radiantly.

"Joel Green, I do believe you've been taking a holiday from your serious and important novels portraying the cancer of today's society and have been dipping into romances."

"Oh I can turn an ardent phrase when I want to. I'll come pick you up around five thirty."

As Kate went on with her work, she found that not only was she enjoying the thought of dinner with Joel, she was enjoying even more not going back to the Meadowbrook house till as late as possible, sleep or no sleep.

"I've always found this bar particularly soothing when burdens pressed on me," Joel said, leading her into a well-known mid-Manhattan pub with a long mahogany bar, a rather male atmosphere and tables at the back covered in white linen. "In my fantasies the seduction scene always starts here."

Kate was just about to comment that as far as she was concerned it would also end there, when she decided that, for once, she wouldn't make loud or sardonic noises of resistance until the signals were far more unmistakable.

"It does have a seductive quality," she agreed meekly.

Joel was on his second drink and Kate finishing her first when Joel said, "What's Kramer like? The receptionist and your Judy say he's been in. I thought he was in California with all the other . . ."

"Crazies?"

Joel grinned. "Yes, like being known to seek like."

"With an attitude like that you wouldn't go far in California."

"That's okay. I have no desire to. Why, do you?"

"Do what?"

"Desire to make a dash in California."

"I don't."

Joel put his elbow on the dark bar and considered her. "Then why are you blushing?"

"I'm not."

"Then you should check with your doctor immediately. You must be coming down with some strange disease whose early symptoms are flushed cheeks. Do you have a fever?" He put the back of his hand on one side of her face. "Did you know that I was in my last year of medical school when I decided that my mission was to save American culture rather than American lives?"

She squelched an almost automatic reaction to push his hand away. If her chief sin—as told to God on her way down the steps of the church—was in not desiring anyone, then in His wisdom He was arranging for her to have a set of experiences that would enable her to test that out. Gently she took his wrist and slid it to one side.

"Don't, Joel. I refuse to receive your advances while sitting at a bar. It's unseemly."

"Then why don't we go to your place?"

"Because I'm not in my place at the moment. I'm up in one of our famous suburbs, helping to cope with my sister's children."

"Relaxing in front of your fire would be much better."

"You have me confused with someone else. I don't have a fireplace. That's one of your other loves. And that just convinces me that—despite your assertions—what I've wounded is not your heart but your conceit."

"And to think I cut my hair just for you!"

"You probably cut your hair like that because it was no longer fashionable. The bank executive trim—as you call it—is back."

Joel gestured to the bartender. "Another round."

"Okay Joel," Kate said. "But let's carry them to the table. The knowledge that I have to catch a train is having an inhibiting effect on me."

Half an hour later, when she was still sipping her second drink and Joel had finished his fourth, they were led to a table for two against a wall.

"I'm starved," Kate said. "The thought of eating a meal cooked by someone else is having a terrific effect on my appetite."

169

They ordered. Joel lit a cigarette. "You haven't answered my question. What's this creep like?"

"What creep?" Kate asked sharply, knowing the answer.

"Your big, best-selling author, Kramer."

"He's not a creep. He's a nice man. I like him."

"You like him because he sells ninety thousand copies. Anyone who writes crap like that . . ."

"It's not crap. I wouldn't bother with it if it were crap!"

"Come on, Kate. What's happened to you? I've heard you say that yourself."

And he had. Kate pushed some peas around her plate. "He has a right to his theories. And if he has a publisher who's willing to publish . . ."

"Publishers are unfailingly interested in books that sell. You know—"

"Joel, do you want to continue what started out to be a pleasant dinner or not? I like Kramer. Maybe he isn't the kook we all thought. End of subject."

"Dick said you were showing a certain maidenly interest in him." Joel said gloomily. "I refused to believe it."

"Dick's full of prunes," Kate said. "He frequently is. You've said so yourself and repeat it almost every week at editorial meetings."

"And that expression went out with the bustle."

"How would you know, unless, of course, you've reincarnated from some libertine who died of excesses on the tenderloin?"

Joel was filled with delight. "You're jealous!"

"Your steak will get cold."

They ate in silence for a few minutes. Kate's mind was where it had been on and off during the day—on the locked trapdoor. Could she have made a mistake, and it was only stuck? Somehow she knew that could not be true—it had opened so easily the first time. Then who locked it? Eliminate Ranger, she thought—he certainly could not be involved. That left Paul and Marie. Paul was in Chicago. That left Marie.

170

Marie with her sulky withdrawal. For a brief while the previous evening the wall she kept around herself had seemed to disappear. Friendliness had broken through. There, over the dishwasher, she had seemed much like any other attractive teen-ager with a chip on her shoulder, not much different from the chip Kate herself had carried for so long. *If* she had been the one to lock the trapdoor, then what was the reason? Kate came to abruptly when she heard Joel's voice, loud and insistent.

". . . not that I mean to disturb your meditation," he said rather angrily. "But if you still intend to catch the eight whatever to your glorious suburb, you're going to have to run all the way."

Kate glanced at the big clock on the wall. The train after, she knew, would not get her into the Lamont house until 10:30. "Good-bye," she said. "And thanks for the dinner." She was still getting into her coat as she hit the pavement outside and started running.

Kate made the train, which started to pull out before she was even in her seat. Then she sat and puffed slightly, pleased that she could still put on such athletic bursts of speed. It was five minutes past nine when she opened the front door.

Bones, by now her friend, greeted her, plumelike tail waving. Kate made her way back to the kitchen. Everything semed exactly as she had left it that morning. Of course Marie and Ranger could have had dinner and cleaned up after themselves so thoroughly that they removed all evidence of having been there. But it seemed unlikely. Furthermore, Bones's dish was polished clean, and by his general prancing around and what Kate had come to think of as his hungry noises, she doubted very much that he had been fed.

That brought Kate's first tinge of alarm. Neglecting to feed his precious dog seemed totally unlike everything she had known about Ranger.

"Where's your master, Bones?"

Bones, now somewhat filled out in the short time Kate had

171

known him, galumphed about, plunging up and down. Kate went back out into the hall, hung her coat up in the hall closet and went upstairs. Neither Ranger nor Marie was there. Kate stood for a minute, battling with a growing sense of guilt. I should not have gone out to dinner, she thought. Paul had left her to look after his children, and however much she thought he neglected his responsibilities, she had agreed to do so. Which did not mean staying in town for a pleasant meal with a friend without calling back to see what Ranger and Marie were planning to do. Why hadn't she called?

Because, she thought to herself, going into her own room, they seemed perfectly content to get their own meal if she was late—even to prefer doing so. Still, she should have called.

Switching on the light, Kate pulled the closet door open just enough to check on Duchess and her brood. They all seemed there and in order, the four kittens, their mouths attached to the milk buttons, sucking busily. Duchess started to purr, her motor getting progressively louder, whether as an expression of the gratifying greed of her children, or pleasure at Kate's interest, Kate didn't know. "Have a nice supper, kids," Kate said.

But when she left the room to go downstairs, she was amused to note that Duchess followed her, padding softly behind as she went downstairs. It was more than likely that Duchess, too, wanted something to eat.

Kate went back to the kitchen, fed both Bones and Duchess, then, when Bones pawed at the door, Kate put back on her coat, snapped the leash into Bones's collar and went out to give him a short walk. She was beginning to wonder if she should check to see if Duchess was able to get to her litter pan, wherever that was, when she noticed, for the first time, a sort of cat port in the kitchen door. As she watched, Duchess butted her head through the little swinging door and went outside.

Walking around a block in the suburbs turned out to be

172

more complicated than Kate thought. What Bones really wanted to do, in his growing state of health and confidence, was to run free. Since Kate had no dependence on his obeying her, and had no idea what code words to use if he had been obedience trained (although that seemed ludicrously unlikely), she didn't dare let him off the leash. Furthermore, Kate thought grumpily, feeling herself hauled along at almost a run, suburbs obviously believed in either narrow sidewalks or none at all. And to anyone used to Manhattan's square layout, the lozenge-shaped blocks in the hinterlands were hard to follow. Twice Kate found herself and her charge standing at an intersection that she had never before seen. At the corner of one of those she was about to ask instruction of someone in a nearby parked car, when the car revved up its engine and shrieked away. "Thanks a lot," Kate muttered to herself. The next time anyone had anything to say about the rudeness of New Yorkers she'd have a few things of her own to come back with. It was Bones who seemed to know where to go, so, in lieu of anything more concrete, she let him lead her. About twenty minutes later she found herself back in front of the Lamont house.

"Good dog," she said approvingly. She might wish with all her heart she was back in her own quarters, but in this area of total unknowns, the Lamont house looked like home.

When Kate opened the back door there was a cry of "Hey, Bones!"

An ecstatic Bones flung himself at Ranger, who went down on one knee and hugged him as though, Kate thought, amused, he feared his pet had been in some terrible danger.

"We only went around the block," Kate said, hanging up the leash. "And by the way, where were you? You had me worried when I realized that your friend here hadn't been fed."

"I've been at Don's house."

Kate felt one of the guilt pangs that were becoming depressingly familiar. If she had got up earlier . . . if she had

173

gone to bed earlier . . . if she had been able, after her nocturnal ramble, to go back to sleep sooner and therefore wake up sooner . . .

"Well, I wish you'd left a note."

Ranger struggled to his feet but didn't say anything. He looked, Kate thought, a little pale. She didn't want to become a nag, so she said conversationally, "I wonder if Marie's home. Maybe she came in when I was walking Bones. Do you know, Ranger?"

"She's not in. Come on, Bones! I'll give you some dinner."

"He's been fed and walked, as you must know since I just came in. Do you know where Marie is?"

"No. How should I know?"

This was so much in his former style that Kate was almost startled. "Are you mad about something?"

"No, but I don't know why I should know about Marie. I mean, after all—she's older than I am. And she's a girl."

Kate looked at him for a moment. Was it her imagination, or was he really paler?

"You may not be mad. But you certainly are defensive. It was only a civil question. It is not outside the realm of possibility that you might know where your sister is."

"Come on, Bones. We're going upstairs."

"Just a minute." Kate stood in front of him and put her hands on his shoulders. "I thought we were friends."

"Sure. What's the big deal? I have to go upstairs." He pushed aside her hands and almost seemed to run out of the kitchen, pursued by Bones.

Kate stared after him. She had not realized how much he had changed in his attitude until this regression to his old self. It was odd. The trouble was, she had known both the children such a short time that she had no way of knowing whether this yo-yo change from hostility to friendship and back to hostility was characteristic of Ranger, or whether something had happened to make him retreat to his former stance. She feared it was the latter. In which case, what had

174

occurred? Had Paul called? Come home? When was he due home? She couldn't remember exactly. And how strange that she couldn't. Shouldn't she be counting the days and hours the way she once would have. Which meant. . . ?

It meant that at some point, between the moment when she had seen him for the first time in so many years and her heart, with remembered obedience, jumped and now, something incredible had happened. She had let go the obsession with Paul that had haunted her since she was twelve and that had underlain every infatuation with every man since. That being the case, shouldn't she be feeling free and at peace instead of hollow and miserable?

It was, she decided, important to find out when Paul was due home. Going upstairs, she knocked on Ranger's door.

When he came to the door and opened it a few inches, she was sure that he had been crying. Instead of asking about Paul, she said, "Ranger, what's the matter? I know you're upset!" She tried to push the door further open but Ranger's foot and sturdy form were behind it.

"I told you. I'm okay."

"You've been crying. I can see it."

"For pete's sake, I got something in my eye."

"Let me see."

"No. I have work to do. All you do is interfere. Leave me alone."

A sudden shove of the door caught her off guard and she heard it snap shut. I handled that badly, she thought. And she still didn't know when Paul was due home. Suddenly finding out became important—for reasons other than just her presence in the household. "All right, Ranger," she called through the door. "I'm sorry if you feel I've poked my nose in your business. I won't do it again. What I came to ask was, do you know when your father is coming back? I forgot to ask him."

There was a pause, then "End of the week, maybe."

"Don't you know the exact day?"

"He wasn't sure."

"Yes, but . . ."

"Look, I've gotta work."

She sighed. "All right."

The hollow and unhappy feeling was now considerably greater. Slowly Kate made her way to her room, disturbed and puzzled by a sensation she could not shake; despite Ranger's presence, she felt strangely alone in the house, alone and vulnerable. Vulnerable to what? she muttered to herself, getting into the shower.

The feeling persisted as she sat on her bed working her way through the Napoleonic saga. Was it because she had not heard Marie come in? Possibly she had while Kate was in the shower.

Swinging her legs out of bed, Kate groped around for her slippers, tied her robe more securely and went back into the main hall. When she knocked on Marie's door there was no answer. After a second knock without response she pushed the door open and stood adjusting to the same sense of culture shock she had had the first time she'd ventured in. There was the monk, the flames around him. Surely, Kate thought, flinching despite herself, he must have felt indescribable agony—or had he succeeded in withdrawing to the point where he could remove himself from all sense and feeling? The light when turned on still produced the blinking glare. This time Kate went over to the lamp, fumbled around and found a switch. Her eyes felt the relief when she turned it off. That left the overhead light, making the room mundane. Rather than exotic or bizarre, it now looked merely uncomfortable. The bedroll was rolled up and tied. The bamboo slats were down. Incense sticks stuck in little sand containers gave off a sweetish odor. Diverted for a moment, Kate stood there wondering why it smelled different from the incense used at so many of the High Masses she had attended. She must ask a priest some time—if she ever found herself talking to one again. There was no real conventional furniture. Instead of a bureau, there was the white raw wood of what looked like overturned orange crates, one serving as a bookcase, another seeming to contain a great number of T-shirts, and another, a miscellaneous collection of boxes, bottles and paperback books. Did Marie possess anything else—this well-to-do child in an affluent suburb? And how passé it looked now. Surely the whole style and mood was late sixties and seventies. Idly, Kate opened the closet door. Certainly the jeans and T-shirt that Marie had worn every time Kate had seen her did not spring from lack. The closet was packed with hangers of blouses and sweaters and skirt hangers, each holding two and three skirts. True, there was only one dress—a full length granny-looking cotton print. But Kate doubted if when she herself was sixteen back in . . . in 1954 she had anything but skirts and blouses and sweaters. The wheel turned and came back to its old place. Almost. Not quite. More like a spiral.

Which made her think of Jed Kramer and his theories of time. What would he make of all this? Kate glanced at her watch, 10:45. It was late for Marie to be out—although she'd been out this late and later before. Still—that was before her father came home and got everybody back into shape. And it was late to telephone someone.

Kate switched off the light and closed the door. To make sure Marie had not come in while she herself was insulated from sound inside her own shower bath, Kate went downstairs, explored the whole lower region and went back upstairs, leaving the lights on.

When she got back to her room she checked on the closet. Yes, there was Duchess, her four children lying in a furry heap, sated and asleep. Smiling a little Kate got back into bed and tried to concentrate on her manuscript. But the unease she had felt before she felt now with even greater intensity. However ridiculous she knew such a feeling to be, Kate could not shake the sensation of being alone in an empty house sitting at the corner of a rather empty suburban street.

"You're imagining things," she said aloud, and forced her

eyes back to page 125. Then she nearly jumped out of her skin. There was a plop beside her, and something soft rubbed against her arm. Looking down, she saw the pointed face with the blob of black coming down over one eye. "Duchess, you almost drove me off the bed." Duchess, who had started her loud purr, turned around and around, as though burrowing a circular hole in the bed clothes. Then she sat down with her back against Kate's side.

"You're a good girl," Kate said, and putting out a hand, stroked her. The purr got louder than ever.

Kate forced herself to read, until the book, after its cumbersome beginning, slowly picked up interest. One hundred and three pages later Kate looked again at her bedside clock, 1:15.

She was conscious of being cold. Well, here, as in most houses, and unlike many apartments, the thermostat probably automatically turned down at night. Kate was sure that Marie could not have come in without Kate hearing. She had left her door propped wide open. But she had been concentrating. Once more tying her robe and putting on her slippers, Kate slipped down her small hall to the main one. The lights were still on. Marie's room was still empty. Without any specific purpose, Kate eased open Ranger's door and promptly heard Bones's bark as a reward.

"Shut up Bones," came a sleepy voice. "You'll wake Kate."

Equally silently Kate eased the door shut and tiptoed back to her room.

So Marie was not home. So what? One-fifteen was small potatoes compared to returning home at four in the morning, according to the nosey neighbor. And Marie had been circumspect for a long time—for her.

Yet as Kate went back to her room, turned off the light and opened the windows, she could not rid herself of the feeling that another element had entered the situation, and that she did not know what it was.

An hour later she was still awake, and Marie had still not returned. Sometime after 3:30 Kate finally dozed off. Marie was still not home. Duchess had long since returned to her family, and Kate spent the last hour before sleep fervently wishing that she had brought her heating pad from home.

She awoke groggily at 8:30, staring at her clock. As she became aware that no means on earth could enable her to catch the 8:44 train, she put on her robe, went down the hall and knocked on Marie's door. After the smallest token wait, she pushed the door open. It was, as she knew in her guts it would be, empty.

"Ranger?" Kate called. He was usually gone by this hour, so she was not surprised when all she received in response was a bark.

Ten minutes later she was downstairs boiling water. While she waited for it to boil she found herself calling the Hilton Hotel in New York. It was so totally unplanned that she had a strange observer's detachment from what she was doing.

"Jed?" she said, when he came on the phone.

"I was waiting for your call."

She hesitated a moment, then said, "I want you to come out here. I feel a terrible hypocrite, because I am all too aware that I spent most of the time while I was editing your last two books making fun of all your theories and now I'm asking for your help. Truthfully, I don't know what I think. So if you refuse, or have to go home, or both, I'll understand."

"That's all right." He sounded as much his old bouncy self as ever. "Most people think people who believe in the things I do are kooks. Glad to help."

"I'm sorry. I still don't understand anything to do with the spooky or psychic or occult or any other related matter. I have no idea why you know what you seem to know. But in my present uncomfortableness, you're the only one that has seemed to make any sense at all." She took a breath. "So I was wondering if you'd come out here this morning. You probably have other things you must do but . . ."

"No, no. I stayed in New York so I could be of help. The moment I met you I knew you'd need it. And aside from the

179

fact that the whole point of life is to be of service, I feel so grateful to you for putting my dreadfully written books in shape. I'll be out there as soon as I can get my car out of the garage."

"You have a car here?"

"Yes. I thought I might need it, so I hired one for my stay."

"I don't drive and don't know how to tell you to get here."

"Don't worry. I'll find the address—as soon as you've given it to me."

"I'm surprised you have to ask—" Kate said slyly. "That you don't know it anyway, by some arcane method."

"I could probably find it, if I concentrated. But giving it to me would be quicker."

As soon as she hung up Kate dialed again. Judy was an early arriver at the office and she might be there even though it was still a few minutes to nine.

"Judy," Kate said, when she answered the phone. "I'm not coming in today. I have this huge opus to read and I think I'll do it here. If anybody really wants me, I'll be at this number." And she gave it to her.

"Do you realize you're down for a lunch with Mr. Maitland?"

"No," Kate said, "I'd forgotten."

"Tut," Judy replied. "He'd be upset if he knew that."

"So don't tell him." Damn! she thought. Graham might be her ex-lover and professional admirer, which gave her a certain sense of leeway and freedom, but he was still the boss, and no employee, however favored, would lightly pass up a lunch with him. "Judy?" Kate said.

"Still here. I could hear your thinking, click, click, click."

"I'll call Graham myself in half an hour. If by any chance he should call me or come to the office before I've had a chance to reach him, tell him that I'm trying to get in touch and that I have a crisis."

"Okay. What's the crisis?"

"I think I'll tell him myself."

"Sure. Are you telling me politely that it's none of my business?"

Kate laughed. Judy, she decided, was an excellent antidote to all the strange and disquieting thoughts drifting in and out of her mind. "I was, but on second thought, I'll tell you. Marie, my niece, has not been in all night. She was out when I got here at nine—because I stayed in town for dinner."

"Yes, I know, with Joel."

"Word gets around fast."

"The tom-toms are always busy."

"Well, I don't know whether I am being punished for not showing up for my baby-sitting job before dinner, or what. But she didn't come home. And I'll have to admit I'm worried."

"Where's her father?"

"In Chicago. And I don't know—and Ranger, the boy, doesn't know—when he's supposed to be back."

"Why don't you call him?"

It was such an obvious statement. Kate was astounded she hadn't thought of it herself. And then she realized that on some level she had, but didn't know where Paul was staying. Which was also surprising. "I'm going to try to," she said now. "I'll be in touch."

She thought back. When did she talk to Paul about her coming to stay and his going to Chicago? The day before she had actually returned. How had they left it? That's where her memory was blank. He was full of thanks and appreciation on the phone. Had he said he'd be gone a week? It was now—she counted on her fingers the sixth day since he had left. And she could not remember his saying where he would be staying. Was it odd?

Dr. McGrath had known where to reach Paul in Tokyo, and when she called she reached him without trouble. So, obviously, it was their common oversight: Paul's neglect to tell her, her neglect in asking. Well, she'd just have to call his office to find out. But first, she'd better get dressed.

She was zipping up her skirt when the telephone rang.

"So," Graham's pleasant voice said. "You're standing me up."

"Graham, I couldn't be sorrier. Did Judy tell you my family problem?"

"She said it had something to do with your niece. Is she sick?"

"No. At least I don't think so. She simply isn't here. She never came home last night."

"Is she given to doing this?"

"According to a nosey neighbor, whom she bitterly resents, she's accustomed to coming home at all hours. But I've never known her not to come home at all. On the other hand, I haven't been around her that much."

"I take it she's something of a wild kid or rebel."

"You take it right. Her room looks like an SDS hideout from the late sixties or early seventies—conflagrating monk and all. There've been a couple of moments when I thought we were making headway—or at least talking. But both she and the boy have had a severe relapse in the past few days. Anyway, rebel or no, I'm worried about her absence. She may be simply staying with a sympathetic friend. But you'd think that the friend, however sympathetic, would have a mother who'd call. . . . Sorry Graham, I didn't mean to go into all that. It's just that I don't know what to do other than to sit tight."

"Where's Paul?"

For some reason his question startled her. How would Graham have such casual knowledge of her brother-in-law? And then she remembered that all during their affair she talked endlessly about the dramatis personae of her life.

"Hello? Are you there?" Graham's voice was a little sharper.

"Sorry, Graham. I thought somebody might have been ringing the bell." The lie fell so easily it was disconcerting.

"And were they?"

182

"No . . ." She stared out the front window from the living room extension of the telephone. "It was a bicycle bell, I think." There was, indeed, a bicycle going past, presenting her with a useful excuse.

"Oh. Well, you'd probably better get in touch with him, hadn't you?"

"Yes. I was just going to do that when you called."

"Where is he staying?"

"I was just going to find out."

"I see. Well, see if you can get him to come back and mind his own store. We need you here, lady. The copy editor is waiting to discuss with you a few minor nitpicks on the Kramer manuscript, and I want your opinion on the Talbot novel."

"Graham, I'll be back as soon as I can. I truly do not want to be here any more than you want me to."

"Besides," Graham said, his voice changing a little. "I miss you."

She saw him suddenly in her mind, leaning back in his chair in the big corner office, the light streaming in on his blond head. It was on that tone of voice, speaking just such casual words, that she had lived for so long, a tone that made the long week of no intimate communication, of no more than a smile on passing in the hallway, bearable, a week during which, of course, he always went home to his wife. That was the way it was with Graham—the intimacy, with all its potent sweetness distilled into a few hours, or nothing at all. We never had time to be friends, Kate thought. We were lovers either on our way to bed within the hour or parting immediately afterwards, or we were employer and employee—nothing else. Not that that couldn't be a great deal. Graham was a subtle, skilled lover, tender and perceptive. That was his power. . . .

"You might at least say 'likewise, I'm sure,'" Graham said, sounding a little jovial.

183

"Thanks Graham. I'll hang on to the thought while I'm wrestling with the younger generation. And I'll be in as soon as I can. Thanks for calling."

She went downstairs, made coffee and toast, and was eating it when the bell rang.

"You got here fast," she said to Jed Kramer as he came in.

"It really wasn't difficult. I asked in the village and they gave me clear directions." His gray brown curls were ruffled. He didn't seem quite as tubby as she remembered. A little taller and compact. Although there was a nip in the air outside, he had simply wound a long muffler around and around his neck.

"Hmmmm," he said, as he came in. "This is really not a happy house."

"I could have told you that without benefit of dowsing rod."

"Yes. You're very sensitive." He grinned. "An amazing amount of what people think is spookiness is a state of high metaphysical development, combined with sensitivity, combined with common sense. Also a knowledge of cosmic law."

"What cosmic law?"

"Boiled down," he said, walking around the living room and looking at the prints, "it is, love God, love your neighbor, serve both, be accountable and take responsibility for what you do."

"That sounds to me like plain old Christianity. Or plain old Judaism."

"It is. Also plain old Buddhism. I don't think this particular room has been used or lived in for a while. It feels empty— empty of thought or feeling or the continuing presence of people who are thinking and feeling in it."

"I'm not quite sure what you mean," Kate said cautiously. "But it's true. It is, sort of, a dead room. Come back to the kitchen. That's better."

"By the way," Kate said, leading the way down the narrow hall. "There's a dog, a puppy really, named Bones who lives in the kitchen. According to Bones's owner, my nephew Ranger,

184

he had an abused puppyhood, which accounts for an extreme case of terminal cowardice the moment he meets anyone new. So if he goes under the table and cries, don't take it personally. He has other reactions too, sometimes, which I hope I don't have to go into."

"Goes all over everything, does he?" Jed said cheerily.

Kate looked back over her shoulder. "You seem to be aware of the phenomenon."

"My wife used to pick up strays and bring them home. Since she died I've continued the practice. It makes for lively living. Ah yes, the kitchen!" He walked in behind Kate. "This is much nicer," he said. "Hello, how are you?" This was to Bones, who had retreated under the table, but had reemerged and was sitting, staring in an inquisitive manner at Jed. At his voice, Bones got up, whiffled a little, walked around in the same spot a couple of times, then came forward. Jed held out a hand. Bones sniffed. Then, cautiously, he licked Jed's hand and went up on his hind legs to make his greeting more personal and general.

"You must really practice some kind of voodoo," Kate said, watching this.

"No. I think he smells my dogs. Besides, he's not as frightened now as he was."

Kate considered. "No. I think you're right. But it hasn't been that long since I first came here—less than a month. That's a big change in a short time."

"Well," Jed said, rubbing Bones between his ears and pulling one ear slowly through his fingers to Bones's obvious gratification, "it may be that those who frightened him are not here. He feels safe with those here right now." He smiled at Kate. "Probably you."

"Thank you. What a nice thing to say! I was having some coffee. Would you like some?"

"Yes. I would. Do you mind if I look out the back and upstairs?"

"Not at all. Help yourself. I'll make some more coffee."

It was ridiculous to feel that everything had improved simply because he was there, when nothing at all had changed. Kate spent the time the water was boiling trying to argue herself out of her improved spirits and failing. A few minutes later Jed was back, and the coffee and more toast were ready.

"Now, tell me," Jed said. "What's worrying you?"

"Marie, my niece, who is fifteen, was not here when I arrived after dinner last night and she hasn't come home since. I don't know where she is. Further, both she and her brother seemed to have regressed in their behavior towards me. We were beginning to be—not friends, maybe, but also not enemies. I felt I had suddenly become, once more, the enemy. That's my first worry. The second is that when I thought of calling my brother-in-law in Chicago to tell him about Marie, I didn't know where to reach him. He didn't say where he was staying and I didn't ask. It's sort of an incredible slipup on both sides. After all, Mark McGrath—the doctor looking after my sister-in-law—knew where he was in Tokyo and gave me the telephone number." She put down her coffee cup. "I truly can't think why I didn't ask."

Jed Kramer nibbled a piece of toast. "Are you as much puzzled as to why he didn't offer the information?"

She stared at him. "Now that you ask, not quite. I wonder why that is."

"Perhaps because you are not completely convinced about his concern—either about his children or about you?"

"There's no reason why he should have any particular concern about me. . . . I was in love with him once, and thought I was for a long time . . . but . . ."

"But you've discovered that is no longer the case." He had taken out half-moon spectacles and put them on, the better to read the small print on the pot of honey Kate had put on the table. Now he looked up at her over their straight tops. Kate found herself thinking that his brown eyes were the clear color of the peat tarns or brooks dotting the highlands of Scotland where she had vacationed one year.

"That's so," she said. "I don't know why, but I just discovered that . . . well, it's like having an old, old wound healed." And as she spoke she remembered the dream she had had when she was a child, of seeing her soul like a green crystal with a fault like a great crack down the middle, and the finger of God touching the fault at its base and searing it closed. "When I was a child I had a weird dream," she said, and told him about it.

"Ummm," he said. Then, "Your dreams are interesting."

She grinned. "Are you going to tell me what they mean?"

"No. Partly because I'm not sure . . . beyond the fact that they are trying to tell you something. But that's true of everybody's dreams. Most psychologists know that."

"I told Mark McGrath, the psychiatrist, about them. He didn't seem to think they were significant."

Jed stared at her for a minute. "Like most doctors, I'm a coward about criticizing a colleague, but I'm bound to say I think that's strange."

"Yes," Kate said, getting up to pick up the coffee pot from the stove. "You doctors are worse than a union."

"You have to remember that goes back to the days when doctors could be hauled into court and criminally prosecuted for every single mis-diagnosis—a state of affairs that, to some extent, seems to have returned," he finished gloomily.

Kate poured him and herself more coffee. "I refuse to weep for a profession that is probably more highly paid than any other in the country. Although," she added hastily, "I don't think it applies to you."

"It doesn't, I'm afraid. My wife thought I didn't take a sufficiently practical view of non-bill payers."

"That doesn't sound like someone who picks up strays."

"Yes, but she felt that she could have picked up more strays, or perhaps founded a home for them, if I'd made more money."

Kate burst out laughing, and Jed joined her.

"Speaking of McGrath," Kate said. "You remember I told

187

you about his coming to my apartment in New York to persuade me to come back here? I keep getting the feeling that it was a slightly weird thing to do. Would you do it?"

"I might. But I'd have to be very sure that it was necessary. That's a lot of interference and meddling into the life and affairs of a patient."

"Even if it's for her good?"

"Who's to say it's for her good? That's what I mean. He's playing God, and that's dangerous. Sometimes it's better, over the long haul, to let things fall apart than to move heaven and earth to patch them up temporarily. People often don't believe that, but it's true. That's why I said he should have an overwhelming reason. Why?"

"I don't know," she said slowly. I suppose because I'm dogged by the feeling that . . . that there was some reason other than concern over Deborah."

"Maybe there was." After a minute, when she didn't go on, he said, "Where's this trapdoor you were telling me about?"

Kate took him upstairs. "Before we go look at the trapdoor, which is in the closet of the master bedroom, I'm going to show you Marie's room. I won't go as far as to say I've become a believer, as far as your theories are concerned, but my mind is more open. Let's see what vibrations you pick up there."

When she opened the door, Jed stood there on the threshold for a minute or two. Such was his concentration, that she felt as though he had withdrawn from her. She tried to speak, failed, then made a bigger effort.

"When I said vibrations, I mean exactly what I said. Behold!" And she went over and switched on the blinking light.

"Yes, I see." He walked in for a minute and moved slowly around the room, touching things—the orange crate, the blinking light, the rolled up bedroll, the granny dress inside the closet. He looked at the picture of the monk. Then he went over to the window and rolled up the bamboo blind. Sun poured in. For the first time the room looked like a room rather than a statement.

"My dear, would you leave me alone in here for a minute or two. It's easier for me to concentrate if I'm by myself."

"Not at all. Just give a shout when you want me again."

She went out and, after a second's hesitation, closed the door. Her feeling of his withdrawal was stronger than ever. It was a struggle for her to hang on to her concept of him as a slightly comic little man. This image was retreating before something else. Not fear, she thought, walking down the hall, but something related to it.

Outside the master bedroom she hesitated, then put her hand out to the doorknob. She might as well employ the time usefully. The place to begin to find out where Paul was staying was his office. Probably in the desk in the bedroom there'd be some kind of letterhead bearing the telephone number. It was not until she was halfway across the floor of the master bedroom that she realized why she needed to look at the letter head of his firm: one of the details with which he had forgotten to supply her was the name of his corporation.

Chapter 8

Twenty minutes later she was no nearer finding out the name of his company. She had looked in every drawer and in the cubby holes above the drop leaf. There was relatively little in the drawers and what there was, was so impersonal that Kate felt as though she could find the same in any desk in Westchester County. There was a small checkbook and a large one with stubs written in what Kate well remembered was Deborah's handwriting. Since she was merely trying to find the name of Paul's corporation, she did not feel justified in looking at the stubs more carefully. There was engraved notepaper, a box of stamps, stacks of plain white paper, envelopes, post office envelopes, boxes of unused Christmas cards, boxes of pencils, clusters of felt point pens held together with rubber bands, a small hand calculator, address labels, a photograph album, stacks of warranties and instruction sheets for various household appliances and rolls of gummed paper tape. The whole thing, Kate decided, looked like a desk in some showroom deliberately filled with a convenient collection of impersonal items that could be found in any stationery store.

"Did you find what you were looking for?" Jed said from the door.

"No, I . . ." She turned and was struck by the fact that Jed seemed troubled. "Are you all right?"

"Yes. I'm fine."

"You don't look particularly fine."

He came slowly into the room and sat down on a chair. "I'm a little worried about your niece."

"What do you mean?"

He stared at her, his round normally cheerful face oddly drawn. "I'm not sure. You know I'm not reading some invisible printout that nobody else can see. All I do is to collect vivid feelings and impressions. My feeling about your niece—what is her name? Marie?—is that she is running away from something that is frightening her almost beyond bearing."

He and Kate stared at each other for a moment in silence. What Kate found dismaying was how totally she believed him. She decided to resist that belief. "But what would she be so frightened of?"

"I don't know."

She replaced the drop leaf with a snap. "That's not exactly helpful."

"I know. I'm sorry."

Kate felt ashamed of herself. "You have nothing to be sorry about, Jed. I'm sorry I was such a . . . a witch."

"You're not a witch. Or even a bitch. You're playing devil's advocate because you're afraid what I'm saying is true, but you don't want to believe it."

"More voodoo."

"No, ordinary perception."

Kate got up and moved restlessly around the room. "If I just knew *what* she was afraid of."

"I have a feeling that if you knew that you'd know the answer to a lot of other things. By the way, did you find out the name of your brother-in-law's firm?"

191

"No." She turned and waved towards the desk. "I've been through every drawer and cubby hole and it was all about as revealing as a display counter in a stationery store. Nothing. Nothing that tells me anything."

"Well, that in itself is revealing, isn't it?"

"What do you mean?"

"I mean, what do you have in your own desk at home? Supposing someone were to go through your desk? What would they know about you?"

She stood staring out the window at a tan car parked across the road. "Well, I suppose, my financial state, that is, my bank balance. I keep my statements and checkbook and cancelled checks in one of the drawers." She hesitated, "Also, who my friends are. I have an address book there. Letters from same. Doodads, knickknacks. Carbons of some letters I have sent. A file drawer." She paused. "Even a couple of old love letters."

"But you found none of those in the desk there?"

"There's a checkbook with stubs in Deborah's handwriting. Since I was looking specifically for the name or letterhead of Paul's company, I didn't feel justified in snooping too closely into the checkbook. But the rest was just supplies. Except for a photograph album."

"Did you look at that?"

"No." She glanced over at him. "I shouldn't think that would reveal any company name, would you?"

"No. I don't think so. Which leads me to the opinion that that desk was deliberately purged of anything that could tell you something about the owners."

"Do you want me to get out the checkbook and the photo album?"

"No. Not now. I may be wrong, but I don't think they'd show anything. If they did, it would be by accident. We can go back to that. Now, to return to your brother-in-law's company. Who would know the name?"

Kate thought. "Ranger, Deborah, possibly a neighbor."

192

"What about the psychiatrist? What did you call him? Mc-Grath? Wouldn't he know, since he knew where to call Paul in Tokyo?"

"Of course! What a dumb head I have! I'll call Mark right away. There's an extension in this room I think. Yes, there, on the night table."

"Do you remember the number?"

"Yes," Kate said, and felt self-conscious.

But when she reached the hospital, she was told that Dr. McGrath was out.

"Well . . ." she said. Surely somebody there would have Paul's number to notify him in case of emergency. "Look, may I speak to whoever is next in charge?"

After a certain amount of clicking and muttering, a female voice said, "This is Mrs. Andrews, may I help you?"

"This is Kate Malory. I'm staying with the Lamont children while my sister, Mrs. Lamont, is there in the hospital. My brother-in-law, Paul Lamont—I know that Dr. McGrath has a business telephone number for my brother-in-law—which I seem to have mislaid. Could you let me have it?"

"Don't you know the name of his company or firm?"

Kate cursed herself for leaving such a wide opening. "Strange as it may seem, I don't. I've never called him at his company office, although I have called him in Tokyo at a number supplied by Dr. McGrath when I was summoned here to help out."

"Well I'm sorry, Mrs. Malory. If Dr. McGrath has that number it's in his office and I couldn't get in there to give it to you even if I would—it's locked."

Kate was beginning to feel the pigheadedness that comes with frustration. "Supposing you had an emergency that required your reaching Mr. Lamont?"

"Then we would get in touch with Dr. McGrath right away."

"Give me Dr. McGrath's present number and I will get in touch with him."

"I don't know what it is, Miz Malory," the nurse intoned, "we would simply have him paged on his beeper."

"Well please have him beeped, then, wherever he is, and tell him to call me at the Lamont house. Thank you." And Kate hung up rather briskly. She turned around to see Jed laughing.

"It's not funny," she fumed.

"I know. But I can't help it. Most doctors at some time or other feel hounded by their patients. It's good for us to see the patient's point of view."

"Most doctors are sadists. A brief but thorough course in the uses of sadism is required before graduation from medical school."

"Tut!"

Kate grinned. "Well, you know what I mean. In the meantime, where else I wonder could I get Paul's number?"

Jed started counting off on his square fingers. "To begin with, the school where his children are. Surely no school would be without a phone number where the father could be reached during the day. If worse comes to worst, call the telephone number you called in Tokyo—it will be expensive—but then call from this phone. You're doing it for his family. You also haven't mentioned the most obvious of all—your sister. Is she reachable? You said you hadn't seen her for eighteen years."

"I did go to see her." She glanced at him and suddenly remembered his saying that it was important that she see Deborah. "As you strongly suggested," she finished dryly.

"Yes. It was important. Well, did she have a telephone you could call her at?"

"Yes. She did. First tell me, why did you think it important that I see her?"

"It's not easy to answer that. It was simply a very strong feeling. On the most basic level, how would you know what you're dealing with if you didn't?"

"All right. I guess I'll have to go along with that. I always

194

have the feeling that you're going to tell me that you know exactly what's going to happen."

"I already warned you that precognition doesn't work that way—it's hard to tell whether something is in the immediate past or the immediate future. Much of it is intuitions amounting to certainties. This does not make me unique, my dear. Most people, if they bothered to concentrate and become attuned would know just as much as I. It's not magic."

Kate smiled. His use of the word *magic* made her remember his saying that he had not bothered to learn the course in his English class because he was obsessed by science and magic. She suddenly saw him as a small, sturdy boy, solemnly practicing taking rabbits out of hats or pulling cards from behind someone's ear.

"Why are you smiling?"

"I was seeing you as a small boy trying to take rabbits out of hats when you should have been parsing sentences and/or reading *Silas Marner*."

He sighed. "Yes, I'm afraid I was the despair of my parents, who wanted me to grow up to be rich, famous and distinguished. Poor Matilda!"

"Your wife?"

He grinned. "No, my pet white rabbit. It was with Matilda that I used to practice my magic—Matilda and my father's dress hat. She was very patient. I'd had her a long time, and she would hop around after me whenever I came home from school. I was afraid at first that she mightn't like being put in and out of a top hat. But she didn't seem to mind."

"What happened to her?" Kate asked, fascinated.

"I'm happy to say she lived to a ripe age and died peacefully in her sleep."

"That was nice. What a pleasant memory."

"Yes. I had a very happy childhood."

"How unusual! And how unfashionable! Even if it is true, no one today wants to admit it!"

"I know. It's a shame. Childhood is a time for learning and

not all lessons are painless. But it's like having measles and tonsillitis—much better have them as a child. If they come in adulthood, they're far more serious."

"I suppose so. But . . ."

The telephone rang. Kate walked over and picked up the receiver.

"Hello?"

"You called me?"

"Oh, Mark—thanks for calling back. Yes. I feel dumb asking this, but I don't know the name of Paul's company—the outfit he works for. So I can't call them to find out what hotel he's staying in in Chicago. And I need to get hold of him."

"Anything wrong?" The concern in his voice was both real and gratifying.

"Yes. I'm afraid so. Marie's disappeared."

There was a pause.

"Are you there?" Kate asked.

"Yes. I was just thinking. That's not good news. How long has she been gone?"

"Well actually, I'm not sure. She wasn't home yesterday evening when I came home here after dinner in New York and she hasn't shown—or called—since."

Another pause. "Have you called the police?"

"No. Not yet. I suppose I'll have to. But what I wanted to do first was to call Paul and tell him, and then maybe call the police. I know he's at some convention in Chicago, and there's nothing around the house here to tell me what company he's with."

"I don't really know either. I have a daytime number for him, but it's back in my office in the hospital. And I'm not there right now."

"And I guess you don't have it with you?"

"No. 'Fraid not."

"Damn!" Kate said. "Well, I'll have to try something else. Thanks anyway."

"Wait!"

On the point of replacing the receiver, Kate paused. "Yes?"

"Let me ask around. I know the Lamonts, if not better, at least more recently than you. I may be able to come up with the names of friends of theirs who'll undoubtedly know where Paul works. So, leave it until you hear from me. I'll be back in touch soon." Suddenly, in her mind, she could see him quite vividly as he talked into the receiver.

"Well, I thought I might try one or two places myself."

"Let me find the number for you. It would be so much better. All right?"

"Well . . . if you think it really would be better."

His voice warmed perceptibly. "I do."

"Very well." Kate hung up. "He wanted me to leave it until he can track down a number for Paul."

"I see," Jed said. There was a sardonic look on his face.

"I suppose you think I shouldn't have agreed."

"I didn't say a word."

"I know you didn't. But you, too, have a speaking countenance, and it conveyed a paragraph."

As he continued to say nothing, Kate sighed. "You know, you're right. I don't know why I'm so spineless. That's the second time he's had that effect. What's the matter with me?"

"A susceptibility to male approval?"

"If I needed their approval that much you'd think I'd have given in more often and more gracefully. I'd hardly ever get out of the horizontal."

For a second he looked mildly shocked. She burst out laughing. "You'll never get away with playing psychiatrist if you're going to be so easily shocked. It's not cool."

He smiled wryly. "No, it isn't, is it?"

Kate found herself walking restlessly around the room. After a minute she said, "You're right, though. Even with Paul. Even now. I can fight with him up to a point. And then I do what he wants. I've always done it with Graham. I don't with Joel, because I can't take him seriously. He's still to me a little boy."

"These are your admirers?"

197

There was something distinctly old-fashioned about Jed Kramer, Kate thought, still unable to think about him as Dr. Marker. "I don't know whether I'd call them admirers or not. They are certainly the men who are—or who have been—the men in my life."

"You'll always have admirers. You're a good-looking woman, and although you don't seem to be particularly aware of it or perhaps even want it, you send out highly enticing messages to any male in the vicinity."

"If that's the case, then why haven't I married at least two by this time?"

"Because you would not settle for anyone except the man you wanted—or thought you wanted—Paul. Jed took out his half spectacles and started polishing them. Then he put his handkerchief away, placed the spectacles on his nose and looked at her over them. "So I take it you don't want to find out what your brother-in-law's company is. You want to wait until Dr. McGrath calls."

"No," Kate said. "I don't want to wait. And I don't think I should. I'll call the school. If I can't find where Paul is, then . . . then . . ."

"Perhaps we should call the police," Jed said. "Your niece may have been gone since yesterday morning, which would be the required twenty-four hours."

"Yes. But I'll call the school first."

At the end of fifteen minutes Kate had talked to the administrator, the secretary to the principal and the principal of the local high school. The first two would not even look in Marie's file without someone else to confirm Kate's identity. "I'm sorry," the administrator said. "I'm sure you're everything you say you are. And I am aware that Marie's mother is in the hospital. But we got in terrible trouble once through giving out a parent's phone number or address to somebody who said he was a relative—something very legitimate sounding—and the next thing we knew we were in court defending ourselves in a custodial fight for having dispensed vital information

198

without checking on credentials. You'll have to talk to the principal."

So Kate talked to him. "Before we go any further," that gentleman said, "I'd like to know why you haven't been in touch with us over Marie's absence from school? We telephoned, we sent letters. There's been no reply."

Kate absorbed this somehow unsurprising information. "I suppose the answer is that neither Marie's father nor I knew she was cutting school. If you tried to call me here during the day, then you wouldn't get me because I'm at work. Her father is in Chicago. If you called his office, then all I can say is, please give me the number—or even the name of his firm. That's what I'm trying to find so I can locate him and tell him Marie has disappeared."

There was a long silence on the telephone.

"Just a minute," the principal said finally.

Kate, hanging on to the receiver, heard various sounds at the other end. "You'd think I was trying to find out the secret code of the CIA," she said to Jed.

"They have to be careful," he said. "More careful than they used to be, what with the growing number of single parents and custody battles. As far as they know, you could be anybody."

"It seems that our precious Marie has not only disappeared, she's been playing hookey and they've been sending off letters and making phone calls trying to reach Paul. I don't look at the mail downstairs. It's always picked up and neatly stacked in a rubber band by the time I get home. I suppose . . ."

"By Marie, no doubt," Jed said. "After removing any correspondence from the school."

"And I thought her father had put the fear of God into her."

"He undoubtedly has. Enough fear so that she'll cover her tracks whenever possible."

"I don't understand it. I, too, was a rebel, but I never behaved this way," Kate said, and then recalled again the anger and sense of inferiority and resentment with which the Légères and everything that belonged to them filled her. "I suppose," she went on more slowly, "if I didn't behave in Marie's fashion, it was because I was too terrorized and convinced I wouldn't get away with it."

"Yes. We were, as a generation, probably better behaved than the present, at least as far as family discipline went. But I doubt if much of that was innate virtue."

"Miss . . . Miss Malory?" The principal's voice came over the phone.

"Yes, that's right. Kate Malory."

"It's very strange," the principal's voice said. "We don't have a business telephone for Mr. Lamont. Just the home phone. I can't understand how whoever checked the form didn't make a point of getting it."

"I see," Kate said. "Is there the name of a company?"

"No. There isn't. I'm sorry. It's most remiss."

"All right. Thank you," Kate said.

"Just a minute, Miss Malory." The principal's voice sounded severe, almost as though he were reprimanding one of his students. "May I say I find it exceedingly strange that you, Mr. Lamont's sister-in-law, living in his home at the moment, do not know the name of his company or where he works?"

"I'm sure you do, Mr. . . . er . . ."

"Grayson."

"Mr. Grayson. And while it is indeed strange, I don't think it is any stranger than the fact that you also don't have a business telephone for him, nor a business address. Thank you. Good bye." And she hung up.

She sat staring at the phone. "Paul was probably in a tearing hurry and a terrible temper when he put Marie in the local school. I suppose I could call Marie's former school. I wonder if they, too, are having custody nerves."

They were. She had to work her way up to the headmistress, who listened to Kate's story in silence. To Kate herself, her own words were sounding steadily less believable. "I'm sorry if this sounds crazy," she finally finished. My God, she thought,

I act as though I expected to be rejected. She was therefore considerably astonished when the headmistress's cool voice said. "Yes, I think we have a business address for Mr. Lamont. Just a minute." There was a silence. Then, "Importing Services Limited, Rockefeller Plaza. Of course," she went on, "the date this information was taken was five years ago. I don't know whether it's up-to-date."

"Thank you," Kate said. "Thank you very much."

"Miss Malory . . ."

Kate was on the point of hanging up. "Yes?"

"Despite the fact that we had to expel her—for her good as much as ours, she couldn't go on as she was—I am very fond of Marie. Have you no idea where she is?"

"None, Miss . . . Miss MacNair." Kate remembered the headmistress's name just in time. "Would you have any suggestions?"

"No. Most of the parents of her friends here would have let you know if she's staying with them. But I will say one thing, even though it's no longer my business and I am to some extent breaching the confidence of our school counselor, I think that Marie has been for too long in an impossible position between her parents. Few girls of that age could retain any balance in her situation. The sooner it is resolved—one way or another—the better for her. Please give her my love." And the headmistress hung up.

"Well!" Kate said. "It may not have been her business, but she didn't hesitate to give me her opinion." She told Jed about the conversation.

"I think she's right," Jed said. "That could explain some . . . some of the feeling I picked up in her room."

"Paul said he'd hung onto the marriage for the sake of maintaining the home for the children, but had about decided that it would be better to get custody and take the children away. I suppose he's right."

Jed, who had opened the closet door and was staring up at the ceiling said, "Is this the trapdoor you told me about?"

"Yes. I'm going to call Information and ask the telephone number of that company Miss MacNair gave me."

Five minutes later Information had told her that there was no such company listed in the Manhattan Directory. After another two minutes of thought Kate called Information again. Shortly after that she had confirmed from the central office at Rockefeller Plaza that there was no such company anywhere in that vast complex of buildings. "Jed," she said finally. "What do you think all this means?"

"It could mean that the person who took the information down at the old school got it wrong. Or the company has moved out of New York altogether—quite a few have . . ."

"But Paul has distinctly talked about his corporation head office or whatever *in* New York." She looked up at Jed. "I agree it could mean that the person at the school could have been wrong. But what on earth reason could Paul have for giving a phony name to whatever company he's with?"

"Unless he doesn't work for it. Didn't you say that the information was five years old? He could have left there. The company could have moved away or folded, and he could be working for someone else."

"I suppose."

"Or perhaps he did work for one of the multinational giants and doesn't any longer, but also doesn't want it to be known. Maybe he got fired, which could account for his not leaving anything in his desk that could reveal the name of the corporation. If somebody called up and asked for him, then they'd be told that he is no longer with the firm. By the way, when you called him in Tokyo, who picked up the phone?"

"He did. When I think about it now, I realize that anybody important enough to be traveling around the world for a company would probably have somebody answer his phone. But I was too taken up with talking to him at all."

"What sort of man is Paul?" Jed asked finally.

Kate found herself thrown by the question. She stared at Jed blankly. All the hours and weeks and years of thinking about Paul had been, she saw suddenly, focused on Paul's relationship to women—notably herself, but also Deborah and, in descending hierarchy, his various other girl friends. . . .

"I mean," Jed went on patiently, "is he a man of principle? Does he have integrity? Would he be a valuable employee in any capacity? Can you take his word for something? And what kind of work did he do? Administration? Managerial? Public relations? Was he an engineer? A chemist? Lawyer?"

Kate felt curiously stunned. She didn't have any idea how even to begin to answer the questions. Paul was handsome, a football player, attractive to women. . . . What was it her father had said once? It was a passing comment, something said at dinner shortly after he and Diane were married. They were in the big, beautiful dining room with its long windows looking out on the live oak tree. Kate couldn't remember what had gone before, but she could see and hear, as clear as though it had been the previous week, her father, busy delicately deboning his trout, say idly, "Paul Lamont reminds me of myself when I was a boy. . . ."

"He was very like my father, my adoptive father," she said slowly. "Handsome, clever, appealing to women. He was good at athletics in general, football in particular. He got a job with the Légère shipping company right after he and Deborah were married. I suppose in some junior executive capacity. I am almost certain he wasn't in any kind of profession such as law or engineering or chemistry or whatever. . . . Isn't it *strange* that . . ."

At that moment the telephone rang. Kate picked up the receiver. "Hello?"

"Kate. This is Mark. I'm at the office. Somehow or other I seem to have mislaid the book where I keep the business numbers of my patients and their families. I'm sure it will turn up . . ."

". . . with the relevant page torn out," Kate said, sighing.

"What?"

"Nothing. Despite your insistence, I did some calling around

203

and have succeeded in finding out zero about Paul's business—even what it is. The high school had no listing. The company listed at Marie's old school has gone out of business or he doesn't work for it any longer. So we have no name, no address, no telephone number. I can't believe it. It's like something out of a spy novel. Anyone would think he belonged to a super secret agency."

"Perhaps he does," Mark said. "And if he does there's nothing you can do about it. The more immediate thing is Marie."

"I realize that," Kate said, beginning to feel irritated. "But I like less and less the feeling that I have the responsibility without any authority. When I tried to find out Paul's business number from the high school I discovered that without going over there with a sheaf of identification papers and letters from the family, they're not going to accept my word as to why I'm here. Apparently they've been stung in the past by giving out information that has landed them in the middle of a custody battle. But in the meantime I have to do what I can to set the wheels in motion to locate Marie. I don't suppose you have that Tokyo phone number you gave me to call."

"I don't—just a minute." A short time later he was back. "No, sorry. I destroyed it when I knew he had returned."

"All right. Then I'll call the police."

"There's no use calling them until Marie's been gone for twenty-four hours."

"She may have, for all I know. I didn't see her yesterday morning and she certainly was not there at all last night."

"Leave it for just a few hours, Kate. Once you call the police in on something like this, you're never going to get rid of them. And sooner or later that kind of thing leaks to the press."

"I'm not a figure in public life," Kate said. "Who'd care?"

"You may not be, but the Lamonts are pretty prominent around here. If you made public your reason for wanting to find Paul—that his wife had been committed for abuse of drugs and that his daughter had run away—it could make things unpleasant and embarrassing for all of them when this is over."

There was so much truth in what he said that Kate was pulled up short. She had worked with journalists and the police on one of the books she'd edited and she had learned that once either one entered any situation, any faint hope of privacy is gone. "You may be right," she said slowly.

"Give it a while."

"And Marie? A missing fifteen-year-old?"

"She might be visiting a friend. Probably is, if she resents your being there."

"I would think the friend's parent would call here and let us know."

"You'd be surprised at the number of parents who wouldn't do that because they'd know their children would consider it an invasion of privacy. Kids are far more independent now, you know."

"Yes. I do know." She hesitated. "All right. You may have a point. I'll give it another few hours anyway." She hung up and stared at the phone and then at Jed. "Was I being brainwashed again?"

"What reason did he give for your not calling the police."

"That if I did the cat would be out of the bag about Deborah's incarceration in a mental institution and about Marie's running away. That once the police knew, then everybody sooner or later would know."

Jed was staring out the window, his hands in his pockets. "To a degree he's right. If the police are going to find somebody, they're going to have to make inquiries, and the moment you do that, then you have to let people know what you're looking to find out."

"Mark seemed to think that Paul might be engaged in something hush hush . . . some sort of intelligence work."

"That occurred to me, too.

"I can just see myself trying to track him down. 'Is this the CIA? The FBI? Forgive my calling, but I am looking for one of your undercover agents, Paul Lamont. Would you have his number?' "

Jed smiled. He had white, healthy-looking, slightly crooked teeth. It suddenly occurred to Kate that most of her friend's teeth were straightened, scraped and capped to a blinding uniformity. Most Europeans' teeth, when not false or atrocious, had the same individual look. "Where your parents foreign?" she asked him.

"Yes. My father was English, my mother Dutch. Why?"

"Your teeth. There was an English actress once. She had slightly overlapping front teeth, which was charming. When she got over here the first thing Hollywood did was put on straight caps. She's never looked as good since."

"I know. Several dentists wanted to straighten my teeth when I was a boy, but my mother wouldn't let them."

"Good for her," Kate said absently. "I still haven't answered your question about Paul, have I?"

"It doesn't matter."

"I have a feeling it does. But to go back to McGrath for a minute. Do you think there's more to McGrath's not wanting the police in than a desire to preserve the Lamonts' privacy?"

"I don't know."

Kate's old suspicions of McGrath, somewhat lulled of late, rose up again. "There's something not quite right about that," she said. "He's attractive, but . . ."

Jed was looking at her quizzically. "But what?"

"I'm not sure. Deborah, who's in his hospital, is acting strange. I mean, even given her problems, she's acting erratically. McGrath himself admits that. Paul seems to give him only guarded trust, and McGrath never really comes out and says what kind of treatment Deborah is getting there. All he says is she's not responding. Yet whenever I'm with him I seem to do what he wants."

"That's a remarkable gift to have," Jed said drily. "As long as it's not abused."

"Do you think it is?" she asked quickly. "Being abused?"

"I would have no way of knowing. But . . ."

"But what?"

"Be careful. Now . . . let's see what's in the attic."

"I forgot to tell you. The night after I first talked to you about it—last night in fact—I came back in here and pulled—or tried to pull—the trapdoor down again. It wouldn't budge. Somebody must have locked it."

Jed stared at her. "I didn't notice any lock in the ceiling, or any bolt. Did you?"

Kate shook her head. "No. But how dumb can I be? I simply pulled on the handle with the pole hook. I didn't even think to check and see where a lock might be. Let's go look."

A minute later they were both staring up at the trapdoor. Jed looked around, found the pole, raised the hook and pulled hard on the door handle. It opened with a jolt and the aluminum ladder fell down.

"Well!" Jed said.

"I swear to you," Kate said.

"It's all right," Jed turned and smiled at her.

"It was *locked*. I pulled *hard*." She paused. "Perhaps it was just stuck," she added uncertainly. "Doors sometimes do stick."

"Yes. They do. But I would be surprised if this one did. While I was standing here before I noticed that it is not that closely fitted. In fact a thin stream of rather cool air was coming from the attic through the cracks. It's probably not heated up there. Most attics don't have heat."

"That's all very well for you, from sunny California. But by New York standards this is spring weather—that's to say, not cold. The thermostat in this house is rather low anyway, and at this time of year little heat is needed in the middle of the day."

"In that case, let's see why it's cool."

Jed pulled the ladder all the way down. The same rectangle that had confronted Kate before seemed to stare at her now, although in daylight, of course, it was no longer black. "I can feel it," she said. "You're right. It *is* cool."

207

As Jed stepped up into the attic, Kate mounted the ladder behind him.

"I can see why," Jed said. "The window over there is open." He pointed towards a dormer that faced them. It was one of several dormers placed at regular intervals in the huge attic that seemed to stretch over most of the top of the house. Even with the window open the low room was somehow stuffy as well as dusty. And because the shades had been pulled down over the other five, there was a dim twilight atmosphere.

"Here," Jed said, and reached for the chain of a light that hung from a rafter. "Let's switch this on." Then he went over to the window and stared at the frame and then peered out.

Kate looked around, fascinated. The attic seemed to cover the entire top of the house, except for one corner where, partly hidden by a large screen, there appeared to be a room. Going behind the screen, Kate saw it was indeed a small room, with wooden, partitioned walls and a door. She tried turning the knob, but the door refused to budge. It was obviously locked.

"I wonder what's in here," she said.

"Where?" Jed's voice came from the other side of the room.

"Here. There's a room behind the screen. But the door's locked."

"Probably records and files. I find this window more interesting."

Kate wandered back to the main body of the room and looked around. Treasures from the Légère past seemed to be strewn higgledy-piggledy everywhere. Needlepoint chairs that Kate had forgotten about were piled in twos in one corner, their wood covered in dust, their seats, those that were visible, faded and dirty. Nearer were plainer, wooden chairs, the kind that are found in kitchens. An old-fashioned shaving mirror that had been used by her father was on the floor. Nearby were a Sheraton sewing table, its inlaid top buckled, and a drop leaf table of intricate ornateness, heavy, ugly, yet in some way elegant. There were chests, bureaus, trunks, screens, one

208

with mottoes in French. Where had that been in the Légère home? In her own bedroom, Kate remembered with a shock. And around everywhere were cartons upon cartons tied with rope, with sheets and screws of newspapers lying around on the floor as though they had been used for packing. She walked over and picked up what looked like curtains spilling from an open chest. Dust poured out. She coughed and withdrew.

"Phew! I wonder why Deborah didn't put these away properly. They used to hang in the living room on Prytania Street. I remember how magnificent they were!" She rubbed a piece of material between her fingers and then made a face. "Once!" Now that she was looking she saw other chests, either open, or, if closed, plainly packed with carelessness, material caught in the openings.

"If your sister has been having emotional problems, complicated by drugs, then she probably started to get careless. Apart from her erratic behavior, was she changed?"

"Yes. Terribly. For one thing she's huge. At first—when I got there—she seemed vague, almost spacey, as the young would say. Then, for a short while, she seemed sane—sane enough to be aware that something was happening to her mind. It was sad and frightening. But she got onto the subject of my stealing Paul—which is ludicrous—and after that appeared to go mad. It was unnerving. A nurse rushed in and accused me of upsetting her."

"Yes. That happens sometimes with people who've been drug addicted. Does she ever have any visitors?"

"Paul, Marie, Ranger."

"Friends?"

"He says no, which I think is odd."

"Not really. If she was an addict for the past several years she would first stop going out and then stop trying to keep in touch with them. After a while, her friends would give up."

"I suppose." Kate turned around and looked at the attic.

"Now that I'm here I'm bound to say it doesn't seem very mysterious. I don't know what I expected to see."

"It may not be mysterious, but there are one or two interesting things I noticed. Such as," Jed said, turning towards the window, "that that particular window is not too difficult to reach from the roof, certainly not for someone who is reasonably agile. Also, it was open. In view of the fact that the trapdoor was locked once you tried it, but had not been the night before and was not this time, it would seem to argue that it was locked from this side. To which I would direct your attention to the bolts on the floor there."

Kate looked down. Sure enough. Bolts, drawn back, were at one end of the rectangular opening. Undoubtedly the fixtures they would slip into if locked were on the door itself, now hanging invisible behind the ladder. "So," Kate said. "Somebody's been up here. What a lovely thought! So reassuring. As far as I can remember the trapdoor doesn't lock from the other side, so X can come down into the house at will, while we can't lock the trapdoor from our side." She sighed. "Are you sure, Jed?"

"Reasonably. Look at the floor. If you stand where the light falls properly, you can see square shapes in the dust that must have held boxes of some kind. Also, I think, although it's blurred, a footprint. Of course it may not—probably doesn't—mean anything except that Deborah or a maid has been cleaning the attic. But from what you tell me, your sister has not recently been in a condition to be gripped by housecleaning fervor."

Kate moved to where she could see the mark where the boxes had been. "Yes, I see what you're talking about. Who . . . what do you think it all means?"

"It could mean anything—or nothing at all."

Kate said slowly, "If it weren't for those noises in the middle of the night, I could easily be persuaded that all this adds up to imperfect housecleaning."

"But . . . ?"

210

"But there's something very unordinary about housecleaning in the middle of the night."

Far below, there came the sound of Bones barking. Then, faintly, the ring of the doorbell.

"I expect that will be the doctor," Jed said.

"McGrath?"

The bell sounded a second time and Bones's barking started up again.

"You'd better answer it," Jed said.

"What's makes you so sure it's Mark McGrath?"

"I just am."

Kate walked across the attic and looked out the front window. "You're right," she said. "That's his car. I wonder what he wants."

"The best way to find out is to go and see."

Kate had a strange feeling that Jed was disappointed or perhaps upset. "Are you angry about anything?" she said, struggling to open the window.

"No." Jed looked at her. "I suppose . . ."

The bell rang a third time. Kate finally got the window open. "Mark?" she called out. The jutting roof beneath prevented her from seeing him, if, she thought, it was indeed the doctor. Then she saw him as he backed away from the front door and looked up. "Hi," Kate said. "I'm in the attic. I'll be right down." She closed the window and looked over at Jed, who was still staring at the floor. "You were right," she said.

"Ummm," he said. And then, as she started down the stairs, followed her.

When she got to the bottom she opened the front door. "Come in."

McGrath looked, this morning, Kate thought, more like the man who had come to her apartment, confident and magnetic, almost arrogant, rather than the tired psychiatrist who had driven her home. Once in the living room he saw Kramer. "Sorry," he said lightly, "I didn't know you had company."

"Dr. Marker, Dr. McGrath," Kate said, introducing the two men, and noted that she had, without thinking, used Jed's real name.

The doctors shook hands. Then McGrath turned to Kate. "I can't stay. I was passing and I just stopped by to see if you'd had any news of Marie?"

"None. Have you come up with any names of friends of the family, or of Marie's, I could call?"

McGrath hesitated. "I'm afraid I've drawn a blank there, I even thought of asking Deborah, but when I went to see her she seemed in one of her more agitated moods, and I didn't want to add to it. I suppose there are others I could ask, but of course that would spread all the unpleasant publicity as quickly as if the police were drawn in." He moved towards the door. "If you can just hold off for another few hours. . . . What about Ranger, by the way?"

"He asserted very flatly that he didn't know where Marie was."

"No, but he might well know some of the names of her buddies, male or female." He hesitated again. "Call the cops by all means if you think it's a good idea. I suppose I am thinking most of Deborah, and what she will have to go through when she comes out of this. The more people know the circumstances of her family, the tougher she may find it." He started to move towards the door. "Nice to meet you, doctor. You practice in New York?"

"No, California," Jed said.

Kate, turning, saw Kramer's almost tawny eyes fixed on McGrath. He didn't look at all like a cheerful monkey at this point. More like a . . . a . . . but the analogy wouldn't come. She glanced up at Mark's face and was again reminded of that moment in her apartment. There was the same frozen look of . . . shock? fright? Whatever confidence and magnetism had been there when he came into the house had vanished, at least for the moment. "Let me know if you hear anything," he said rather hurriedly, nodded to them both and let himself out the front door.

"Did you notice," she said, turning to Jed, "how sort of strange he looked just now?"

"Yes. I did."

"I've never seen a man who could radiate so much sort of psychic energy—" she glanced at Jed and made a wry face, "you should excuse the expression—one minute and look absolutely hollow the next."

"I don't think he was happy when I said I was from California," Jed said.

"Why on earth not?"

"I don't know. But I'm pretty sure I've seen him at some point, or at least a picture of him, and the sensation that association evokes in me is not a happy one."

"But you can't remember?"

"No, the whole time he was here, I was wracking my brains to try and trace him in my memory. But it was no use."

Kate's old suspicions of the psychiatrist were well activated by now. "Can't you remember at all? I have a feeling it's tremendously important."

Jed shook his head. "No. Sorry."

"Well what's the good of being able to read people's minds and vibrations and knowing how they are from touching their possessions if you are just like everybody else in not being able to remember something crucial?"

"No good at all," Jed said. "I agree, it's deplorable. But I never claimed to be anything but an ordinary human being."

"Yes you did," Kate said. She felt her temper give under a variety of pressures, including her suspicions of McGrath, her concern for Marie, her frustration at not being able to find Paul and, within herself, a maelstrom of stormy and upsetting confusions. "Anybody who writes books about other levels of consciousness and time not being continuous but something else and reincarnation is claiming to be something more than human, but when you could really be a help in an ordinary way, you suddenly can't remember something." She had meant the words to sound half-joking and was herself astonished at how belligerent they came out.

There was a silence that seemed to go on and on. Then Jed said, "That's really the root of the problem, isn't it? Someone comes along and for reasons within yourself you endow him with a whole package of personality and abilities he doesn't have. And then when you discover that, you get angry." He paused, and there was more silence as they looked at each other. "I'm sorry your handsome psychiatrist cannot be put above suspicion. But you yourself thought there was something fishy about him."

Jed went over and started winding his long scarf round and round his neck. "I'll be going now," he said, and went towards the door.

Kate, furious at him and at herself, watched in stoney silence. Just as he was about to go through the door she said, "Any more words of wisdom?"

"Yes." He paused and looked back. "Call the police." Then he closed the door.

Kate stood in the middle of the living room, hearing his rapid steps retreat down the concrete path and feeling curiously abandoned. She glanced at her watch. A quarter to three. What time did Ranger come home?

Slowly she made her way upstairs and into the master bedroom. Jed had tidily closed up the aluminum steps in the big closet and shut the trapdoor. For a while she stood there staring at it, her mind not so much on the trapdoor as on her display of bad temper a few minutes before. What on earth had got into her? Jed had been nothing but helpful. He had given her what was in his power to bestow. And she was like a spoiled child putting on a tantrum because, having received a doll, she didn't also get a doll's house. Except . . . except that wasn't the reason. Somewhere she'd read—was it in one of his books?—that most anger is fear of loss. What was she afraid of losing? The answer was there, not far from the surface of her mind. Even so, it eluded her. . . .

After a minute or two she became aware of the total silence of the house. How unlike an apartment in the city it was. There was really no such thing as silence or solitude in the city—loneliness, yes, but not aloneness. At any time of the day or night, even if there were not voices, there were other sounds: elevators going up and down, police, fire or ambulance sirens, the belowground rumbling of the subways, the cars, the car horns, feet in hallways, along sidewalks. Here there was silence. . . . She shivered.

To be in the house with only Ranger for safety, and with the knowledge that someone could come in from the roof and walk at will down into the rest of the house was a thought she decided she could not live with in peace. Getting a chair from the bedroom, she dragged it into the closet and stood on it. Then she put her hands up and felt the trapdoor. Although painted the same color as the walls—a curious dull purple—the door itself was wood. She could screw a bolt into this side of the door all right. But how would she affix the latch into the ceiling itself. With a toggle bolt, of course. Kate had not spent sixteen years living on her own in New York without becoming handy at small bits of carpentry and mechanics that in previous eras had had to wait for the male touch. All she had to find out now was whether Paul had such an electric tool in his possession. If he didn't—well she'd contrive some-. thing else. But she was not going to leave that trapdoor open for anyone to use. Where did people usually keep their tools? In the cellar, of course.

She was approaching the cellar steps when she heard the front door open. Going back into the hall, she saw Ranger making for the kitchen.

"Hi," she said.

He stopped. For a moment—she would swear it—he showed panic on his face.

"Why does that scare you?" she asked quickly. "Why are you frightened that I should be here?"

"I'm not, for Chrissake," Ranger said, and started to move towards the swing door.

"Ranger, as I'm sure you know, Marie didn't come home last night. Do you know where she is?"

"How should I know?"

"I didn't say that you should. And please try not to be so defensive. I don't know why you should be so angry. To my knowledge I haven't done anything to cause it. I'm still the same person who brought Bones in from the doghouse. If you're mad at me, at least tell me why." She paused, in the hope that Ranger would reply in some way. But he stood silent. "Marie hasn't come home today, either. I've been here every minute. I'm not trying to intrude into your life—more than I have to, that is, considering the circumstances, but you're old enough to know that for a fifteen-year-old girl to disappear today is not a good thing. She could get into all kinds of messes. Do you have any idea where she is?"

Ranger was staring down at his sneakers. "I don't know where she is," he said sulkily. "Why ask me?"

"Who else is there to ask? I can't find your father. Do you know what his company is named, or what his telephone number is?"

Ranger simply shook his head. That a self-absorbed twelve-year-old should not know by heart the title of his father's corporation was not remarkable. But it seemed to her that a more typical reaction would be to make a stab at it. Simply to shake his head seemed to her to betoken something else.

"Do you have any idea what kind of business he's in?"

This time he shrugged. "Import-export, I guess."

That seemed accurate enough. There was a loud whine from behind the kitchen door. "All right," Kate said, correctly interpreting Ranger's glance, "you can take him out for a walk."

Ranger had lunged towards the door when Kate suddenly thought of something.

"Ranger, just a minute," she said. "I take it Marie has often stayed out in the past when you had a housekeeper. Is that right?"

"Yeah."

"Would you know the names of some of her friends? She might be with one of them and I'd like to check."

He paused, hand on door, long enough to appear to be thinking over her question. Then he said. "There's Tippy Lawrence. She was in the same class at St. Hilary's."

"How about her boyfriend? What's his name?"

"Andy. Andy Brigham. He's at St. Matthew's." He started to push open the door.

"Aren't you worried about her at all, Ranger?"

"What's to be worried about?" He was through the door now and audibly greeting Bones, who seemed to be rising to new heights of hysterical delight.

Kate sighed. Jed's strong push for her to call the police was sitting in the back of her mind. What am I waiting for, she wondered? Why don't I go ahead and do what he says? Because of what Mark said: the moment the police came in the whole thing would cease to be a private matter? Why did she care? Because it would make things harder for Deborah? Wasn't it more important to find out where Marie was and get her back? Of course it was. Still, she sat there, her eyes on the telephone extension in the little hall. With part of her mind Kate heard the back door slam. Though the window she could see Ranger tearing across the lot, leash in hand, following the horizontal line of Bones's nose, ears and tail, as he galloped, flat out, up the street. A pang smote her. She had become fond of both Ranger and Bones. Together, they seemed to make up one of the great twosomes of nature: a boy and his dog. What was it she feared, that they might be coming to the end of their pastoral togetherness? That unless something was done. . . . What? The threat was amorphous, yet none the less real. Suddenly, as though he were standing beside her, she remembered Jed's sense of urgency.

Deliberately she turned and went to the phone, putting her hand on the receiver. She was about to lift it and dial 0 for the operator to get her the police when a small scribble on the white wall seemed to pull her attention. It was upside-down writing. What did it say? Kate twisted her head. "Andy 682-5097." What was it Ranger had just said? Marie's boyfriend was named Andy—Andy Brigham.

On an impulse, Kate dialed the number. It rang three times, then a woman's voice said, "Hello?"

"Is this Andy Brigham's home?"

"It is."

"Is Andy there?"

"Who's calling?"

"My name is Kate Malory. I'm Mrs. Lamont's sister and I am staying here with the family while my sister is . . . while Paul and Deborah are away. I was wondering if . . ."

That was as far as she got before the storm broke over her head.

Chapter 9

T he infuriated woman at the other end of the telephone turned out to be Mrs. Brigham, Andy's mother, a highly articulate woman who considered Marie a dangerous combination of Carmen, Delilah and a Symbionese Liberationist. "No matter what anyone says, I *know* Andy did not smoke pot or stay out half the night until he got mixed up with that wild niece of yours . . ."

"Now wait a minute . . ."

"And if he did have a glass of wine or beer at home, that's *all*. It's only been since he took up with that female libertine you call a teen-ager . . ."

"I take it your son is neither feebleminded nor a dwarf," Kate snapped back. "In which case whatever he did, he chose to do, and I'd a lot rather have a niece like Marie, who at least takes responsibility for what she does, than some overprotected mother-coddled wet noodle who spends his whole time blaming others. . . ."

The phone slammed down.

Kate stood there holding the receiver. It was a little late, she thought bitterly, to remember that she needed all the help she could get, including that of Andy and his sulphurous mother. But she felt cheered and invigorated by discovering how profound was her instinct to come to Marie's defense. However, after that delay, there was now no question, she had to call the police.

She tried to remember everything she'd ever heard or read about reporting someone missing. For some reason what she did remember was not encouraging: a depressing looking precinct, endless forms to fill out and the demand for a photograph. Where was the photograph? She could not recall seeing one, not even in the master bedroom where most couples usually covered at least part of one wall with pictures of their offspring. Marie had only her burning monk. The pictures in Ranger's room were all of humankind's near relatives—not of any human. And there were none in the guest room. In fact, Kate wouldn't know where to look. . . . Of course, she thought, the photograph album in the desk in the main bedroom.

Aware that she was still postponing calling the police, Kate went upstairs. The album was exactly where she remembered it to be, in one of the two top long drawers of the desk. Taking it out, she sat on the chair, turning the pages to find a photograph of Marie that would serve for identification. Most of the pictures were snapshots of the family, two and three at a time, obviously taken by the missing member. Several were of Marie and Ranger, together and separately, but all very young. Paul, who photographed extremely well, seemed unchanged throughout. He aged little, and what ageing there was, was beneficial. Like many good-looking men he was even more attractive in middle life than he had been as a youth. His big frame and strong features improved as he got older. The children, even as babies, were immediately identifiable as themselves. The jolt to Kate's system was Deborah. With the recent memory of the heavy, half-demented woman in the psychiatric hospital in the forefront of her mind, Kate had forgotten the Deborah who had been such a torment to her youth; the fair, slender dryad who smiled and effortlessly took away what Kate herself most wanted. But in several of the early snapshots that young Deborah was there, her magic intact, the azure eyes under heavy lids staring dreamily into the camera. Then there was a shot taken in Rome, with Deborah seated beside one of that ancient city's noted fountains—the one of Neptune and the dolphins in the Piazza de la Republica. It was a color shot, and Deborah's spun gold hair showed up clearly.

Kate went on looking and turning the pages. It proved to be a telescoped chronology of the intervening years, with the passage of time indicated by the stair-step jumps in growth of the two children and the deterioration of their mother. It was not, at first, apparent. Then the waist was thicker, the hair seemed ungroomed, dull. In the last snapshot, Deborah was wearing tent dresses. Some of the pages of the album were dated, although towards the end there were no dates. However, it was possible to calculate, mostly from the sizes of the children, that the downhill slide had begun three to four years previously.

Kate held the book and stared ahead for a while, filled with a curious ache, which she could not identify. It was almost a sense of loss. But what had she lost? It took a while before it came to her that what she had lost was her envy. And until that moment she had never realized how much envy had fueled her forward drive. Would she now, if she could go back, change places with Deborah? The "no" that came was so instantaneous that it shocked her. So what did that make of her lifelong obsessions?

I can't stop and figure that out now, Kate thought. She had come up here to find a photograph of Marie. None was really good. There was no single head shot that could serve as unmistakable identification. She flipped back the pages and started to reexamine all the photos that revealed Marie during the past two years. Curious, she thought. She hadn't noticed it before, because it was less obvious than the deterioration of

Marie's mother. Yet, in a less noticeable way—less noticeable because of the obvious tendency to attribute any change in a child to natural growth and development—Marie, too, had altered. She had not only grown obviously taller and more mature. Her whole expression had changed. And it had started to occur about the time that her mother's deterioration was becoming apparent. Flipping back and forth in the album, Kate chose two photos to contrast with one another. One revealed Deborah, Marie and Ranger standing together in the back yard. Deborah had not yet graduated to tent dresses. Her hair, while no longer the deceptively casual fall of silk that indicated meticulous grooming, looked moderately clean and brushed. Nevertheless, the radiant girl had long gone. In her place was a middle-aged woman, who was losing the battle against time and calories. But the real difference lay in Marie. Looking up at her mother, her face had an openness, a fresh expectancy, that was hard to associate with the Marie Kate had met. What had caused the change? Was it just adolescence? When was this photograph taken? It was easier to see that Ranger was about nine than to be sure of Marie's actual age. But there was a three year difference, so that would make her about twelve. She still had her stork legs, plainly visible under her shorts. Her breasts were two almost invisible mosquito bites under her T-shirt. Her hair was in ponytails, one over each ear. She looked healthy, normal and well-adjusted. Or did she? Kate leaned forward. Then, her memory stirring, she remembered a magnifying glass in one of the cubby holes in the top part of the desk. Sitting back, she lowered the drop leaf and looked around. There it was. She took it and looked through it at Marie's face in the picture. Under magnification, the face showed anxiety as well as normality. Perhaps that was why she was looking at her mother. Kate moved the glass to Deborah's face. The mouth smiled, but the eyes looked blank. What was the current word? Spacey.

Kate put down the glass and moved on again. She found a picture taken about two years later. The metamorphosis in

Marie was almost complete. And it wasn't just the frizzy hair and thrift shop outfit. The young face was hard, the mouth clamped together and defiant. It was a picture of Marie alone. Kate wondered who had taken it, and whether it could be used for identification. The answer to the second question was definitely no. It was too small, the glare was too bright, and anyway, she was only about fourteen. Without thinking, Kate moved the glass closer. What was that she was holding in her hand? Well, Kate thought, as I live and breathe! Her own experience with marijuana had been confined to one experimental occasion and it had made her feel queasy, so she had not repeated it. But that little squashed together object looked very much like a joint. Kate moved the glass up to Marie's face again. The mouth was clamped together all right in a defiant grin. No wonder. Obviously Marie's belated but holy war with the establishment had started.

Kate riffled through the album once more. There was no head shot of Marie either stuck on the page or loose. Well, the police would have to go to one of the two schools Marie had attended for a yearbook photo. She closed the top of the desk, opened the drawer beneath and replaced the album. So much for that, she thought to herself, and went downstairs to the hall telephone.

She had put her hand out to call the police when the telephone rang. "Hello?" she said.

"Is somebody named Malory there?" A young male voice asked.

"This is Kate Malory. Who's this?"

"Andy. Andy Brigham. I heard you called me."

"I did. Did your mother tell you?"

"Well, sort of. My sister heard her and told me. Then I asked Mom, but she said she was so mad she didn't wait to find out what you wanted. She doesn't like Marie."

"So I gathered. Andy, Marie hasn't been seen around here for at least twenty-four hours—maybe more. I got up yesterday morning after she'd gone, and she didn't come home last night.

I'm worried about her and was just going to call the police when you called."

"Yeah, well . . ." His voice trailed off.

"Do you know where she is?"

"No. She wouldn't tell me where she was going. She said somebody'd be asking me."

"So she did run away."

"Yeah."

Andy's laconic, noncommunicative attitude was beginning to get on her nerves when it occurred to her that if he wanted as little connection with Marie's flight as he seemed to, he would never have telephoned her.

"Andy, why are you calling me?"

Silence. Then, "Is she okay? I mean, nothing's happened to her, has it?"

"How would I know? All I know is, she's gone. That's what I want to find out from you. Why did she run away? I'm going to have to call the police, but maybe if I knew the reason it would help."

More silence. "Look," Andy said. "Don't call the cops. If they find her, she could be in real trouble."

"You're going to have to tell me more than that, Andy, to keep me from trying to discover where she is and in what shape and why she's run away. I'm *responsible* for her. That's why I'm here."

Andy's voice suddenly became urgent. "Mom's coming in the front door. I'll call you back." And he hung up.

Kate stood there staring down at the phone, understanding, for the first time in her life, how people felt when they beat their heads against a wall. Frustrated. According to Andy, if she called the police, Marie might be in real trouble . . . whatever that meant. If Kate did not call the police, then not only might Marie be in trouble, but Kate herself would be doing nothing to get her out. And Paul was not available. McGrath. . . . Kate stared at the wall behind the phone. Whatever her doubts—and Jed's—Kate remembered the psychiatrist saying he would go on trying to find a number where Paul could be reached. Kate dialed the hospital's number, and asked for Dr. McGrath.

"I'm sorry, Dr. McGrath is not here."

"Is there anywhere you could reach him?"

"No. I'm afraid he's out of town today."

"Well if he is, it's pretty recent. I saw him not two hours ago."

"He was called out suddenly," the voice said rather smugly.

"Can you get in touch with him wherever he is out of town?"

"No, I'm sorry. We can't."

Why, Kate wondered, did doctors' offices, secretaries and answering services sound so triumphant when informing some anxious inquirer that their medicine men were irretrievably, irrevocably out of reach. There out to be some final cosmic court, she decided, which would condemn all doctors to a short or long term of calling numbers only to find out that whoever they're calling is not there, has just left, cannot be reached, is out of touch, and will not be back in touch for several turns of the eternal wheel. And only when the ex-doctor finally achieves contact will he (they would all be men, Kate decided) be allowed into the heavenly kingdom where he would be permitted to take out eternal appendices, which would grow eternally back. . . .

"Thank you," she said, and hung up.

She was still standing in the little downstairs hall, staring at the telephone when the doorbell sounded. She crossed the living room and was about to open the door when her New York City caution prodded her. "Who is it?" she called out.

"Andy. Andy Brigham."

She opened the door. A tall, lanky boy with curly, brown hair and brown eyes was facing her. "All right, Andy, come in. Now," she said when she had closed the door and they were both inside. "What did you mean that if I called the police Marie would be in big trouble? I can't *not* call the police if she's missing an hour longer, you must know that."

"Marie was scared. That's why she ran away. She . . . she didn't tell me much, but she said she found something that . . . like . . ." He fumbled and stopped.

"Yes?" Kate said kindly. She knew he was having a hard time, and her heart softened towards him.

"Look, you're gonna think I'm crazy. But she thought . . . Mom came in when she was calling and I had to get off the phone. You know how Mom is about her. Anyway . . . she'd discovered something about her mother getting drugs at the hospital. That's why she ran away. She said she'd found something that'd prove it." He stared at her face. "Honest, it's true!"

It was queer, Kate thought. She should have been shocked, surprised. But she wasn't. On some unconscious level she must have suspected it. If Deborah was being fed drugs, the most logical explanation was that the hospital was supplying them. It would explain so much: Deborah's wild behavior, McGrath's exaggerated reaction to Kate's mild (and ironic) suggestion that he was a specialist in drugs, meaning, of course, drug abuse treatment, and his insistence that she not call the police. But if that were the case, why all the phony worry about Deborah and talk about her erratic behavior and lack of response and insistence that Kate be at the house for the children? . . .

"It doesn't add up," Kate said aloud.

"I'm only saying what she said to me."

"No, Andy, I'm not disputing it. I just meant . . . why did Marie take off then? Why didn't she tell the police, or me, or, if she knew where to reach him, her father?"

"I dunno . . . I told you, Mom came in then. But she did say that if some people knew she'd found out about the pills—and I don't think she meant the cops—they'd be out to get her. That's why she ran away."

"But you have no idea where she ran to?"

"No. If she could've talked a little longer, she'd have told me. But Mom . . ."

"Yes, all right." To Andy, his mother figured as a combination of Lady Macbeth and Medea. But having encountered the lady herself, Kate felt his view of her was understandable and realistic.

"Who's they?" Kate asked. "The ones who'd be out to get her."

"I dunno. Somebody. Maybe drug dealers."

It was beginning to sound to Kate like an old movie or some television detective show. She was about to say so when it occurred to her that, given all the circumstances, it might be possible. Of course, McGrath as a doctor would surely be able to get all the drugs he needed quite legitimately. Kate remembered Jed's doubts about McGrath and suddenly shivered.

"If Marie ran away because she discovered something criminal at the hospital, then it is even more important the police be informed. If also, as you say, she's afraid of an unnamed party or parties, she'll need the police." Kate realized her knowledge of drugs and drug dealing came from what she'd read in newspapers and magazines and seen on television. Still, taking even the most low-keyed view, the possibilities were considerable and unpleasant. From all accounts people who dealt in drugs usually protected themselves and their clients. Marie seemed a frail opponent. "Does anybody but you know about her discovery?"

"I dunno. Maybe Ranger."

Ranger, Kate thought. If that were true it would account for a lot in Ranger that had puzzled her. "Would she tell a twelve-year-old boy?"

"They are pretty close. They have to be, with her mother being the way she is and her father being away so much."

"I suppose . . ."

Kate stared out the window, trying to wrack her brains over Marie, over Paul's whereabouts, over what she should do next. After a minute or so it occurred to her that she was gazing at the same tan car that she had seen there since . . .

227

when had she first seen it? She couldn't remember.

"Just a minute," Kate said, going over to the living room window and pulling aside the white muslin curtain to look through. "Andy, come here."

When he was beside her she said, "Do you have any idea who that car belongs to? Would you know if it's the neighbor's across the street?"

"No," he said, sounding sure for the first time. "The Montgomerys live over there. They have two cars, one a Jaguar and one a Volks. That's a seventy-eight Ford."

"Does it belong to anybody else around here that you know?"

"No. I haven't seen it before."

"Can you see if anybody's in it?"

He, too, moved a little. "There could be. I could go out and make sure if you want me to."

"No. Not right now."

Kate watched as a streak of yellow fur raced over the grass towards the back door, followed by Ranger. "Here's Ranger, he might know. Ranger!" she called out as soon as she heard the back door slam, "could you come in here a minute?"

There was the sound of steps in the kitchen, but no answer. Kate walked rapidly to the swing door and opened it in time to see Ranger going out the back again. "Ranger, come here! I want to talk to you!"

But he was gone, and the door slammed shut. Bones, sitting down, gave a bark, then flung himself on Kate. "Not now, Bones," Kate said, going back into the living room. Bones slid through the door before it swung back. "I was too late. He'd gone. I wish I knew why he's avoiding me. I think he knows something."

"I'll catch him," Andy said. And he was out the front door before the last word was out of his mouth. Kate made a leap at Bones, but he, too, had gone. She stared at their headlong flight up the street. Andy's long legs were pumping manfully, but Bones was well ahead and gaining. Feeling curiously bereft, Kate closed the front door. What she needed, she thought, was some coffee. Making her way back to the kitchen, she put some water on to boil, and as she spooned instant coffee into a cup and waited for the water to come to a boil, she tried to organize her thinking while waiting for Andy to return with Ranger and Bones.

Jed told her to call the police. Mark and Andy told her to hold off, with Andy adding to the weight of the argument by claiming that, according to Marie, it could get her in trouble. Which did not make sense. Any more than it made sense for her to run away because she had discovered that her mother was being fed pills in that so-called hospital. . . . There was some piece missing somewhere, Kate mused, as the kettle started to screech. Furthermore, she decided, she didn't wholly believe that bit about Marie being afraid of drug peddlers. Why didn't she believe it? Kate wondered, as she poured the boiling water into the cup and then got some milk from the refrigerator. There really wasn't any reason, except that it sounded too much like a whodunit. No matter what Andy thought he heard over the telephone before his mother came in and scared him off the phone. . . . At that point, the wall telephone rang. She took off the receiver. "Hello?"

"Miss Malory?" Andy's voice sounded out of breath. "I couldn't get them. By the time I'd got to the intersection they'd gone."

"Have you any idea where they'd be? Does Ranger have any special friends between here and the intersection?"

"I dunno. I'm not too up on his friends."

"No suggestions as to whom I could call?"

"No . . . we go to different schools. I don't know who're his friends."

"Okay. Thanks anyway, Andy. I just hope they haven't run away, too."

"I gotta go now. See ya." And he was gone.

As she stood at the kitchen table and sipped the coffee, it occurred to her that this was the first time she had been entirely alone in the house. At least before there'd been Bones. And even when he was being walked by Ranger there were Duchess and the kittens. Kate put down the cup. Where was Duchess? Probably up in her closet. For some reason, and without being able to explain it, she became quite convinced that Duchess and family had also left the house. "This is insane," Kate said aloud. She stood sipping from the cup for a few minutes. Then, pushed by some strange compulsion and feeling absurd, she went upstairs, into her room, opened the closet and looked in. There was no Duchess and no kittens. Plainly, Duchess had once again moved them. Kate went back down the stairs and into the kitchen and looked in Duchess's box beside the old refrigerator. Empty. She was standing, staring at it, when the telephone rang again.

She snatched the receiver off the wall extension. "Hello?"

"Hello," Mark said. "My answering service said you'd been trying to reach me."

Kate startled, only just prevented herself from blurting out what Andy had told her about Marie's discovery. Ordinary caution told her that if it were indeed true, it would be wiser not to let Mark know she knew. Who knew what measures he would take to halt further exposure? As long as Deborah was there under his aegis, it would be better to play it safe. It was possible, of course, that she was being unjust to him, that some pusher on the hospital staff was giving Deborah pills without Mark's knowledge, which would account for his puzzlement at her failure to recover. But surely as a doctor he would know what her strange behavior meant and make very sure of finding out who was doing this?

"Hello?" Mark said. "Are you there?"

"Marie is still missing," Kate said finally, choosing her words with care. "I think I have to call the police immediately."

"Well, if you think that's the best thing to do."

"Mark, she's a fifteen-year-old girl, and however sophisticated she would like everyone to think she is, she's still a child. I don't know where she is. She may be here with a

230

friend or she could have gotten on the train and gone into New York—a thought that does *not* fill me with ease of mind. And if it's the latter, she could get into the kind of trouble that could destroy her."

"Marie's pretty cool. If she were from some midwestern small town I'd tell you to call the police immediately. But even if she has gone to New York—though there's nothing to say she has—well, she's spent her life going in and out of the city to the theater, to museums, concerts, department stores. One of her best friends is the daughter of a buyer at Saks or somewhere. She knows her way around. Anyway, maybe she hasn't gone there. She could be at a friend's house here. I know you think the friend's parent should have called you and she—or he—should. But lots wouldn't."

"But . . ."

"Look, I'll call back in an hour or so. If you haven't heard from either Marie or Paul, then we'll both go to the police. Take care."

"Mark . . ."

But he'd gone.

Kate stood in the kitchen staring at the receiver, from which was coming the sputtering of static. Then she hung up and walked slowly to the middle of the kitchen where she stood, gazing across to the back window. It suddenly occurred to her that she'd had no lunch. Perhaps that was at least partly why she was feeling so hollow, so much alone.

Taking some bread and cheese out of the refrigerator, she sliced the cheese and made herself a sandwich. Then, when more water boiled, she poured herself a second cup of coffee and sat down with the morning paper, which she had not yet had a chance to read.

The trouble with her mind, she thought, trying to concentrate on foreign affairs, was that it seemed to be circling around and around like a merry-go-round. She would read something about the Middle East, but before she knew it, her brain was scurrying about trying to figure out where Marie might be;

was she with a friend in Meadowbrook or in New York? If in New York, where? Should she, Kate, call the police? Or would that make everything worse for the family? Would it, as Andy thought, endanger Marie? What should she, Kate, do about Deborah if Mark were feeding her drugs? If only Paul would call . . . This would be followed by a rising anger against Paul—Paul who should be faced with these decisions, if only he could be found . . . Paul who, according to Mark—who himself was almost certainly not trustworthy—might be involved in some kind of intelligence work . . . Paul who might just as easily be with his girlfriend in New York, what was her name . . . ? Angela Griffin . . .

Kate sat bolt upright, the paper slipping off her lap to the floor. How on earth had she missed such an obvious place? Angela Griffin would undoubtedly know where Paul was. "Stupid, stupid, stupid," she said to herself, getting up. But where would she find Angela Griffin during the day? She could start, at least, by checking the Manhattan directory, if she could find one.

Kate went out to the hall where the main telephone rested on a small table with slots below for directories of various sizes. Kate pulled out the fattest, which was, indeed, the Manhattan listing. Angela Griffin had an address on East 57th Street. Without much hope Kate dialed the number, glancing at her watch as she did so. A quarter past four. Predictably, there was no answer. Kate put the receiver down and stood, staring at the wall, thinking. Marie had said something about Angela Griffin being connected with television. It was, of course, possible to call up every one of the networks and local television stations and simply ask for Angela Griffin. Still furious with herself for having taken so long to reach the obvious, Kate tried to think if she knew anyone who had contacts in the world of television. With continuing chagrin at her obtuseness, Kate realized she did; Judy Roth, whose boyfriend worked for one of the networks. She'd try Judy.

"Hi," she said, when Judy came on the telephone. "Did you tell me that your boyfriend—what's his name—?"

"Simon," Judy said lovingly.

"Does Simon work in television?"

"He does. He's one of the super flunkies that work in the newsroom at Central Broadcasting."

"Would he know somebody called Angela Griffin?"

"Sure. She works at Central Broadcasting too. Good heavens, Kate, don't you ever watch the tube? She's even subbed on the air when their chief harpy, Melissa Grant, is on assignment."

"Well I don't catch Central Broadcasting too much," Kate said, feeling unaccountably guilty. "I probably should."

"That's all right," Judy said in a kind voice. "One day Simon will be top banana at one of the major networks."

"That's what I like, faith. Anyway, where would Angela Griffin be now, this minute?"

"Possibly out with a mike cornering some citizen who'll find himself on prime time saying things he never thought he thought. But maybe at her desk. I can give you Simon's extension and he can switch you. It's 598–6423."

"Okay, Judy. Thanks."

Kate hung up, then looked up and dialed the television station and asked for Angela Griffin. After some static, there was a low buzz, then a male voice said, "Newsroom."

"Angela Griffin, please."

"Who's calling?"

Kate had been thinking about that. Her name would mean nothing. She did a little editing. "I'm Paul Lamont's sister. His daughter is missing and I have to reach him."

There was a pause. "Just a minute. Hang on."

Kate heard the sounds of the newsroom coming over the receiver: other phones, typewriters, voices. Then the phone was picked up. A woman's cool voice said, "This is Angela Griffin. May I help you?"

"My name is Kate Malory. I'm Paul Lamont's sister-in-law.

233

I've been staying at his home with his children while he's been away in Chicago and his wife is in the hospital. One of his children, his daughter, has run away. I am going to call the police because by now she's been missing at least twenty-four hours. But I would like to reach Paul before I do, and I have been told you are a friend of his." It was as nonaccusatory a statement as she could make it. After all, quite apart from anything else, she was certainly in no position to pass judgment on Angela or anyone else.

"Who told you to call me?"

A lot, Kate thought, could be conveyed by a voice. Angela Griffin's voice was well modulated and reflected good background and good schools—whether from reality or from careful elocution lessons, Kate couldn't tell. But underneath was a quality that Kate was quite sure made Angela Griffin a tough reporter.

"Marie Lamont, several days ago, before she ran away, mentioned your name. Since I cannot find any office number for Paul and I do not know where he is staying in Chicago, if indeed he is there, and no one else around here seems to have any ideas on the subject, then I decided to call you. I felt a lost daughter was sufficient reason."

Pause. "I'm curious," Ms. Griffin said, and this time there was amusement in her voice, "because I haven't seen Paul in a while."

So Paul was telling the truth, Kate thought, when he said he and Angela Griffin had broken up. "I see. Do you have any idea where I could find him? As I said, this is something of an emergency."

"He's always been pretty closemouthed about his activities. He's involved in some kind of industrial investigation—that's all I really know. I have a couple of numbers where I might reach him. I'll give it a try, but I don't hold out much hope. What did you say your name was?"

This time Kate was amused. Perhaps Ms. Griffin really hadn't caught her name, though it was a fairly ordinary one.

234

Still, it was a classic bit of one-upmanship. "Kate Malory—with one l," Kate said clearly. "And thanks for anything you can do." She hung up first, which gave her a small, if admittedly petty, sense of satisfaction.

Half an hour later the phone rang. Kate picked it up. "Hello."

"How are you, Kate?" Paul sounded as cheerful as the rising sun. "How're things?"

Kate took a deep breath and told him. ". . . and I haven't seen Marie since—well, since two nights ago. She went to bed. I overslept the next morning and didn't see either of the two kids. Then I went to work. She wasn't here when I got back, her bed was not slept in, and I haven't seen her since."

"Damn it to hell!" Paul said, sounding as upset as a father should. "I was afraid of this since her mother went to the hospital, especially with me having to be away so much on business. Which is why I thought you could take a few days off and help us out. However, since you didn't . . ."

Kate recognized this ploy for what it was, and for the first time in her life, at least as far as Paul was concerned, decided to put a finish to it before it really got off the ground.

"Come off it, Paul. I did as you asked, in so far as I could, given that I, like you, am gainfully employed—that is, if you *are* gainfully employed and do owe my employer something. And speaking of that, Paul, I have not only not found an office number for you anywhere, I haven't even found the name of any firm. Marie's old school gave me the name of a company that, according to the various authorities I called, doesn't exist, at least not now. What's happening?"

"Nothing's happening. I'm involved in confidential work and prefer not to broadcast every move I make."

"All this talk about your head office in New York . . ."

"Do you want to discuss Marie or not?"

Kate swallowed. He had a point. Paul had a lot to explain, but he was right about the priorities; for the moment, Marie's crisis came first. But she couldn't stop herself saying, "McGrath implied you were involved in intelligence work. All I can say is, all the intelligence people I've ever known—and I've come across a few in connection with books I have edited—usually call themselves something quite unextraordinary, like vice president in charge of public misinformation. And they always have telephone numbers where they can be reached."

"So do I. You didn't ask me for it, so I didn't give it to you."

"I should have thought that for an emergency, and a missing daughter could certainly be called that, you would have supplied me with a number where you could be reached."

"And I'd have thought you'd ask for it. I'm sorry—it was an oversight on my part. Here, do you have a pencil?"

"Yes," Kate said grudgingly. There was a pencil and pad beside the phone. "Shoot."

"Here's a number: 783–2111. That phone is manned twenty-four hours a day. If I don't answer it, then anyone who does will know where I am at any given time. Okay, now," Paul went on after a short pause during which she wrote down the number. "What made Marie take off? She's volatile, imaginative and not the most stable teen-ager in the world. But she's never done that before, and she's had worse provocation than anything that has happened in the past few weeks. You must have had words, and you forgot . . ."

"Whoa—come off it, Paul! You're turning this into my fault, instead of helping me arrive at an idea of where I can start looking for her. Let's not go into whose fault it is. You—and Deborah—have had years, in fact her whole life, in which to build a situation where she feels all she can do is run away. Don't put it on me. Where do you think she is?"

"I don't know!" Exasperation made his voice explode on the other end of the telephone. "If I knew that I would be going to get her, not listening to all your rationalizations."

The funny part was, Kate thought, because of Paul's open hostility she had the strong feeling that he was being honest in a way that he had not been—to her at least—before. Further, she believed his concern.

"What triggered it?" he asked now. "Something must have happened."

"Well, Andy, her boyfriend, whom she called just before she took off, seems to think she found something . . . something that made her think Deborah is getting drugs at the hospital. Paul, I know you said if you didn't trust McGrath you wouldn't leave Deborah there, but the evidence against him seems to be mounting. According to Andy this was why Marie ran away. Apparently she's scared somebody will find out she knows. And Jed . . . Jed Kramer, who is really a Dr. Marker from California—he's one of my authors and I'll explain it to you some other time—anyway, Jed was here when Mark turned up and he—Jed—half recognized McGrath as mixed up in something unsavory, but he couldn't remember what."

"Did Andy have any idea where she'd gone?"

"No. Apparently his mother came in the room at the wrong moment . . . I had a memorable talk with Mr. Brigham, by the way. That's one angry and unpleasant woman! And she doesn't think too much of Marie."

"She ought to be flattered that a girl like Marie would go out with her clod of a son. This Jed, whoever he is, couldn't remember where he remembered McGrath from?"

"No. But when you put that together with the fact that Marie has discovered Deborah getting drugs at McGrath's hospital and running away because she's afraid, it puts Mc-Grath in a pretty poor light."

Paul let out a sigh. "You're right. I'd better get back as soon as I can. Maybe I can locate something or somebody that would know where she is. I'll be there tomorrow morning."

"Can't you come out tonight?"

"Kate, I can't. I have responsibilities here, too."

"Yes. I just talked to her."

"Who?"

"Angela Griffin, of course, who just called you."

"I haven't talked to Angela in weeks."

"Paul—I called her to tell her to have you call me. Half an

237

hour after I hung up you called. That's too much of a coincidence for my comfort."

"I can't help that. If you'll just calm down and think, you'll remember that I told you I'd call you Tuesday. Today's Tuesday."

"I don't remember," Kate started, when she did. True enough, Paul had said he'd call that day. "It's still one hell of a coincidence."

"They do happen."

"Can't you come out tonight so we can get started on calling around to locate Marie?"

"For Chrissake, Kate. What do you suppose I'm going to be doing a large part of this evening? It's just as easy to call from here as from the house."

"By the way, where are you?"

"Chicago. I have to go now. Just keep cool. We'll find Marie. And Kate, don't talk to anybody about what Marie's supposed to have found out."

"Why not?"

"Because she could be right. It could be dangerous for her."

"What about the police?"

"Hold off on calling them until I get there. If you call them, you'll have to tell them about Marie's so-called discovery. That could set all kinds of things in motion, including their tramping through the hospital and trying to interrogate Deborah, which could be the final thing to push her over the edge."

"You don't seem to have much faith in their competence."

"You're right. I don't. If I think it's necessary, we'll call them when I get there. But wait until I can see the situation and do a little investigating on my own."

"All right. She's your daughter."

"That's right. She is. How's Ranger?"

"He's taken off, too. With Bones, his dog. I have no idea where he is."

238

"I must say you have a powerful effect on my two children. I leave you in charge and they take off!"

"In that case you won't mind if *I* take off right now and go back to my own apartment. Perhaps then Ranger will come home. But if I were you, and he were my son, I'd make some phone calls around to find out where he is, too!" And Kate hung up.

The temptation to return to her apartment was overwhelming. It was beginning to get dusky outside. The house felt empty—extremely empty, and vulnerable. Whoever was entering the house by the attic window still had a clear passage. She had meant to mention that, too, to Paul, but had forgotten. And she had been on her way down to the cellar to see if she could find a tool to put in a bolt on the lower side of the trapdoor. Instead, she could now pack her one bag, call a taxi and be home in her own living room in a couple of hours. Yet Kate didn't make any effort to. Somehow the idea of either Marie or Ranger coming back to the empty house was something she could not tolerate. In other words, she thought with some bitterness, her captivity was complete: she had become hostage to her own fondness for them.

Now what, Kate thought wearily? She closed her eyes and realized that for the past half hour she had been aware of a steadily growing headache. A tight band was beginning to form over one side of her head. During her teens she had been subject to such onslaughts, and some of them had run the full gamut of severe pain and nausea, to be exorcised only by lying down for twenty-four hours. Later, after she left home, she learned that certain aspirin compounds, taken early enough, could stop the headache. But she hadn't had a headache like that in a long time and had certainly not thought to bring any remedy with her. So she would have to call the local drugstore to see if any could be sent out because—to her knowledge—the nearest pharmacy was beyond walking distance. Or, she thought, opening her eyes, she could find some in one of the upstairs bathrooms.

The obvious one was the first. The bathroom attached to the master bedroom was large and luxurious, with two medicine cabinets and several sliding cabinets beneath the double basin. There was, indeed, a bottle of aspirin in the first medicine cabinet, along with the usual spray antiseptic, antacid tablets, multivitamins and some other capsules in a container with a prescription label. Vaguely hoping to find her usual remedy of choice, Kate slid open the other doors. But the remaining medicine cabinet space was taken up with razors, blades, bars of soap, toothpaste, deodorant and other familiar bathroom items. The cabinets underneath stored rolls of toilet paper and boxes of tissues. It would have to be the aspirin. After all, Kate told herself, most objective reports united in stating that one headache remedy was as good as another.

She took two tablets out of the bottle, hesitated, and put one back, quite why she wasn't sure. After swallowing the one, she decided that the better part of valor would be to return to her room and relax her mind and anxieties by working with the manuscript she had brought home. An hour or so of Napoleonic saga would serve as a refreshment to emotional wear and tear. Going into her room, she glanced once again in the closet, seeing, with a pang, that Duchess and her family had not returned, although the old sweater on which the family had been resting still bore the imprint of their bodies.

Collecting her manuscript from her tote bag, Kate crawled up on the bed with it. Ten minutes later she was absorbed. Twenty minutes later she was sound asleep. The last thing she remembered before she drifted off was that she had meant to go to the cellar for an electric drill to drive home a bolt for the trapdoor. The realization that the door was still unlocked sent a snail of worry through her mind, but it was not enough to halt her slumber.

It was dark when Kate woke up. For a minute she thought it was the middle of the night and she was in bed in the usual way. Then she realized that what woke her up was the fact that she was cold. She was lying on top of the covers, and her hands and feet were chilled. She sat up and looked at the illuminated dial of her electric clock. It was a quarter past midnight. My God! she thought. What happened to me? She had not slept like that during the day since her last attack of flu, four years previously, and then she had had a high fever to account for her somnolence. Even napping during a weekend day had never been a habit, not because of any inherent puritanism, but simply because the thought of sleeping during the day had almost literally never occurred to her. Like most people who slept well at night, she had never felt the slightest need for anything further.

Well, she thought now, I must have been more tired than I thought. It was not hard to imagine why. Anxiety, tension, conflict and a strange bed could account for a lot. Still . . . it was discombobulating.

Fumbling for the switch to her bedside lamp, she slid off the bed, found her shoes, stood up, and then fell back again. She had lost the headache, but had been visited instead by a strange cotton wool feeling, as though her brains had been replaced by wadding of some kind. She was also dizzy and put her head down. After a minute, the floor steadied. What she wanted to do more than anything else was to get inside the covers, lie down and go to sleep. The desire was almost overwhelming. But by this time she was also thinking about Ranger. He surely must have come home, although how he managed to get himself and Bones in without waking her, she couldn't imagine. Furthermore, she hadn't been up and around to fix him dinner. Guilt added its prod to her lethargy.

Slowly, and with much less precipitate action, she stood up and remained there a minute or so to make sure that the room would remain steady. Then she made her way, turning on lights in the dark house as she went, to the main upper hall. Ranger's door was closed. Going up to it as softly as she could, she turned the knob and eased it open, pushing it far enough for some light to fall on the bed.

Ranger sprawled on his stomach, one arm flung around Bones, who was lying beside him. The boy didn't stir, but the dog's ears went up. His tail started to thump. Then sliding from under Ranger's arm he jumped to the floor and came over, tail waving.

"Shhh!" Kate said, hoping he would understand the sound and intention. Then she bent down and patted his silky head. He jumped up and licked her face. "No, no, down Bones," she whispered. Then she walked silently over to the bed. The light from the hall was on Ranger's face, showing the track marks of tears. Kate put her hand on the pillow beside his cheek. It was damp. Poor baby, she thought, poor little boy. His mother was in the hospital, her personality distorted and twisted, his father gone, his sister run away, having, according to Andy, first shared with Ranger her terrible suspicions as to what was happening to their mother. . . . A strange aunt, whom he had never seen before, was in the house. . . .

Kate stood there, staring down at the boy. Always in the children she had seen their parents: Marie was a young Deborah. Ranger, a young Paul. But he wasn't, she saw now. He was himself. Perhaps the eye of the beholder was far more controlling than she had realized, but at the moment she scarcely saw the resemblance. She heard again Paul's sardonic statement to Marie, *"I'm sorry you have such a rotten life."* At the time she'd thought it was funny, a fittingly sarcastic comment to an overaffluent, overindulged suburban child. Now she saw that it was merely accurate. At this point, Ranger was indeed having a rotten life. Pity filled her, and admiration for a stoicism she sensed in him. Sitting beside him as gently as she could, she smoothed the fair hair off his forehead. He stirred. "Mom?" he said. She didn't reply, hoping he would go back to sleep. But his eyes opened. "Mom?" he said again.

"No, it's Kate," she whispered.

"I thought maybe it was Mom. I thought maybe she'd come home."

Kate felt the tears in her own eyes spill over. "I'm sorry,

242

Ranger, I'm sorry. Maybe some day soon." Without thinking, she put her arms around him. He sat and clasped his own around her. She held him, his face cradled against her shoulder. For the first time in her life, she felt a tearing regret that she had chosen, whether by design or circumstance, not to have children. "It'll be all right, Ranger, I promise." She kissed his head. "It'll be all right."

After a few minutes she felt him relax against her and sigh. He was, she thought, almost asleep again. Whatever painful knowledge she was sure he was carrying could wait until the morning. She wanted him to sleep because there was the rest of the night to be got through. The morning seemed far off. After another minute or two she lowered him to the bed. He was asleep before he reached the pillow. Then she crept out, seeing, as she closed the door, Bones jump up again on the bed.

The downward riptide of whatever had been in that tablet she had taken was still operating. She knew, now, that it wasn't aspirin, or it wasn't only aspirin. Thank heaven she'd taken only one. But the thought of slipping into another drugged sleep was as frightening as being up and awake in the dark house in the middle of the night.

I have to think, she muttered to herself. But to do that, she would have to clear her head. Slowly, and holding onto the bannister, she crept downstairs, turning on the light in the living room as she reached the bottom. For a moment she hesitated. Was it a good thing that the now brilliantly lit house was pouring light onto the outside lawn all around? Going to the living room windows, she drew the heavy curtains and for a moment stood between the drawn curtains and the windows to see if any other house lights were on in the street. But all the houses were dark shapes dimly visible against the sky. It made the Lamont house more isolated to be lit up like that. Yet the light itself was a fortress against the dark she had always hated so much.

Stepping back, she closed the curtains and made her way to the kitchen. There the curtains were short and made of a blue and green striped denim. Pulling them together, Kate filled the kettle from the tap and put it back on the gas stove, lighting the jet as she did so. Coffee would undoubtedly mean no sleep for the rest of the night, which was not a pleasant prospect. But it was better than another narcotic induced sleep with the trapdoor open to the attic . . . and beyond that the window . . . and beyond that the roof. Besides, she had always had a morbid fear of drugs, and nothing she had heard about Deborah's years of addiction in the house made her feel any better about the pill she'd taken, however innocently, from the medicine cabinet. She glanced at her watch. Ten to two. There were approximately five more hours of dark, of night, before morning. Well, there was always her manuscript. She was behind on that anyway.

She remembered then that she had been on her way to the cellar to find an electric drill so she could put a bolt in the ceiling next to the trapdoor. When she had drunk sufficient coffee she would resume her search and, if she found all the necessary tools, put up the bolt herself. In the meantime she wanted something to read while she drank her coffee. A lifelong compulsive reader, it was inconceivable to her to sit, drinking coffee, and not reading something. She went into the living room to look over the bookshelves there. The two walls on either side of the fireplace were covered with books from floor to ceiling and, from a cursory glance, seemed to be divided into fiction on the left side and nonfiction books on the right. Nonfiction, Kate decided. What she wanted was history or biography or autobiography. But, on examination, those on the Lamont shelves she had either read or had no interest in reading. Her eyes working down to the lower shelves, she found herself among the reference books. Quotations courtesy Oxford and Bartlett. A huge tome on family medicine, another on nutrition. Whose interest was that, Kate wondered? Deborah's in a better day? Or Paul's? Somehow she thought Deborah. Taking one out at random, Kate decided she was right. The copyright dates were six and seven years old, predating Deborah's addiction. Kate put the books back and returned to the kitchen as the kettle started screeching.

Making herself a strong cup, to which she added both milk and sugar, she came back to the living room. After nutrition came *Gray's Anatomy*. What an odd collection of books to find in a living room owned by Paul and Deborah, she thought. Yet why? These reference volumes, with which she had been surrounded both at her office and her apartment all her life, were standard items. Atlases, world almanacs, *Physician's Desk Reference*. Why on earth would Paul and Deborah want that? This was followed by an even fatter book, *Pharmaceutical Guide*. Putting the cup down on an upper shelf, she pulled the book out. No wonder it was so fat, she thought. The volume contained several hundred glossy pages in full color, bearing photographs, to size, of what must surely be every known pill, tablet and capsule ever manufactured. Trying to hold the book with one hand, Kate took the cup in the other, meaning to transport both to the kitchen. The book crashed to the floor. In the total quiet of the house, the thump sounded inordinately loud. Kate took the half-empty cup and went back to the kitchen, putting it on the table and lighting the gas under the kettle. Then she returned for the book, which required both hands to transport.

With a fresh cup of strong coffee, she opened it up and started perusing it. She was about a third of the way through when she jumped. There was a click followed by a swishing sound at her back. Whirling around she saw Duchess sitting on the floor looking at her, the cat port in the back door behind her flapping gently.

"You scared me, Duchess!" Kate said aloud. And her voice sounded to herself like a thunderclap. "Where have you been?"

Duchess arched her back, stretched, extending her claws, and then paced over, her supple body moving like a miniature calico panther. She rubbed against Kate's leg in one direction, then turned around and rubbed herself in the other. Kate, her eyes on the page in front of her, gently stroked her tail.

Duchess pawed at her lap and, when she had Kate's attention, meowed pitifully. Kate looked down at her. "Yes, you're eating for about seven or eight, aren't you?"

Getting up, she searched through the various cabinets for cat food, opened a can when she found it and warmed some milk. Leaving Duchess swallowing hungrily Kate was about to sit down when an idea that had been with her compellingly since she had seen the book directed her feet back upstairs to the master bedroom and thence to the bathroom. Grasping the bottle of aspirin, she turned and went back to the bedroom. She was about to leave when she paused and turned to look at the closet door, which was shut.

Was it her imagination, or did there seem to be a cold draft of air coming around her slippered feet? Standing there, clutching the bottle, Kate fought within herself a fearful battle. More than anything else she did not want to open that closet door. Behold, the compleat coward, Kate thought. And besides, it was the middle of the night and a cold draft along the floor was to be expected in chilly spring weather. Hadn't she felt it the other night when she had come in and discovered the trapdoor in the closet ceiling? Truthfully, she could not remember. All she did recall was the cold that she felt while standing on the aluminum ladder facing the black rectangle in the ceiling. And what if she discovered the cold air was indeed coming down from the trapdoor? Kate closed her eyes and summoned an old and usually effective maxim. *If something has to be done, don't argue about it, do it.*

She opened her eyes, marched to the closet door and opened it. The trapdoor in the ceiling looked exactly the way it did the night she discovered it. And yes, there was chilly air coming down, but that could mean . . . it could mean that the attic was unheated, as well as the other possibility, that the attic window leading to the roof had once again been opened.

It was an unbearable thought. I should go up and find out, Kate thought. And knew she wouldn't. When she and Jed had gone up it had, at least, been daylight. Even more, Jed was there and had gone up first. Dear Jed, Kate thought, why oh why had she let him leave?

Closing the closet door, she also closed the bedroom door, but left on the light inside for reasons she did not stop to analyze. Then she paused outside Ranger's door. What if the prowler came in and Ranger heard him and got up to investigate? She couldn't allow that to happen. Slipping the bottle of aspirin into her jacket pocket, she went downstairs, got the pharmaceutical tome and coffee cup and came back up again, then she stood, uncertain.

If she returned to her own room, she might not hear any noise from the master bedroom before Ranger did. If there were a prowler, if her fears had some root in reality and not just her overheated imagination, then Ranger could be in potential danger. Why, she thought, didn't I do what Jed said and call the police? Aside from her concern over Marie, she could have mentioned her worry over the prowler and the police might well have put a lock on the trapdoor for her or even sent a cop out to watch the house . . . but she hadn't. And her present anxiety could be the timidity of an urban dweller who walked the crime filled New York streets with a bearable degree of worry because it was a danger she was used to, but panicked at the thought of the silence and solitude of the country.

Well, if she was not going to sleep and wanted to peruse that pharmaceutical reference, the hall sofa was as good as any place. She could bring a blanket and a pillow out from her room. Five minutes later she was propped up on the sofa, one pillow at her back, her legs up with another pillow under her knees, the blanket over them and the reference on her lap. It really wasn't too bad, and tomorrow morning at dawn she would call the local police and talk to them. And she would call Jed. But that thought, which brought a flush of pleasure, also brought pain. There was more than an even chance that he had returned to California by now. After all, she hadn't been that warm and welcoming at their last conversation. She could always write him . . . she could even telephone him. . . . After blowing her nose, she collected her attention and opened the pharmaceutical guide and started a careful study of any photographs of white tablets. As the next hour and a half wore on she was mildly surprised that she felt no inclination to sleep, whether out of anxiety or because she had been slept out or because of the coffee she had drunk, she didn't know. But as time passed, she found no white tablet that matched the ones in the bottle lying on the sofa beside her. One thing that she felt her long and profound sleep had established beyond question: those innocent looking white pills in their bottle with the familiar label bore no relation to the bottle's usual contents. They were no form of over-the-counter analgesic.

Kate was about halfway through the book when she thought she heard a noise coming from the master bedroom. She froze. Seconds and then minutes passed while she hardly breathed. But there was no further sound. Lowering the heavy book gently to the floor, she swung her feet down and sat there for a moment. The noise, of course, could be anything—and quite innocent. Her inner argument continued; there might be someone in there. On the other hand, if she went in and found out what had caused the noise and established that it meant nothing sinister, she could come back out here and relax, instead of thinking that at any minute she might have a heart attack from fright.

Standing up, she walked in her stocking feet to the master bedroom door. The whole thing, she thought, would have been so much easier if the bedroom door had had a lock. But, like most modern houses, it had instead a device for locking the door from the inside, but nothing from the outside. Taking a deep breath, Kate thrust the door open. The room looked exactly as it had when she had been there before, taking her spurious aspirin. Her eyes slid towards the bathroom. Something was different. She had left the light on and the medicine cabinet door open. Beside the aspirin bottle and vitamins, there'd been a container of capsules—blue and brown, she remembered. The container had been next to the aspirin bottles, but it was not there now. Trying to calm her inner shaking, Kate made herself walk across the room to the bathroom. And then she let out her breath. The noise she had heard was caused by the plastic container of capsules that had fallen down into the basin. Probably she had half pulled it out when she was getting the aspirin bottle and some stirring of air had finally overbalanced it. Impatiently, Kate put the container up on the shelf. As she did so, she found herself staring at the capsules and at the prescription label pasted to the container. "Take one at bedtime." The doctor was McGrath.

Kate took the container and went back into the hall. Picking up the reference book, she started turning the pages once again. This time she was successful. She found the capsule's duplicate in size, shape and color on a glossy page. But it was in the international section carrying pictures of drugs manufactured in other countries. The one in her fingers was made in Germany, and it was a powerful tranquilizer. Listed for it was a long paragraph of cautions. Below the warnings, she found a statement to the effect that the drug had not been passed for usage by the Food and Drug Administration because one of the elements it contained was still considered too dangerous.

Kate lowered the book to the floor again and stared at the container in her hand, knowing she needed no further proof of McGrath's almost certain involvement in illicit drugs. Plainly he had given these to Deborah when she was seeing him in his office as a patient prior to her suicide attempt and hospitalization. She—Kate—should have listened to Jed . . . she should have called the police. She glanced at her watch. Three-thirty. Police precincts stayed open all night, obviously, since so many crimes were committed at that time. Could the prowler have anything to do with the little container of dynamite in her hand?

No. Plainly McGrath gave the pills to Deborah. Marie had

discovered that and she had fled out of horror and fear for her own safety.

But *cui bono?* Kate thought. What good accrued to McGrath by giving a patient like Deborah these illegal drugs? And even more (back to an old question) why would he insist that she, Kate, be in the house? Above all, why hadn't Paul tumbled to this, and taken his wife out of McGrath's clinic?

To anyone who had known Paul, the answer was obvious—because he was taking the line of least resistance. That was what he had always done . . . bright, attractive Paul, to whom everything, but especially women, had come so easily. Kate knew she did not believe for a moment that he was engaged in any kind of intelligence, corporate or governmental. He was a good front man, a public relations representative, and as long as that was all he had to do, he was adequate. But his grandiosity and ambition had always been matched by his laziness. The chances were, he had been fired, and didn't want to admit it to his family or anyone else while he found himself another job. And as for Deborah being ill and needing better treatment . . . she went to the easy, nearest place. It wouldn't occur to him to look into the kind of pills that had been prescribed for her. If she didn't recover . . . well, she didn't recover. And Paul would inherit a tidy amount of money.

Kate found herself gripping the container. And she found she was, after all, tired. If she sat outside the bedroom on the sofa much longer, she'd go to sleep. And she didn't want to do that.

Making a sudden decision, Kate glanced at her watch. A quarter to four. Then she started down the stairs. It might be the middle of the night, but she was going to call the police to see if they had an officer who could come out and sit there so that she and Ranger could spend what was left of the night in peace and safety. Maybe he would dismiss her as an hysterical woman, but maybe he wouldn't. At the expense of looking as hysterical as the worst Victorian heroine, she was willing to give it a try.

Lifting the receiver from the hall phone, she waited for the dial tone. There was none. Impatiently, she put the receiver back a few seconds, then lifted it again. Still no tone, no static, no sound. She tapped the button on the cradle a few times. Nothing. Once again she replaced the receiver, let it stay there, and lifted it. There was still no dial tone. She stood there, holding the receiver to her ear, and dialed anyway. Sometimes the dial tone started after the number had been dialed. But there was no dial tone and no ringing at the other end. She tried then just dialing 0 for the operator. But she knew, as she did it, that it was no use. The phone was dead. It had been cut off, and with it, herself and Ranger.

At that point fright, something far worse than anything she had experienced so far, flowed through her. She knew then what was meant by the description she had sometimes read about watery knees. Her own seemed to have lost their function and were shaking. She felt overwhelmingly in danger. . . .

I must get to Ranger, she thought. There was another noise, this one immediately behind her. Then everything went black.

Chapter **10**

S he opened her eyes to absolute blackness. Her headache had returned with a vengeance and extreme nausea with
it. It was as she fought the nausea that she realized a gag was
around her mouth. Real panic ensued then. People choked to
death on their own regurgitation if they couldn't eject it.
"Please God," she thought. "Help me." Her strange theological
preoccupations of the past now seemed wildly irrelevant. She
found that whatever else she doubted, she did not doubt the
existence of a Presence, or that she needed help, and she
prayed fervently and with conviction.

It—or something—must have calmed her because the rising
nausea retreated. She had the mental leisure then to note that
her hands were tied behind her back and that she was lying
on a floor. Dust seemed to be coming in her nostrils and she
could feel wood under her cheek. I mustn't sneeze, either, she
thought, and tried to sit up.

It was a mistake. The headache, which she had momentarily
forgotten, reminded her of its presence by a pain that seemed
to streak through her head, and the nausea returned. She lay
still, waiting for the pain and the sickness to abate and for her

head to stop swimming. While doing this, she passed out again.

The next time she awoke, she felt better. Slowly she tried to raise herself, not an easy task with her hands bound. Finally, and at the expense of bruising her elbow, she managed to sit up. Her greatest fear was that something would block her nose. If that happened, with the tight gag around her mouth, she would not be able to breathe. How short a time, had she read recently, did it take for the brain, deprived of oxygen, to become permanently damaged? Panic over that didn't help, either. She concentrated on breathing slowly and deeply. Then, little by little, the terror retreated, at least enough for her to be able to think about figuring out her situation. Where was she? Did the total darkness mean that it was still night? Or was she somewhere without windows, or with windows curtained? Without thinking, she leaned back further than she intended and started to fall over backward, thrusting out her bound hands to stop herself. Her hands slid along the wooden floor, gathering splinters as they went.

"Ouch!" It wasn't a sound, of course. Her tongue hit cloth. But the word formed in her mouth. With a thrust she pushed herself forward again. As she sat, she tried to think where a splintered wood floor would be. The floors throughout the house, those areas that were not covered by carpets and rugs, were parquet and highly polished. Gingerly, she pulled her arms to one side and leaned slowly back again, feeling the floor with the tips of her fingers. The wood was rough, unfinished and unpolished. Had she been in any room whose floor that would describe? Not the kitchen, which had a vinyl covering, nor the bathrooms, which were tiled. What did that leave? Nothing except the attic, which she had been in, and the cellar, which she had not.

Concentrating, she tried to remember the attic floor. She and Jed had examined it, while Jed pointed out the patterns of dust that would indicate square objects recently removed. But she did not remember whether the attic floor was as dry and splintery as the surface under her fingers now. And didn't cellars usually have concrete floors? The only two geographical areas she'd lived in during her life were New York and New Orleans. In the latter, because New Orleans was originally drained from swamp, most houses did not have cellars. They were more liable to be raised on short, square stilts. This was certainly true of the house on Harmony Street. What about the house on Prytania Street? She could not remember. And as for New York, the floors of the cellars she had been in, containing washing machines and dryers, were, indeed, concrete. Of course, she could be away from the house entirely, somewhere by herself, where no one would be able to hear her or know to look for her. . . . The panic surged back, and she once again strove to calm herself.

Who had done this? The two candidates that leapt to the mind were McGrath and the prowler. . . . The prowler's purpose would be simple: tie her up and put her away where she couldn't alert anyone, and then take everything from the house that he could carry. . . .

But what about the nosey neighbors?

In view of that, Kate decided, it must be still night outdoors, unless, of course, the thief had taken everything he could and had left, leaving her for somebody else to find, if indeed she were still in the house. And McGrath? Somehow that did not make sense. His motive, if it were he, would certainly not be theft in the ordinary way. . . . Then why would he be entering the house by the roof . . . and what would he be taking away? And if he were not doing that, what would he be doing? There was no answer to that.

And what about Ranger. . . ?

It was time to make some effort to identify where she was, and the only way to do that was to feel. Getting to her feet was not easy. It involved an old trick she had not tried since her school days—crossing her legs and rising on them. Once, when she was in college, she became quite skilled at it. But her bones were now twenty years older.

254

As she rocked back and forth, trying to get purchase on the floor, the word "Bones" reminded her of another of the house's inhabitants. Wouldn't he have barked if someone had come in? Unless, of course, whoever it was had taken measures to silence him. . . . At that thought her heart felt sick again. But before she had time to think about it, her momentum had built up and she stood, wobbling, on her feet. The fact that she had succeeded there gave her a burst of hope. Moving slowly in the dark, she walked forward, stepping carefully. And then, without quite knowing why, she stopped. Sliding her foot forward, she encountered what was obviously a wall or barrier of some kind. Evidently what she had read somewhere was true, people have some kind of ability to estimate when they are near a wall or door. Turning around, she backed to the wall, feeling it with her hands. That, too, was wooden. Where, if anywhere, had she seen a wooden wall? The hope she had felt was now gone, because a wooden wall seemed to argue that she was no longer in the house, but in some shack somewhere else. Unless . . . suddenly her mind produced a picture: herself, standing in front of a wooden door, turning a knob, finding the door locked, and saying, "I wonder what's in here?" That door was in a corner of the attic behind a large screen. . . .

Slowly Kate moved along the wall, feeling her sweater catch on more splinters. But, after a few steps, her shoulder banged against something that stuck out. It was much too high for her hands to feel. If she felt it with her face, would she be able to identify it? There was only one way to find out. Turning, she stepped back and brought her face down to the level of whatever it was, moving too fast. Her nose encountered a sharp edge. Once more the silent "ouch!" filled her mouth. Raising her head, she waited until the pain subsided. Then, moving more slowly, she lowered her head again and touched the protuberance with her face. It felt cold, colder than wood. It was metal of some kind. Steadily, and trying not to overbalance herself, she moved her forehead and sore nose around it. Whatever it was, was small and stuck out from more metal, which protruded—as far as she could tell—from the plane of the wooden wall. Raising her head, she tried to imagine what it might be. Suddenly, she remembered something she had not really registered at the time. Above the doorknob outside the locked door was a shiny Yale lock. The metal she was feeling was the right shape, in the right place and at the right height to be the reverse side of that lock—a square, drop lock arrangement. This somehow confirmed her growing certainty that she was in the corner room in the attic.

Shuffling her feet and moving as soundlessly and as slowly as she could, she moved around the room. After several minutes of this she knew that whatever might have been in the room before, was gone. It was empty. She leaned back against the wall and tried to think clearly. Her head still ached at the back, although the shooting pain had gone, and so, mercifully, had the nausea.

She tackled another question. If she were in the attic and daylight had arrived, would she see a light under the door, instead of the complete blackness around her? Not necessarily. A closely fitted door would prevent that.

She made her slow way back to the door, and, bending even more slowly, so as not to bang her nose again, she was about to see if she could push the knob around in some way, with the faint hope that it might unlatch the door, when the door opened abruptly.

"Kate!" It was an urgent whisper.

The light that poured in almost blinded her. Blinking, she backed. She had the impression of a curly head not much higher than her own outlined against the light. Then a hand pushed her back into the room and the door was quietly shut.

"It's Jed," he whispered, a second after she realized who it was. Tears started to flow out of her eyes and she tried to make sounds from behind her gag.

"I'm going to open the door again," he whispered, "just an inch, to get some light. Don't make any sound."

She heard the lock turn, then the door opened again.

"Turn around," Jed said. "Let me undo the gag."

She turned, and felt his hands groping at the back of her head. After a minute that seemed like ten, the pressure against her mouth slackened. The outside binding fell off and he pulled the wadding out of her mouth. It wasn't until that moment that she realized how terribly dry her mouth was.

"Now," Jed said. "I'll undo your hands."

That took somewhat longer, but while she swallowed and tried not to cry noisily, he finally got the knots undone and her hands fell free.

"Poor darling," Jed said. "There, there."

She had no sense later of what happened then, except that her arms were around his neck and he was kissing her and stroking her back. It was he who started to pull away. "We have to get out of here," he said. "Immediately. Before he comes back."

Kate, still clinging, kissed him again. "Oh Jed. I'm so glad to see you! How can I thank you!"

"Later. You can thank me all you like, and I have several ideas of just how, all of them pleasant—at least to me. But we must get out of here before he comes back."

"Who?" She spoke more loudly than she meant to.

"Why me, of course, Kate dear." A tall head had loomed up behind Jed.

Jed turned. "Where did you come from?"

Paul smiled. "From the roof, my dear man, on soft and sneakered feet. I saw you lurking in your car across the street, but hoped you would wait a little longer before dashing to the rescue."

"Paul," Kate said, through her thick mouth.

"None other. What a pity! If your Lochinvar had just tarried another hour, he could have rescued you in peace and quiet and I would have been on my way to Rio. As it is, I can't loiter on the roof any longer. And now I'm going to have to do something about the two of you."

"Why, Paul?" Kate walked out into the sunlit attic and blinked.

"Why what, Kate?"

She stared at him, as everything, including her stupid blindness about him fell into place. Then she made a gesture with her hands. "Why *everything?*"

"That's pretty all-embracing." He was dressed in jeans and sweater, and his hands were covered with dust. Fastidiously, he brushed them against each other.

"Obviously, it was you who shut me in the room there," Kate went on. "So it's been you up in the attic all along. What was in those boxes? Narcotics?"

"Yes. I should have thought that answer fairly leaped at you. Pills, pills and more pills. You'd be surprised at the black market there is in those—especially the foreign ones you can't get here. Thanks to the old women who run our FDA, they've been very profitable. But the time has come, as the walrus said —to get out." Almost casually he took a pistol out of his belt, hidden under the voluminous sweater.

"So that's what you've been doing in your travels? Smuggling drugs."

"Well . . . arranging for their—er—transport. It's not that difficult. There are ways—if you have the right connections, and I developed those when I was, as you put it, gainfully employed." He grinned. "That's how I was able to retire."

"It was you who cut the telephone wires, wasn't it?"

"Yes."

Kate put up her hands and rubbed her head. "My head still feels full of mush. I suppose that's because you hit me on the head. But it was feeling cottony before. What was the white pill I thought was an aspirin? It was in a bottle marked aspirin in the medicine cabinet."

"Probably one of Deborah's old sleeping pills or maybe a tranquilizer. I'd have to look at it to identify it. She had access to them all and took what she wanted."

"Took what she wanted? From your store? Didn't McGrath

prescribe those? What about those powerful German pills? I saw them in a container with McGrath's prescription on it and looked them up in that pharmaceutical guide."

Paul grinned. "Old Mark? I don't think so. After the terrible trouble he got into in California I doubt if he'd prescribe much more than the safest of safe pills. He's in enough of a jam as it is."

"What trouble?"

Paul made an impatient gesture. "I don't have time to go into it. He had a super rich clinic out near Hollywood. It catered to a few minor movie and rock stars, but mostly the rich playboy jet set. Somebody, who was mad at him, hinted to the police that an awful lot of his patients were on drugs. Then, before the cops got going, one patient of his died of an overdose. There was no real evidence that Mark was directly responsible. Most of his patients were heavy pill users before they went to him. And he claims he was trying to get them off. Anyway, when the cops wanted to take a closer look, all his records mysteriously burned, and witnesses clammed up or disappeared. The police had nothing solid to go on. So they couldn't do anything when he decided to pull up and come east and start up a new clinic."

Kate turned towards Jed. "Is that what you were talking about?"

"Yes. When I saw him, his name and face set off warning signals, which is why I told you to be careful, and I finally recalled that I'd seen them both in a newspaper. So after I left, I called my office. My secretary remembered the whole thing."

"So McGrath didn't prescribe those illegal pills for Deborah?"

"I told you, she helped herself and put what she wanted into any handy container—aspirin bottles, vitamin bottles—anything. God knows what you took. It may have been some harmless sleeping pill McGrath gave her before he knew what an addict she was. She switched things around so much, there's no telling. But if you're not used to dosing yourself with sleeping pills or tranquilizers, you're lucky it only made you sleep a few hours. Let that be a lesson to you—don't go helping yourself from other people's medicine cabinets."

"I hardly expected to be taking up residence in a drug den. And, incidentally, that habit of putting powerful narcotics in any old container could be pretty dangerous with children around, couldn't it?"

"For the past years Deborah was past worrying about that."

"But you weren't. And they're your children, too."

"You don't have to preach to me about my children," he snapped. "They're doing fine."

"I wouldn't say Marie—wherever she is—is doing fine. And if you'd seen Ranger crying over his mother tonight you wouldn't be so sure of his condition, either."

"Ranger . . ." his voice dismissed his son. "He's too old to be a crybaby . . ." He didn't mention Marie.

"Besides that," Kate interrupted, "knowing what you did about McGrath, you let Deborah go to him?"

"Encouraged her to go to him, I would say," Jed said. "He'd hardly let his wife go to a regular and legitimate doctor who'd know immediately she was on pills and want to know what they were." Jed looked at Paul. "I imagine you could blackmail McGrath into taking Mrs. Lamont in the first place and then later keep him quiet about the drugs you were sending her by your children."

"Sent drugs by Marie and Ranger?" Kate said, in her shock forgetting to wonder how Jed knew this.

"That's right," Jed said, "telling them that they were taking their mother some super vitamins unobtainable here."

"That's really the bottom," Kate said. 'It's sick."

"Not sick," Jed said calmly. "Evil, in the old sense of the word. Completely amoral." He turned to Paul. "And you kept this high wire act going by threatening to expose McGrath, didn't you?"

"Sure. One good newspaper story in an eastern paper would

destroy his hospital. People would take their near and dear out of there as fast as they could snatch them."

"How did you know about McGrath?" Kate asked.

"My—er—distributors gave me that piece of information. They, too, had a stake in keeping Deborah quiet. If I hadn't kept her supplied, she would have blown the whistle. If I'd been here to watch her, she wouldn't have tried that suicide and wouldn't have gone to the hospital in the first place. But she was there when I got back." He paused. "I think it would be well to clue you in on reality, Kate. By sending her to McGrath when she first said she wanted to go to a doctor, I saved her life. If I hadn't sent her there," Paul went on, slowly emphasizing his words, "Deborah might, in my absence, have met with a fatal accident. The people I'm in business with protect their interests. They had nothing to fear from a Deborah, who needed her drug supply. But if she had ever even looked as though she were thinking of getting off, or of going to a doctor who'd try and get her off, she might have been—would have been—in serious danger."

"And you let everything get that far? Why—just sheer greed?"

Paul shrugged. "I've always been a libertarian." He had put the pistol back in his belt. Kate felt sure that he had taken it out only to show them that he had it. He stooped and picked up a coil of rope on the floor and started to wind it. "I believe if people want to take drugs, they should be allowed to. I've never forced anybody to take them. I simply supplied what they already asked for."

"You don't take responsibility for Deborah?" Kate said. Her eyes had at last become used to the light. All the boxes had gone from the attic, although the sheets and curls of newspaper still littered the floor, plus various pieces of rope. The furniture that was left looked spare: chairs dotted around, chests, tables, mirrors. But the higgledy-piggledy look had gone.

Why are we standing here talking, Kate thought? Why don't Jed and I make a run for it? But Paul, apparently relaxed, his athlete's body still graceful, had placed himself squarely in front of the trapdoor with its stair.

"It's no use your trying to get down those stairs," Paul said amiably, easily reading her mind. "You'd never make it. Nor would your friend here."

How much he's enjoying himself, Kate thought, and felt disgust, not this time at him, but at herself for her long obsession with him, a piece of emotional stupidity that should have vanished with her adolescence. She had been absently rubbing her face where the gag had been. Suddenly she noticed the reddish brown stain on her hand. "What's on my face?" she said.

"Blood," Jed said. "Your nose bled. With that gag on, you were lucky not to suffocate with blood coming down your nasal passages." His voice had a quality to it that Kate had not heard before, but that reminded her of a look she had seen on his face. Being considerably less magnificent than all the men who had had such power over her emotions—to whom she had given such power—she had not thought of him as having authority, except that once, when he was in Marie's room. Yet it was there now. Jed was looking at Paul.

"Short of our willing cooperation," he said, "there is really no way you can get completely away."

"And I wouldn't depend on your so-called willing cooperation for five minutes. You're just the man who would call any promise the result of coercion and phone the police the minute I got out of the street. Wouldn't you?"

"That depends. Not if my life, or Kate's life, depended on it."

Paul looked at him and shook his head. "But they wouldn't, would they? With me on the way to Kennedy Airport, I could hardly hold your lives hostage. I'm going to have to be cleverer than that."

"If you kill us both," Jed said in a matter-of-fact voice, "you won't get away with it."

"I haven't said I was going to kill you. But, for the sake of argument, yes, I would get away with it. I'll be at the airport in a couple of hours, and my plane takes off not too long after that. There's no extradition between Brazil and the U.S. Once up in the air outside U.S. territory, I'm as safe as I would be if I were in Rio. Undoubtedly, somebody would discover your . . . your bodies . . . within a few hours, but I would be gone."

"You'd do that to us?" Kate asked. Even after what she'd heard it seemed impossible.

"I'll admit, violence has never been my thing," Paul agreed.

"Except remotely," Jed said dryly. "But I expect you don't include the violence that results in the sale, distribution and taking of those medical baubles you bring in. Or the violence committed by people you do business with and who, as you put it, know how to protect their interests."

Paul behaved as though he hadn't heard. He was wrapping a third coil of rope. "You keep trying to pin responsibility for Deborah on me," he said. "You have the shoe on the wrong foot. I didn't addict Deborah. Her perfectly legitimate doctor back in Tokyo—an American doctor—gave her quite legitimate pills, which, however, she proceeded, after a while, to use in ways and amounts that the good physician didn't intend. After that, all I did was to keep her supplied. But it was the Légères, strictly speaking, who got me pill-running."

"The Légères?"

"Yes, the aristocratic, all-powerful, all-desirable Légères. One of them had discovered it was easy to bring various contraband in along with their shipping interests. In a very genteel way they were as crooked as they could get away with. And they were sniffing coke and puffing grass and taking uppers and downers long, long before the kids discovered them and the drug culture became generally fashionable. Didn't you know that your dear father got hooked?"

"I don't believe it," Kate said automatically.

"Don't you? He was going to lose his job for a combination of laziness and a touch of fraud at that handsome brokerage

263

house. But by that time he had married Diane, and the Légères decided they could use him. So they paid his debts and got him out of his slight stock manipulation trouble, and after that he was theirs. After you'd gone up north, they started having all kinds of parties to which I was invited. Then, after marrying Deborah, I went to work for them. Of course, as I told you, I'm now in business for myself. Have been for a while. In a quiet way. I have a small office, a phone, somebody to take messages, that kind of thing. But I found working for somebody else . . . restrictive." He grinned.

"So all that talk about needing to be in Tokyo and lost contracts and conventions in Chicago was so much malarky."

"It sounded reasonable, though."

Jed was right. He wasn't immoral. He was amoral. And she remembered Jed's question: "Is he a man of principle?" Under the circumstances it seemed almost ludicrous. "Why did you ask me out here, then, in the first place, or have McGrath do it?"

He glanced at his watch. "Because of the damn nosey neighbor. She was threatening to call in the child welfare people, and I couldn't have that. So I put a little pressure on McGrath to call you. I thought coming from him the request would have a certain imperative quality. And when you walked out after I arrived, I put pressure on McGrath again. This time he went to see you."

"I see," Kate said, and she did. "I always did think it was fishy. Wouldn't another housekeeper have done just as well?"

"We'd had housekeepers. They had a way of leaving after Marie had been rude enough. . . . And she was beginning to get out of hand . . . and anyway, I remembered how persuadable you were." His voice trailed off. "I'd like to have seen Marie before I went . . . well, I can keep in touch with her. I want her to come to Brazil."

"Do you know where she is?"

"With one of her friends, probably. She's run away before and always turned up and was found to be staying with one of her buddies." But he sounded less certain, and Kate didn't believe he believed that.

"She may have stayed with buddies before, but this time she found something out—possibly that you were supplying her mother with narcotics. Possibly that you were using her and Ranger as couriers."

Paul shrugged. "She'll come around."

"And Ranger?" Kate glanced at her watch. Ten past nine. She had no idea so much time had passed. "Where is he now?"

"At school. Where else would he be?"

So she had spent a longer time tied up on the floor than she realized. Which reminded her of an immediate need. "I have to go to the bathroom," she said, and started to move towards the stairs, which meant moving towards Paul.

"Sorry." He put out his hand and stopped her.

"Paul—I have to go. Now you can come with me if you insist. But I *have* to." As it happened, the need, although present, was not quite as urgent as she was making it sound. But she was banking on her hunch that it was the kind of request that the civilized Paul could not refuse.

He hesitated, then took out his pistol. "Okay, both of you, downstairs. You first, Kate. And you, whoever you are—I suppose you're that author Kate was talking about—remember that if you try anything at all, Kate gets a bullet."

When they were in the master bedroom Paul said, "All right, Kate. You can use the bathroom. But just remember what I told your boyfriend here. I don't know what you could try, but if you try anything, then your would-be rescuer gets a bullet."

How much he was relishing his sarcastic jabs, Kate thought, hurrying to the bathroom. In the few minutes it took to accomplish her mission, she wracked her brain to see if there was anything she could do to help herself and Jed. But there seemed nothing. She could lock the door. But what would that accomplish? It would leave Paul free to concentrate on Jed, and, if he were foiled, he might be a lot nastier than if she were there. Jed was shorter, older and less athletic. What match would he be for the ex-football hero, who, unlike so many, seemed to have kept himself in trim?

Nevertheless, as she was flushing the toilet, her eye was caught by the medicine cabinet, the door of which was partly open. Facing her was a razor . . . and blades. She didn't stop to think what she was doing, but quickly wrapped two blades in toilet tissue and hid them in the top of her panty hose, devoutly hoping they wouldn't slice her flesh. Then she came out.

"Just as a precaution," Paul said genially. He was still holding the pistol on Jed, who was standing in the middle of the floor. But he thrust the other hand in the pockets of her jacket and patted her all around.

"My, my," he said. "What a nice shape you still have. How about coming to Brazil with me?"

"No thanks."

Having satisfied himself that she was not hiding something, he backed off. "Why not? I have more than enough money to keep us in luxury for a long, long time. Deborah, without my tender help, will finally get off drugs somehow and be okay. The children . . ."

Kate was watching him, and saw a spasm of pain cross his face. "And Marie?" she said, making a fairly easy guess.

"As I said, she can join me. She and I are the same kind of person."

"I don't think so," Kate said. "I don't think she'd be so taken with the idea of joining you when she learned that you were the one who kept her mother hooked. Learning that her mother was getting pills was what sent her running away, anyway."

"And she's not with a friend," Jed put in. "She's with a policeman with the narcotics squad in New York."

Paul had been holding the pistol, trained on both of them, fairly easily. It did not look like a toy, but he had been holding it as though it were. Now he gripped it, and it didn't look at all like a toy. It looked like a gun that could go off. "What the hell are you talking about?"

"I called a policeman friend of mine in the city," Jed said evenly, his eyes on Paul. He was standing so the light fell on his face. His clear brown eyes had a compelling, almost magnetic quality, Kate thought. She found it hard not to watch them. . . .

". . . I told him about Marie. It turns out he's on the narcotics squad, and he managed to have her picked up at Grand Central Station. After a while she told him the whole story, how you had given her and Ranger pills—vitamin pills, you called them—to take to their mother when they visited her. Children are not as carefully monitored as adults when they visit a psychiatric hospital—not the way an adult friend might be, at least they weren't in this one. Although, of course, I imagine that McGrath, with your threat over him, could pretty well be depended on not to make too many waves, no matter what he suspected. That was a dirty trick, though, to play on your children, leading them to believe she needed those strong vitamins that could only be supplied from abroad. That's why your daughter ran away. . . . According to the cop, Marie felt she saw you as you really were for the first time, and realized how you used her . . . that was what hurt."

Paul made an impatient gesture. "Deborah didn't want to be taken off her pills. If I'd threatened to withhold them, she'd have told the hospital and anybody else who'd listen about my effort at—er free enterprise."

"That may have been true once," Jed said. "But from what Marie said, I don't think it's true now. Marie said her mother was ill some months back—genuinely ill—and during that time was mostly withdrawn from some of her narcotics. But I imagine an unaddicted wife, beginning to resume her responsibilities, was a threat to you, so you helped her back on."

Paul made an impatient gesture. "I don't have time to listen to all this. Marie will do as I ask. She'll come to Brazil when I send for her. She's always done what I asked her to."

267

He believes that, Kate thought. Why shouldn't he? Didn't I? Didn't probably every other woman?

"I don't think so, not this time," Jed said. "She really cares for her mother."

Kate had been figuring out a few things. "While I thought you were in Chicago, you were here, getting those narcotics out. You were the noises I heard during the nights."

Paul grinned. "Even so, I was pretty quiet. Things were beginning to get a little close and uncomfortable. I knew I'd have to make a break sooner than I'd planned. Of course, I could have carried the cartons out and pretended they were files for the office or something. Unfortunately, I had been told by one of my—er—contacts . . . that I was being watched. And cars I hadn't seen before started being parked around the street here. Also, I had a few business deals to tie up, so it had to be night work, carrying the damn things down, out the back door and into the garage. There were times when it was easier to use the roof and the porch roof—even once, your room, Kate. I didn't figure you'd be such a light sleeper. However, the fact that we'd had a prowler was useful. There was one time I barely managed to get down the back stairs to the kitchen while you were poking around the master bedroom. . . ."

"Yes. I heard you in the kitchen. . . . I was with Bones. Something about him made me feel somebody had been there. . . . Why is he so afraid of the master bedroom?"

"Because he made a mess there once and got one hell of a beating. I'd have sent him to the pound a long time ago, if I'd been home more."

Kate shivered a little.

"And besides, I didn't want him nosing around. God knows what he might dig out. . . ."

"I'm surprised you kept the stuff here," Jed said.

Paul shrugged. "It seemed safe. My distributors thought so, anyway. And it was, until you came, Kate. That's the one mistake I made, getting you here. A couple of the housekeepers complained about noises in the night. But with you, I thought . . ."

"That you could keep me quiet," Kate said. "Or maybe get me hooked, too. The way you readdicted Deborah. In my book that's tantamount to murder."

"Deborah would have gotten off the stuff when I left," Paul said. "Marie'll see to that."

"You'll miss your flight," Jed said.

"For a variety of reasons, I don't want to leave here too early. For one thing I don't want to be hanging around the airport. But it seems time to go. Upstairs, both of you."

"Why not leave us down here?" Jed suggested.

"That much nearer to the outside? No, I think not. Up the ladder. Kate, you go first."

When they were at the top, Paul lit a cigarette and looked at them both for a minute. Then smiled. Kate had a sudden memory of his smiling at her across the Sunday school class. She would never forget that moment. He was the most beautiful creature—next to Keith—that she had ever seen. And somewhere there was always the feeling that if she couldn't make Keith love her, she could win Paul. They were so alike. But Paul then didn't have the invincible aura of adulthood.

"Come with me, Kate," Paul said. "Better late than never."

It was astonishing. She wasn't even tempted. "No," she said.

He drew on his cigarette. "We should have been together long ago. Come with me and I'll tie your boyfriend here up lightly enough so that he'll get free, but not in time to stop the plane."

"No. I prefer to stay with Jed."

He made a grimace of distaste. "You must have a taste for the banal and the second-rate. You are certainly not going to claim that you prefer him to me."

"I certainly am. And I do."

"Well, well, it must be age or the desire for security. Who would have thought it? I'll have to tie you both up." He balanced his cigarette on the edge of the table behind him.

269

It was all so good-humored that Kate couldn't take him seriously. Not until he grabbed Jed with one hand and swung him around bringing down the butt of the pistol as he did so. Jed made a grunting noise and crumpled to the floor.

"Jed!" Kate ran forward, only to receive Paul's hand against her throat so that she choked.

"Sorry about the unchivalry and all that." He looked down and kicked the toe of his sneaker against Jed's side. "I owe him one for making Marie go against me. She never would have by herself."

"Oh yes she would. Before Jed ever came into the picture she nailed you for a two-timing fraud. It hurt her to do so. But she has guts, that girl, more than most of us. She . . ."

The slap when it came stung her flesh and snapped her head around.

"For your own good," Paul said, dragging her to one of the chairs, "just keep your mouth shut."

"At least let me see if he's badly hurt."

"Why the hell should I? As far as I'm concerned he's entirely expendable."

At that moment Jed groaned and moved. Kate, taking advantage of a moment when Paul's grip had slackened, darted towards him. But she didn't get there. She was pulled back so hard her arm felt as though it were wrenched almost out of the shoulder socket. She let out a scream, then felt the sting of Paul's hand again. This time the blow was so hard it almost knocked the breath out of her. Then cloth was pushed into her mouth and she thought for a moment that she would die, because it seemed as though he were plunging it down her throat.

"No more drama, Kate," Paul said, and was winding rope around her arms and knotting it again and again. Then he bent over her and stared into her eyes. "So you prefer an over-age crazy to me. That's a little too much, you know." He laughed than. "I think you'll finish up with neither."

It wasn't cruelty, she decided, in the sense of sadism for the

270

sake of sadism. It was self-indulgence taken to the far extreme. What Paul wanted, he got. His fury was evoked when he was foiled. Whatever narcissism meant, he had it to the ultimate degree. Nothing that did not serve him or his desires had reality. He didn't really want Kate. He simply could not endure the thought that she—or any woman—didn't want him.

"Dad!" Ranger's voice came from below.

Kate stiffened. She heard Paul swear under his breath. He strode to the trapdoor and bent down. "Ranger?"

"Dad, you're home!"

"Briefly. I have to go abroad again, right away. What are *you* doing home?"

"I forgot one of my papers that I have to turn in. I had a free period, so I came back for it. I saw your car in front. Has Aunt Kate got up yet?"

"She went to her office in New York. Why?"

"Oh, I wanted to ask her if she could take Bones for a walk this afternoon. I'm supposed to do extra gym. Where've you been, Dad? Aunt Kate's been trying to find you."

"I was in Chicago. She knew that. She just forgot it. You can leave her a note about Bones."

"Marie's run away." Ranger's voice was getting nearer. Kate tried frantically to think of a way she could attract his attention without endangering him.

"She's okay, Ranger. She called me. She's just staying with a friend."

"Well, I wish she'd let us know. Aunt Kate's been worried."

"She will. She'll call you. She meant to. But she was mad at Kate. You know how Marie is."

"What are all those boxes in your car?"

"Oh, stationery for the Tokyo office, printed memo pads, that kind of thing. I've got to fly out again later this morning. Hadn't you better be getting back to school?"

"It's okay. I got permission to come home. Are you sure Aunt Kate's gone?"

271

"Of course I'm sure." Paul's voice, which sounded further away as he descended the ladder, reflected irritation.

"Well, her work, the book she was working on and kept bringing back home, is all over the hall sofa. It's funny she'd leave it."

"She probably had a good reason. Now go back to school, son. In fact, I'll drive you. It's not too far off my road. I want to see you safe at school before I go to the airport."

Kate, by straining her ears, could hear his voice. They must be talking in the hall outside the master bedroom door. Paul wasn't in such a hurry to tie her up that he didn't remember to place her chair well away from any danger of being seen from below.

"I'll just close up my closet and be with you in a minute," Paul said.

Then his head appeared above the trapdoor.

"You're a fool not to come with me," he said in a low voice. "But then you always were."

She was staring fixedly over at the table where he'd put his cigarette. A thin perpendicular thread of smoke was ascending to the rafter, and a half an inch of ash had accumulated.

"Dad!"

There was a tense, anxious quality about Ranger's voice. His steps sounded, coming nearer to the base of the ladder.

"Coming, son!"

With her eyes Kate tried frantically to direct his attention back to the cigarette. In a second or two it would fall onto the curls of newspaper underneath.

Paul tipped an imaginary hat to Kate. "Adios!" he mouthed silently. And he disappeared down the steps. In a moment, the aluminum contraption that represented the folded stair rose up as the trapdoor closed.

Chapter 11

K ate, her eyes straining, watched the cigarette. The ash was beginning to be longer than the cigarette. A breeze blew gently from the window. The cigarette moved. It was inconceivable that it would not drop, and dropping, light a fire. Fear was a dry, sticky taste in her mouth. She couldn't scream. She couldn't move. Panic was a giant beast with a hundred talons, all of them embedded in her.

"Jed," her mind said. Somewhere she'd read that something in the mind remains awake, even in sleep, even in coma, even when unconscious. According to his writings, Jed believed that minds could communicate with one another without the use of any of the senses. "Now is the time, Jed, to prove it," she implored silently, half in irony. "Wake up, my darling. Wake up!"

With a huge effort she rocked her chair forward, but instead of shifting it, she and the chair, bound together, fell. Pain shot up her arm as it struck. Her face felt bruised. For a second she lay, trying to recover, and then started breathing in dust from the floor. Turning her head away, as far as she could, she drew in gulps of air and knew then that the cigarette must have fallen because she smelled burning paper.

"Jed!" her mind screamed. "Wake up! Jed, Jed . . ."

She felt rather than heard him move, for the floor carried the slight vibrations.

"Jed," she implored silently from behind her gag. "Jed, wake up!"

"What . . ?" His voice sounded thick. She heard a dragging sound. There was no way, lying under the chair as she was, her face jammed against the floor, that she could see how much of the paper had caught fire. She slid her knees across the floor a few inches, driving splinters into them. But she still couldn't see.

"Kate! Oh my God!"

His steps, stumbling at first, came over to her. She felt herself pulled up and the chair righted, so that she was once again sitting in it. She could see now. The flames were licking up the papers all around and searching hungrily for the furniture. Suddenly she remembered Ranger's dream: his mother taking pills and the man amidst the column of smoke and flame.

Jed took off his jacket and started slapping the flames to the right and left, extinguishing many of them, then he turned, ran back towards her and pulled the gag out of her mouth.

"Are you all right, Kate?"

She nodded. "Yes." It was hard to speak. Her tongue felt swollen.

"I'll try and undo that rope in a minute. But he's really knotted it, and I want to get as much of this fire out as quickly as possible."

Kate finally got her tongue working. "There are a couple of razor blades just under the top of my panty hose. I put them there when I was in the bathroom. You can slide your hand inside the top of my skirt. I have on a half-slip, so it should be easy."

He eyed the flames that seemed, for the moment, constant rather than growing. Then he slipped his hand down one side under her panty hose.

"No, the other side," Kate said, "And a little behind."

He found them, "Clever girl," he said admiringly. "Though I wonder you don't have blood streaming down your side. At least you wrapped them in tissue."

She could feel him saw through the rope binding her to the chair. Suddenly, and quickly, it gave.

"Now run downstairs and call the fire department. Immediately." And he went back to work with his jacket where the flames had licked up the legs of two of the chairs and were burning torn upholstery.

Kate found she was numb and that her legs didn't work as well as she wanted, even after so short a time. Her right arm ached agonizingly. Somehow, using the other arm, she opened the trapdoor, pushing down the stairs, which opened immediately. And as she did so found herself considering one of life's ironies. If, as she had wanted, she had been able to lock the trapdoor from the underside, she and Jed would be trapped. Then she went down. She found that if she held her arm in a certain folded position against her body, it didn't hurt as much. As she lifted the receiver with her left hand and her mind automatically registered the lack of dial tone, she remembered that Paul had cut the line. For a second she stood there, frozen with horror. But then, as the wind blew from the attic down the steps, she smelled burning again and saw that a piece of newspaper, smoldering, had dropped down the steps to the closet floor and was licking up towards the clothes hanging there. She slammed down the dead receiver and ran into the bathroom, glanced around, and saw an enamel pitcher. Slowed by being unable to use her right arm, she filled the pitcher and ran back to the closet and threw the water on the paper and boxes of clothes that seemed to be smoldering. Then she called to Jed. "The fire's down here. Come down quickly, Hurry, hurry!"

But it was too late. The clothes were now burning, and where plastic containers held them, the flames were reaching up. Jed's face appeared above the flames.

"I'll get onto the roof," he said with unbelievable calm.

"Oh Jed darling—but can you. The window's small."

"I'm not that fat," he said, and disappeared.

"The phone's dead," she cried, "I'm going next door!" She turned and ran into the main upper hall, which was now smoky, and down the staircase and out, hearing Bones's frantic yelps as she went. Knowing that he was not in immediate danger, she ran as fast as she could across the fifty yards of lawn to the house next door, aware with every pounding step of the sickening pain in her arm. When she got there, she pressed the bell and then pounded on the door. What if they're not in, she thought? But the door was opened immediately by a gray haired woman.

"Call the fire department," Kate blurted out.

"I already have," the woman said. "I did that as soon as I saw the smoke coming out of the attic window."

Kate turned. Smoke was indeed coming out of the window. "Jed!" she whispered, and ran back across the grass. As she flew in the front door, she barely noticed people coming out of houses on either side and from across the street, and then she heard the most beautiful sound in the world, the siren of the fire engine. For a second, she broke step, hearing Bones's yelping. Then she hurled herself down the little hall and against the swing door and felt, rather than saw, him streak past her.

The kitchen was relatively free of smoke. Running to the sink, Kate, forgetting her arm for a moment, tried to yank the dish towel off its hook and winced with the pain. Using the other arm, she took the towel, turned on the tap and soaked the towel. Then she started up the back steps. Probably because the back door wasn't open, those stairs were relatively free of smoke. But when she got to the upper hall, she rammed the wet towel against her face.

"Anybody up there?" a loud male voice yelled from downstairs.

"Yes," Kate cried and then started to cough. "In the attic," she yelled, between coughs. "A man."

"Where are you?"

"Back stairs."

"Go back down and out the back. We'll take care of the man in the attic."

She didn't want to, but she could hardly breathe. At that moment, a man, looking enormous in his fire hat, loomed up in front of her.

"Come on," he said. "I'll take you."

"Jed—upstairs."

"He's okay. Come on."

"But . . ."

The fireman picked her up. Pain shot up her arm and took her breath away. For a minute she thought she was going to be sick. By the time she recovered she was being dumped feet first on the lawn in back of the house.

"Go round there and you'll see," the fireman said. "You okay now?"

She nodded and hobbled around the back of the house annex. As she came out on the side she realized that she had done Jed—or rather his figure—a disservice. He was sitting on top of the roof, well away from the smoke coming out of the window, watching everything with a calm she found, perversely, maddening.

"Are you all right?" she yelled, almost as though it were an accusation. Relief, she noted, was making her irritable.

"Quite all right," he commented, as coolly, she thought, as though he had gone to the roof to meditate.

The fireman placed the ladder just beneath him, and with no fuss Jed climbed nimbly down and came over to her.

"I didn't dream you were that athletic," she said.

"I jog," he replied simply. "Not far and not fast, but every day."

Unable to stop herself, she leaned forward and kissed him,

oblivious of the firemen and the neighbors and various other people who had appeared from nowhere and were watching.

"I love you," she said, astonished at herself. How free she felt saying that, and how different from previous occasions when the words had been counters in a game; you pushed them forward in the hope of getting a bigger counter back.

"And I love you," he said, and turning, put his arms around her and hugged her.

She heard her own cry, then she fainted.

When she came to, she was inside a strange room lying on a sofa. Jed was sitting beside her, and the gray haired woman was standing at the end of the sofa with a glass of water in her hand.

Kate stared at them. "The fire!" she said.

"It's out." Jed replied. "Without too much damage, although the attic and the master bedroom are awash. Also the upper hall is pretty wet."

There was something else bothering her a lot. "Bones!" she said. "I let him out."

"He's all right, too. It seems he ran straight to the school yard, where he wandered around barking until somebody saw him, looked at his collar and got Ranger. He and Ranger ran up right after you fainted. They're in the house downstairs now. How do you feel?"

Kate tried to sit up, and was reminded, strongly of her injured arm. "I hurt my arm," she said, and felt her right upper arm with her left hand. "Ouch!"

Jed bent forward and touched the arm, feeling it gently. "It's broken," he said. "No wonder you fainted when I hugged you."

"Did you think it was the potency of your charm?" Kate said feebly.

"One hopes. But somehow I believe the arm is the better explanation. Mrs. Fitch has been very helpful," he said, getting up and glancing up at the gray haired woman.

278

Kate sat up, wincing. "Yes. Thank you. Did you say Fitch?" The name prodded a memory. "Fitch-bitch," the nosey neighbor, Marie had called her. "Mrs. Fitch," Kate said. "I believe we owe you more thanks than just today. Didn't you call people's attention to Marie's wild goings-on."

"I did. Earning your niece's undying enmity. But it seemed to me that somebody who would take responsibility should be there."

"You were right," Jed said. "Kate, I'm taking you to the nearest hospital to get that arm taken care of."

"I don't want to stay in the hospital," Kate said. "I hate hospitals."

"That's a healthy attitude. I hope you keep it. I don't think you'll have to stay. Unless, of course, it's a complicated break. But it doesn't look that way to me. They'll have to X-ray it and put it in either a cast or a sling. You can come home, then. But you may find it a little awkward trying to do things, especially in the house as it is now."

"Is it a mess?"

"As I said, the downstairs is pretty much all right. A little damp here and there and streaked. The annex is all right, too. But the front of the upstairs is fairly waterlogged, and the attic's a mess."

"But livable?"

"Oh yes."

"Where's Marie?"

"On her way home, courtesy my cop friend in New York."

Kate put her feet on the floor. Mrs. Fitch said, "Is there anything I can get you?"

Kate shook her head. "Not right now, but again, thanks. I'll come over and see you tomorrow."

A few hours later Jed drove Kate back from the hospital. Her right arm was in an elaborate supporting sling, and in her other hand were clutched some pain-killing tablets given her by the hospital dispensary.

279

"It isn't hurting as much as I thought it would," she said.

"If you have to have a break, it's the best you can have, high up in the upper arm, clean and with the bones still aligned. That's why they didn't put a cast on. But be gentle with it. Let Marie do most of the arm work in the next few days, or a neighbor."

"How did they know to pick Marie up—I mean, you hadn't even seen her, so how could they just suddenly pounce on her in Grand Central. She could have been in New York for a couple of days—from the time I missed her."

"It was luck, combined with some ingenuity. You called me yesterday morning. She had probably been missing for twenty-four hours, although possibly less. I called my cop friend later that morning after I left you. He asked me if I knew what she looked like and I had to admit I didn't. So my friend called the police here who did know Marie Lamont by sight because she'd been in minor trouble with pot and other wild parties. They also assumed she was still at the private school. So they called and got a picture. After giving a detailed verbal description of Marie, they put one of their people on the train with two copies of the picture, and he gave them to the cops in Grand Central. A couple of hours later, they picked Marie up and called my friend, who went to see her and after getting her story out of her, took her to his home with his wife and several children until he could reach me."

"That *was* lucky. She could have gone in the day before."

"Well, she didn't. She stayed with some friends whose parents were away. That's how you didn't know."

They drove for a while. Kate, looking out the window, said, "I'm still vague about directions out here, but I don't recognize any of this."

"That's because I'm taking the long way back to the house. In the past two days I've driven around this village quite a lot, what with one thing and another, and some ways are longer than others. Kate, I'm sorry. But I have some bad news. While you were being put into your sling, I called the phone

280

company to see if they would get your line mended, because I didn't want you to be in the house without being able to phone out, particularly if you're one-armed. Then I called Mrs. Fitch to see if everything was still all right. She said a local cop had come looking for you. And he told her what he'd come for." Jed took a breath. "I'm afraid Paul's dead. The police have been watching the house for the past twenty-four hours. When Paul left they gave chase. In trying to outrun them on the parkway, he got careless and drove the car across the divider and into a concrete wall. He was killed instantly. I'm sorry." He paused. "I also think I have to take some responsibility for that. When I called the police about Marie I told them what I thought Paul was up to and that he had a lot to do with his wife's present condition. After I left you I started putting things together in my head. And it seemed to me more likely that Marie would run away if she thought her father were implicated in what was happening to her mother than if she simply suspected her mother was back on narcotics. What I kept feeling about her—especially when I was in her room—was her terrible distress. But she had known for a long time that her mother had been on and off pills. So it had to be something else. Something new that she couldn't face. Then I thought about those odd squares in the dust of the attic, and the room behind the screen with its locked door that you tried to interest me in, and the story started coming together. So I told my policeman friend what I thought, and he took it from there, telling the cops here. Apparently they weren't too surprised. They'd had their eye on him, anyway. And on McGrath, too, apparently. The California police have been in touch with the New York and Westchester cops over him, asking them to keep a watch on him as well. As far as anyone can make out, his operation here is clean, except, of course, for turning a blind eye when he knew—or strongly suspected—drugs were being brought into the hospital for Deborah."

"I suppose he'd argue he was being blackmailed."

"He could have gone to the police."

"True. So they, the police here, know about . . . Well of course they do, if Marie's been telling them."

"Yes. McGrath can, I think, be held as an accessory to Paul's supplying Deborah with illegal drugs, even though he was being blackmailed, because, as I said, he could have gone to the police. But whether or not they're actually going to arrest him I don't know. I suppose it all depends on what he can tell them and whether or not the California police have come up with any more evidence about his connection with the overdose, and if so, whether he can be extradited out to the coast."

"I wonder if he really was responsible for that death."

"Well, you've been with him. What would you say?"

Kate thought about McGrath, the occasional almost hypnotic quality in his personality, his excellent (and expensive) tailoring, his finely furnished study, his talent for making people (especially women) do what he wanted them to do.

"I don't know. He likes power, and he likes to feel himself controlling people. That could lead him into doing things he probably would not start out to do. Maybe."

"Even if they don't extradite him, this is going to finish his clinic. Once the newspapers know—and I'm sure someone will see to it that there is a leak—that'll be the end."

After a minute Jed said, "I hope you're not too upset about Paul."

The odd part was she was not. If she felt anything, it was relief, relief for Paul's family. Paul in jail or Paul living it up in some South American country could be an unhealing abscess in the life of the family. And for herself? Sadness, she thought. Sadness because of the waste. Could there have been some time when he might have taken a different path?

"Paul once said that I walked out on him. In a way, he was right. Of course, I did so because I thought he'd already left me for Deborah. I may have been right. I may not have been. But if I hadn't been so neurotic, if I had stuck with him

. . . I wonder if things for him would have been different?"

"You can't play God, Kate. Before you go into self-torture over that, why not ponder how much of your obsession over him was manufactured by, say, your father? If he had treated you differently, would you have been as blinded by Paul as you were? Wouldn't you have been able to free yourself so that you would have seen Paul for what he was? And if your natural mother had not felt she had to put you up for adoption, etcetera, etcetera . . . I think that's what the Bible means by that much maligned quotation about the sins of the fathers. It seems to me it's a simple statement of fact about the intricate web of responsibility that links people not only at the present, but with the past and the future."

"Well," Kate said, and reaching out her left hand grasped his right one. "I'm free now."

After another minute she said, "Speaking of my father, there's always been something about him that baffled me—at least it has since I've been an adult. He was the one who sparked my interest in religion—for all the fact that he obviously didn't like me. He loathed church, which was an ongoing bone of contention between him and mother. But he was fascinated by . . . well, God and speculated about Him all the time. He read voraciously on the subject and the only time he ever really talked to me was about that. Yet all that interest never seemed to trickle down into the way he behaved. You heard what Paul said: he was ambitious and not too scrupulous, and I know he married Diane Légère because she was who she was and had money. But Mother was the opposite. To her God was a set of rules. She was completely bored with any sort of speculation. In fact, she thought it was wrong."

"Well, your parents seemed to represent the two aspects of religion that have often warred against each other and split religious communities down the middle. Gnosis, or knowledge, and morality. Ideally they should be taken together. There've always been people with a thirst for religious, or spiritual or esoteric knowledge, but no sense that once gained, it should affect their behavior. Then you have the moralists to whom God is a kind of angry parent."

"I always thought—or at least Mother always thought—you couldn't love God and be morally lax."

Jed smiled. "That leaves out large parts of quite religious humanity. I don't find hypocrisy so much in your father's weaknesses. We all have them. I do in what I suspect was his unkindness to you. You haven't told me about it too much, but I see and hear echoes of it in you."

"What's going to happen to Deborah, I wonder?" Kate said, after another few minutes.

"You'll have to talk it over with the children. My suggestion would be that she go into New York to one of the good psychiatric hospitals there. If you like I can get in touch with the head of one of those. I went to medical school with him."

"Thanks. I think that'd be a good idea. And the sooner, the better, for the children's sake, as much as her own." After they'd driven another few minutes Kate burst out, "There are two things that still bother me. One is, if McGrath was being more or less blackmailed by Paul, why was he, too, so enthusiastic about getting me out to the house? Because Paul's foot was in the middle of his back?"

"Of course. But also for his own sake. I'd be willing to bet that McGrath wanted nothing more than to get Deborah out of his establishment. She could be nothing but trouble, even under the best of circumstances. His staff was probably not of the highest order, but even they'd begin to wonder what was going on with Deborah. And under the worst circumstances, she could land him in more trouble than he'd been in in California. I think you looked like his one hope; a strong-minded sister would do a lot more than a housekeeper could to decide to take the ailing sister out of there and place her in another clinic. I expect he was praying daily that that would happen. Then he'd be off the hook. On the other hand, he had to be careful just how much he said to you. If you ran with it to Paul, then he could be in a jam over that. I don't have much respect for him, but I must say I don't envy him this particular problem."

"Yes, I suppose so."

"What was the other thing bothering you?"

"Whether Paul deliberately left that burning cigarette on the table, the one I told you about. Whether he'd really forgotten it or knew it was there?"

"On some level he certainly knew it was there. But whether consciously or not, we'll never know."

"But wouldn't he care about burning up his own house?"

"His children weren't in it. He probably argued that it was insured—if he thought about it at all. As for you, well, you gave his vanity—his most vulnerable area—a bad blow."

"But I'd read him out of my life years before when I got drunk at my last and most catastrophic party in New Orleans." And Kate told Jed about it.

"But he could rationalize that by attributing it to wounded love. This time you were guilty of the unforgivable—you chose me over him. And further, you proved his gamble wrong. He dug you out from the past because he thought he could control you. You showed him you had escaped—permanently."

"You remember," Kate said. "You once asked me if Paul was a man of principle? That question really stunned me. I'd never thought of him—or any other man—in those terms. Just as to whether they were more attractive or not attractive; even more, how I did on some pass-fail test that assumed all men had it in their power to administer to me."

"In other words," Jed said, turning into their street, "men with you were sex objects pure and simple and nothing else. The way women are always accusing men of looking at women."

"Yes. I suppose so. Although it seems to me my motivation was somewhat different. Mine came from a terrible sense of

285

failure, engendered, I think, by my father. The most important thing I could get from a man, therefore, was acceptance, on a purely sexual basis."

"Well, it's not too far from the so-called male chauvinists. If what you needed from the man was not to be rejected sexually, then what the equivalent male needs from the woman—any woman, individuality doesn't count—is the reassurance of his maleness that her submission will bring. Both are extremely self-centered and spring from an assumed lack."

"Yes, doctor."

Jed grinned, but didn't say anything.

Suddenly Kate remembered her experience when she tried recently to go to confession. "Did I tell you, Jed. Every now and then I remember I'm a Catholic and go to confession. Only the last time I went the only thing I really wanted to confess was that I didn't desire anybody. Does that sound crazy? Or is it related to that profound comment you're just finished unwinding?"

"Sort of. I think you were tired of the wrong kind of desire for the wrong kind of reason. Which is healthy. And I don't think you've had much experience with the right kind. People can decide to adopt chastity for perfectly good reasons—most of the major religions state that. But the reasons have to be positive, not negative."

"You'll have to explain that to me, along with your other kooky notions. Speaking of which, I wonder what your distinguished medical friend in New York would think of the latter, your notions, I mean."

"What makes you so sure he doesn't share them?" Jed glanced at her as they drew up in front of the house. "Along with my cop friend. That's how I know him, you know. He read my books, became a fan and wrote to me."

"Too much," Kate said, and opened the car door with her left hand.

"You'd better let me open that for you and help you out.

No need to fall in the street and do a really good job on your arm."

There was nobody downstairs when Jed and Kate went into the house. The carpet was wet and smeared where the hose had been dragged across it, and smears were streaked on the walls. Other than that, there wasn't too much damage. But the moment Kate put her foot on the stair carpet, she felt the material squelch beneath her feet. Upstairs the carpet was waterlogged, and the pale walls liberally stained. The remains of the manuscript were a sodden mush. Thank God it was a copy, Kate thought devoutly. Hesitating, she knocked on Ranger's door.

"Come in," he called, and she heard Bones's bark.

Ranger was sitting cross-legged on his bed. His eyes looked red, and his face showed the tracks of tears. Bones loaped up on Kate. She patted him and kissed him between the ears. "Good boy," she said. "Now that's enough. Get down."

She went over and sat on the bed. She was pretty sure that Ranger knew about Paul, but she said, "You know about your father, Ranger?"

He nodded.

"I'm sorry."

He didn't say anything.

"Try not to judge him too harshly." It was a pat phrase, and she felt hypocritical saying it.

Ranger's reaction was immediate. "Why not? He got Mom addicted again . . . Marie told me. Just because he was scared that she'd blow the whistle on him if she got well. And he kept giving us those phony vitamin pills to take her in the hospital. She'd still be taking them if Marie didn't see her almost have a fit one day because she was late and Mom had taken her last so-called vitamin. Mom snatched the bottle out of her hand and went to the john and took one and then came back and in two minutes was fine. Marie knew what that meant. So she got Andy to take one of the pills to a friend of his at a lab to find out what it was . . ."

Ranger's voice broke. He rubbed his eyes with the heels of his hands, making his face even more streaked than it was. "I'm glad he's dead. He deserves to be dead."

Kate sighed. It wasn't too far from her own conclusion. But to hang on to such fury could mean untold trouble for Ranger in the future. Well, she thought, I can't do anything about it now.

"Ranger," she said. "I'm going to need all the help I can get from you two. My right arm is broken, not badly, but it's uncomfortable and I won't be able to use it that much for a while."

Ranger gave a gigantic sniff. "Sure. I mean okay. We'll help. Marie isn't as bad as she sounds sometimes. How'd you break it?"

"I fell." She reached out her left hand and clasped one of his. Then she leaned forward and kissed him. "Thanks."

She then went to Marie's room and knocked.

"Come in."

Marie was sitting on a cushion, her back to the wall, which had long dark patches on it, where the water from the attic had soaked through and run down. The floor also was wet.

"Isn't that cushion you're on wet?" She asked.

"Yes," Marie said indifferently.

Kate turned and stared around. It took a minute or two for Kate to realize that, as well as dark patches, a big rectangular light patch represented the area previously covered by the photograph of the monk.

"What happened to the monk?" She asked.

"I decided he was a jerk and an idiot. What he did was cop out. Big gesture. Then nothing."

"I'm sorry about your father," Kate said.

"Yeah." Unlike Ranger, her eyes were not puffy, and her cheeks were not streaked. "Big hero, wasn't he?" Then, in a

288

wrenching echo of her brother, "I'm glad he's dead." But on the last word her voice broke.

"He loved you," Kate said. "I think you were probably the one person he really did love."

Marie blew her nose on a tissue she had grabbed from a box on the floor near her. The box, Kate decided, looked strange in this pseudo-oriental room. She said, "I'm glad you're back. I was worried about you."

Marie wiped her nose and raised her head. "I had this romantic notion of going to New York and paying everybody back by being a call girl."

Using her left hand to balance herself, Kate sat down on the wet floor. "Somehow I think the romance of that might have worn a bit thin."

"Yeah. That's what the cop said."

"Which cop?"

"Wouldn't you know it! Other kids go to the Port Authority or Grand Central and get picked up by pimps. I was sure at least three would try. After all, I'm not bad looking. But of course Grand Central isn't like the Port Authority. Anyway, the person who picked me up turned out to be a cop. Called by your buddy—some busybody doctor called Marker or something, or at least that was what I thought. But it turns out this cop had read his books on really cool subjects. I told him I was into that and never read anything by a Marker, and he said this doctor wrote under the name of Kramer. Kate, you never told me you knew Jed Kramer. I mean, he's a terrific cult figure. Only nobody's ever met him. I want to meet him."

"Well," Kate said, a little stunned by this. "You can have your wish. He's downstairs."

"Is he? Well, anyway, the minute I knew it was Kramer, I felt better about the cop. I mean anybody who reads that kind of book can't be all fascist. He took me back to his house to meet his wife and kids and have dinner. Some deal. They were pretty nice, though. Anyway, he talked and talked and talked, until I got tired of listening. And then I thought, well, you'd run away, and where had it got you? Not that you don't have a good job and all that. But you're still hung up on the same things you were then—like Daddy." Her voice quivered again.

For a brief moment Kate once again had the eerie feeling that their lives—hers and Marie's—were running parallel, counterpointing one another. . . .

"Oh hell," Marie said, and started to cry. "It was such a rotten lousy thing for him to do to Mom."

Kate eased herself up, then went over and sat down again on the other side of Marie. After a minute, she put her left arm around the girl. Marie stiffened at first, then finally leaned against Kate's shoulder and cried steadily for about five minutes. After that she straightened, pulled some more tissues out of the box and blew her nose again. "I felt so *crummy*. I'd been taking her more pills thinking they were vitamins. What a fool I was! Daddy had this big game that I wasn't to mention it to anybody at the hospital because these were extraspecial strong vitamins that weren't allowed over here. And the reason they weren't, he said, was because the government was in with the drug manufacturers, who were afraid the better vitamins might hurt their bleeding profits."

Well, Kate thought, it took me longer, but we're both free of Paul now. She said drily, "He certainly knew how to give the right reason to the right person. But I'm curious. Where did Deborah keep the pills? Surely a nurse would want to know what they were?"

"Sometimes in the bathroom, but mostly in the locker where she kept her coat."

"I see. Well, Marie, I can't pretend your father was a man of solid character. He wasn't. But try not to forget his good points. He could be fun, he was here—sometimes—when you needed him. Most of all, he really loved you."

"It's enough to put you off men," Marie said.

"Not permanently, I trust."

After a minute Marie said, "I called the hospital. Mom's better."

290

"She's going to another hospital for a while. One in New York which is supposed to be one of the best in the country."

"You're going to stay until she gets home, aren't you?" Marie said, sounding panicky.

"I am. Thanks for the concern."

Marie sniffed again. "I guess I haven't always been full of love and sunshine towards you. But—I'm glad you're here." She paused. "I suppose when she gets home Mom's going to need a lot of support."

"Yes. Maybe you could get some help with that. The people at Deborah's new hospital probably have family group sessions or something." After a minute, Kate, removing her arm, said, "To return to the practical for a moment, you can't sleep in this room tonight. It's soaked. Why don't you come into the other room in the annex?"

"Yeah. I was thinking that. I was going to do my room over anyway. I think I'm about to go into another phase."

Kate, rising to her feet, suppressed a grin. Marie took herself seriously, and this wasn't the moment to tease. "I wouldn't be at all surprised. Good night, Marie."

When she went downstairs Jed was winding his scarf round and round his neck. "I think I'd better be getting back to the hotel," he said.

Kate, feeling let down, watched him button his jacket. "I'm sorry you have to go. If the master bedroom and Marie's room weren't soaked, I'd invite you to stay here. Marie'd be thrilled. She says you're a cult figure. As it is, though, she's going to have to use the one dry extra room. I wish you didn't have to leave."

· "So do I. But my patients out on the coast—those who haven't defected to another doctor—need me. Besides, I can't afford those hotel prices much longer."

"You could stay in my apartment. Nobody's there. In fact," Kate hurried on before Jed could reply, "You could stay in my apartment if somebody—me for instance—*were* there."

He paused. "That's very nice," he said. "If, indeed, you were there, I'd accept. My patients could get better without me. In fact, they probably would anyway."

"What a thing for a doctor to say. What about the great priesthood of medicine, without which we would all be dead by the age of six?"

"Grossly exaggerated. Given enough time, most things would get better. I'll grant the power of medicine in wiping out the scourges—smallpox, typhus, typhoid, scarlet fever and so on. But the body, particularly the body and mind combined, make up an incredibly wonderful machine. Left to itself, and given the right attitude, that machine can often effect its own healing. The daily bath and decent sanitation have done more against the various plaques we've been heir to than all the antibiotics put together."

"You'll be thrown out of the AMA if you don't watch out."

"I know, I know." With his scarf rising like a Regency cravat, Jed hesitated. "Thank you for the offer of your apartment, especially the offer to stay with you." He blushed a little.

"Would you have accepted?"

"I certainly would. You don't have to be young and beautiful to want to love and be loved."

"I know. I've just discovered that." She smiled at him. "I'm so glad you were here when all this business started. What a wonderful coincidence!"

"There's no such thing as coincidence."

"How so, Swami?"

"I mean that I've always loathed the idea of conventions: large numbers of people milling around making hearty noises, drinking too much, eating too much, making statements they don't really mean and promises they know they can't keep. So I've always put the announcements about conventions straight into the wastebasket. But this time, after I had done that, I had a strange dream. I dreamed about my wife, which I had done before, of course. But she seemed to be telling me 'goodbye.' And instead of being upset, as I usually was when I dreamed about her, I felt—released. The next morning I fished the literature out of the wastebasket, filled out the form and sent it in."

"You're going to have to explain the whole thing to me, slowly."

"Gladly." He came over to her and kissed her, carefully avoiding her bandaged arm. Her heart gave a quiver and then started beating rapidly. She felt warm all over. He was right; it was wonderful to love and be loved.

At that moment Marie appeared, coming downstairs. Under her arm were two books. She stopped. They looked up at her.

"Jed," Kate said, "this is Marie, my niece. Marie, this is Dr. Marker, alias Jed Kramer."

"I know." She came down the rest of the way. In her faded jeans and baggy sweat shirt she looked younger than her fifteen years. "I heard your voices. Kate said you were here." Suddenly, and with a child's gesture, she held out the books. "Would you autograph them for me?"

A look of gratification came over Jed's face. He became, in that instant, Kate reflected, the compleat author. "With pleasure."

"Why don't you stay here?" Marie said. "You don't have to rush back."

"There's a slight shortage of room," Kate said. "Otherwise I'd invite him."

"What's wrong with your room?" Marie said. "It has a double bed. You were kissing a while ago."

"In my own apartment, yes. In this house, no. It's—er—inappropriate."

The younger generation, Kate noticed in the middle of her embarrassment, was much more *dègagé* about this than either Jed or herself. She could feel the heat in her own cheeks and see the red in his. "We're too young," she went on. "Wait till we grow up to your age."

"That's hypocritical *and* archaic." Marie said. "Nobody thinks that way today."

293

"When your mother comes home . . ." Kate started.

"Yeah, well, how long's that going to be? She's been real sick."

"A month, six weeks," Kate said. And knew that it sounded short.

"It'll probably be longer than that," Jed said gently. "From what you tell me she's been very ill indeed."

"And you *said* you'd stay until she could cope."

She and Marie had come a long way, Kate saw. There was again an anxious look on Marie's face, as though she were not sure that Kate would keep her word. Kate put her arm around her. "As I promised you, I'm not going to leave till your mother is truly well and home."

Relief flashed briefly across Marie's face before she assumed her preferred air of sophisticated languor. "In that case, it's a pity you're so Victorian."

"Yes. But you have to be tolerant with us," Kate said, and found she also was not anxious for her role in the house to be extended indefinitely.

"I have a revolutionary suggestion that might well meet all contingencies." Jed nervously wrapped his scarf once more round his neck. "I'll come back in a week or two and we can get married." He eyed Marie. "You can give Kate away."

"I'd rather be a bridesmaid."

"All right," Kate said. "I accept." Odd, she thought, there was no doubt in her mind at all.

"What about your career?" Marie said.

"When you find something you like very much, it's a good idea to grab it."

"That's not very liberated."

"I've been liberated for years. I'm ready for a little bondage."

"Chicken!" Marie sauntered towards the kitchen. "I'll leave you two alone," she said airily. Then, just short of the door she stopped. "What about Daddy? Won't there be some kind of service?"

"Of course." Kate felt a stab of guilt for not thinking of it herself. "Did either Paul or Deborah attend any church here?"

"Mom sometimes went to St. Andrew's, the Episcopal Church."

"We can call on the rector this afternoon, then."

"I'm afraid you're going to have to go into the city, Kate, and identify him," Jed said. "Then you can arrange where to have the body sent."

Marie's mouth twisted. She swallowed. "It seems funny to be calling Daddy 'the body.'" She looked at Jed. "Do you believe he's dead dead. Or do you think something of him is alive, somehow?"

"I do believe something of him is alive, very much so," Jed said.

"Do you think he was wicked, evil? Like he's been sent to hell?"

"I think he put his values on the wrong things. And that led him to do worse things. But I also think the point of being alive somewhere is that he will be given another chance to learn that, to choose the right things."

Marie nodded. "So do I."

Kate walked to the door with Jed. "Luckily," she said, "on the theory that it's easier to move me and my editing pencil than you and all your patients, they have publishing houses out there in California, along, of course, with the kooks and the oranges."

"You're very prejudiced. Not to say bigoted. Once your sister is home and functioning, you can come out and see for yourself."

"I intend to. After all," Kate said thoughtfully. "I've always liked oranges."